"I PROMISE YOU'LL NOT FIND MARRIAGE TO ME TO BE DELIGHTFUL," LILLIANE SWORE.

"Now I see why you remained so long unwed. Despite your fairness and your considerable inheritance, you are quite the shrew," Corbett mocked.

Lilliane backed away from him, keeping the table between them. "Then perhaps you should follow the example of your betters and seek a wife elsewhere."

"My betters?" He laughed. "More than likely they were merely boys. You are dealing with a man now, Lily. And it is you I want. Taking you to the marriage bed is a pleasure I sincerely anticipate."

MY
GALLANT
ENEMY

~∾∾✦∾∾~

REXANNE
BECNEL

A DELL BOOK

Published by
Dell Publishing
a division of
Bantam Doubleday Dell
Publishing Group, Inc.
666 Fifth Avenue
New York, New York 10103

ISBN: 0-440-20621-9

Printed in the United States of America

Published simultaneously in Canada

August 1990

10 9 8 7 6 5 4 3 2 1

OPM

For Brian and Katya
  It started as a bedtime story . . .

With loving thanks to David
  for your support and faith in me

Swete maidè of the bowr,
   as diamaund so bright,
As saphyr in silver,
   seemly on sight,
As jasper the gentil
   that glemeth with light,
As gernet in golde
   and ruby wel right;
As Onyx she is
   on beholden on hight,
An emeraude of morning;
   this maidè haveth might . . .

      Anonymous medieval verse

1

September 1273

The scene in the bailey was golden. The sun caught the swirling remnants of dust stirred by the knights' mock battle. Over and over they had fought their way back and forth across the dry, hard-packed dirt until their bodies had glistened with sweat and their arms had become almost too heavy to lift. It was only then that they had retired from their practice, weary yet satisfied with the day.

Stepping lightly across the now-empty courtyard, Lady Lilliane of Orrick fancied she still heard the shouts of the men: their cries of victory, their oaths upon defeat. Orrick was the same as it had always been, and she felt as if she had not been gone these two long years. But there were differences, she reflected as she made her way to the broad-limbed chestnut tree that shaded the far end of the bailey.

It was not her father who led his men in their daily exercise, for he was no longer the vibrant, healthy man of her youth. Sir Aldis had led Orrick's knights in their practice today. Her younger sister, Odelia, had married him just prior to Lilliane's departure, and although her father had yet to relinquish his authority to his son-in-law, Lilliane feared it was only a matter of time.

Still, there was young Tullia's husband-to-be. After her wedding four days hence, Sir Santon might very well make a play for stewardship of Orrick Castle. And yet Lilliane sensed that her father did not hold either of the two young knights in very high regard. But then, it was seldom he approved of the men his daughters favored.

Across the bailey two women made their slow and stately way toward the great hall. Odelia and someone Lilliane didn't know, she noted. A small frown marred her normally serene features. The wedding guests had already started arriving from as far away as Farrelton, and Odelia was quite clearly in her glory playing the role of lady of the castle. She was more than content to leave all the practical aspects of the preparations to Lilliane while she entertained the guests.

At first Lilliane had been hurt by Odelia's coolness toward her. It was obvious that neither Odelia nor her husband, Aldis, was pleased with Lilliane's return. As long as she remained unmarried, Aldis and Odelia were the logical ones to inherit Orrick Castle. But if her father should find her a husband . . .

Lilliane scoffed at that idea. The subject of her marriage was one neither she nor her father was willing to bring up. Indeed, they'd stepped very carefully around that topic these past few weeks.

She sighed, determined to ignore Odelia's bad humor. Tullia's sincere welcome had more than made up for it. If it hadn't been for her youngest sister's letter desperately pleading for help with the wedding preparations, Lilliane would still be at Burgram Abbey.

And yet she was glad to be back. Lilliane let her eyes slowly sweep the bailey, taking in the familiar sights and noticing every little change. There was something special about Orrick, she admitted as she leaned back against the ancient tree's solid trunk. All her memories were tied up in this castle, both good and bad. Not one day had passed at the abbey without her thoughts dwelling on Orrick Castle.

It would be even harder to leave this time than it had been before.

From a window opening in his receiving chamber, Lord Barton of Orrick watched as his eldest child brought a hand to her eyes. Was she crying? He leaned forward with a hand on the center mullion, straining to see. He watched as she straightened up and walked toward the storehouses. Then he slapped the granite sill in frustration.

"What is it, Father?"

Without taking his eyes from the slender figure below, Lord Barton opened an arm to Tullia and then held her affectionately close. He planted a kiss on her smooth brow.

As she hugged him she spied Lilliane. "She's not going to stay, is she?" she asked wistfully.

"It seems unlikely." He sighed. "Unless I force her to."

"Maybe you should. Maybe that would be best."

"My mistake was in letting her go in the first place."

"You mean you should have let her marry Sir William?" Tullia looked up at her father in surprise.

"No. Sir William was not for her. I meant I should never have let her go to Burgram Abbey. She would not have kept her anger at me alive this long if she'd been here. But now . . ."

"She's not angry with you," Tullia said earnestly. "Truly she's not."

He only snorted in disbelief.

"You're just as stiff around her as she is around you," Tullia accused with soft brown eyes. "Why, 'tis clear that you and Lilliane are so alike in temperament as to irritate one another endlessly."

"A daughter should obey her father."

"She did," Tullia replied with faultless reasoning. "She did not marry William, did she?"

"No, but she makes it clear she will not marry another. Does she yet pine for him?"

"I don't think so," Tullia replied pensively. "But we shall know soon enough. Sir William and his wife, Lady Verone, arrived this afternoon. Odelia is with her now. Lady Verone is—" She hesitated. "She is with child."

"With child? And William brought her traveling this far?" Lord Barton's heavy brows lowered in a scowl. "I hope I do not rue the day I invited William back to Orrick. I have never trusted that fellow. He's a peacock. A man who'd rather dawdle about King Edward's vacant court than see to his lands and his people. I don't want him alone with Lilliane."

"You've never a kind word for anyone," Tullia reproached him gently. "You sent poor William packing when he courted Lilliane. And her with a broken betrothal already. You very nearly did the same to Sir Aldis when he courted Odelia."

"I let him marry Odelia, didn't I?" His frown deepened but his grasp on her tightened. "And now I shall let you marry that boy, Santon."

Tullia pressed her face against her father's wide chest and smiled. "I love him. And that's why you said yes, isn't it? You let both Odelia and me marry where our hearts lay. Why could you not do so with Lilliane?"

Disturbed, Lord Barton patted her head tenderly and let his gaze stray to the late-afternoon glow that rested over the stone fortress and the fertile lands beyond it.

He was a man of actions, not of words. He was a man of war. Though he might wrestle with his feelings and reason with his daughters, his decisions invariably were made for the good of Orrick and its people. He could not put into words his mistrust of William of Dearne. But he had been adamant in refusing the man his eldest daughter's hand as well as in denying him dominion at Orrick. And so the rift between him and Lilliane had been formed.

But it had been the right decision, he reassured himself as he led Tullia toward the great hall. William was not for his Lily.

The great hall was nearly filled to capacity, abounding with both guests and servants. The arched ceiling resounded with laughter and conversation as Lilliane paused at the landing of the main staircase to look at the gathering below.

It was as it should be, she thought with a small, satisfied smile. A great ox and two huge boars had been turning on the spits since the previous evening and were now being prepared by teams of meat carvers. Other servants bustled about with platters of pheasant and quail, duck and eel. Great tureens of leek soup as well as overflowing baskets of breads were centered on each of the many tables, and wines and ales flowed freely. Trays of delicate fruit pasties and bowls of stewed pears waited in the kitchens to be passed about later.

Lilliane could not ignore the feeling of pride she took in the display she saw before her. Not three weeks earlier she had been appalled at the drab condition of this very same hall. The two massive hearths had been black with encrusted soot and home to a myriad of small crawling creatures. The great shield of Orrick, which should have gleamed proudly, had been gray with smoke and cobwebs, the blue and silver colors hardly discernible.

The hall had been little used for entertaining in recent years, and Lilliane could not blame Tullia for its shabby appearance. After all, the girl had been but fourteen when both of her older sisters had left Orrick. The castle was a large and rambling one. Seeing to its daily routine and upkeep was a considerable task, one that never seemed to end. There were servants aplenty to see the work done, but Lilliane knew that pretty, soft-hearted Tullia would never be one to control her servants well. At least Tullia had had the foresight to send for her prior to the wedding.

It had taken every minute of Lilliane's time to see Orrick made ready for the guests' arrival. Every scrap of bed linen had been washed, whitened, and hung to bleach in the sun. The kitchen storerooms had been purged of their moldering contents and replenished from the ripening late-summer fields. Every room, from the finest honored guests' chambers to the meanest servants' niches, had been swept and scrubbed. Each sconce and torch base had been removed and scraped of old drippings, then polished until it shone. A team of women had toiled for days preparing beeswax and wax berry for pouring hundreds of candles.

At her command seamstresses had labored at new hangings for the great hall and all the major chambers. They had swiftly stitched the fine new garments expected of the wedding host family. From dawn to dusk she had worked, overseeing each task until there was not a servant she did not know, nor one who had not come to know her high standards. She did not doubt that they all bemoaned her return to Orrick, but that was only because they'd grown lazy under Tullia's inexperienced hand.

Content now that even the most exacting of their guests would find naught amiss with Orrick, Lilliane leaned forward over the carved stone balustrade and peered at the gathering below.

"Do you seek any particular face?"

Her father's voice took her by surprise, and she whirled to face him. He was dressed as befitted the lord of the castle in an overtunic of rich blue silk, trimmed at the neck, hem, and armholes with wide silver embroidery. A short mantle was pinned back over one of his shoulders, held by a large sapphire brooch set in heavily worked silver. A heavy silver chain circled his considerable girth.

On first returning to Orrick, Lilliane had been struck by how much her father had aged in her absence. But tonight in his regal attire he looked more the man she remembered.

"I was only curious about which of Tullia's guests had arrived," she answered.

"But no one in particular?" he persisted.

"No. No, why do you ask?"

Lord Barton lowered his gaze then and moved to grip the balustrade with his two beefy hands. "Sir William of Dearne arrived today. His wife is with him," he added pointedly.

Although Lilliane stiffened at his words, understanding at once the warning he gave her, she refused to acknowledge it. "Well, I do hope Odelia placed them in a comfortable chamber."

Her father eyed her suspiciously, and she knew he was not at all fooled by the sweet tone of her words. She could not deny, at least to herself, that the thought of seeing William again caused her heart to quicken in anticipation. But she would keep that fact from her father if it killed her.

"I still have hopes of settling you with husband." Lord Barton spoke cautiously, as if uncertain of her reaction. But his bright-blue eyes were canny as he waited for her response.

"I would agree, and eagerly," she retorted, lifting her rounded chin bravely. "But I would marry a man I love . . . or at least respect."

"Would I choose a man of no honor for you?" he demanded, waving one hand angrily in the air. "Would I leave my eldest child and my ancestral home to the care of a man of no honor or respect?"

"But I thought Aldis . . . or mayhap Santon. Why, Odelia has great plans for Orrick when you . . ." She trailed off in embarrassment.

"When I die?" Lord Barton laughed and his face softened as he gazed at her. "Aldis is not a leader. Oh, he leads the men well enough. But to tend a castle and its lands and people requires much more than skill with the mace and broadsword. No, his ability on a war steed will not help him on that score. And as for Santon." He shrugged and let his eyes stray to the boisterous company below. "Santon is good for Tullia. But he could no more see to the demesne's needs than Tullia can properly tend the castle's. So you see"—he smiled gently at her—"nothing has really changed. I still must find you a husband."

Lilliane was momentarily silenced. She had not sought her father's company since she'd returned to Orrick. Indeed, she had avoided him as much as was possible, although it pained her greatly to do so. She loved him deeply even though his decision about William had broken her heart. But while his honest revelation now surprised her, it did not anger her, for her thoughts on her sisters' husbands had followed nearly the same path as his.

"I love Orrick," she admitted in a hushed tone. Her hand ran slowly along the rough stone wall beside her as if she stroked a beloved pet. "I've missed it sorely."

"Then you shall stay."

He did not seem to expect an answer from her, and for that Lilliane was much thankful. He merely took her arm and led her down the broad stone stairs to join the gaiety below and lead their guests to the dinner table.

Many eyes followed father and daughter as they crossed through the throng greeting relatives and acquaintances, for they made a striking pair. Lilliane in many ways favored her father with her erect carriage and confident air. Although his hair was heavily laced with silver and his eyes were no longer the piercing blue of his youth, those who had known Barton of Orrick in those years saw his reflection in Lilliane. Her hair was the same deep chestnut color as his, glinting with deep gold in the light from the many torches. Her wide cheekbones and firmly set jaw were cast from the same mold as his. Only her eyes had she gotten from her mother, a rare shade of green and gold, as likely to sparkle in humor as to flash in anger.

And it was known to all that she bore the same temper as her father. What else would keep a girl almost two years away from her home?

Lilliane was aware of the speculative looks her entrance on her father's arm created. She knew the gossip their estrangement had caused. But tonight she felt no estrangement at all. It was simply good to be home and in this company.

She smiled warmly at Tullia and Santon as she ascended the steps to the head table. But as she moved her gaze to include Odelia and Aldis, she was taken aback by the fury in her other sister's expression. Sir Aldis as well seemed soured by her appearance. With a sigh she let her father seat her in the chair next to his own. When his hand squeezed hers, she glanced warmly at him and vowed to ignore Odelia's foul mood.

As the guests found their own seats, Lilliane's eyes swept the assembly, and it was then that she saw William. He was staring directly at her as he stood next to a woman he had just seated. For a long moment their eyes met, until his attention was drawn by the woman. He slowly sat down beside her on the wide bench seat, but not before he sent a last, lingering glance toward Lilliane.

There was something in that look that disturbed her, and Lilliane turned her attention to the servant who poured wine for her. Grateful for the distraction, she sipped at the liquid and glanced covertly back at William.

He was as handsome as ever, she noted, tall and elegant-looking with his hair in tawny waves upon his collar. He was dressed in an intricately detailed tunic of red and gold. The woman with him wore the same colors, and Lilliane realized at once that she must be William's wife. She was a small, pretty woman, with hair nearly as pale as Tullia's. It did not surprise Lilliane at all that William had married well. She had heard of Lady Verone and knew that she had brought a fine castle and many serfs to the marriage. That she was also beautiful seemed only right, for William of Dearne was as beautiful a man as a woman was ever likely to find.

At that moment he looked toward her again, and she immediately lowered her gaze. For two long years she had kept his memory alive, knowing that they would never marry but still needing some romantic imaginings in her young and confined life. Yet now, faced with his clear interest in her, she was uneasy.

"Yon William seems most distracted by your presence here." Her father spoke in her ear. "That is his wife at his elbow. She is with child," he added pointedly.

"You do me an injustice," Lilliane retorted curtly, a faint blush coloring her cheeks. "Do you think I have less honor than you? Do you think I would dally

about with a married man?" She shot him a sharp
look before picking up her goblet once more.

Lord Barton leaned back in his carved chair and
scrutinized her angry face. "Nay, daughter," he replied softly. "I know you would not dishonor yourself nor your family in such a poor manner. But as
for William . . ." He shrugged. "I hear much of him
and his antics at court. You have been away from
such doings a long time." He reached out a hand and
touched her cheek tenderly. "And you've grown even
more beautiful in your absence from Orrick."

The fond expression in his eyes dissolved every bit
of Lilliane's anger. She had no trouble standing up to
his wrath or his displeasure. But his gentle affection
was her undoing. Impulsively she clasped his hand
and smiled ruefully. "Your eyesight must surely be
failing. I'm quite the vestal now. Quite the aging
maiden. You've set yourself a Herculean task if you
hope to find me a husband."

She had thought to make him laugh, but Lord Barton seemed preoccupied and he only squeezed her
hand tighter. "It's too bad," he said slowly.

"Too bad?" she asked, not understanding his
words.

He seemed to rouse then. "About Colchester. It's
too bad your betrothal to him could not be consum-
mated."

For a moment Lilliane did not respond. The name
Colchester brought a myriad of near-forgotten images to mind. Once she had dimpled and blushed at
any reference to the handsome young knight chosen
for her so many years ago. Corbett of Colchester had
been tall and well muscled, enough to make any
young girl tremble with pleasure. She'd been the

envy of the other women in the castle. But that had been before. Before the trouble. Before the bloody wars that had turned the houses of Orrick and Colchester into bitter enemies. Now the name Colchester was anathema, a name she despised. They had stolen the innocence of childhood from her. And they'd killed her dear cousin Jarvis.

"Colchester?" Lilliane pulled her hand from her father's grip and stared at him reproachfully. "You dare mourn his loss as a son-in-law? Why, those barbarians from Colchester are a curse upon the earth and most particularly upon Windermere Fold. Can you forget the five years of misery they've brought upon the people of Orrick? Can you forget that they murdered Jarvis?"

"I forget nothing," he answered with a warning light in his eyes, "Jarvis was as near to a son as I had. But as lord of Orrick I cannot allow my personal feelings to interfere in what is best for my people. And it would have been best—"

"If the lot of them had died in the birthing!"

"Is that the bloodthirsty lesson they've taught you at Burgram Abbey? If so, you may be sure Mother Mary Catherine shall hear from me. I send her a sweet and innocent maid and she sends me back a warrior wench willing to curse a family and see it ruined—"

"You did not send me to her," Lilliane retorted hotly. "I chose to go. And she did not send me back, I decided to return. And if you've any thoughts of approaching that offspring of Colchester on my behalf, I assure you that I shall flee to Burgram Abbey and take the vows of sisterhood!"

"Calm yourself, daughter. Calm yourself. 'Tis sad

to say but my musings are only that, musings. Young Colchester has been gone these past years to the crusades. I know not if he even lives." He paused and gazed out at the gathering below them. "But he was a strapping fellow was Corbett. I'll warrant that he's done fair well for himself in the East. He's the sort of fellow Jarvis would have turned out to be." Lord Barton picked up his goblet and drank deeply from it as memories pressed in on him. "It would have been a good marriage between Orrick and Colchester. Corbett would have made you a good husband, and this valley would have finally been at peace."

Lilliane stared down at her platter, disturbed by the same memories. "But they chose instead to make war on us."

"They believed Lord Frayne was murdered at my bidding. What else could two loyal sons do but seek to avenge their father's death? If Jarvis hadn't fallen in battle against them, I believe the war would proceed yet."

"An eye for an eye?"

"So it seems. Oh, do not misunderstand. There's no love lost between us even still, for they yet thirst for revenge against me. To pass beyond the Middling Stone and into Colchester lands, any man of Orrick would surely be inviting death. And likewise should they venture here. But there's been no outright fighting since Edward drew so many knights away on his crusade."

"They're still our enemies," Lilliane asserted.

"Aye, they are that." Lord Barton sighed. "And it seems unlikely any change shall be forthcoming."

The remainder of the meal passed in relative peace. The difficult subjects of William, Sir Corbett of Colchester, and her future were assiduously avoided. Sir Aldis made a point of capturing his father-in-law's attention on a number of matters pertaining to Orrick's defenses, and Tullia did her best to keep Odelia, Lilliane, and Santon entertained. But Odelia seemed bent on being difficult, and Tullia ultimately retreated to the sanctuary of the adoring Santon's attention. Left to her own devices by Odelia's studious exclusion of her, Lilliane watched those assembled in the great hall below the raised family table.

Once the meal ended the amusements began. Several minstrels entertained the crowd with their witty songs and bawdy lyrics. Dogs darted beneath the tables, seeking cast-off morsels, while children teased and ran about, plaguing both adults and beasts with their pranks.

Still, there was an atmosphere of harmony and good cheer over the entire gathering. The summer had been one of good harvest and relative peace. They gathered now to celebrate a wedding. Except for the conspicuous absence of everyone from their nearest neighbor's domicile, the Castle Colchester, Lilliane would have described it as a perfect evening.

The thought of the Colchester family brought a frown to her piquant features. She had not thought of her betrothal to Sir Corbett of Colchester in years, and it bothered her that her father had brought it up tonight. She'd been but fourteen at the time. Her father and Lord Frayne of Colchester had hoped to seal their shaky friendship through the marriage of Orrick's eldest daughter to Colchester's youngest son.

He'd been much older, of course. Twenty-three years to her fourteen. But she remembered well the tall, quiet youth. He'd been so dark and solemn he had somewhat frightened her at the time. Still, he was so handsome and dashing that she'd been quite pleased. As a betrothal gift he'd given her a matching silver hair comb and looking glass, and she'd cherished it. She'd been quite the envy of her sisters, and even her mother, Lady Edlyn, had been impressed.

But that was long ago, Lilliane reminded herself sharply. The following year her mother had died in a late childbirth. Her father had been mad in his grief, and he had quarreled quite violently with Lord Frayne over a shepherds' dispute. The next day Lord Frayne had been found killed. Although witnesses had accused Lord Barton, and indeed much evidence pointed in his direction, he had taken an oath of innocence.

The ensuing war between the two houses had raged up and down the long valley of Windermere Fold. The river Keene had more than once run red with blood. It was not until her only cousin, dear Jarvis, had fallen that any semblance of peace had come. But it had been a peace built of pain and lasting scars. Even now she remembered those days as the worst of her young life.

The duties of chatelaine she'd taken on well enough. After all, her mother had trained her in all facets of running a castle. But the death of the young cousin who had been like a brother to her and the long and painful recovery of her severely injured father had taxed her sorely. Those had been bleak days at Orrick. No laughter and song, no pleasantries to ease a young girl's labors.

But they had survived, and they always would, she thought with fierce pride. Let Colchester do its worst;

Orrick would always come through. And despite her father's maunderings, she had no cause to fear the return of Corbett of Colchester. If the good God in heaven were truly just, then surely He had sent some heathen's sword straight through that knave's black heart!

Disturbed by her memories, Lilliane rose to go. She bid her father good night then gave brief instructions to the steward and made a cursory inspection of the kitchens before ascending the stairs. From the great hall the sounds of gay shouts and singing echoed, and she even began to hum along with one familiar tune. It was as she was turning to mount a narrower stair to her personal chambers that a man moved from the shadows to block her path.

"At last you have come."

At her startled gasp Sir William stepped farther into the torchlight and extended a hand to steady her. "I could hardly believe my eyes when I saw you."

His voice was quiet, barely above a whisper, and when she did not at first respond he gently pulled her toward him and into the dimmer recesses of the stairway. But as his hands tightened on her upper arms, Lilliane recovered from her shock.

"You should not seek me out," she admonished him softly. Then she pulled away. "It does neither of us good and most certainly is a disservice to your wife."

For a moment his eyes ran over her and Lilliane felt her heart quicken. "It was only that you are even more beautiful than ever, Lilliane. Even my memories could not do you justice," he vowed with one hand held earnestly to his velvet-clad chest.

"Please, William. You must not say such things to me."

"May I not speak the truth when I see it?" he reasoned, taking a step forward. "May I not say how like the fields your eyes are, amber and forever changing? May I not say how like the autumn's russet leaves your hair is, red and brown and golden? May I not—"

"No!" she rejoined sharply as a knife seemed to twist in her heart. "You may not say such things to me, now or ever. It got us nowhere before, and now you have a wife."

He seemed to come to his senses then, for his face became harder and his smile faded. "Yes, I do have a wife. But you have no husband. Is it still your father's plan to find you one? Or will you continue at the abbey?"

Lilliane shook her head slowly. Her decision was suddenly easy to make. "No, I shall stay here. Whether he will see me wed I cannot say. But for now I shall stay."

For a long moment William only stared at her, and she feared he meant to throw all caution to the winds and take her in his arms. A small part of her would have welcomed his domination: it had been so long since she had felt beautiful and desirable. But there was another side of her that found his amorous pursuit completely distasteful. He had a wife. His moral duty must be to her and to no other. Oh, she knew that many married men dallied with other women. But she would never stoop to participating in such perfidy.

Her disapproval must have shown on her face for William seemed to become annoyed. "You'll have no say in whom he chooses, you know. He'll use you for whatever purposes best suit Orrick."

"Can you say you would do otherwise with your firstborn daughter?" Lilliane challenged him in quick defense of her father. "Can you say you will not use that babe that even now grows beneath your wife's heart to achieve what you cannot get in any other fashion?"

Surprise registered in his face then, but his answer sidestepped her words. "I would have made him a good son-in-law. I would have made Orrick a good lord and I would have made you happy."

"That may have been, but it's too late now."

Frowning, William turned to leave, but then he paused and peered closely at her. "Perhaps I should warn you that I've seen Sir Corbett at court, not three weeks past. He's back from the crusade. He still has no wife."

With that parting comment he left.

She heard the sound of his descent. She heard the faint echoes of the gathering below. But Lilliane did not heed any of those things. Instead it seemed that a dreadful weight of foreboding lodged in her chest. Like a web, the threads of her past seemed to wind about her and imprison her.

Then on swift feet she hurried to her own chamber and pulled the heavy paneled door closed behind her. Her fingers trembled as she unlaced her over-dress, then removed her stockings and slippers. She loosened her wimple and unwound her hair from its tight coil, then shook its luxurious length free. Absentmindedly she began to plait it for bed when a sudden thought gave her pause.

She moved to an oaken chest beneath the narrow

window and knelt before it. Within its depths were the memories of her entire childhood: the linen garments she'd stitched for her wedding, the fabric she had laid aside for her eventual husband's wedding costume, and the tiny garments she'd begun for her babies. A chain of daisy flowers, withered and dry, a scapula that was torn but too sacred to discard, and a collection of pebbles also were buried within its depths, but it was not any of these she sought. In the far corner of the chest, wrapped in a rough bit of fustian, old and softened by countless washings, she found the package she searched for.

Lilliane sat back on her heels and stared at the abandoned bundle for a long time before she opened it. When she brought the two items into the light, she was almost disappointed with their shining beauty. They were an ornately designed hair comb and a silver looking glass, both engraved with curling tendrils and lily flowers. On the back of each a fanciful letter *L* was formed, set with sparkling chips of meridian. The lavender gems were from the Middling Stone, she recalled, the stone that marked the dividing line of Windermere Fold.

She traced each shape as she'd done so often in her youth. Somehow she'd expected them to be hideous now, as ugly and awful as the terrible state between their two families. But no, the two pieces were as exquisite as they'd ever been.

With an angry oath she pushed them away from her.

She had no reason to fear Corbett of Colchester's return, she told herself. He would never seek out his enemy's daughter. Never.

Calming herself with that thought, she retrieved

the silver glass and brush and quickly wrapped them back in their coarsely woven cloth. Then she thrust them into the deepest corner of the chest and piled the other items over them. She slammed the chest closed and quickly blew out the candles, then she hopped into her high curtained bed.

Then, as if for good measure, she pulled the heavy fur cover up over her head.

2

A tray clattered from the servant's hand. He cringed as his master sharply cuffed him, but he obviously knew better than to run from his lord's anger. Every servant at Colchester was well aware that left without an outlet, Sir Hughe's fury would increase tenfold. In spite of his quaking fear, the poor man only bowed his head and inured himself as best he could to the rain of blows.

Sir Corbett of Colchester could not hide his disgust at his older brother's display. His face darkened in a frown and that, taken with the wicked scar that marred his brow, gave him a fierce expression. With three quick strides he entered the hall and crossed directly to Hughe.

"Do you have trouble with the servants? I recall no such problems at Colchester Castle in the past."

Hughe drew himself up immediately. When he turned to his brother there was no trace of anger on his face, nor chagrin either. But the smile he forced to his lips was also devoid of any warmth. Corbett had to steel himself against the distaste he felt for his brother, the last living remnant of his family.

"He is lazy," Hughe explained with a shrug. "As is the lot of them. I should send them all to work in the fields. Then they might appreciate my generosity, which they now take so much for granted." With a flick of his hand he signaled the hapless servant to leave.

On the surface it was nothing of any great merit: a careless servant reprimanded by his master. But Corbett was finding too many disturbing incidents at Colchester for him simply to ignore. On the surface the castle was finer than ever it had been; rugs, tapestries, and even window glass made Colchester impressive indeed. Yet beyond the fine trappings all was not as it should be. Corbett had been home but three days, yet he'd not been able to miss that fact.

The conversation was strained as the two brothers made their way toward the bailey. Hughe spoke of inconsequential matters, of hunting and his prize falcons. Yet Corbett had the uneasy feeling Hughe was avoiding something. On the steps of the hall Corbett turned to face his brother. Although he was troubled, he kept his face carefully composed.

"There was not much talk of the northern shires in London. And you've said little enough. Does this mean nothing has changed in the years I've been gone?"

Hughe studied his tall younger brother through narrowed eyes. Then he pursed his lips and looked away. "We do well enough considering we do it without benefit of a king."

It was a curious statement and Corbett was puzzled by his brother's odd tone. "Edward has England's good at heart. As a loyal citizen you can hardly doubt that. If he is not definite about his return from the East, we must trust that it is a well-considered decision."

Hughe peered sharply at Corbett. But when his brother's stare did not waver, Hughe's dark eyes darted away. His lips thinned and sarcasm edged his voice when he replied. "There are those who say England is better off without his presence. I only hope the mad Scots to the north are as patient in awaiting his return as we 'loyal citizens' must be!"

There was an awkward silence between them as they descended to the bailey. Then Hughe recovered a modicum of good grace.

"Now that you depart Colchester, shall you make your way to London? Or perhaps return to the East?"

It was a polite question, forced perhaps, but polite nonetheless. Most certainly it would have been natural for Corbett to answer his only brother with the truth. But there was an uncomfortable tenseness between them, and Corbett responded with a caution he'd never thought to use with his own flesh and blood.

"London holds no real appeal. And I've no longer the stomach for the wars against the Turks."

"Edward is said to be much in your debt. He is clearly enamored of Normandy. Mayhap he will settle you with some well-dowered Norman bride."

Corbett could not help but note his brother's satisfied expression, and he felt an inexplicable sorrow. It was clear Hughe was eager for him to leave Colchester. Only the reason behind it was hard to determine.

Their parting was not fond, although Hughe forced a jovial mien. For three days Corbett and his band of knights and men-at-arms had sought the comfort of the home they'd left four years earlier when they'd joined Prince Edward's crusade. But there had been a coolness to their welcome just as now there was a subtle but undeniable relief about their departure.

Before Corbett would leave, however, he made a final visit to the family's tomb. The chapel was cool and dim. And musty. Another change from the days when his mother had seen every least portion of the castle clean and well aired, Corbett brooded. But his mother was dead now. She had not long survived her husband's death. Only he and Hughe remained, and there was a strain between them that he feared was caused by more than merely years and distance.

Corbett sighed and rubbed the jagged scar that marked the side of his brow. Whatever he had expected of his return to Colchester, this most certainly had not been it. He could always return to London and await the new king there. He was sure that was precisely what Hughe expected him to do. But that did not fit into his plans. Instead he would have to move his men into the Colchester fields and set up a temporary camp. Some more permanent arrangement would have to be made before winter fell in earnest, but for the present he had no alternative. Hughe was clearly ill at ease with him at Colchester and equally uneasy about King Edward's tardy return to England.

With another sigh he turned to leave. He had long ago grown tired of the miseries of war, of the suffering and the slaughter. Still, at least in war one knew what one must do and who the enemy was. Here in the northernmost reaches of England his purpose was vague and his enemies unknown. And yet, he was the prince's—the new king's—man. He would do as his liege lord required, and he would do it well.

When the contingent of soldiers departed Colchester a short time later, there was none of the gaiety that more commonly marked such activities. No horns sounded or flags waved, save the standards Corbett flew. They rode north, and once they were well away from the castle, one of the knights joined Corbett at the head of the double column.

"Blessed relieved I am to be leaving," the burly giant muttered. " 'Tis very like a morgue there. What ails the place?"

"Hughe," Corbett replied curtly. He shifted in his saddle and looked at his second in command. "My brother was always a strange one, Dunn. You can recall that. Often given to moods. But this. . . ." He shrugged. "He was thoroughly unsettled by my return."

Dunn snorted. "His knights—if you want to honor them with that title—have all grown fat and lazy. 'Twould be an easy task . . ."

Corbett smiled grimly. "If it were that simple. But that's not our purpose here."

" 'Tis our purpose to quell the opposition to King Edward in northern England—"

"Our purpose is to put down any treasonous plots. That has nothing to do with Hughe."

"Nothing apparent," Dunn intoned somberly. "He was not happy to see you. God's blood, man! If it is not you he fears, then who?"

It was a question Corbett was to ponder long and hard. During the gruesome years of fighting at Edward's side, then throughout the perilous return journey across the European continent and the dangerous crossing of the channel to England, he'd been sustained by thoughts of this beautiful, green valley. Windermere Fold had been like a shining beacon in the forest, promising peace and respite from the end-less horrors of war.

His gaze swept slowly across the valley, taking in the wide sloping fields divided neatly by low stone fences and dense green hedgerows. It was this very place he had longed for, and yet now that he was back he found it mired in secrecy and deceit. His mouth turned down as he thought of the name he'd earned: the king's Bird of Prey. He'd gladly protected his liege from the threats of the infidels. But now it was a threat from within that he must quell. And his enemy might be anyone—even his own brother.

The sun was well into its downward arc when Corbett broke ranks with his men and pushed his rambunctious destrier forward. Just ahead of them was the Middling Stone, and he urged his mount up the narrow trail that led toward its peak. Little more than a ledge protruded from the great stone outcropping, and it provided scanty footing for the mighty steed. Yet neither man nor beast was deterred. Upward they went, passing beyond the view of the men who waited at the base of the stone.

When the heavy destrier reached the end of the rugged path, he stood obediently while his rider dismounted. Then hand over hand, with his leather-shod feet struggling for a hold on the cold jagged rock, Corbett hauled himself up toward the peak. His breath was coming hard and fast when he finally reached his goal.

Far to the south, almost beyond his view, the gray granite towers of Colchester Castle rose, and the sight brought a frown to his face. He had thought to make Colchester his home base as he followed through on Edward's orders to ferret out the root of treason that brewed in northern England. It was natural that he would return there, and no suspicions would be roused by his presence at Colchester. But Hughe clearly did not wish to have his brother under his own roof any longer.

For several more seconds Corbett stared south to the distant fortress, his expression harsh, his eyes somber. Finally he turned away to begin his descent.

It was then that a shaft of sunlight pierced the leaden gray layer of clouds that hung low over the northern end of the valley. Like a golden finger of light, it touched on the pale walls of faraway Orrick Castle, and it gave him pause. Equidistant from the Middling Stone, Orrick governed the northern half of Windermere Fold, and Colchester ruled the southern half. Yet he'd not thought of Orrick in years.

Now, as the sunlight glinted off the solid limestone walls, he could not tear his eyes away. An early autumn wind ruffled his dark hair but he did not notice, so intent was he on that distant vision. Then a slow smile lighted his face, softening his hard, masculine features. He started to leave but was suddenly stopped by a remnant memory from his youth. In short order he cleared away the accumulated moss and lichen that covered a crevice near the base of the top jut of stone.

Even in the dreary light of the overcast day the narrow ribbon of lavender rock seemed luminous. Corbett rubbed his finger once then again down the rare vein of meridian. When he straightened up he looked back to the south.

Colchester Castle lay south. But perhaps, he thought speculatively, perhaps the best way to get there lay north. Through Orrick.

* * *

There were only two days left before the wedding, and Lilliane was determined to have all in readiness. Let Odelia entertain the chattering guests; Lilliane was hard at work in her oldest gown and kirtle. Her thick chestnut hair was bound in a length of plain linen to keep it out of her way.

She was in the storerooms with the pantler and the seneschal when the bell sounded the alarm. After abandoning her tasks, she scurried out into the bailey. There Lilliane found all in chaos. Foot soldiers rapidly scaled the stairs to the battlements. Animals were being herded inside the protective walls of the castle as the villagers fled their fields and cottages. Women frantically rounded up their children, counting heads to be sure none were missing. But despite the noise and confusion and the blinding dust, Lilliane heard her father's bellowing voice and saw his broad figure striding across the yard.

"Father! Wait!" she cried as she lifted her skirts and ran swiftly to his side. "What is it? What's happening?"

"Don't worry." He patted her arm distractedly, his eyes anxiously watching the hasty preparations. " 'Tis nothing you need worry about. Just take the ladies to the great hall and try to keep everyone calm."

"But can't you tell me what's going on? I must know," she pleaded as she held tightly to his arm.

He seemed to hear her then, and at last he met her worried gaze. "A full complement of armed men approach. Mounted knights, foot soldiers, and a caravan behind." He paused. "They fly banners of black and red."

As Lord Barton hurried away, shouting as he went, Lilliane stared after him in shock. Colchester flew black and red. Colchester was attacking Orrick! There could be no other cause for them to march so boldly up the hard-packed turnpike. There were no wars to the north, nothing to require such a display of strength.

They should have known better than to become complacent during the recent peaceful years, Lilliane fretted as she turned to find Tullia and Odelia. The Colchesters were an evil and cruel lot. Not in word or deed could anyone from Orrick trust them. Now it was clear they meant to humiliate Orrick by trapping all the wedding guests and holding the castle to siege. Angry and frustrated, Lilliane had no outlet for her emotions save the efficient management of the frightened guests.

It was two long hours before any word filtered down to the women and children gathered in the great hall. Even then they were left with more questions than answers, for the orders Lord Barton sent Lilliane bade her to clear the hall and to set out a jug of the finest ale the alewife had on hand and two tankards. Beyond that curt demand there was nothing.

The bailey was crowded with family, guests, and retainers when the bridge across the moat was lowered. Every protesting creak of the seldom-used cranking mechanism resounded across the multitude, but all else was hushed. Even the sheep and cattle penned temporarily between the stables and the tannery seemed to know better than to raise their voices.

As ominous as the bells of doom, the heavy measured tread of a large animal was finally heard crossing the bridge. When two other sets of horse hooves were also heard, Lilliane cringed in spite of herself.

The first rider who emerged through the gatehouse was an impressive sight. His steed was a deep-chested destrier, a war-horse clearly bred for strength, endurance, and speed. As black as coal, the animal's high arching neck and near-prancing gait seemed almost a challenge to the silently gaping crowd.

Sandwiched between her sisters, Lilliane was no less impressed by the magnificent destrier. But it was the huge knight astride the beast that truly awed her. He was clad in a bissyn shirt and a black leather sleeveless tunic, cut short in the warrior manner. Tall and erect, he wore neither armor nor chain mail, yet there was about him an air of invincibility, as if not arrow, blade, or mace could stay him from his goal. His head was bare of helm or hood, and in the light breeze his black hair lifted slightly.

It was the only part of him that appeared soft.

From his black leather boots to the piercing stare of his eyes, he looked as hard as forged iron. Lilliane had to prevent herself from making a quick sign of the cross as he passed where she stood. As brave as Daniel in the lion's den, he rode purposefully to where her father stood at the steps of the great hall. Then he dismounted and arrogantly preceded Lord Barton into the hall.

When the doors closed with an audible thud, the entire company in the bailey seemed to let loose their collectively held breath. The two riders who had followed their lord did not dismount, but only turned their steeds to face the curious throng.

Inside the great hall, Lord Barton offered his unexpected guest a chair, then he took his seat as well. It was not until his aged servant, Thomas, had poured out two tankards of ale and then backed away that he spoke.

"Your messenger said your business with me was urgent. I must confess, Colchester, that your presence here surprises me."

"And I will allow that I am equally surprised that you granted me safe passage."

Lord Barton took a swallow of ale as he studied the stern young man before him. A fine warrior before leaving to join Prince Edward, Corbett of Colchester was clearly a well-seasoned veteran of Edward's campaigns. The handsome face of his youth was no more, for no boyish quality remained. A long, puckered scar slanted across his brow and gave him a fierce expression.

He looked fit and strong, broader than before, but without an inkling of excess flesh. For the second time that week Lord Barton regretted that the young man's match with Lilliane could not be. What magnificent grandchildren they would have given him.

"I offered you safe passage only because I find myself puzzled. Colchester and Orrick remain bitter enemies. Or did your brother, Hughe, not remind you of that fact?"

"It does not take Hughe to remind me of the murder of my father."

It was said quietly. And yet Lord Barton felt a twinge of fear as he met the other man's unwavering stare. He had no doubt that Sir Corbett could easily best him. With the long Damascene steel blade that hung from his belt, the younger man could easily disembowel him before a single guard could be raised.

Still, Lord Barton had faced death many times, and while he sensed Sir Corbett's animosity, he did not detect any immediate threat.

"I stand by my vow of innocence on that score as staunchly as ever I did," he declared as he lowered his tankard to the oak table. "But surely you've not come here to discuss the past. State your business."

Sir Corbett's eyes narrowed and their clear gray seemed to darken almost to black. But he kept whatever emotions he felt well contained from the old lord's scrutiny.

"On that count you err, Lord Barton. It is indeed unfinished business from the past that brings me here."

"Then state it quickly and be gone from here. I've a vast assemblage gathered, come to celebrate my daughter's marriage."

"Her marriage?" In an instant Corbett came out of his seat. His face was creased in anger as he leaned over the table and glowered at Lord Barton. "The contract still stands. No one from Colchester consented to break the agreement. You cannot illegally wed her to another!"

Lord Barton was taken aback by Sir Corbett's violent reaction to his words, but a canny light quickly crept into his faded blue eyes. " 'Tis Tullia I speak of. And she's no contract save with Sir Santon of Gaston. Perhaps in the long years that have passed you've forgotten which of my daughters it was you were betrothed to. 'Twas Lilliane you were to wed. Lilliane, my eldest." He picked up his tankard and quaffed the last of his ale.

"Lilliane." Corbett repeated the name as he slowly returned to his seat. The anger had disappeared from his face. "Yes, I remember her. A puny child with eyes overlarge for her little face." At the stormy look he received from the older man he smiled slightly. "I've heard that she yet remains the maiden while her younger sisters marry. Perhaps that is why. But puny or no, I've come to exercise my betrothal rights."

Lord Barton did not answer right away. He was torn between fury at this impudent upstart and thankfulness that the match he'd always wanted would finally be made. But it would not do to reveal any eagerness, he realized. When he did speak he called first for more ale. Thomas silently refilled first his master's tankard, then the young lord's.

"So you wish to wed Lilliane. Why should I allow it? The house of Colchester has waged war on us for five long years. Jarvis, my beloved nephew who was more a son to me, fell to Colchester steel—"

"As my father fell to the Orrick assassin's foul blow," Crobett countered grimly. "I'll not pretend to any liking for this proposal. I've no desire for your spinster daughter beyond the castle and lands that go with her."

"Then I'll be damned if I'll see the spawn of Colchester sit in my place!" Lord Barton angrily swept his tankard of ale from the table with a loud crash.

"Whether by your consent, old man, or by war, I'll have her to wife. And you may be certain King Edward will support my suit!"

For long silent moments the tension stretched between them. Even the aging servant knew better than to move. Then Lord Barton waved Thomas away and, with a crafty glint in his eyes, turned to face his young adversary. "What if she will not have you? She has no love for Colchester."

"She is a woman. She has no say in this," the knight replied derisively.

An expression akin to amusement passed over the old lord's face, but it was quickly gone and he once again appeared the wary baron. "You've the right of that. The decision will be mine. But as I see it, I've no reason to agree. Colchester has been our enemy too long for me to turn my daughter over to you. She is my eldest child. My own flesh." He paused. "She has ever been my favorite."

"Why has she not married before now?" Corbett asked bluntly. "I'll tell you why. She is poorly favored else you would have been besieged with suitors. 'Tis clear I do you a kindness to take her out of your keeping."

"You do me no kindness with this offer. You would have my child and then my castle and lands. And you would have me dead in my sleep as soon after the wedding as possible. No." Lord Barton stood as if to leave. "I have two sons-in-law already. And I'll not send my Lilliane to Colchester Castle."

"We'll live here."

Corbett had stood as well and Lord Barton eyed the towering man assessingly. "Does this mean you're not welcome at Colchester? Or is this a plot yon Hughe has prepared?"

Sir Corbett tensed at that and his expression darkened. But when he spoke Lord Barton noted that he held whatever bothered him well in check. "My marriage is mine own affair."

There was a short silence.

"My son-in-law Aldis would not take kindly to your presence here," Lord Barton warned.

"Ah, yes. Aldis of Handley. Let me concern myself with Aldis and any others who object."

A dull ache had begun in Lord Barton's side, and he quickly found his chair. "I'll not say yea nor will I say nay so quickly. This is a matter that affects every soul in Orrick." He lifted one shaggy brow. "I'll not be hurried."

Corbett shrugged and also sat down. "So be it. But when Santon weds Tullia, then also will I wed Lilliane."

The suspense in the courtyard was unbearable. More than one person had identified the daring rider as Sir Corbett of Colchester, lately returned from Edward's crusade. But Lilliane would not let herself believe it. Sir Corbett had been such a handsome young fellow, she recalled. At one time he'd quite captured her girlish imagination. Although he'd been quiet and rather somber, she remembered none of this fierce and terrifying demeanor. Besides, she reassured herself, Sir Corbett of Colchester had no reason to come here. What business could he possibly have with her father?

It was old Thomas who was to provide the terrible answer to that question. When he emerged from the keep, he was crowded about and bombarded with questions. But he ignored the curious throng and made his way to where the ladies clustered beneath the chestnut tree. Like the piper leading a mesmerized crowd, Thomas made his slow way to them. And as his eyes remained locked on her, Lilliane began to feel a cold chill of dread.

When he stood directly before her, the crowd hushed and everyone waited anxiously for his words.

"Lady Lilliane," he began, his old eyes infinitely sad. "They have—"

"No! Not here." Lilliane would hear the terrible news in private, and no matter how Odelia and the other ladies complained, she ignored them. She was beside herself with worry as she slowed to match the old man's pace. But even as she passed through the crowded courtyard, she could hear the gossip begin.

"All right, Thomas," she began when they had reached the privacy of the falcon room. "What is it those two are about in there?"

"'Tis your betrothal contract, milady," he explained. "Young Colchester demands that you wed him."

Lilliane took a deep shaky breath. "And . . . and my father? What does he reply?"

"Well, he hasn't rightly said yes. But . . ."

"But?" Lilliane whispered, aghast. She put a trembling hand to her throat.

"I've been with Lord Barton since I was a mere lad and he a mere babe in his mother's arms." Thomas shook his grizzled head. "He'll agree. 'Tis what he's always wanted."

"But why! There is simply no logic in it at all."

She was suddenly struck by an awful thought. "It could even be a terrible trick, Thomas! A way for Colchester to get close enough to strike my father down and finally get their misguided revenge upon him!"

The old man seemed to consider her words, but then he spoke up. "You discredit Lord Barton if you think he could so easily be taken in."

"But why would he want to see me wed to our enemy? Has he forgotten how they accused him and sought to murder him? Or how they cut down poor Jarvis? Has he no pride?"

"Beggin' your pardon, milady, but 'tis Orrick that must come first with the master. And such a union would benefit Orrick."

"It would ruin us once and for all," Lilliane contradicted him angrily. But she knew her anger was poorly directed at Thomas. It was her father—and that barbarian he bargained with—who deserved the force of her anger. Bound to do just that, she hastened from the falconry. The grim determination on her face deterred anyone from questioning her, and she proceeded uninterrupted to the large pair of carved wooden doors that led into the great hall.

She went to push one of the heavy panels open. But at precisely that moment it swung inward, and she stumbled into the hard chest of the man who was just leaving. His powerful hands grabbed her and prevented her from falling. As she looked up, appalled, her vision was filled with the disapproving expression of Sir Corbett of Colchester. His dark eyes narrowed and he seemed to see right through her as he pulled her upright. Then he set her aside and turned back to his host.

"It appears Orrick is in need of a firmer hand if serving wenches are free to interrupt their lord during his deliberations!" Then with a last frown in her direction he quit the hall.

Lilliane was so stunned at the absolute gall of the man that she could formulate no retort until he was mounted and riding away. In anger she went to slam the door, using all her strength. But as if to mock the futility of her fury, the massive panel only screeched in slow protest as it closed with a dull thud.

She was angry and frustrated; her heart was pounding and her breath came fast as she turned toward her father. But the contented expression on his aged face drained all the emotion from her. Already knowing the answer to her question, she slumped back against the solid wooden door.

"Father, what have you done?"

He did not answer at once but peered keenly at her. "I've only done what any overlord worth his salt would do—"

"Sell your own daughter to the devil himself?" she whispered in anguish.

"He may not be precisely to your liking, daughter, but he'll make Orrick a good master. And you a fine husband."

"I'd sooner take vows at Burgram Abbey," Lilliane retorted in freshening anger. "You cannot truly mean for me to wed him!"

"Indeed I do mean it, Lilliane. The betrothal contract was never officially broken. And he and I are in agreement."

Impotent rage gripped Lilliane. "But I am not in agreement! When I said I would marry as you directed I knew it unlikely it would be for love. But you said you would seek a man of honor for me. Someone I could at least respect!"

"Do you now question my word?" Lord Barton thundered. "Sir Corbett is a man of honor! He has fought long and hard for his country and his faith! By God, woman, if you choose not to love him, then so be it. But you'd best learn to honor him, daughter.

And to give him the respect a wife owes her lord husband!"

Lilliane was speechless. Her father continued to stand at the end of the table, his thick brows lowered as he dared her to contradict him. But no words would come, and she turned and scurried from his presence. She did not hear his heavy sigh, nor was she there to witness the sorrowful expression that crossed his lined face. With a groan that mingled frustration and pain, he pressed a hand to his side and leaned heavily on the table. In an instant old Thomas appeared to ease his lord back into his chair.

" 'Twas you, wasn't it? 'Twas you told her," Lord Barton said, wheezing.

The servant frowned but his hands were no less gentle as he made his master comfortable. "Aye. But 'twould have been out soon enough. She needed to hear it from someone other than the gossips."

"Meddling old fool! Don't you think I know that? I'd have told her in good time."

"So you say. But you would have put it off and off. Now 'tis done," Thomas answered with flawless reasoning.

" 'Tis done indeed," Lord Barton said with a growl. "But she bears watching, that one does. She loved Jarvis dearly. His death was a hard blow for such a young girl. She's never forgiven the Colchesters. She'll not take this lightly."

"Shall I post a guard near her chamber?"

Lord Barton nodded, his face grimacing in pain. "Their marriage must be soon, Thomas. This rot in my gut gnaws at me night and day. I would see Orrick secure before I go."

"And Lilliane?" the old man prompted.

"Aye." Lord Barton's faded blue eyes met the other man's gaze. "I would also see my Lily settled before I go."

3

Lilliane worked like a demon. There was not a servant who did not jump at her first bidding and tackle whatever task she set before them with a fervor. She knew their diligence was born of fear of her angry countenance and brusque manner. But she could no more disguise her anger than she could ignore it. Let Odelia and Tullia see to the guests and prattle at small talk, she fumed. If she had to be civil to anyone, she knew she would explode.

Although the work in the pantry and storerooms proceeded with little talk, even so castle gossip managed to find its way to her. By the late afternoon when she dismissed the weary servants from their work she knew that the contingent of Colchester soldiers had established their camp in the fields just beyond the moat. She had found some small solace in hard work and anger, but now she could almost feel the chill hand of doom hovering over her.

Her father was seated in a chair near one of the hearths when she entered the great hall. Like fretful children, Odelia and Tullia fluttered around him. Beyond them Sir Aldis thrust an iron poker in and out of the fire. His ruddy face was redder than usual, and Lilliane knew at once that he was no happier than she about Sir Corbett's arrival. Although she certainly knew it was his own interests that concerned Aldis, not hers, she was nonetheless encouraged by his support.

As she approached the group Tullia spied her and immediately rushed to her side.

"Oh, Lilliane! Tell him I cannot do it. I cannot!" Her young face was so distraught and her words so desperate that Lilliane turned to her father in alarm.

"What do you plot now? What have you done to so upset her?"

"She has been mistress here for two years now, ever since Odelia married and you left," Lord Barton replied determinedly. "It is only fitting that she should see to our most esteemed guest's bath."

"That's not a custom in common use any longer. We've not followed it since Mother died," Lilliane countered as she put an arm around Tullia's trembling shoulders.

"We've had few enough guests since your beloved mother died. And none of such importance."

"Was Aldis of no importance?" Odelia cut in. "Are Santon and the rest of Tullia's guests of no importance? That man is most likely an assassin come to lower your guard so he may strike you a death blow, and you court him like some—"

"Silence, daughter!" Lord Barton roared. "Sir Corbett is the betrothed of my firstborn daughter. He will rule at Orrick when I'm gone and he has traveled long and hard. That is reason enough to honor his request for a bath."

"If he's come from Colchester then he's not come so far," Aldis bit out the words.

"His stay at Colchester was brief. I doubt Hughe gave his younger brother much welcome."

"And so he beat a hasty path here?" Lilliane put in. "Well, he can just as easily be on his way."

"He stays! And if Tullia will not attend his needs as a good chatelaine, then it falls to one or the other of you two."

"Don't look to me," Odelia hissed. "I'm only a guest here now. You've made it quite clear that Lilliane and her husband shall rule Orrick. Let her tend her bridegroom," she said with a sneer.

Lilliane was so taken aback by the venom in her sister's tone that for a minute she was speechless. Lord Barton was equally stunned. As Odelia stormed away with her husband hurrying in her wake, the old lord turned to face his eldest child. "Then it must fall to you. I trust you will not shame me or Orrick with some childish display of temper."

"You call it childish to show a temper when you would wed me to our enemy? Well, I shall see to his needs," she snapped. "I shall see his bath prepared. But if he expects a warm welcome, he'll be sorely disappointed."

But her father only shrugged at her sharp words. "He's a man. 'Tis unlikely a woman's waspish ways can unsettle him."

Her father's easy dismissal of her feelings seemed to pierce Lilliane's heart. She had to bite her lip to still the sudden quiver in her voice. Forcing a wan smile, she gave Tullia a small squeeze. "See that Magda heats water and send up the biggest tub and adequate linen. I'll go and prepare a chamber."

"I already instructed Thomas to have the tower

room prepared for him," Lord Barton stated as the two women turned to leave.

"What?" Lilliane whirled to face him. "You had him put in the tower room?" Absolute shock reflected in her disbelieving eyes.

"Am I not still lord here? Can I not put a guest where I will? I said the tower room. And Lilliane," he added, "do see that he's very comfortable."

She was too furious to reply. As she mounted the stairs that led past her sleeping chamber and up to the tower room, she seethed with resentment.

The exalted Sir Corbett—their enemy—was receiving her father's every attention. He was to be installed in the very room that had been her parents' domain all during their wedded years. Her father had not set foot in it since her mother's death. Yet this . . . this . . . this usurper was to be given free rein to it.

And to her.

A chill coursed down Lilliane's spine. That dark, glowering man was to become her husband and to be given complete control of her life. Unbidden an image came to mind of Sir Corbett as he'd appeared when their betrothal had been announced. She'd felt small and insignificant next to his tall frame. But if he'd been pained at the thought of marriage to such a skinny child, he'd hidden it admirably. They'd supped from the same trencher, and he'd been most patient with her shy bumbling.

But she was not that same impressionable girl, she reminded herself. Nor was he the cavalier of her dreams.

Lilliane was in a dither by the time she reached the iron-hinged door to the master's chamber. With hands that trembled, she eased the door open. The room had already been swept and aired. Thomas had been most efficient, for new linens lay over the high bed and a small fire now burned in the stone fireplace.

Lilliane had always loved this room, and although she'd not been in it in years, its effect on her was profound. For a moment she was caught in time, remembering a long-ago life that suddenly seemed as real as yesterday. Her mother had used the room as a retreat, a place for solitude or quiet conversations with her fast-growing daughters. It had been warm and inviting, and very special.

As quickly as that, Lilliane's anger fled, leaving in its stead a sad longing for a time that could never be again. She let her eyes sweep the room, noting the familiar furnishings and rugs. There were differences, though, she saw. The tapestry stand had been put away. Now only a chair stood before the tall, narrow windows.

Then she spied the heavy leather pouch leaning against the large trunk in the corner, and she felt a returning surge of anger. He had ridden into Orrick in the most arrogant manner. He had dismissed her as a mere servant, a maid of no importance whatsoever. And now he was using this room as if it was his due!

Swiftly she crossed to the pouch and shoved it away from her mother's long-emptied trunk. It fell with a dull thud, spilling a few garments and a sheaf of papers from beneath its loose flap.

Lilliane did not care one whit about his belongings. However, the papers did catch her interest. For a moment she hesitated. Then, with a wary glance over her shoulder, she knelt down and lifted the packet of tied papers into her lap.

Her slender hands were quick as she sifted through the documents. They were all written in the flowing hand of a scribe, she determined, with flourishes and wax seals in profusion. But it was in a language she could not fathom. Not French, nor Latin, nor even English, the words were completely foreign to her, and her brow creased in bemusement.

She was sitting on her knees, puzzling just what it could mean, when she felt the fine hairs on the nape of her neck raise. With a gasp she looked over at the door only to be met with the dark scowling vision of Sir Corbett.

He did not speak a word, but his fierce stare pinned her to her spot. Helpless and horribly embarrassed to be found thus, she nervously made to rise. But with three quick strides he was across the room and had planted one leather-booted foot on the skirt of her faded work gown.

At such an insulting gesture Lilliane's embarrassment fled. But when she tugged unsuccessfully to free herself, her anger began to rise.

"Is this the welcome all Orrick's guests receive? Their belongings rifled through?" At the quiet menace in his voice she paused, suddenly less sure of herself.

Mutely she stared up the long muscular length of him. He was a big man, but as he towered above her, his arms folded sternly across his massive chest, he appeared enormous, and she shrank back from him in fear. With a sudden movement he bent down and snatched the packet from her lap, then handed it to a brawny knight who had followed him in.

"What's this?" the other man exclaimed. "Has Orrick already loosened his pilfering horde upon us?"

"She may just be a pilferer. Or else a spy. But I'll soon have the truth of it, Dunn." So saying, Sir Corbett grabbed the back of Lilliane's gown and lifted her rudely to her feet.

Faced with his sinister glower and the equally clear animosity of his companion, Lilliane fell back a step, her mind empty of any retort. Her heart was pounding painfully and a small bead of icy sweat trickled down between her breasts. All she could think was that this terrifying man was the one she would be forced to marry. That threatening realization shook her to her very core.

"Speak up, girl," he ordered curtly. "What did you think to find by searching my belongings?"

"I . . . I only . . . It fell—" Lilliane stopped her babble abruptly. She took a deep breath. "I came in to prepare your bath and—"

"She has neither tub nor water," the man called Dunn scoffed.

"They're on their way," Lilliane snapped back at him as her anger returned.

"That's of no matter," Sir Corbett cut in. "The fact is you've shown yourself to be a thief or, even worse, a spy. I'll have neither in my household."

"Your household!" Lilliane sputtered. "Your household! You've no rights to Orrick—"

"Hold your tongue!"

Sir Corbett's thunderous command stilled her words momentarily, and it was during that quaking silence that a timid knock sounded.

Sir Corbett's man opened the door with a jerk, and the group of servants in the hall seemed to tremble as they viewed the two warrior knights. Their mistress's pale face did nothing to strengthen their resolve, and it was only the threat inherent in Dunn's gesture for them to enter that prevented them from fleeing.

The silence in the room was dreadful. Dunn watched keenly over the procession of servants bearing tub, water, soaps, and bath linens. Sir Corbett, in contrast, ignored the rest and kept his eyes trained on Lilliane. Conscious of his steady stare, she fought to regain her composure.

Orrick was her home, she told herself. She understood the need to have a strong and just lord to see to its well-being. Neither Aldis nor Santon would do; she would not argue her father on that score. But neither would this hard and suspicious knight do, she vowed. Unable to prevent herself, she lifted her downcast eyes to him.

She was immediately sorry. Sir Corbett's expression was no less forbidding. His tall, muscled form was no less threatening than before. But his dark eyes had cleared to an even gray and they were slipping now over her trim figure in interested scrutiny.

She'd been frightened of his anger before, but of a sudden Lilliane felt a far different sort of fear. Trying to restrain her panic, she clasped her arms tightly around her waist and licked her dry lips. But at precisely that moment Sir Corbett lifted his gaze from the fullness of her breasts to her face, and his eyes seemed to heat as he watched the swift darting movement of her small pink tongue.

She looked away at once. But it was only a matter of seconds before the servants were dismissed and she was once again alone with the two knights.

"See to your own quarters now," the dark knight bade his man, although his eyes did not veer from Lilliane. "And see guards well posted in the camp."

"I'll make a pallet in the hall at your door."

"It won't be needed."

"Damn it, Corbett! Isn't this chit's pilfering proof enough that it *is* needed?" Dunn stared balefully at Lilliane. "She may be a small enough threat, but think you that Orrick's sons-in-law will take your presence here lightly?"

"Neither of them look to be much opposition. Besides, I think our curious little maid may prove quite a boon." Sir Corbett smiled and revealed white even teeth. Yet Lilliane felt no relief at his smile; she was sure it bode ill for her.

"If you mean to bed her, it may be precisely what was intended."

Corbett laughed out loud. "She would no doubt fit quite neatly beneath a man. But I've no intention of spoiling the marriage before it's done. No." He caught Lilliane's wrist in his large palm and pulled her closer to him. "She shall assist me at my bath and nothing more."

There was something in his touch that disturbed Lilliane, although his grasp did not actually hurt her. She tugged at his hand, trying vainly to be free, but he only caught her chin in his other hand and tilted her face up to his. "You're the chit from this morning, aren't you?" he asked. Then he turned to Sir Dunn without waiting for an answer. "She came tearing into the hall as Lord Barton and I sealed our pact. Rather bold for a mere serving wench, wouldn't you say?"

The two men's eyes met and Lilliane knew some understanding passed between them.

"Well, then, I leave you to your sport." Dunn shrugged. "But bear in mind that she's got the advantage. She no doubt knows exactly which way the wind blows. She's on her home ground."

"It's my home ground now as well," Sir Corbett countered. He released his hold on Lilliane and watched as she scurried across the room. "I'll soon know which way the wind blows also."

Lilliane had to fight down her panic as the other knight departed. As frightened as she'd been at being caught in such awkward circumstances, there was something in her that feared much more being alone with this tall, battle-hardened knight.

Nervously she started to identify herself, then stopped and gathered her courage. He thought her a servant? Well, she would just play the part and see where it might lead. It seemed he was a man who had an eye for a comely maid. If he should become too free with her, she might be able to convince her father that the great Sir Corbett of Colchester was no better than a common, lusty soldier. Certainly he was not worthy of being lord of Orrick!

She peered at him through partially lowered lashes. It would not be easy. He was inordinately tall with muscled arms and shoulders that would put even Orrick's armorer to shame. But it was more than his physical strength that concerned her. There was a dangerous quality about him. She could not define it any better than that. She only knew he would not be a good person to have as an enemy.

Still, she reminded herself, they were already enemies. He might not recognize that fact, but she did.

And she was fighting for her very life. She weighed the circumstances and decided. If she could prove him a dishonorable man, her father would have to break the betrothal. He would have to!

She was standing against the rough limestone wall. Sir Corbett had not moved a step closer to her, and yet when his smoky gray eyes swept over her she felt his gaze as profoundly as a long, lingering touch. To her chagrin she felt a blush heat her cheeks, and she wished devoutly that she could simply disappear into a crack in the wide plank floor.

"Whether a thief or spy, you are surely a pleasure for the eyes," he commented quietly. Then he abruptly turned away from her and crossed the room to pull a velvet hanging back from one tall, arched window. He peered out into the late-afternoon sunlight.

"I should not be surprised that the 'lady' of the castle isn't here to attend her guest." He snorted. Then he shot her a sardonic look over his wide shoulder. "I'll have my bath first, then you can unpack my belongings. Those two tasks should satisfy your curiosity fairly well."

Lilliane almost snapped an angry retort back at him. Did he truly think she would assist him any further in his bath than seeing that everything he needed was at hand? But she wisely decided caution might be the better course, at least for now. Still, he must have seen the rebellious look in her stormy golden eyes, for his grin widened.

"You've a bold manner for a mere serving wench."

"If you were familiar with Orrick you would know that I'm no 'mere serving wench,'" she replied, unable to keep a note of belligerence out of her voice.

"Oh?" One dark brow lifted knowingly and his eyes seemed to take in every aspect of her appearance.

For a brief vain moment Lilliane wished she were dressed as befitted the lady of a castle. She knew her gown was serviceable at best, its soft blue long ago faded to drab gray. The linen that bound her hair was plain as well, and without even a wimple to add some dignity.

But then reason returned and she lifted her chin haughtily. She didn't care what he thought. She would never care what anyone from Colchester thought.

Noting her arrogant expression, Sir Corbett's eyes swept her willowy form, lingering at the soft white hollow of her throat then following the sweet curve of her jawline to meet her angry glare. "Any other maidservant would be shuffling around, never daring to meet my eyes, let alone argue with me. But you," he said as he strolled toward her. "You dare much with the new lord of Orrick."

He let his gaze drop to her breasts, then ever so slowly lower to her toes. She felt burned by his frank appraisal of her, and she bit her lip in vexation. Then his eyes made a leisurely return up her feminine form, pausing at her rose-hued lips before raising to her now-furious eyes.

"You must be Lord Barton's . . . personal servant." He grinned. "I'll give him credit for good taste. But I should think he'd dress you in finer gowns if you treated him well. Don't you treat him well?"

Although taken aback by his innuendo, Lilliane managed to respond in her iciest tone. "I treat him well enough. I'll have you know the lord of this castle is an honorable man—"

"But a man nonetheless," he taunted.

"No doubt he has his flaws," she retorted angrily. "For instance, he was sorely mistaken when he selected such a base and lowborn fool as you for a son-in-law!"

It was the wrong thing to say.

In an instant he had her by the arms, and she was completely unable to break his grasp no matter how she struggled.

"You'd best take a care and not anger he who shall soon be your master."

"You'll never be my master." She panted as she fought him. But he only clasped her against his broad chest until her breasts were pressed hard against him.

"Oh, I'll master you, my pretty little maid. But which will be more effective?" He mocked her with a gleam in his dark eyes. "Strength or seduction?"

His face lowered and for a wild instant she thought he meant to kiss her. She tensed, determined to avoid him, and closed her eyes tightly. When he chuckled, however, then suddenly released her, her eyes flew wide open and she stared at him in surprise and suspicion.

His eyes were warmer now, lighted from within as from a low and smoldering fire. But his words, when he spoke, were as arrogant as before. "You've a fair face, and even that dreary gown cannot completely hide your soft, rounded form. But it's your mistress I'll be bedding. You'll have to be satisfied with the old lord."

Then he unbuckled his leather sword belt and set it aside. He sat down on an upholstered bench and stretched his long, muscled legs before him. "Help me to my bath. I've weeks of travel to wash away. And a new bride to impress," he added sarcastically.

Lilliane did not respond at once. Her mind was working so quickly she did not know how to react. A part of her wanted to tell him in no uncertain terms what she thought of his appalling manners. He had been at Orrick but a few hours, and already he chased the serving maids. He didn't even have the decency to wait until after the wedding. The fact that her father fully intended to marry her to this wretch and, further, considered him a man of honor was galling beyond belief. A knight indeed! This great grinning brute who sat before her most assuredly knew not one whit about chivalry!

But then that would be his undoing, she reminded herself.

With her resolve firm she faced the arrogant man. A faint smile played upon her lips. "It's unlikely you can do anything that would impress the Lady Lilliane."

He did not immediately respond and she realized he was staring at her softly curving mouth. Disturbed, she looked away, a frown returning to her face.

"It is no matter how particular she proves to be. She will submit to her husband's will. Now come here and remove my tunic."

It took all her willpower to hold her anger in check. Only by reminding herself of her goal to rid herself of him once and for all could she force herself to do as he ordered. Still, her reluctance must have been apparent, for when she stopped near his outstretched feet he grinned.

"Come closer. I'll not bite you."

Lilliane's heart was racing in her chest as she edged closer. His gray eyes were steady on her, and she wondered what thoughts churned beneath their hooded surface. He did not move to make it easier for her, and it was with a frustrated sigh of resignation that she reached to loosen the silver-edged leather girdle at his waist.

She had to bite back an oath as her fingers fumbled with the buckle. Instead of acting cool and detached, she was trembling like a child and, what was worse, he was quite aware of it. When she finally had it unfastened, she pulled it from around his waist and hastily put it aside.

His tunic was next and he obligingly leaned forward to make her task easier. But if removing his belt had made her nervous, sliding the soft hide tunic over his shoulders rattled her completely. Like a living extension of him, the leather retained his body warmth. Lilliane nearly flung it away, she was so anxious to be free of the strange feelings it caused in her.

He looked up at her when she hesitated to remove his shirt, and she was sure it was amusement that sparkled in his eyes. "My shirt," he prompted smugly. Then when she did not respond he grinned. "Remove my boots then."

"Remove them yourself," she snapped.

His gaze grew warning and his words were low and steady. "Lord Barton may be lax with you. But I will not."

It took all her willpower to choke back her fury. He was no more than an arrogant fool! Yet she knew she must play this role of servant. Just do it, she told herself. It will soon be over.

Gritting her teeth, she knelt down and turned her attention to his boots. As she concentrated grimly on her task, she noted that they were of an unusual style, rising almost to his knees and hiding most of his hose. The leather was heavy and yet it was amazingly supple.

Once he was clad only in his hose, braies, and shirt, and she was faced with the choice of what to remove, Lilliane balked at last. After scrambling to her feet, she backed away.

"My shirt. Come, pull it off," he ordered from his relaxed position on the bench.

Lilliane swallowed convulsively then shook her head.

"You'd best learn now that I demand obedience of all my servants and retainers." His face was unreadable and his voice even, yet Lilliane felt a tremor of fear shake her. She was suddenly sorry that she had elected to play this dangerous game.

"I . . . I cannot," she whispered in a cracked voice.

"You mean you *will* not." Slowly he rose to stand tall and threatening before her. "Now come here and do as I say."

How she hated him at that moment. She hated him for the strength he had, so much greater than her own. And for the arrogant manner in which he was making the castle his. But most of all she hated him for the power he would soon have over her as her husband.

Trembling as much in anger as in fear, Lilliane approached him. With both hands she lifted the hem of the fine bissyn fabric and, with extreme care so as not to actually touch him, she slid it up his back. His bare skin was covered with a light sheen of sweat, making it a gleaming bronze in the afternoon light, and she closed her eyes to the disturbing sight. In her haste to finish her loathsome task she tugged the garment free of his shoulders, then, with a final yank, pulled it over his head. His arms slid easily from it, and she stepped back from him at once, unaware that she still clutched his shirt in her arms.

She'd known he was a big man, not only of rare height but of brawny muscle as well. But having him standing before her, bare to the waist, took her completely aback. She'd not often seen a man's naked chest, and yet she knew beyond all doubt that any man would envy him his powerful form. He was solid muscle, carved as a marble statue might be. But she knew he was warm to the touch.

Unwillingly her eyes slipped over him, from the heavy muscles of his broad shoulders, down his dark-furred chest to the rippling muscles of his trim waist. Her eyes stopped there, refusing to be drawn any further. The bunched fabric of his braies hid his hips and thighs from her view, and yet somehow she knew. His thighs would be like iron, finely wrought from years of horseback riding even as his arms were developed from endless practice at his battle skills. And the narrow line of hair that ran down his belly would end . . . She swallowed hard.

"Shall my bride find me as appealing as you seem to?"

She raised her eyes to his face with a jerk at his amused taunt and a wash of color flooded her cheeks. "As unappealing, you mean," she snapped. But she feared he saw past her angry retort, for his eyes were dark and smoldering from some heat from within. She watched in helpless fascination the tick of a muscle in his jaw. The moment seemed to stretch out forever, and even her breathing was suspended as if she waited for something.

Then, as if it were an effort, he turned away from her and toward his bath.

She heard but did not watch as he removed his remaining garments. It was only when she heard him step into the tub, then lower himself into the heated water, that she dared turn around. He was lying back in the hammered tin tub, his head against the rolled edge. His eyes were closed and he was so still she might have thought he slept. Yet somehow she knew he was quite alert. He was a knight, well trained and well seasoned, and she knew from her father's constant lectures to his own troops that this man had not survived by chance. He might rest, but the least sign of danger would bring him at once to the ready.

She wasn't sure what she should do. She had the soap and cloths in her hands, yet she could not force herself to approach him. Then, as if he sensed her dilemma, he spoke.

"Unpack my bags now. Put out suitable garments in which a bridegroom may meet his bride."

There was a tension in his voice that belied his relaxed position, but Lilliane was too relieved to note it overlong. With swift hands she emptied the satchel that had caused this awkward situation in the first place. Besides the sheaf of papers that he'd placed on the bed, there were only what she might expect a man to carry. Two shirts, extra braies, chausses and their bindings, and three handsome tunics.

She chose an iron-gray tunic, woven in a rare silk

cloth she'd seen only once before. Silver threads ran through it making it glimmer in the light, and she could not resist running her hand lightly over it.

" 'Tis made of Camoca. I had it stitched in Turkey."

Lilliane shot a sidelong glance at him. "It's lovely work," she allowed in a muted tone.

"I've trunks of such goods in my wagons."

It was a statement made with no particular inflection. Yet Lilliane sensed at once that there was much hinted at in his words. His eyes were no longer closed but were fastened upon her. Did he mean to tempt a poor serving girl with a length of fine cloth? She could not be sure, and his expression did not reveal his meaning.

When she made no reply, he raised himself to a sitting position, his arms resting on his bent knees.

"I've jewels, spices, perfumes." He splashed water onto his chest and slowly rubbed his hand on the wet, curling hairs. "Rugs, tapestries. Rare furs." He continued speaking but Lilliane made no note of his words. She was too intrigued by the absent movement of his hands. Around and around they moved in soothing circles as he washed. Her eyes skimmed lightly over the bronzed torso exposed above the softly steaming bathwater.

Despite the invincible image he'd presented earlier when he'd ridden so arrogantly into the bailey, she could see clearly that he was, after all, only a man. She had noticed then the nasty scar that marked his forehead and gave his left eyebrow its wicked arch. It had in some perverse way only made him seem less human. But the scars she saw now were not like that. One long gash tore its way across his chest from his arm almost to his throat. Another neat crescent marred the smooth skin of his side. It was the odd raking scar that ran across the back of one shoulder that caught her interest the most, however. Three parallel scars, they most certainly must have been caused by some huge beast's claws.

Unwittingly she shuddered at the thought of some wild creature's curving talons catching on that warm flesh and ripping it open. Then she felt his eyes upon her and she reluctantly lifted her gaze to meet his. There was a faint cynicism on his face and his tone was biting. "So tell me, will your sheltered mistress be repulsed by the honest scars that mark me? Shall she also quiver in fear at the very sight?"

Lilliane could not answer him for she felt a bewildering confusion. If she were to be honest, she would admit that, yes, Lady Lilliane of Orrick would—and did—indeed tremble in fear of him and his hard, battle-marked body. But it was not revulsion at the scars that affected her so. She could not say precisely what it was, but there was something about him that brought all her senses alert. Like some bird of prey's poor quarry, she knew she must be careful not to make a single misstep else he would have her in his merciless grip. Maid or lady, he was dangerous to either of her poses.

When she remained silent he snorted in disgust. Then he gestured to the wooden bucket. "Douse me thoroughly. Lady Lilliane awaits."

With hands that trembled she lifted the water bucket high and dumped it without warning full upon him. But this water was icy cold, and it brought him to his feet in surprise.

Lilliane jumped back in alarm, averting her eyes at once. With an oath he stepped out of the tub and wrapped a length of bleached linen around his waist. She was certain he must be furious. When he only stared at her with an odd, speculative gaze, however, her heart's pace increased and she swallowed convulsively.

She felt devoured by that gaze but it was going as she planned, she reminded herself nervously. If he would but show his base and dishonorable side, she could rid herself of the burden of marrying him.

He pushed his wet hair back from his face and slowly smiled. It crossed her mind that despite the hard planes of his face—the proud straight nose, the steel-gray eyes, and the solid jaw—when his lips softened in a smile, the harshness almost disappeared. Almost. But she would be a fool if she allowed that smile to deceive her, she told herself.

"You've a saucy manner." He paused. "What shall I call you?"

"You've no need to be calling me at all," Lilliane answered warily.

"Ah, but I'm a man who enjoys his bath. I think I shall often have need of your services."

"I've other duties—"

"Your first duty is to your master." He took an easy step forward.

Lilliane took a step back. "And what of your lady wife?" she goaded.

A brief shadow passed over his face. "It's doubtful my lady wife wants any more to do with me than I want to do with her."

"What a heartless attitude you bring to your marriage! You know naught of Lady Lilliane."

"I know she was a scrawny red-haired girl with eyes too large for her face. I know she has remained unmarried long past the time most maids are wed and with babe. And that with a considerable estate to commend her." He shrugged. "I can only reason that she has not grown into a particularly well-favored woman."

"But you will wed her nonetheless? Sight unseen?"

"A wife has little appeal for me. It will suit me most admirably if she chooses to surround herself with her women and their endless chatter, and leave me to attend my own duties."

Despite her anger at the dreadful picture of her he painted, Lilliane felt a wild flicker of hope. "Does that mean . . . well, I mean . . . what of an heir?" she finally blurted out in complete embarrassment.

He laughed out loud and advanced a step closer to her. "Begetting an heir will also be one of my duties—"

"Even if you are repulsed by your wife?" she interrupted in a tense voice.

"And even if she is repulsed by me."

"No doubt she will be," Lilliane retorted. But her words lacked the venom she'd intended, for she was suddenly overcome with emotions. He saw Orrick as a prize to be won. The wife he must take to get it was of no matter to him. No matter at all.

Abruptly she turned to leave. But Sir Corbett was quick to block her passage with one brawny arm across the door. "Where do you think you're going, wench? I haven't dismissed you yet."

His words, spoken with such infuriating confidence, seemed to bring all her confusing emotions to a boil. Without even thinking about it she struck out at him.

It was very likely that the sharp crack of her palm

•

against his cheek brought her more pain than it did him. Still, when he grabbed her wrist then pressed her roughly against the cold wall, her heart sank to her feet. His eyes were dark and threatening and his lips, which had curved in such a deceptive smile before, now were rigid with anger.

"You overstep your bounds," he said with a growl. His face was lowered so that only inches separated them.

"Let me go," she whispered in desperation. "Please just let me go." Her amber eyes were wide upon him. There was no hiding from his scrutiny in such close circumstances.

"Would Lord Barton let a serving girl—even one he holds in such high esteem—go unpunished for striking him?" He lifted his scarred brow skeptically. "Somehow I cannot believe it." His hand tightened on her wrist although he did not go so far as to hurt her. She was terribly aware that he wore only the damp linen toweling to cover his loins, and for that reason she did not lower her gaze. Yet his eyes boring into hers were equally disturbing.

Lilliane was frightened. She realized her plan to catch him in a dishonorable act had been quite mad, and she now saw how at his mercy she was. If he chose to act dishonorably there would be no way for her to stop him. In desperation she decided he might release her if he knew her true identity. But before she could speak, he moved even closer and she was shocked by the feel of his body pressing full length against hers.

"I have in mind a particular punishment," he whispered in her ear.

"No . . . no, you mustn't do this," she pleaded in a quivering voice.

"Indeed. But I fear I must. Beneath that plain gown I suspect I might find quite a delectable morsel." His lips moved closer to her ear until his breath heated against it. Frantically she tried to escape, but he would have none of it. "Let your hair free of that cloth you bind it in."

"No!" She looked up at him, aghast at his boldness, and said the worst thing she could think of. "You are a man of no honor!"

For a moment he tensed and she feared the repercussions he must surely send down upon her. But to her complete surprise, he heaved himself away from her and took a step back. For a long tense moment their eyes remained locked. Hers were a flashing gold, vivid with emotions, while his were a smoky, opaque gray. And yet she knew emotion boiled within him by the way he stood so rigidly as he stared at her. Then a bitter smile lifted his lips.

"I would have this incident kept between us and no others."

"What?" Lilliane stared at him increduously.

"There is no need for Lady Lilliane to hear of this," he said stiffly.

"It's rather late to think of your betrothed, wouldn't you say?" she jeered.

"To tell her of this can only cause her grief," he explained with a frown.

"And perhaps give her cause to call this farce of a marriage off," she taunted.

At that he smiled. "The marriage will go forth as planned. Never fear that." His face grew more serious. "Although I do not relish the thought of your spinster mistress in my bed, she will nonetheless be my wife. You may reveal to her our sport and make the marriage even more difficult for her. Or you may be a better servant to her and keep your silence. Who knows?" he added. "As time goes by you may find yourself becoming more agreeably inclined toward me."

"That will never be!" she spat venomously. "Now let me pass."

When he finally did step aside, she moved cautiously toward the door. Her gown was wet from where he'd pressed against her and her head linen was loosened and falling askew. As she passed him, holding her arms self-consciously across her wet bodice, he plucked the trailing end of her headrail.

Her hair needed no more than that to come completely unbound. In a thick curtain of chestnut and bronze it fell free about her shoulders and tumbled down to her waist. The sight drew him up short. But while he stared at the glorious cascade framing her pale face, Lilliane did not hesitate. In an instant she whipped around, pulled the door open, and fled into the hall.

He came to the door to stare after her, but she had disappeared down the stone staircase. Echoing in the still air, however, he heard her swift footsteps.

And a heartfelt oath wishing him cast to the devil.

4

~~~~~~~

She had put off going down to the evening meal
long enough. Ever since she had fled to the safety of
her chamber, Lilliane's anger had been festering. He
was as bad—no, worse—than she'd imagined! He
was arrogant, self-centered, and he had no heart
whatsoever. He wanted Orrick, not her.

No, she amended. He wanted her, just as he probably wanted any pretty little serving girl who crossed
his path. But it was not Lilliane of Orrick he wanted.

How she despised him, she fumed as she jabbed a
slender wooden hairpin into the woven crespin that
held the thick chestnut coils of her hair. She'd not
enjoyed the bath set out for her at all, barely cogni-
zant of the warm, rose-scented water. Only one
thought had consumed her, and that was the very
real need she had to put this heathen in his place. He
expected his betrothed to be a skinny spinster, plain
and unattractive—except for the very attractive
desmesne that went with her hand in marriage. Well,
she was looking forward to setting him straight.

She had decided to wear her most flattering gown
and her most elaborate girdle to this, their first real
meeting. After all, she reasoned spitefully, it was
only natural that a bride should want to impress her

future husband. Still, now that it was time to go down to the great hall she was hesitant.

She ran her hands nervously down the skirt, smoothing away an imaginary wrinkle, then patted her coiffure. She felt elegant and important in the exquisite samite fabric. The aqua silk was shot through with gold threads, and an intricate gold braid trimmed the neckline and the tightly laced sleeves. A finely embroidered girdle of gold metal worked into a russet silk cord emphasized her small waist and dangled in two long tassels nearly to the floor. Satisfied with her appearance, she reviewed once more the several sins she would lay at his door.

Her only hope for freeing herself from such an unacceptable marriage arrangement lay in convincing her father that Sir Corbett of Colchester would not make a suitable lord for Orrick. She would have to show him that the man was common and crude. That he was greedy and would very likely pauper Orrick.

She took a deep breath then lifted her head a notch. She was sure her father would agree with her once he had a chance to think about it. He would have to.

Lilliane sensed the difference even before she had reached the great hall. The gaiety of the previous evenings since the guests had started to arrive was gone, replaced now by a more subdued drone. People spoke in quieter tones with frequent glances toward the head table. When she reached the bottom step of the stone stairs, she quickly discerned the reason: her father and Sir Corbett sat there, side by side, surveying the vast gathering below them.

But if she thought the crowd subdued before her

entrance, the quiet that fell as she made her way through the maze of tables was truly astounding. Like a wave it preceded her so that before she reached the raised area where the family ate, the hall was completely silent. Even the dogs that wandered in search of an occasional bone or bit of fat seemed to sense the tension in the room and shrink away.

A part of Lilliane was pleased with the impact her entrance made, for wasn't it just such a showing she had hoped for tonight? But another part of her cringed at the spectacle they made of her. Everyone waited with bated breath for the introduction of the betrothed couple. Everyone wanted to see how Lord Barton's willful daughter responded to the enemy knight her father would have her wed.

Did they expect to see her deny him before the entire company? she wondered in rising agitation. Or did they relish seeing her cowed and obedient to her father's will? And her betrothed's?

Although she trembled from the emotional turmoil it brought her, she resolved to give the anxious crowd neither pleasure. She would not. With her head held high, she assumed her most regal posture as she continued through the hall.

Before her a sea of faces stretched, yet Lilliane would not look at them and could not have said who they were. Her gaze was drawn to the man who sat beside her father, and she was unable to break the hold of his dark eyes. She was gratified by his surprised expression and by the clear appreciation she saw on his face. Her lips even lifted slightly in a smug smile. But his faint answering grin brought a feeling of distinct unease to her. She paused before the table aware of a quiver deep within her, but she could not tear her eyes away from him.

He looked incredibly powerful at the lord's table, as if he had every right to such an honored seat at Orrick Castle. The steel-gray tunic gave him an air of invincibility and made his smoky gray eyes even more intense. Cleaned and combed, dressed in his finery, he did indeed appear the grand lord. And yet Lilliane refused to be deceived by his courtly attire. She knew that the warrior in him lurked beneath the façade he had donned. He might appear the gentlemanly knight this evening, but just a short while ago he had revealed his true self. He was selfish and arrogant, a hard, unfeeling man who did not care for anything—or anyone—but himself.

It wasn't until Lord Barton stood up and raised his heavy goblet that she was able to break the compelling hold of his eyes. But the pleased expression on her father's aging face cut her to the quick. He was truly happy with this union, she realized hopelessly. In his esteem it was the best thing for Orrick.

But it wasn't best for Orrick, Lilliane vowed. It wasn't! And it certainly wasn't best for her.

"Lilliane," her father began, his smile fond as he looked down upon his eldest daughter. "I know you must have met him earlier, Lily, but now I would like to properly present you to Sir Corbett of Colchester." He turned to the tall, scarred knight who now rose to his feet as well. "Sir Corbett, I present to you Lady Lilliane of Orrick."

The hall was in complete silence as the betrothed couple faced one another. Every eye watched as Sir Corbett lifted his goblet to her. Every ear strained to hear his words. But only Lilliane recognized the sardonic gleam in his eyes and the faint ring of sarcasm in his voice as he toasted his bride.

"To Lady Lilliane, the most beautiful . . . maid in Windermere Fold—nay, in all of northern England. I would have all of you drink to our happy union."

Every arm raised a drink to them, and yet Lilliane was not warmed by the gesture. She had succeeded in surprising him, both with her appearance and by her identity as the uncooperative maid he'd met earlier in the day. But that success tasted bitter now as she recognized the light in his eyes for what it was. He was still the victor in this battle of wills, for now he would have the saucy maiden who had caught his fancy right where he wanted her: in his bed.

It was with a grim expression that she mounted the three steps and made her way to the high-backed chair reserved for her. Sir Corbett was nothing but gallant as he saw her seated, but she knew he mocked her with every gesture. When he resettled himself beside her, she was quite aware of the dangerous glitter in his eyes.

"So we meet again," he whispered for her ears only. "And so soon. I'd thought you would be more difficult to find."

When she did not answer but only stared at the salt bowl on the table before her, he leaned a little closer. "I cannot tell you how much I anticipate our wedding."

"You did not anticipate it so readily before!" she snapped as she turned to face his baiting.

"Ah, but I had no inkling how delightful Lord Barton's eldest daughter was." One corner of his mouth lifted in a mocking grin.

"I promise you will not find marriage to me to be

delightful," Lilliane hissed. She was mindful of the curious gazes upon them, and she was hard-pressed to keep her expression civil and her tone low. But oh, how she wished to put him in his place!

"You will soon be brought to heel," he murmured. Then before she could prevent it, he took her hand in his and brought it to his lips. The kiss he pressed upon it was fleeting, light, and not entirely unpleasant. But when she tried to pull her hand free, he tightened his grasp and turned her hand over. The next kiss was not as fleeting nor as light. This time he pressed his warm lips against the tender flesh of her wrist. Her pulse jumped in shock, but that only seemed to encourage him. In a bold move he let his tongue flick over her suddenly heated skin. As he sought to move the kiss to her sensitive palm, she gasped in true alarm. His touch seemed to burn her flesh and her nerves tingled in reaction. Instinctively she curled her hand into a ball, and this time she succeeded in freeing it from his warm hold.

But she was not reassured by her meager success. Sir Corbett seemed, if anything, encouraged by her resistance. His face was relaxed in an irreverent grin and his eyes were alight with some heated emotion that she was sure boded ill for her.

She was growing less and less assured of her ability to send this barbarian on his way, but she knew more than ever that she must. Whatever it took, she vowed she would do, and yet, beyond tossing insults at him, she had no realistic plan. Still, she was preparing to do just that when her father leaned around Sir Corbett, a huge smile on his face.

"I knew the two of you would suit," he said with great satisfaction. "Why, 'tis clear as could be that your union will settle the trouble in this valley once and for all. With such a peace only prosperity can result."

Sir Corbett did not respond to Lord Barton. Indeed, it seemed that the reference to the ill-feeling between Orrick and Colchester had sobered him, for his jaw tightened and his eyes narrowed. With a motion that she suspected came of long habit, he rubbed the scar that split his brow. Unable to help herself, Lilliane followed the movement of his hand with fascination.

She had been prepared to denounce him to her father, but all at once she stopped. No words quite came to mind. Besides, she reasoned, it would not do to argue with her father in the company of so many guests. As much as it galled her, she knew she must save her angry accusations for a more private moment. Then she would not hesitate to tell her father of this heathen's lack of manners and his crude approach to her in his chamber.

But as if he read her very thoughts, Sir Corbett leaned back in his chair and turned a carefully bland face to his future father-in-law. "I don't think I thanked you properly for the splendid chamber you settled me in, Lord Barton. I found it more than comfortable. And the bath you had sent up was most refreshing."

"You may thank Lilliane for that. She has a way with the running of this castle. There's not a servant who does not jump at her bidding." The older man signaled a servant to fill Corbett's goblet and his own. "She is a jewel is my Lily."

Corbett's eyes moved easily over Lilliane and she squirmed under his casual perusal. Had he no shame? she wondered angrily. But Lord Barton could not see the disturbing gleam in Corbett's eyes, and he continued speaking. "Why, under her firm hand everything at Orrick Castle runs smoothly."

Corbett's gaze dropped to those very hands of hers and, to her chagrin, caught her in the act of rubbing the spot on her wrist where his lips had caressed. Then his eyes raised slowly to her face. "I have no doubt of what you say. The young maid she had attend to me was nothing but courteous and efficient. She saw to my needs so well that I felt quite at home. If I but knew her name I would commend her to you. But, alas, when her work was complete she quietly withdrew." He smiled at her then, showing a devastating charm.

"That is good, that is good." Lord Barton beamed as he settled back in his chair. "Now, Lilliane, let us begin the meal."

Lilliane was too incensed with Corbett's clever remarks to respond to her father. It was all she could do to signal the chamberlain to start the long procession of servants with their trays of food. In stony silence she watched the results of her efficient management as the meal was served to the huge company. But her mind was not on the elaborate dinner or the many guests who set to the fine meal with hungry vengeance. It was the man beside her who occupied her every thought.

She was excruciatingly aware of his nearness. As if the heat of his body reached out to surround her own, she felt a slow warmth envelop her. Unwillingly she sent a sidelong glance toward him only to be unsettled by the frank manner in which he stared at her.

"Do not look at me so," she snapped in a low tone.

"And how is it I am looking at you?" he asked as he leaned towards her.

"You know how! As if . . . as if . . ." Lilliane floundered and she felt color stain her face.

"As if what? As if I could hardly believe my good fortune at finding my spinster bride to be the very maid who attended me today? As if I were heartily relieved to find my bride to be so fair of face?" He reached out a hand to touch her cheek but Lilliane jerked back to avoid him.

She sent him a quelling stare. "And if you had not . . ." She struggled for words. "If you had not found me so fair of face, how quickly would you have begun dallying with the maidservants?"

"Jealous already?" He arched his scarred brow in a taunt. "If it's our earlier meeting you refer to, I don't see why you should fret. It was you, after all, who misled me."

"I misled you!" she hissed. "Why, if you hadn't—"

"If I hadn't come into my room when I did you would have had time to finish searching my belongings."

"It's . . . it's . . . it's not your room!" Lilliane sputtered.

"Oh, but it is," he contradicted her. "And as much as I did enjoy the bath, I still wonder what you thought to gain by disguising yourself so."

"It was no disguise—"

She stopped abruptly as a servant brought a platter of meats to them. She watched in simmering anger as Sir Corbett calmly selected cuts of roast capon, slivered eel, and grilled pork for them to share from a communal plate. From another servant's tray he added herring, raisins, and several cheeses. Then he poured a generous amount of an amber-hued wine into his goblet and offered it to her.

But Lilliane would have none of his mocking gallantry. Nor would she honor him by sharing a plate with him as was expected of a betrothed couple. She anticipated an outburst from him; if the truth be known, she would have welcomed it, for she was utterly frustrated by the farce they played out before the company. But the objection to her obstinate behavior came not from Sir Corbett but from her father.

"Eat, daughter. Eat and do not shame your father or your bridegroom with such a temper! Would you have the gossips carry tales of your behavior?"

Beyond her father, Tullia and Santon looked on, their meal forgotten. But it was Odelia's satisfied expression that finally goaded Lilliane into acquiescence. She did not know why Odelia felt she must be so spiteful toward her, but it was quite apparent that both Aldis and she took delight in Lilliane's dissatisfaction with her marriage.

With the utmost care not to let her fingers touch Sir Corbett's, Lilliane selected the capon. But she took no pleasure in it, nor was she even aware of the cook's considerable efforts. Her enjoyment of the meal was spoiled completely by the overwhelming presence of the man at her elbow. Her stomach was knotted with anger and her mind raced with churning emotions. With every morsel of food he took from the well-filled plate, with his every expression of satisfaction with the elaborate repast, Lilliane's rage only intensified. It was all she could do to choke down the capon and maintain a reasonable expression.

Corbett did not speak to her during the meal, preferring, it seemed, to converse with her father. They spoke of the fields and the serfs, the hunting to be had in the surrounding forests, and the conditions of the castle's defenses. There was still a strain between the two men, a discomfort based on too many years of suspicions. But in spite of that the conversations flowed smoothly and the tension between them seemed to lessen.

As the two men relaxed under the spell of good food and ample wine, so did the rest of the company slowly revive their gay mood until the hall resounded with all the festivity expected with an approaching wedding.

But Lilliane's mood did not lift. How could she be lighthearted when her life was being ruined? she fumed. And then as if to insult her further, the big lummox was ignoring her as if she and her feelings were of no account at all. Indeed, it was quite clear that the two men had reached this agreement with absolutely no concern for her opinion.

It was only when the platters of fresh fruit and golden-baked pastries were brought out that Sir Corbett finally turned his attention back to her. She was fingering the empty goblet in agitation when he suddenly placed his large hand over hers. Lilliane was completely taken aback by this unexpected move. With a gasp she tried to pull free of his unwelcome touch, but his fingers only tightened more securely about hers.

Disturbed as much by the penetrating warmth of his grasp as by the presumption of his action, Lilliane turned a glittering glare upon him. "Release me at once, you wretch!" she hissed. "You dare much when—"

"It is expected that I should be drawn to you." He gave her a wicked grin and his scarred brow lifted devilishly. "I daresay your father will be ecstatic that I should be so overwhelmed by his 'Lily.'"

"Don't you call me that!"

"It is your name, isn't it? I'll concede that Lilliane better befits the heiress of Orrick. Lily bears more the ring of a sweet and simple young girl, one who might be servant to a noble lord." His eyes sparkled with amusement at her benefit. "I prefer Lily."

Lilliane was outraged. "Perhaps then you should select from among our many servants for a wife if that is what you seek. 'Tis certain it would not break my heart!"

"Ah, but it happens that I've an eye for a certain maid already. Perhaps you know of her?" Before she was aware of it he had slipped her fingers from the stem of the goblet and had deftly entwined them with his own. "She is sweet-faced, with a form soft and alluring. Yet she has a saucy way about her and a sharp tongue." He chuckled at her impotent anger. "She would not give me her name, and yet I feel sure I will eventually find her."

"Not if she can avoid you," Lilliane muttered as she struggled to free her hand.

Sir Corbett did not respond at once. When he did speak his voice held a warning note. "Both maid and lady as well as the demesne shall be mine. Never doubt that." He released her hand. "Whether you be willing or not matters nothing to me. You will do your duty as a daughter and a wife, as I shall do mine as a husband."

It was said with such conviction and finality that Lilliane's heart filled with dread. At that moment he was her enemy, pure and simple. And he was announcing his victory before the battle had even begun.

Lilliane could not reply. Worse, she felt the sting of foolish tears behind her eyes. Knowing only that she must get away from him, she abruptly rose from the table, nearly toppling her chair in her haste. She did not pause to excuse herself. Indeed, she feared that should she speak, shameful tears would overwhelm her.

As at her entrance, the great hall quieted at her leaving. She knew that speculation abounded and that the gossips would find her abrupt departure generous fodder for their mills. But she could not stay. She could not!

She should never have returned, she told herself as she mounted the stone stairs. She should have remained at Burgram Abbey and never returned to help with Tullia's wedding.

But what was done was done, she had to admit as she wiped her tear-dampened cheeks with the back of one hand. She had come and her father had decided to honor the betrothal. A heavy sigh caught in her throat and she slowed her frantic pace to catch her breath. The wall was cool and smooth against her flushed cheek as she leaned against it. It helped to clear her racing thoughts. She needed to think and to be away from the wedding furor that seemed to have taken hold of the entire castle. How she wished she could just leave and find a peaceful clearing in the forests to be alone in.

But she knew it would be useless for her to try to leave the castle. The guards would never grant her passage alone at night. But neither did she wish to sit idle in her chamber, fretting and worrying.

Then she remembered the look-over. Above her parents' old chamber, the look-over was a small roof court, surrounded by battlements. At one time it had been the highest point of the castle. But a new section added to Orrick by her grandfather more than fifty years before had made the old Lord's Look-Over, as it had been called, unnecessary to castle security. As a child she had used it as a place to daydream or else to lick her wounds. Just as then, she knew it was precisely what she needed now.

Up the solid stone steps she went. Up, winding past her chamber, then past the tower room. She averted her eyes as she rushed past that particular door. Beyond it lay the chamber claimed by Sir Corbett, the room she was expected to share with him. With a grimace on her lips she hurried past that offending portal and up the last steep flight of stairs.

Lilliane was out of breath when she finally stepped into the cool night air. Autumn was upon the land and the crisp September weather raised goose bumps on her arms and shoulders. But she did not care about that at all. Beyond her lay the lands of Orrick bathed only in the meager light of the waning moon. She could see the dark shapeless mass of the forests far to her right. Before her stretched the fields and meadows, silent and still. The village at the base of the long hill that led up to the castle was only a dark jumble of shadows, and yet Lilliane was comforted by what she saw.

It looked the same as it had ever been, and she hugged her arms tightly around her waist. Orrick Castle had survived over three hundred years. From Saxon stronghold to Norman castle it had grown and prospered, and the people of Windermere Fold had prospered as well. Even the last five years of unease could not stifle that prosperity, and she took heart at that. Most certainly Sir Corbett of Colchester would not.

The decision was suddenly easy: she would run to Burgram Abbey. She could delay the wedding in no other way. She knew that if her father came for her, the abbess would not shelter her overlong. But Sir Corbett was a proud man—arrogant if the truth be told. It would humiliate him before all the gathered nobility if his bride did not apear for the wedding. And perhaps, just perhaps, he might abandon this plan in disgust.

Lilliane wiped away the last of her tears. It was not much of a plan, she knew. But it was all she had. And somehow, just having decided on a course of action restored her spirits considerably.

As she had when she was young, Lilliane took a deep breath of the cool night air then rested her palms on the corbeled wall and leaned far out over the edge. Below her was the green water of the moat, and if she craned her neck a little farther she would be able to see the great block of stone that was said to have been the earliest part of Orrick Castle. But she was prevented that view when a hard-muscled arm grabbed her without warning and yanked her roughly from the parapet.

"What do you contemplate, woman!" a harsh voice demanded. "Would you burn in hell forever rather than be wed to me?" Then she was spun around and subjected to Sir Corbett's furious glare.

In a rage she tried to shake off the heavy hold he maintained on her two shoulders. But she might as well have tried to tumble the castle walls down for all the effect she had on his grasp.

"Unhand me now, you vile blackguard! Am I to be allowed no privacy at all?"

"Not until after we're wed and you've produced an heir," he retorted through clenched teeth. "I'll not have you spoil my plans with some foolish idea of throwing yourself from this tower!"

"Throwing myself?" Lilliane sputtered with indignation. "You flatter yourself overmuch if you think I'd end my life on your account. I plan to be quite alive and quite well for many, many years after you're gone from Orrick!"

Perhaps it was that he expected weeping and hysterics from her. Perhaps it was that he was amused by her angry reply. For whatever reason, Sir Corbett slackened his grip on her, and she immediately pulled away from him. The look-over was not large, and his presence there made it seem even less so. In the darkness Lilliane could make out very little of him, but she could tell by his rigid posture and clenched hands that he fought to contain some mighty emotion. Every muscle in his powerful body seemed tensed as if for battle, and she cringed inwardly. But the very fear he inspired in her fanned her anger anew. She would not allow him this power over her. She would not!

"Now that you've 'saved' me from myself," she be-

gan in a sharp, sarcastic tone, "you may leave. You
have no reason to be here anyway."

"Oh, but I do," he answered in an equally biting
tone. "It's my responsibility to know every crook and
cranny of Orrick. I felt the rush of air up the stairhall
and so I came to investigate. Since we are both here,
however, I suggest we make the most of it."

"I cannot determine a single benefit in spending
time with you!" Lilliane spat in anger. "You're greedy
and arrogant. You're suspicious and you jump to
conclusions when you've no cause!" Incensed, she
turned to leave. But Sir Corbett was quicker and with
a swift movement he caught her by the arm.

"You have much to answer for, Lady Lilliane," he
said with a menacing growl. "You've searched my belongings in the guise of a serving wench. Then you
maintained that farce throughout my bath for some
unnamed reason. Now I find you perched over the
moat seemingly bent on leaping to your sure death."
He arched his scarred brow and peered at her as if
she were some strange, never-before-seen creature.
"Are you mad? Is it for that reason your father has
been unable to see you wed?" He shook her until her
teeth chattered in her head. "Is it a mad wife I must
suffer to have Orrick?"

Tears had started in Lilliane's eyes when he finally
released her. She would dearly have loved to throw
any number of insults and accusations at him, but
she feared her voice would reveal how distraught she
was. He wanted Orrick. Only Orrick.

Her knees trembled as she backed away from his
huge shadowed form. "I am not mad," she vowed in
a small voice. She reached for the iron ring to pull
the door open. "But 'tis certain you must be, for to

marry one who hates you and make your home among your bitterest enemies marks you completely without any wits."

She feared he would follow her as she flew down the steep stairs, for she knew she'd angered him terribly. It was only when the door to her own chamber was slammed closed behind her that she felt at all comforted. But not two minutes later she heard his tread at her door and then that of another man as well. Her heart leapt in panic but it turned in an instant to icy fury when he spoke.

"I've posted my most trusted man at your door, Lady Lilliane. He will keep you safe—and allow me to sleep without fear of you picking through my belongings. Or trying to fly!"

The evening had been bad enough, but his final poor attempt at jest was simply too much. With a cry born of both frustration and fury, she grabbed the nearest item at hand and flung it wildly at the door. But after the resonding thump on the oaken panel had quieted, there was only the sound of muffled laughter. Then she heard Sir Corbett's steps departing and the other man settling himself against her door.

It was then that the futility of her situation finally hit home. In absolute despair, feeling more weary than she could ever recall, Lilliane sank to her knees on the cold stone floor. Unaware, she picked up the small copper bowl she'd thrown so violently at the door. Over and over she turned it in her hands, and it came as no real surprise that it had suffered very little for her anger. In truth, it seemed somehow ludicrously appropriate that only a tiny dent indicated there had been any trouble at all.

5

Early the following morning Lilliane shoved at her door, then shoved again even harder. It gave her great satisfaction when the large varlet Sir Corbett had left to guard her roused himself with a muffled curse, then stumbled to his feet. With neither glance nor word did she acknowledge his presence as she marched regally past him, her slender nose in the air, her jaw thrust forward.

For his part, Sir Dunn seemed amazed at her haughty composure. Then as she made her way briskly down the stairs, he bounded up the steps; no doubt, she suspected, to inform his master of her movements.

As she made her way to the kitchens, Lilliane could only wonder at the speculation racing through everyone's mind. But she was determined not to speak of the matter to anyone, and the distant businesslike manner she adopted forbade anyone's broaching the subject of her wedding. Even so, she could not ignore the many looks sent her way. From sympathetic to indignant, to blatantly curious, the guests watched her every move, as did the servants. It would have been enough to send her in tears to her chamber had she not some promise of release from her fate.

But she did have that promise, and it kept her relatively calm. In the long hours of the night she had plotted and schemed. Now she was able to maintain her serene façade, even to the point of seeing the final wedding details attended to, for she knew she would not be at that wedding.

It seemed the only way. She knew Odelia and Sir Aldis were furious with Sir Corbett's sudden appearance at Orrick. They had obviously thought to control the castle, since Lilliane seemed unlikely to wed. But the arrival of Sir Corbett and his considerable showing of armed men had changed all that. Still, Lilliane was certain her brother-in-law would not meekly allow Sir Corbett to stay if his marriage to Lilliane should fall through. And even as belligerent as he was, Sir Corbett would not risk the censure that would follow should he take Orrick by force. Even the absent King Edward would not condone such action.

With a frown on her face, Lilliane concentrated on her task of calculating the quantity of food needed for the evening meal. She was determined not to worry about Sir Corbett's reaction to her flight. It didn't matter. All that mattered was that Orrick Castle and the green northern half of Windermere Fold not be handed over to him so lightly.

She still could not fathom her father's reasoning in agreeing to such a union. Her father was a good lord, fair in his treatment of his people, astute in planning for their welfare. To bring such a warlike son-in-law to inherit the demesne would only guarantee discontent and strife. Lilliane could not imagine Sir Corbett bowing to her father's rule. Neither could she envision Lord Barton stepping aside meekly for his new son-in-law.

No, she assured herself. Any marriage between Orrick and Colchester would be a grave mistake. Between herself and Sir Corbett it was unthinkable.

With a flourish of her quill pen she made the final notation in the kitchen book, then lay that task aside. She had deliberately delayed her return to the great hall until she was certain all the knights would have completed their morning meal. Only one knight was she truly reluctant to face, but he might be lingering for the very purpose of assuring himself of her continued presence—and continued good health—in the castle. But even if he was still there, she reasoned, it would only work to her advantage. For if he saw her busy about her daily tasks, then he might become complacent and her escape would be made more easily.

Resolute, she stood and shook out the flaring skirts of her close-fitting gown. The maize fabric was rich in its figuring and contrasted handsomely with the fine ivory linen of her kirtle beneath it. She was ornamented with no more than a gilded girdle around her waist and the simple net caul that held her heavy hair in a thick coil at her nape. However, as she made her way across the bailey toward the keep, she could not know how the morning sunlight turned her hair to deep red, nor how it highlighted the flush on her cheeks. But more than one head turned at her passing.

When she entered the great hall, her anxious eyes scanned the room quickly. As she'd expected, only a few guests yet lingered over their meal. The others had all adjourned to the many and varied activities planned for their amusement. Servants scuttled around the hall, cleaning the tables, gathering the remains of the meal for the dogs, and returning the serving dishes to the kitchens. All was as it should be, she noted with the satisfaction of a good chatelaine.

Yet she felt a vague dissatisfaction she could not put a name to. Had she looked forward to another battle with the dreadful warrior knight? Had she anticipated sparring with him and perhaps nicking his pride with her sharp accusations and insults?

She did not have time to decide for without warning William stepped from behind a broad column and she stopped, her heart leaping in surprise.

"Oh, my!" She gasped, aware that she was even more dissatisfied now than before. "You should not come upon me on such stealthy feet!"

"I feared you were avoiding me," he answered bluntly, his still-boyish face watchful.

"I'm not avoiding you," she exclaimed. "I'm not avoiding anyone."

"Not even the king's Bird of Prey?"

"The king's Bird of Prey? What do you mean?"

"Then you've not heard of his great exploits?" William's tone turned sarcastic. "Your bridegroom is a great friend of Edward's, or so the gossips in London prattle. Though it is true he rode with Edward in the East, I discount all the deeds I've heard credited to him."

"But . . . the king's Bird of Prey? Why, Edward has not even been crowned yet."

"Exactly. He dallies in Normandy when he should have been here this year and more. England is a ship without a captain," he said in disgust. "But Edward sends Corbett, his hunter, on some errand," he added musingly.

"If Corbett of Colchester were truly a confidant of the king, uncrowned though he may be, why would he concern himself with Orrick? And me?" she added, doubt etched on her delicate features. "Surely Edward would reward him with a demesne more important than Orrick."

At that William's handsome face lifted in an odd smile, and he looked at her more closely. "Do not judge Orrick Castle so lightly, dear Lilliane. There are few English strongholds so secure along the border to the Scottish hills. While I judge our new king to be a fool to linger so long abroad, I do not completely discount his judgment. No, he knows what he is about. And Sir Corbett does nothing so much as serve his king."

"Then that is why my father so easily agreed to this abhorrent union!" Lilliane deduced at once. "It was done at the king's bidding!"

"Perhaps," William murmured, drawing nearer to her. He cast his eyes about, but spied only three servants busy at their tasks. "You should have been mine," he whispered more quietly. He took her hands in his earnestly. "I cannot bear the thought of him taking you to bride."

Lilliane blushed hotly at his bold words and sought to free herself of his hold. But he tightened his grasp.

"If there were but a way to avoid this marriage I would gladly seek it," she admitted.

"So you find his scarred visage hideous too. Many of the ladies at court were frightened by his brutal appearance, although there were a few who seemed perversely intrigued by his battle marks. I'm glad to see you number among those who would turn away from him in disgust."

Lilliane did not reply to this. It was true that Sir Corbett frightened her. But she could not put the blame for that on his ravaged flesh. Those marks she had found terrible, and yet not hideous. Unwillingly she thought of the three raking claw marks on his shoulder, and she felt the same shiver of horror and awe.

Unnerved by the memory, she peered at William, trying to drive Sir Corbett's image from her mind. Sir William of Dearne was an incredibly handsome man. Perfectly formed features and smooth, unblemished skin had kept him a favorite among women of all ages. And yet Lilliane did not feel the same fascination for him that she had once felt. There was a petulance to his lips now. Or had it always been there?

Frowning, she turned away from him and moved briskly to the massive double doors. But he followed her. Before she could descend the few steps to the bailey, he stopped her once again.

"Lilliane . . ." His blue eyes were direct upon her. But when her clear gaze did not waver, his fell away. He reached his hand to lightly caress her cheek. "This is not how it should have been for us."

"No," Lilliane agreed in a soft whisper, her heart heavy with longing for the past. "No, it is not."

By the time Lilliane had crossed the bailey to the rookery, she was fighting back tears. The doves rose in a flurry at her entrance, raising a swirl of dust. She watched as the birds slowly settled back upon their roosts. Like so many other things at Orrick, time had not changed the rookery at all. Many was the time she'd sought solace here from the heart-aches of childhood. The soft cooing of the doves had always calmed her.

But even this soft reassuring remembrance of times past could not ease Lilliane's troubled mind. With an angry gesture she dashed her tears away. It was not fair. It was not! She was denied even the luxury of mourning her lost love for William, for somehow he was not the same young man she had thought she'd loved. He had changed.

Or perhaps she had.

Lilliane picked up the hem of her kirtle to dry her face, heedless of the renewed commotion among the doves. Her thoughts tumbled disjointedly around her lost dreams, her crushed idealism, and the bitter truth of reality. Then it seemed reality was truly re-morseless for a large hand caught hers, and she looked up into Sir Corbett's glowering face.

She gasped, she was so startled. But he did not al-low her time to collect her wits. "So, 'tis William of Dearne you pine for. And to think I gave you credit for being a pure maiden."

"How dare you!" she cried in true shock. "You have no right to accuse me of such things—"

"If not in deed, then most assuredly in thought," he cut in. "Do you deny your tears?" With his other hand he rubbed his thumb across her cheek, erasing the trail of one last tear. It might have been an inti-mate gesture, but the cruelty of his suggestion made it cold and insulting.

She turned her face stiffly away from his touch. "He is married."

"Precisely," he answered in a dark tone.

She was silenced by his implication, appalled that he could think such a thing of her. Then her frozen wits were restored and with a swift yank she freed herself of his grip. "You have the mind of a low-born . . . a low-born . . ." She struggled for an insult bad enough for him.

"A low-born bastard?" he supplied with a cold chuckle. "I assure you, I am neither low born nor a bastard. You will have to accept my word, however, for my parents cannot verify it. They are both dead, a crime I lay at the doorstep of Orrick."

"My father did not kill your father!" Lilliane cried with much vehemence. "And he most certainly had nothing to do with your moth—"

"My mother died of a broken heart," Sir Corbett said with a growl. "She pined for her husband, preferring death to his absence from her."

His angry interruption gave her pause, and when she retorted it was in a more subdued voice. "You will not listen to the truth. You seek only revenge, and now you would even marry to get that revenge."

Sir Corbett did not reply at once, only shrugging as if in mute acceptance of her words. But his eyes were sharp upon her, their gray as hard and opaque as slate. "My reasons for this marriage are many. But they are of no matter to you."

"Of no matter to me!" Lilliane cried. "Is my life of no matter to me then? Is my entire future of no matter? How casually you disrupt my life as if I were of no account! As if I were no more than some poor beast of burden!" Her anger was in full flight as she stood in the dim rookery. Her eyes flashed golden fire as she faced him with her chin arrogantly raised and her clenched fists on her hips.

" 'Tis your father's will." He shrugged again then let his eyes slide slowly over her. Lilliane felt an ominous shiver as if he had truly touched her with his close scrutiny, but she determinedly ignored it. When he met her eyes once more he smiled, but with no real warmth. "As for being treated as a beast of burden, I remind you that your primary duty as my wife shall be to bear my heir. Small enough burden that shall be, and as I see it, one you are well suited to."

"And what of the burden of your lustful attention?" she cried recklessly. "I despise you and do not want you for my husband!"

In a moment he had her in his iron grasp and forced her to meet his icy glare. "It does not matter to me that you abhor my touch or my attention. You will be my wife. You will share my bed. You will bear my children. If you cannot stomach my scarred face or my battle-marked body, close your eyes. But do not think to shirk your wifely duty!"

She could feel the heat of his anger down the whole length of her. Only inches separated them, and yet he might have held her close against him so vivid was the feeling. Then without warning he captured her lips in a hard and demanding kiss.

It was of no use for her to struggle: he held her immobile, as if her strength were no more than a kitten's. In rising panic she fought to avoid his lips, but he quickly stilled her with a hand at her head. He slid his tongue along the full curve of her lower lip with an expertise that made her gasp. Then he forced entry between her startled lips.

Lilliane could not breathe. She could not think or even marshal her frozen body to react. His tongue was heated velvet, plundering her mouth with an intensity that left her confused and weak. She felt his hand move to the small of her back and press her close against his hard frame. As he molded her body against his, so did he seem almost to mold her will to his own.

But Lilliane would not submit to him so easily. In impotent rage she pounded on his shoulders, pushing against his superior strength. She kicked at his shins, but he only moved his hand to her buttocks and lifted her clear of the floor. And all the while he deepened the kiss until his tongue was searching out her own.

Lilliane was helpless against such an onslaught. Her struggles were futile and indeed, with the intimate press of his hard-muscled body against hers, she found it almost impossible to think. Her mind cried in protest at such an uncivilized handling, but in her belly a languid heat was robbing her muscles of the ability to fight any longer. Like a fever it seemed to overwhelm her, spreading its deceptive heat until she was limp in his arms and pliant beneath his kiss.

His hold seemed to change then. His hands became gentle, stroking up her back as he held her pressed to him. His lips became less demanding and more enticing, teasing her mouth into a freer acceptance of his tongue. She was not conscious of curling her fingers around the smooth kersey of his tunic, nor of the softening of her mouth under his.

But when her tongue crept forward to meet his, she was wholly aware of the exquisite pleasure that seemed to fill her entire being. She felt almost as if she had melted into a hot, glowing version of her cold, former self. It was terrifying to lose such control. It was terrifying but it was fascinating. And she would have more . . .

"Where are your protests now?" Corbett whispered in her ear as he nibbled seductively at her lobe.

Lilliane fought for her breath and her reason as he continued his assault on her senses. "Let me down," she managed to gasp.

"You'll have to loosen your hold of my tunic, then," he pointed out.

Horrified at her own wantonness, Lilliane released his tunic at once. He obligingly lowered her to the ground, but before he released her he pulled her close against him. Lilliane could clearly feel the thickening beneath his braies pressed hard against her belly, and she tried to squirm away. But his slow grin seemed to mock her as he stared at her appraisingly.

"You say you despise me but . . ." He shrugged. "Still, it is of no matter. You may dread our marriage above all things, but your father and I have already agreed." He paused and his eyes became cool and sardonic. "You *will* become my wife on the morrow."

He released her then and she stumbled back a few paces. He was so unfeeling, Lilliane thought. So completely indifferent to how she felt. She wanted to cry but pride held her back. Then as if she might erase the disturbing feel of him from her, she wiped her lips with the back of her hand. "Perhaps I shall become your wife," she muttered. "But I shall hate you just the same!"

Her eyes were brilliant with repressed tears as she watched a frown darken his face. When he spoke again his voice was low and calm, but she did not mistake the sarcasm rampant in it.

"We shall see. But mark my words, Lily, you will not rid yourself of my taste or my touch in so easy a fashion." He turned to go, then paused and swept her with an icy look. "But if you truly find me so offensive, you need only close your eyes and imagine it is your pretty William who stirs you to such heat!"

Then with a look of complete disgust he stalked from the room.

6

"Three squab, a knot of dried beans, a portion of cheese, a large squash." Lilliane placed the items one by one into a covered basket, hoping neither Tullia nor Ferga, the serving woman, took note of the tremor in her hand.

She was shaking so badly she feared she might drop something and thereby reveal all. Her desire to escape to Burgram Abbey had multiplied tenfold since her dreadful encounter with Sir Corbett in the rookery. Knowing that her trembling was caused as much by the power he'd exerted over her as by the anticipation of her flight to freedom served only to increase her fury.

No matter how she tried to forget what had happened between them, she simply could not. She'd not been able to leave the dim rookery, she had been so shaken by the terrible feelings he'd aroused in her. Fear and rage fought for dominance as her emotions tumbled about madly. But worse was the awful suspicion of the incredible power he seemed to have. With just his kiss and a gentle hand upon her he was able to control her. Neither his anger nor his threats did nearly so much damage as did his passion. She shivered in remembrance of it even now.

If it had not been for Thomas, she might be hidden away among the doves even still. But he had discovered her and brought word that she was needed in the hall. Since then her sisters and their lady guests had not allowed her to attend her duties as chatelaine. Instead, she'd had to accompany the women on a hawking party, taking an excruciatingly long meal in the meadow. When they'd returned to the castle at midafternoon, the men had all been at the hunt. And it was then Lilliane had vowed to slip away. She considered it an omen of the best sort when Tullia mentioned that Mother Grendella, the wisewoman, was abed with a recurring affliction to her eyes. Lilliane now prepared a basket of delicacies from the wedding feast for the old woman.

"Wrap several of those pastries and a big loaf of white bread in that cloth and add it to this," Lilliane said to Ferga.

"You need not go yourself, Lilliane," Tullia remonstrated. "Why, any of the servants could be sent down to the village with this basket."

"Tullia, if I must stay in this castle and in this company one more minute, I vow I shall scream. 'Tis cruel enough I must marry this vile knight, our enemy. May I not even spend the last hours of my girlhood as I wish?" Her amber-hued eyes were wide, and the tears that started in them were not contrived.

Moved by her sister's plight, Tullia could not but agree. "As you will, dear sister. But pray, do not linger. And take a groom with you."

But Lilliane had no intention of having a groom accompany her. Taking full advantage of the confusion brought on by the wedding festivities and the servants' many extra duties, she led a horse out from the stables. As she settled herself on the steed, Lilliane was filled with both relief and remorse. She'd not been sure she could keep up the pretense of having accepted her fate one minute longer. Yet she could not pretend to feel no guilt at the terrible deed she planned. For, desperate as she was to avoid this marriage, Lilliane well knew that she wronged her father horribly by such defiance.

It was not her way to be a disobedient daughter. Although the talk ran freely about her long absence from Orrick and her willfulness at staying at the abbey, it was nevertheless a fact that she had obeyed her father in not marrying Sir William. Still, the gossips concerned themselves more happily with her stubborn temper than with her ultimate obedience.

But she could not rationalize her behavior on this day as anything but the most blatant disobedience. Her escape would shame not only her bridegroom, as she wished, but also her father. For a moment, as she passed over the heavy drawbridge, she almost reined in her mount. As it was, the delicate creature danced and skittered in a high-spirited circle until Lilliane settled her with a gentle hand on her neck.

"Easy now, Aere. Easy, my girl." She ran her fingers through the filly's bronze-colored mane. "I know you're anxious to be off. Just as I am," she added more softly.

As she turned past the ancient bridge and onto the smooth-worn road, Lilliane had the strongest urge to look back at the castle. She knew what she would see: pale limestone walls, tall and sturdy, older than anyone's memory; the nut-laden branches of the chestnut tree peeking over the crenellations; and the ever-present watchmen pacing off their allotted rounds.

But something in her would not let her look. It was her home and she loved it dearly. Still, she had the terrible feeling that it would never again be quite the same place she'd taken for granted for so long. If she ever returned, she feared it would be vastly different. Resolute, she urged the willing mare forward, unmindful of the wind tugging at her as she cantered down the road.

Lilliane sat upon Aere stiffly, her maize gown of caddis cloth in deep folds around her knees. She carried the heavily laden basket before her, for truly she did want Mother Grendella to have the delicacies. But she knew she could not tarry. When she reached the edge of Orrick village, however, a simple solution presented itself. Not far from the community well, a number of women had gathered. Young mothers and unmarried girls made the trek there twice daily. First light saw them there with their soiled linens and garments, scrubbing them in large wooden troughs made for that very purpose. Then they would spread and drape the garments over shrubs and branches to dry.

Now they were making their return trip to gather their laundry before the clouds welling up in the west could loosen any rain upon it.

"Hello, Meg, Bertha." She nodded to two women she knew. "Hello, Theda."

" 'Lo, milady." Theda bobbed a swift curtsy. "May I say, 'tis pleased we are t' have you back t' Orrick."

"Why, thank you," Lilliane answered. She was touched by Theda's sincerity, although it made her feel even more guilty for planning to leave.

"We've all heard about the doings on the morrow. 'Tis to be a fine time for us all." Theda nodded. "And both sisters t' wed at once. 'Twill truly be a grand day."

Lilliane forced a smile, while all the while her heart was thumping with excitement. "Theda," she began nervously. "I would have a favor of you."

It was easy to tempt simple Theda to deliver the basket to Mother Grendella by offering her a share of the delightful contents. Although the woman looked at Lilliane with curious eyes, Lilliane knew that neither she nor any of the other villagers and serfs could ever imagine deliberately disobeying Lord Barton's will. It would never occur to Theda that Lilliane might disobey her father. At worst she might be meeting a suitor who had lost out to the mighty Sir Corbett's return. That Theda could understand and even condone. But outright opposition to Lord Barton? Never.

Unwilling to linger and torment herself with her own duplicity, Lilliane quickly turned the eager filly. With another grateful thanks to the good-natured Theda, she urged Aere into a gallop.

Lilliane took the low road that led past the sluggish creek and around the apple orchard. It was longer to the turnpike that way, but it kept her safely out of view from the castle. Only when she had quit the orchard and was beyond the harvested wheat and barley fields did she pull the filly in at all. She was as winded as the horse, but she was too afraid of pursuit to stop and rest.

She'd raised many a head as she'd galloped by, her elegant skirts billowing, her rich chestnut hair streaming behind her. She knew her passing had been well marked and that there would be many to report her direction. But she was counting on time as an ally. With any luck her father would not hear of her escape until his return from the hunt at nightfall. If she was sufficiently away by then, any followers would be hard-pressed to trail her in the dark.

And followers there would be, she realized with a shiver of apprehension. Her father's anger would be terrible. And Sir Corbett's . . . his fury she refused to dwell upon at all.

Lilliane was well along the turnpike, heading at a steady pace toward the craggy Middling Stone and the turn-off beyond it that led to the abbey. Heavy clouds over the valley had brought an early dusk to the land so that all was covered in a dim violet shadow.

Lilliane cast a worried eye to the sky. She'd left without mantle or hood, for she'd not wanted to raise a suspicion. Now she feared she'd receive a thorough soaking before the night was out. Still, she decided, that was far better than a lifetime spent as wife to an enemy knight. With determination she urged the tiring animal on.

She was still a good way from the river crossing when the rain began. It was only a sparse splattering of drops, but when Lilliane looked at the sky behind her, her heart nearly stopped. An ugly purple cloud moving relentlessly across the valley hung low over the land. Like a threatening wave it came, heavy and even, backlighted by the erratic flash of lightning.

A thunderous roll sounded, then another sharper crack made her jump. The horse began to shift nervously, and when Lilliane did urge her on they seemed to fly down the turnpike. But the storm was not to be shaken so easily. Before they were even half the remaining distance to the river they were caught by a blast of wind. Lilliane bent low over the horse's neck, trying to soothe her, but she was almost as frightened as the laboring filly. The storm was whipping her hair and skirts around her and huge splatters of wind-driven rain stung her face and arms. It was all Lilliane could do to crouch low over the terrified horse's neck, her small fists gripped tightly in its mane.

In a panic the animal tore down the muddy roadway as if pursued by all manner of demons. They were quickly drenched. Soon even Aere seemed to become disoriented, and her wild flight slowed. But Lilliane was unable to gain control of the frightened horse until they suddenly met with the boiling waters of the river Keene. With an abruptness that sent Lilliane careening onto the horse's neck, the animal came to a stiff-legged halt. Breathing hard, her eyes rolling in terror, she seemed too frightened to run any farther.

It was only with the most stringent self-control that Lilliane resisted succumbing to panic. Trying hard to control her own trembling, she struggled to calm her mount enough to ford the river. But the beleaguered Aere would have none of it. Snorting and balking at Lilliane's every urging, she danced in a tight circle, turning away from the rushing waters.

Lilliane was beside herself. Everything had gone so well. Even the storm had aided her by preventing the progress of those who must surely trail her. But if Aere would not cross the river . . .

Determined not to be so easily thwarted, Lilliane slid from the saddle, all the while keeping a tight hold on the reins. Her skirts hung about her in a sodden mass and threatened to trip her at every step. Her hair was a wet, streaming cloak about her face and shoulders. But Lilliane ignored these encumbrances. Fueled as much by fear as anything else, she began to pull the horse, trying to lead her through the roiling river water.

At first the horse refused to budge, only tossing her head wildly. But Lilliane would not give up. "Dear Lord, help me," she implored through her chattering teeth.

Finally, as if only from pure exhaustion, the horse followed her lead. The water was icy on Lilliane's legs, and her skirts swirled around her knees. But still she forced herself out into the river. She was making slow progress, but she was close to rejoicing at having made the crossing when it happened.

A small log, scratchy with branches, came careening along in the quick current. Lilliane did not heed its sudden appearance, but for Aere it was the last straw. The branches whipped her forelegs, then jostled around to strike her hind legs. In violent protest, the filly jerked back, rearing and scrabbling around for firmer footing.

Lilliane was completely unbalanced when the reins tore through her hands. She fell forward into the freezing water, then was carried swiftly away from the horse. By the time she could catch herself and struggle to her feet, the filly had bounded from the river, and with a wild neigh of fear, dashed madly away into the storm.

Suffering equal portions of despair and anger, Lilliane staggered toward the riverbank. Both her kirtle and gown were sodden and dragged heavily at her.

She was chilled to her bones, and her teeth chattered violently. With no thought now but to find relief from the horrible cold, she pulled herself toward a slick, muddy bank. The rain beat furiously upon her and the wind seemed bent on defeating her. Even the river seemed determined to hold her down as it swirled her heavy skirts around her ankles. But doggedly she fought her way out of the water.

By the time Lilliane was out of the river, she was trembling. Tears mingled with the rain, and she had to cling to the gnarled trunk of a yew tree for support. There was no sign of Aere, and Lilliane abandoned all hope of finding her. She could only hope the flighty animal would find her way safely home.

As she leaned heavily against the tree, the sobs she had suppressed finally surfaced, and she succumbed to a terrible wave of self-pity. It wasn't fair that this storm should have ruined her escape. It wasn't fair that she should have to flee her own home in this way. And it wasn't at all fair that her father had so adamantly decided that she must wed that beastly Sir Corbett! Neither Odelia nor Tullia had been so dreadfully treated, she recalled as she wiped ineffectually at her eyes. They'd been allowed to choose where their hearts had led. Why not her?

It was a question with no answer, at least none she cared to accept. Miserable as she'd never been before, Lilliane huddled in the meager shelter of the yew.

It seemed hours before the rain abated. By then it was dark. Only the faintest hint of moonlight darted from behind the high clouds that trailed the storm. But Lilliane now was presented still another problem, for the intense rain had filled the river to near overflowing. The crossing would have been dangerous on horseback; certainly it could not be made on foot.

The sound of the surging waters filled the night, drowning out everything else as she stared hopelessly toward the far bank. She could not cross, she admitted dejectedly as she turned slowly away.

It was then she saw the giant apparition.

Mounted on a huge steed, a man watched her in silence. The dark night did not reveal his identity, and yet Lilliane did not need to see his face to know who it was. For a moment her heart seemed to stop beating, and she could not move at all. Sir Corbett had found her. In the darkness of the night, in the fury of the storm, he had still tracked her down. It was impossible, and yet here he was. What manner of man was he? she wondered in frightened awe.

The moment seemed to stretch out interminably, for he did not speak or move. He and his war-horse might have been carved from the blackest granite, they were so still. Yet Lilliane could not mistake the anger and hostility that emanated from him.

She did not stop to weigh her alternatives. She did not consciously decide that the river and its surging floodwaters offered her more mercy than would this vengeful, cold-hearted knight. She only reacted instinctively in stepping back from his furious silence.

Her feet were so cold already that the icy water was barely noticeable to her. The water caught at her skirts and pulled at her legs, yet still she backed into it. Then the horse began to move toward her in slow steady steps and panic set in.

Like a woman possessed she whirled and ran into the frigid black waters. In two steps she was tripped up by her skirts. She floundered, yet still she struggled away from him. Then his horse was upon her and she felt a hard hand grab the back of her gown. Before she could stop him, he lifted her free of the river.

"Let me down, you vile bully!" she screamed as he plopped her unceremoniously before him. "Unhand me or I shall see my father flog you within an inch—"

"It is you who shall be flogged," he said as he forced her arms to her side then clasped her hard against his broad chest. "Whether that honor shall fall to your father or me is still an unanswered question, however."

The threat in his voice gave her pause, and a shiver coursed through her. "You'd best not lay a hand on me," she warned in a voice that trembled despite her every effort to sound brave. "No matter our differences, my father will not countenance—"

"Your father," he muttered in her ear, "wished me Godspeed in finding his wayward daughter—my wayward bride. Do not forget that our wedding day is at hand. Once the vows are spoken, neither your father nor anyone else shall have a say in the discipline of my wife!"

If she had been frightened before, it was nothing as compared to the pure terror his menacing words struck in her now. With a cry of complete despair she wriggled to be free of his steely hold and to slide off the horse, but that only unbalanced them both. Then the huge horse stumbled in the uneven footing of the river, and with an icy splash, they both were dumped into the water.

Lilliane came up first, mired within her skirts and

blinded by her hair. But before she could find a foothold or even try to swim, his hand found her and with one swift tug he had her once more. As if she were only a pitiful bit of river debris, he hauled her ashore and dragged her up an embankment.

She was gasping for breath when he finally deposited her on an overgrown grassy clearing. He stood above her, silhouetted in the faint moonlight, breathing as heavily as she. He was every one of her childhood nightmares come vividly to life, she thought fearfully. A silent, faceless demon, blacker than night, more menacing than any daytime imaginings. And he was determined that she become his wife!

With a sob of defeat Lilliane buried her head in her arms. She did not want to cry before him, and yet there seemed no help for it. She had done all she could, but it had not been enough. With cold efficiency he had tracked her down and now she was truly at his mercy.

She wasn't sure what she expected. Vile accusations and threats at the least. A beating at the worst. She was vaguely reassured that he would not kill her after fishing her from the river, although he most certainly must have been tempted to. When he neither spoke nor made a move toward her, she raised a muddy, tear-streaked face to him.

Sir Corbett, however, was not looking at her at all. Instead, his eyes were directed to his huge destrier. Barely discernible in the dark, the horse had made its slow, painful way onto the riverbank. But with every step it heavily favored one of its forelegs.

Sir Corbett started at once for his horse, but then he stopped and turned back to face her. He bent down on one knee next to her and lifted a heavy tangled lock of her hair, pulling it slightly.

"You have done your best to mock me. To bring shame upon me." He pulled a little harder on her hair. "To drown me." Then he bent low until his face was only inches from hers. Even in the dark she was terribly aware of the menace that glittered in his cold gray eyes. "But if you have caused permanent harm to Qismah I shall make your life miserable beyond your imagination!"

He did not give her a chance to respond, and indeed, Lilliane had no wish to. Cringing, she could only remain as she was, watching with frightened eyes as he gently led the horse up an easier incline. Then he tenderly checked the leg, running his hands expertly over the animal and all the time speaking in soft, indecipherable words.

In spite of her fear, Lilliane could not mistake the bond that existed between the horse and its master. It was a rare thing, she knew. Something she would normally admire. Yet it only increased her sense of dread, for she was sure that this hard-bitten knight had all his meager affection tied up in his war-horse.

Lilliane was sitting up, huddled miserably with her arms around her knees, when Corbett led his horse past her.

"Get up and walk," he commanded curtly, not even bothering to look to see whether she obeyed. But Lilliane knew better than to thwart him further. No other words passed between them as they began to make their way back up the road: the silent knight, the limping horse, and the miserable, drooping girl.

7

Lilliane did not dare to question Sir Corbett, but her mind circled with a hundred thoughts. How would he punish her? Did he plan for them to walk all night in order to get back before the wedding? Would she have any chance to escape him? But he did not speak at all, and left to her imaginings, she began to assume the worst.

It wasn't until they approached a darkened cottage that Corbett broke his angry silence. He roused the sleeping shepherd, who quickly agreed to help the forbidding knight. After seeing to Qismah's comfort in the sheep shed, Sir Corbett turned to the man and handed him a gold coin.

"You will receive another such coin for your trouble if you heed what I say. Make straightaway to Orrick. Speak only to Sir Dunn and Lord Barton, and do not fear to disturb them." He sent a penetrating stare toward Lilliane. "Tell Lord Barton his daughter is with me. I will personally see that she is delivered in time for the wedding."

There was something in the choice of his words that set Lilliane atremble. The dark and frightening night she could handle. Even the chill wind that sliced through her freezing body was not beyond her ability to deal with. But to be left alone with this hard, vengeful man . . .

Without being aware of it, she began to back away from the weak circle of lamplight. She was exhausted by her ordeal, she was miserable with the cold, and terror seemed to overwhelm her. But for all his attention to his injured horse, Sir Corbett detected her movement at once.

"Stand where you are, woman! Do not think to escape this time."

With a gesture of dismissal he sent the shepherd on his way. Only Lilliane was left to face his ill temper. She was braced for the worst, prepared for his furious outburst and even his heavy blow. But when neither came she chanced a quick glance at him.

Sir Corbett had not moved any closer to her. He still stood straight and tall, his muscular form outlined in gold by the wavering lamplight. But instead of the furious glare she expected, his expression seemed more speculative and assessing. And expectant.

Her heart's rhythm doubled as she met his disturbing stare, but then his expression changed. It had been a trick of the light, she told herself as she watched him rub the great war-horse's muzzle one last time. When he turned back to her, his face was a mask of control, and Lilliane did not know whether to feel relief or greater fear. But as she made her shivering way to the shepherd's simple stone cottage, she was uncomfortably aware of his every step behind her.

The cottage was only one room, clearly the home of an unmarried man. A generous blaze burned in the little hearth, and it drew Lilliane immediately to it. As she knelt before it, stretching her frozen fingers to the welcome warmth, she glanced uneasily around. Aside from a simple square table, a three-legged stool, one armless bench, and an ancient wooden trunk with worn leather hinges, there were few comforts. But the cottage was reasonably clean. And it was warm.

She heard Sir Corbett set the bolt across the door, then started when he dragged the heavy trunk to block it as well. Then he sat down on the trunk, stretched his long legs before him, leaned back against the door, and contemplated her.

Lilliane did not at all like the smug smile that lifted his lips, for there was no measure of warmth in it at all. Nor could she long bear the endless silence.

"Shall you now seek your revenge upon me, Sir Knight?" she asked in as brave a voice as she could muster. "Shall you threaten me and accuse me and beat me?" She lifted her chin arrogantly, fully aware that her wet and bedraggled condition probably made her haughty air ridiculous. But she was Lady Lilliane of Orrick, she reminded herself. Daughter to the brave Lord Barton. It would be unseemly for her to grovel, no matter how great the threat. Sir Corbett had brought her to tears once this night. He would not do so again.

"It's unlikely harsh words or even a beating will make you an obedient wife." He shrugged as if it were of no matter to him at all, and Lilliane's eyes widened in surprise. "Warmth is what I seek now," he continued. And with that he tugged off first one boot, then another. His sodden tunic was next, and he flung it over the bench to dry. Then he looked at her.

"If you think to avoid our marriage by bringing on a deadly cough or fever, I vow you shall fail. Just as you have failed in your other plans to thwart me. Now remove your wet garments. Now!" he added when she did not comply at once.

"It is not . . . it is not . . . seemly," Lilliane managed to choke out as she stared at him, aghast.

"We shall be wedded before this day is finished. I don't see—"

"No!" she cried as she rose to a shaky stance before the hearth. "Betrothed or wedded, it doesn't matter. I would willingly cast these wet garments from me were I alone. But not while you are present. Never!"

She did not know what he would reply to her words, so contradictory to his own. But the determination in his dark gaze as he rose from his makeshift seat gave her no doubt of his intent. Before she could gather her wits, he had her by both arms. His face was only inches from hers as he glared at her.

"Have you not yet learned? You will never win against me, woman. No matter how you rail or struggle, the outcome is set."

Indeed, his words rang terribly true to Lilliane at that moment. Hadn't he convinced her father to honor their betrothal, despite all her pleas? Hadn't he found her when every logic said the storm should have slowed him down?

And now, trapped in this little cottage with him, could she truly hope to stop him if he decided she must remove her gown?

She averted her eyes from his slate-gray gaze and a violent shudder coursed through her. Suddenly she felt colder than she had the entire evening; even her teeth began to chatter. But when he relaxed his tight grip on her she became aware that his hands were amazingly warm. Where he touched her skin she was heated though an awful chill enveloped the rest of her body.

When Lilliane pulled away from him, he did not stop her. It was as if he knew he had won. Again.

Unable to bear his scrutiny as she removed her ruined gown, she turned away from him. But the laces along both the sides of her gown had become tighter from the soaking they'd received. Although she struggled with the knots, they would not give, and Lilliane felt a perverse satisfaction. When she glanced over at him, her face had regained a measure of its mutinous expression. But it was completely erased when he pulled a long double-edged dagger from his girdle. It took all her willpower not to cringe from him as he approached her.

Lilliane stood rigidly as he fingered the knot at her side. He knelt on one knee, his head bent right before her breasts. She caught her breath when he placed one finger in the laces then pulled them away from her side to catch with the blade. Again that astounding warmth.

Then he turned her, his hand riding upon her waist. "You can always replace the laces," he said in a quiet voice.

"The gown is probably ruined," Lilliane replied numbly. But still, she did not dare breathe. With another expert flick of his wrist he sliced through the last resisting knot. Then he raised his head to look at her.

In the close atmosphere of the cottage, lighted only by the fire dancing in the hearth, he seemed a different man from before. Perhaps it was the absence of his dark tunic. In his pure-white chainse he was no less large, but somehow less menacing. Or maybe it was his hair, black as a raven's wing yet glinting now with golden lights from the fire. Or perhaps it was only that he looked up at her from his half-kneeling position, not down on her from his normal lofty height.

Whatever the reason, Lilliane sensed the difference in him. Yet that too frightened her. She did not want to feel any softening for this man. He was her enemy and his rights to her through marriage did not change that.

She started to step back, but he had other plans. In one smooth motion he gathered a handful of her skirt in one hand, pulling it taut so that she could not take even one step. Then his other hand found the small gaping space at her waist where the laces were now coming undone. Lilliane's breath caught in her throat, and she could not stifle a gasp of alarm. She looked down at him with wide eyes that could not help but note his scarred brow, the gleaming black of his hair, and the aura of controlled power that seemed so natural to him.

He tugged at the wet skirt, pulling her nearer, and all the while he kept his watchful gaze upon her. Then he slipped his fingers beneath the opening of her gown and Lilliane trembled from his light, possessive touch.

His hand was so warm; it burned her with its bold caress, and it seemed to sap her of the ability to move. Yet she knew it was madness not to tear away. She moved her hand to his wrist, determined to put him from her. But she knew as soon as she had her slender fingers wrapped around his broad wrist that she would not succeed. He would remove his hands from her only when he wanted to. Not before.

Lilliane's heart was pounding a painful rhythm in her chest as her dark, golden gaze locked with his. Then he loosened his grip on her skirts and stood up. But it was clearly not his intention to let her go; he moved his other hand to her waist as well and pulled her closer to him.

"No!" Lilliane gasped as she pushed hard against his chest. But she might as well have thought to push down the solid little cottage for all the impact she had on him. He continued to stare down at her with those dark, penetrating eyes while she grew more and more aware of the heavy thud of his heart beneath her fingers. He was warm all over, she noted distractedly, and she shivered again.

A slight frown shadowed his brow then, and it was he who finally took a step away. "That gown must come off now," he said as his deft fingers plucked the laces free at each side of her waist. Then before she could gather her shaky wits, he was lifting her heavy skirt.

"Wait!" Lilliane cried in alarm as she tried to still his busy hands. "I'll do it." She tugged the water-logged fabric from his grasp and backed into the darkest corner of the room. There, horribly aware of his watchful gaze, she struggled out of the freezing garment.

When it was only a sodden heap on the floor she wrapped her arms protectively about her. In spite of the chill that seemed to go to her core, a heated flush of embarrassment swept over her. She had never stood before a man—even her father—in only her thin kirtle. But this man, this unfeeling brute! Her anger flared again as she saw his eyes slowly sweep her. Then he took a lazy step toward her, and she could not contain her wrath.

"Do not think to come any closer," she hissed. "You think you may do as you please—take what you want. Well, I shall thwart you. You will not have me to wife. And you shall never have Orrick!"

It was madness to speak to him so. She knew it even as she said the words. But she had gone through too much to repress even one angry word. Indeed, she would have continued on even more recklessly had he not begun to laugh.

It was the final insult. With a cry of complete rage she picked up a wooden bowl and flung it at him.

It would have struck his head had he not raised his arm just in time. As it was, it brought his laughter to an end. But the scowl on his face did nothing to appease her either.

"You do not seem to understand, woman. No matter your will, I will possess Orrick. And you."

He advanced on her with the slow, measured steps of a hunter, and she backed around the table. "You will become my wife this very afternoon in the church at Orrick." His eyes swept over her slender form, revealed so clearly by the wet and clinging linen. Then he grinned. "But I think perhaps I shall make you my wife now. It will forgo any further attempts of escape on your part."

Lilliane's amber eyes widened in terrible realization as he continued to stalk her. "You . . . you would . . ." She faltered over the words. "If you force me my father will seek revenge—"

"No, he won't," he replied confidently. He started forward but then he paused as if reconsidering his actions. When he finally did address her, his grin had been suppressed and his tone was deceptively calm and reassuring.

"Ah, but you misunderstand. I only thought to teach you what I shall expect of my wife." He gestured toward the fire. "Make us a broth to chase away the cold."

Lilliane stared at him warily. His expression was bland; his posture was relaxed, not threatening at all. Yet somehow she knew better than to trust him. She glared skeptically at him, trying to read the truth in his eyes. But whatever he thought he kept well hidden.

Lilliane hesitated, unsure of what to do. Then another shiver coursed through her and her stomach growled. "I've need of a supper myself," she muttered as she cautiously stepped nearer to the toasty hearth. "You may have what I do not finish." Then she turned away from him, furious with herself for making even this concession.

There was little in the simple cottage to work with, but Lilliane found a sack of dried beans, a basket of carrots, and one of onions. She put these into the one pot the shepherd owned, then added a half measure of the man's meager supply of salt. She made a mental note to send another portion to the poor fellow when she returned to Orrick.

But thoughts of Orrick only made her frown, and she shot a sidelong glance toward her nemesis. To her dismay, he was watching her quite openly, and when he caught her eye he grinned once more. There was something in that one-sided grin that disturbed Lilliane and made her heart pound in her chest.

Daunted, she bent studiously back to her task. But

even as she heated water in a crude kettle and added a measure of the shepherd's dried linden flowers, she was conscious of his eyes constantly upon her. She was close to panicking when she finally removed the tea from the flames.

He did not move to help her as she found two wooden cups. After pouring them each a measure of the steaming tea, she placed his cup on the small square table and backed across the room.

Lilliane did not want to look at her powerful captor. Most certainly she did not want to watch him looking at her. Yet in the small cottage there were few other options. Determinedly she moved her eyes to the softly crackling fire, but despite her resolve she again slanted her eyes back toward him.

Although Corbett remained silent as he drank his tea, she knew his mind was not idle. His scarred brow gave him a fierce appearance and his carefully bland countenance did not relieve that impression. But she suspected that was a ploy he used to intimidate those who confronted him. She was determined it would not sway her.

When she finished her tea she moved self-consciously back to the fire to stir the boiling vegetables. Her hair had begun to dry, and she pushed a curling lock behind her shoulder before she bent to check the broth.

"You have beautiful hair."

His words brought her up short, and she turned abruptly to face him. She didn't know what she expected of him, but this compliment and his thoughtful mien were surely not it. For a long awkward moment they only stared at one another.

Conscious of the quickening pace of her heart but

determined to appear calm and composed, she turned back to her task. "You may save your pretty compliments for a more foolish woman than me," she retorted boldly. "I am not interested."

She heard what sounded like a soft chuckle, but she angrily refused to acknowledge it even with a glance.

Once more there was silence. When the vegetables and broth were finished, she served them each a generous portion and again placed his bowl on the table. But as she drew away he caught her wrist in his hand.

In sudden fear she tried to shrink away from him, but he held her securely. Then he reached out and ran his hand lightly down the length of her tangled hair.

It was a curious gesture, not at all threatening. Yet Lilliane's heart thundered in her chest. If he was gentle it was only a part of his craftiness, she told herself. Be careful and don't trust him at all.

Then he released her wrist and let her move beyond his reach. She was shaking as she took up her bowl. She did not dare to even glance at him as she tried to eat, for she was too flustered. It didn't make her feel any better to examine her own strange reactions to him, for she felt as if he had touched more than her hair and wrist. She frowned and stared down into her bowl until he spoke.

"Tell me why you are so determined to disobey your father."

Lilliane looked up at him in surprise that quickly darkened to anger. "Are you a fool then not to already know the answer? You are of Colchester. I am of Orrick. Your family has made war on ours for five long years. And you murdered Jarvis. 'Tis simple enough for even you to understand."

"That is your view of the situation. Your father does not see that as sufficient reason. Nor do I."

"Then you're both fools!" she snapped.

"Ah," Corbett replied, standing as he did so. "Now I see why you remained so long unwed. Despite your fairness and your considerable inheritance, you are quite the shrew."

Lilliane backed away from him, keeping the table squarely between them. "Then perhaps you should follow the example of your betters and seek a wife elsewhere."

"My betters?" He laughed. "More than likely they were merely boys. You are dealing with a man now, Lily. And it is you I want."

His words were low and husky. His eyes had darkened to a smoky shade that made her shiver despite the warmth in the cottage.

"It is not me you want but Orrick," she retorted in a voice less firm than before. "Surely there are other, richer demesnes that would suit you better."

Corbett's steady stalking of her slowed and his brow lowered in a slight frown. "There is no demesne that suits me so well as Orrick," he countered darkly. "Neither you nor . . . anyone else shall hinder me in my task."

"Your task? You make a mockery of the holy sacrament of marriage and call it your task?" Lilliane accused. "If it is so unpleasant a prospect, by all means seek another more pleasant one."

"You misunderstand me, fair Lily. Taking you to the marriage bed is no task at all, but a pleasure I sincerely anticipate."

At her look of shock he grinned and leaned forward over the table. "Shall I show you now how much you will enjoy marriage to me?"

"You are mad!" Lilliane cried as she backed away from the clear intent in his warm gaze.

"Perhaps I am, but not in quite the manner that you mean. No." He straightened up. "It is not madness at all but is, in fact, the only way to keep you from running away again." Then he picked up the table she'd kept between them and easily shoved it against the wall.

Left with no protection between them, Lilliane panicked. "What you contemplate is rape! If you do this my father will never allow our marriage—"

"I have never found rape to be necessary, my pretty little maid. As for your father, he would not have his grandson born without benefit of a father's name. In any event, it would be unwise of you to cause discord between your father and me. Do you doubt who would be the victor if he and I should do battle?"

Lilliane could not bear to hear one more word. In anguish she ran for the door, desperate to be away from him. Every word he spoke was true. She hated his horrid logic. But she knew he spoke the truth.

She had her hands on the trunk and was pulling at it fruitlessly when his arms came around her. Though she twisted to be free and kicked wildly at his legs, he held her snug against his chest. His arms were wrapped around her waist, holding her arms down. His hands were under her breasts, and he kept her back pressed tightly against him until she was utterly exhausted by her fury.

"Ah, do not fight me so," he whispered. " 'Tis not so unpleasant as you think."

His warm breath sent an unexpected tingle through her. She squirmed against his bold embrace, but that only made her more aware of his masculine contours. Against her softness he was hard, and when he shifted his hold about her waist she seemed to fit almost too well into his arms.

Then she felt his lips moving within her hair, seeking her neck, her ear, and her shoulder.

"Let me go," she cried in spite of the little quiver that shook her.

"Never," he whispered as he nibbled at her sensitive earlobe. He turned her easily within his arms then pressed her shamelessly against him.

"I hate you," Lilliane muttered, stubbornly avoiding his seeking lips. "I hate you and I always shall."

"We shall see."

One of his hands tilted her face up to his, and his eyes met her hostile and accusing gaze. " 'Tis a pity you did not stay skinny and shy," he murmured, almost to himself. Then his lips narrowed and quite unexpectedly he turned away.

Left to support herself, Lilliane's legs nearly buckled. She was weak and confused, not liking the odd sensations he'd raised in her. She raised one shaking palm to her flushed cheeks as she watched him cross to the far corner of the room. He took an armful of sheepskins from a neatly stacked pile and spread them on the floor before the hearth. Then he added still more to form a bed. Only when he was finished did he look to her.

"Remove your kirtle and come here," he ordered

as he pulled his chainse off and draped it over the stool.

Lilliane had stood frozen where he'd left her, stunned by her shameful response to this man. She hated him as she hated everyone from Colchester. Yet once again she'd gone pliant in his embrace. She was ashamed of her wantonness. But more than anything, she was terrified of where it might lead.

When it was clear she would not comply, he moved toward her. "There is no place for shyness between man and wife."

"But I'm not your wife," she whispered.

"After tonight you will be," he stated as he lifted her heavy hair from her shoulders.

Lilliane did not try to run, but she could not prevent flinching when his hand drew near, and it darkened his features. Then slowly and deliberately he cupped her face in his broad palm and bent down to her. For a long trembling moment he stared deeply into her eyes until Lilliane closed her lids in self-defense. When his lips captured hers it was in a kiss of pure possession. She wanted to resist him, but Corbett would not relent. His lips moved over hers with an expertise that left her gasping for breath. He seemed to envelop her: with his body, with his very will. He was as hard as granite, his arms were like steel bands, and his hands would not give up their hold.

And yet his lips were soft. In spite of her wish to deny him, her mind still registered that fact.

When his tongue traced a sensuous path along her lips she felt weak; if he had released her she knew she would have collapsed. But it was not a part of his plans to free her from his embrace, she thought even as she grew more and more pliant beneath his kiss. He planned to precede the wedding ceremony with the wedding night. He would have her and plant his hated Colchester seed within her and love be damned.

A sob caught in her throat. Even worse, respect be damned. She'd not expected to find love with her chosen husband, at least not at first. But surely respect!

Yet despite all logic, Lilliane could feel herself responding to him. Without warning he swept her off her feet and crossed to the sheepskin bed. She tried to twist away as he lowered her, but it was futile. He flung himself down on the pallet and trapped her at once beneath his long, heavy frame.

"No! No, don't do this," Lilliane protested as she tried to evade his quick hands. But he was swifter than she and he easily removed her loose kirtle from her. She heard his sharp intake of breath when he flung the kirtle aside.

All the fight left her then. Her only concern was to hide her nakedness from him. But Corbett would have none of it, and he quickly captured her hands.

"I hate you!" she whispered as he planted a kiss on the side of her neck. Her soft tone did not disguise her heated emotion, for she sought to convince herself of the truth of the words as much as she hoped to hurt him.

"You may very well hate me. But beneath your coldness I have seen your fire. It is your choice, Lily. Stay cold and unresponsive, doing only your minimal wifely duties. Or be a true wife and meet me with all the passion I know you have within you."

But she was not his wife, she told herself. Nor

would she admit that she felt any passion for him at all. She closed her eyes tightly, willing herself to feel nothing. But when he gently caressed her cheek then slid his fingers down her neck, she could not control the terrible trembling that shook her body. Nor could she prevent the two tears that squeezed from beneath her dark lashes. It was the final humiliation, and her throat constricted with her effort not to sob.

Then she felt a tender kiss on first one eye and then the other, and she came completely undone. Like a torrent the tears came, hot and salty, and seemingly endless. She felt the shift of Corbett's weight as he drew a little back from her. With his thumb he tried to wipe her tears away. When that did not work, he used his shirt. Yet the more he tried to banish her tears, the harder they came.

She heard his soft muttered oath, then he lay down beside her and pulled her close against him. With hands at first awkward he began to smooth her tangled hair and gently stroke her back.

"Hush, Lily. Hush," he whispered in her ear. "It's nothing to fear."

When her weeping did not abate, he tried to make her face him. "You must stop this crying. You're making yourself sick."

But she did not want to hear. She was afraid of him and the way he made her feel, first so angry and then so weak and warm. Like a miserable child she tried to hide her face from his astute scrutiny. Corbett, however, would not allow it. With hands that were gentle but firm, he rolled her onto her back and positioned himself above her. Then he began to kiss her.

First her eyes. Then her cheeks and forehead. Her

chin was next, then down along her jawline in small nibbling kisses. And all the while his hands played with her thick, waving hair.

Beneath her the curling sheep's wool tickled her skin while above his weight was disturbingly warm. Her hands were no longer imprisoned, and yet she did not think to fight him off. Sensing her new pliancy, Corbett moved his kiss to her throat. Lilliane felt a quiver inside her as his lips slid down her tender flesh. At the small hollow of her throat his tongue made a small wet circle and her heart began to beat more rapidly.

The thought occurred to her that she should end this utter madness, and she squirmed in mild protest. But that only brought his weight more firmly against her belly and sent the most alarming sensation coursing through her. Then his mouth moved in the most enticing patterns to her ear. Around the delicate pink edge his tongue licked and explored as his hot breath set her atremble.

Suddenly Lilliane was no longer chilled at all. Instead she was hot and restless and tense with anticipation. A small part of her recognized that he was seducing her. He knew exactly what to do and he'd probably done it many, many times before. But she could not make herself stop him.

When his hand found her bare breast, a small cry escaped her. But just as quickly his lips were on hers to quiet her, to please her, to make her forget her fear. His tongue slid along her lips, gently forcing entrance into her sweet mouth and making her quiver with delight. On two fronts he pressed his advantage, teasing her nipples with agonizing patience even as he coaxed her into returning his kisses.

The feel of Corbett's tongue against hers was staggering. Deep within her feminine core something wonderful and terrifying was happening. She fairly ached with some unknown need that heated her through and through, and made every inch of her skin sensitive beyond belief. She was not aware of his knee forcing her thighs apart, for she was too intoxicated by the exquisite feel of his tongue dancing with hers. She did not protest when his hand swept heatedly across her belly, for that was when he began to kiss her breasts.

First down the smooth valley between them, then slowly up to one aching nipple and then the other. Lilliane was arching off the sheepskin bed, offering herself to him fully as she felt the excitement building within her. Somehow her hands had found him, one tangling in his hair while the other moved shakily over his shoulders and back.

Then she felt his hand move between her thighs. As if he knew precisely where this need of hers was centered, his finger slid along her wet woman's place, driving her nearly to madness. Around and around his finger circled the sensitive nub until she was mindless with the sheer pleasure of it.

She was trembling; her skin was covered with a fine sheen of dampness, shining gold in the fire's light. She wanted more of this wonderful terrible madness, and she groaned in agony when he paused to remove the last of his own clothing. Then she felt the heated length of him press hard against her. Slowly, ever so slowly, he slid his body down along hers, letting her feel the thick shaft of his masculinity. Her breath caught and she stared into his face, suddenly alarmed at what was happening.

But it was far too late for her to try to stop him. She felt him, hot and probing, as he sought the entrance to her most feminine and private place, and she started to protest. But his mouth silenced her even as he slid into her. His kiss was exquisite, deep and passionate, drawing all that was sweet from her and giving her back passion and fire. But even that was not enough to block out the sudden tearing pain of his complete entry.

"No!" She twisted her face away, unaware of the tears that sprang to her eyes. But it was useless. She could not escape the heavy weight of him, nor the painful reality of his complete possession of her.

In vain she pushed at him, trying to drive him away. But he did not even flinch at her attack; indeed he began to move over her in a slow, rhythmic cadence that she was sure would rip her asunder.

"Oh, please!" she cried weakly, reduced to pleading with him. "Please, don't do this."

"Hush, my sweet," he replied as his lips found hers in a long, lingering kiss. "Don't fight it, Lily. Don't fight me. Just let yourself enjoy it."

"No . . . I cannot." She gasped as she tried to avoid his searching mouth. But she should have known better than to oppose him. As he slowly increased the tempo of his movement within her, so did he begin to draw her into the kiss. It was deeper than before, more heated and passionate, and it seemed to touch something primitive within her.

She was not at once aware of the changes happening to her. All she knew was that where she had felt only fiery pain a new sort of heat was building. Long and slow, it grew and grew until she could not find it in her to resist any longer.

Corbett's hands were in her hair, holding her face between his callused palms. She arched eagerly into his kiss, welcoming the sensuous lick of his tongue against hers even as she welcomed the increasing thrusts of his lovemaking. Her hands slid over his back, glorying in the strange slick feel of his hot skin beneath her touch. She found the three ridges on his shoulder, the scars of some beast's claws upon him, and in mindless ecstasy she slid her fingertips along them.

She was dizzy with exhilaration and frightened by the way he pushed her beyond her own control. But still she could not deny him. She felt as if she must burst from pure bliss. Then she felt his movements increase to a furious tempo as he seemed to touch the very center of her. His body, so strong and well muscled, tensed over hers, and she felt, then heard, the deep groans of his satisfaction. In a gradually easing pace he slowed his rhythm. His breath was fast and hard in her ear, yet she sensed that he would soon be ending their lovemaking and she felt a stab of intense regret.

She was so close to some elusive, enticing answer. She did not know what it was or how she even knew it existed. But she did not want him to stop. Her arms wrapped tightly around him as if by sheer will-power she could prolong this moment forever. He was like some magnificent, mythical creature sent down to earth for her pleasure. Yet she feared some jealous god was taking him back now, and she was not ready to let him go.

Lilliane's eyes were tightly closed. Reality was not something she wanted to accept just yet. But when Corbett pulled a little away from her, she could not prevent a small cry of disappointment from escaping her. Still, when he rolled onto his back, bringing her to lay on top of him, she could no longer ignore the fact that she had just behaved like a wanton with this man—and that she had not wanted it to end.

She was in a quandary. Her body still ached with a need she did not at all understand, but her mind was horrified by that very need. She was disloyal and sinful, she told herself as she lay still trembling in his arms. Disloyal to the people who had suffered for five years for the Colchesters' hatred, and sinful to have enjoyed an act so clearly forbidden by the church outside the boundaries of marriage.

She tried to push away from him, but his hand moved possessively down her bare back to rest at her waist. His other hand held her head gently against his chest.

"Be still now," he murmured. "Be still."

His voice was a low rumble in her ear, deep and strangely comforting. When he pulled another of the sheepskins over them, she did not protest. Her mind was whirling with contradictory thoughts, and she fully intended to slip away from his intimate embrace once he fell asleep.

But as his breathing slowed to normal Lilliane relaxed as well. By the time he lifted her hand to his lips and kissed her ringless finger, she was soundly asleep.

8

Lilliane awoke to a muffled curse and the chilling wash of crisp morning air across her bare skin. For one moment she groped for the source of heat that had kept her warm all night. Then an impatient pounding at the door brought her fully awake, and she scrambled for some cover for her nakedness. Sir Corbett was already up, pulling on his braies as he called out to their noisy visitor.

"Hold, man! Give me a minute!"

"Be quick, Corbett" came the voice of Sir Dunn. "Aldis rides not far behind me. He is none too happy with your marriage to begin with. It will take very little to push him to violence if he should find out you've—" The man cleared his throat as he considered his words. "If he should find you abed."

Lilliane's cheeks flamed in embarrassment at his words, and she pulled her meager cover tighter beneath her chin. Across the room Corbett grinned at her rose-flushed features and tangled chestnut hair. With quick efficiency he pulled on his hose and boots.

"Rouse yourself, Lily. Your brother-in-law will soon be upon us, and he's itching for a fight." He paused and let his eyes roam over her. "It would not do for him to find you thus, as appealing as I'll admit you are."

Lilliane had no reply nor did she appreciate his poor attempt at humor. She was too mortified by the memory of her passionate response to him, and too awestruck by the vision of him in the early-morning light, to think clearly. He was bare from the waist up; every muscle was lovingly outlined as he bent to pick up his chainse and slip into it. His black hair was falling in his face and curling at his nape, but he was obviously not concerned with his appearance. As he shrugged into his stiffly dried tunic, he turned to face her.

"Dress quickly. I'll wait outside, but not for long," he warned, his expression turning stern. He wrapped his girdle about his waist then paused. "You may tell your tale of woe to your father, but no other. Is that clear? You're to keep any complaints about me to yourself when we join Sir Aldis. I'll not have my men endangered because of our differences."

Lilliane wanted to rail at him as he stood there so calmly preparing to face this day, as if nothing of any importance had happened in this cottage. And to further insult her, he expected her to be silent. To save him from Aldis's wrath! Lilliane's eyes glittered with anger as well as pain when Corbett moved the trunk away from the door and left the cottage without a backward glance.

For several long seconds she just lay among the wool-covered hides, petulant in her need to disobey him. But the thought of Sir Aldis and his men finding her completely unclothed quickly drove her to rise. Although her gown was somewhat damp, Lilliane was forced to don it on top of her poor kirtle. That pitiful garment had been tossed unceremoniously into a far corner, and she blushed to remember everything that had happened after that.

She was without hose or shoes, having lost them both during her failed flight. She managed to lace her gown with what remained of her laces, then tried to put her hair into some order. But when she heard the distant sound of horse hooves, she gave up on that task and hurried outside.

The early-morning sun was so bright as to blind her. The ground was still wet and very cold on her bare feet, but the sky was a clear and vivid blue. In the brilliant morning light the massive Middling Stone rose huge and forbidding beyond the shepherd's fields.

Near the shed Corbett was speaking to a small group of his men. They were all mounted save for Corbett and an older man who was examining the injured Qismah. It seemed a calm enough scene, but as Sir Aldis and his group of eight knights rode into the small yard, Lilliane sensed the tension in the air.

"I see you received word of my safe recovery of Lady Lilliane," Corbett began. His tone was friendly as only one who truly does not fear his opponent can be friendly. There was no threat in his words, and yet his very size and confidence seemed to make Sir Aldis hesitate. The contingent from Orrick outnumbered Sir Corbett's men by half. But even Lilliane was sure they were not anxious to cross swords with the more experienced knights.

Sir Aldis glared at Corbett then shot an angry glance toward Lilliane. "And has she been, thus, safely recovered? Has there been no . . . no damage done her?" he asked with a sneer.

Corbett stiffened. "Do you cast doubt on the honor of that fair maid—sister to your own wife—that I intend to marry this very day?" This time the menace in his quiet words was unmistakable.

For a long tense moment the two men stared at one another. It was Sir Aldis who broke the silence. "It is not Lady Lilliane's honor I question."

"Then perhaps mine?"

On both sides the knights were alert, and Lilliane was certain they would erupt into battle. It occurred to her as she ran across the yard to them that she was once more succumbing to Sir Corbett's will, but she knew she could not bear to have anyone's blood spilled over her.

"Hold, Sir Aldis. I beg you!" She placed a hand on the bridle of his horse as she stood, a small, slender figure in the midst of the mighty knights. "I am unharmed, as you may well see. And I want no more than to return to my father's house."

She knew Sir Corbett's eyes were upon her, but Lilliane refused to look at him. She kept her wide amber-gold gaze locked upon her brother-in-law's ruddy face, determined that he should back down from his belligerent position. She knew she looked very much the wanton with her bare feet and wildly tangled hair. Never had she appeared in public so, and Sir Aldis did not miss that fact. But thankfully, he seemed to reconsider the situation and he finally relented.

"As you will have it, Lilliane. But your bridegroom has much to answer for."

"His horse was lamed," Lilliane explained, at last glancing toward Corbett. To her chagrin, a small smile was curving his mouth and she bit her lip in vexation. She was playing right into his hands, and he was enjoying it immensely! She was irked to no end that she must play mediator when she would like nothing better than to see him put in his place. Still, if she did not calm Sir Aldis, she risked seeing bloodshed, and that she would not do. "We were fortunate to find shelter here," she finished weakly.

Sir Aldis only grunted, then signaled one of his men to lift her up behind him. But it was a quiet group that made their way up the turnpike to Orrick.

The sun was past its zenith when they finally made Orrick Castle. Lilliane was mortified to be returned thus: sitting sideways behind an aging knight, her bare feet dangling, her derriere sore beyond belief, and her hair a wild tangle of chestnut and gold. The fields were empty, and the village little better. It wasn't until they entered the castle walls that the full extent of her shame was driven home. Every last citizen of Orrick—from tradesman to servant, freeman to serf—was dressed in his finest, prepared to celebrate this great wedding of two of the old lord's daughters and to witness the introduction of the new lord. And once she ran this humiliating gauntlet, she still must face her father and all their highborn guests.

As they rode across the bailey, a low hum of whispers followed them. Lilliane's cheeks were stained with color and her eyes were bright with the threat of tears. But she would not cry. Her head was high and her back was straight as they rode to the entrance of the great hall.

Her father was not there to greet her, and she could only wonder at his terrible anger with her. But Odelia was there, and her horrified expression cut

Lilliane deeply. She and the other women guests drew back in seeming distaste as the knights halted before them with the recalcitrant Lilliane.

Lilliane was not sure what to do. She was almost ready to slide from the high rump of the old warhorse without waiting for assistance when a hand reached out to her.

Sir Corbett stood respectfully before her, the epitome of courtly manners and gallant behavior. Lilliane's breath caught in her chest as she stared down at him in surprise. Indeed, the entire company seemed to wait with bated breath for her response to his gesture.

A part of Lilliane wanted to ignore him, to slap away his hand and throw his manners back in his arrogant face. But there was still the long walk to be made through the disapproving throng. She was sure they all knew of her disobedience, and although many might privately disagree with the decision her father had made, they would be united in their conviction that a daughter must always obey her father's will.

Her face must have reflected her indecision, for Sir Corbett stepped nearer until his chest brushed her bare feet.

"If you would truly be mistress here you must pass this test they set before you now," he murmured quietly, for her ears only. "Take my hand and let us present a strong and united front before this company."

She did not want to take his hands. She did not want to touch him or be near him or . . . or present a strong and united front with him. All through the long uncomfortable hours of the ride back she'd been haunted by memories of what he and she had done in that humble cottage. No matter how she had wanted to forget it or pretend it had not been real, she had only to look at the broad-shouldered knight who rode at the head of the column of men to know how very real it had been. And a strange quiver would snake through her, leaving her insides trembling and her emotions tied in knots.

Now as she looked down at his dark unsmiling face she wondered what thoughts were hidden behind those slate-gray eyes. With a sigh Lilliane squared her shoulders. Her eyes swept the watching crowd one last time before she hesitantly reached her hand to him. For one electric moment they remained thus, seeming to meet in truce yet fully aware of the terrible hostility—and powerful attraction—between them.

Then with one easy motion he moved his hands to her small waist and she leaned down to him, her hands braced on his shoulders. He did not lower her quickly to the ground. Rather, he seemed to linger at his task until her heart was thudding in her chest. When at last he did set her on her feet, he deftly tucked her hand under his arm and led her into the great hall.

Neither of them looked at the gaping assembly save to ascertain that Lord Barton was not among them. Corbett led her directly to her chamber, his expression defying interruption from anyone. Once there, however, he turned to her and placed a hand on each of her shoulders.

"I will speak to your father directly. You shall prepare for our wedding." One of his hands moved to stroke her thick, wind-tossed hair. "Although it is no longer the fashion, I would have you wear your hair loose, Lily."

Lilliane's emotions were too tangled for her to respond to his words. He was her enemy. And yet he was to be her husband. He was arrogant and greedy. But he had seen to it that no one should belittle her for her ignoble return. She hated him. Yet they had been lovers.

The weight of his hands on her was warm. But his touch disturbed her, and she quickly escaped into her room. She heard him descend the stairs, no doubt in search of her father, and her heart sank. What would he say to her father? she wondered. And what would she say?

Lilliane leaned against the door, her forehead against the hard, grainy surface. A dull ache pounded in her temples. She had never felt so weary. Every emotion seemed to have been drained from her so that now only numbness remained. Against her will she had been betrothed and bedded. Now she was to prepare for her wedding, and she felt nothing at all. No anger, no despair. Not even fear. She held no control over her own life—she never truly had, she admitted. Her stay at Burgram Abbey had created the illusion that she might not marry until she so chose, but the truth was clear now. Her father had let her stay there because it had suited him to do so. Now it suited him to have her wed Sir Corbett of Colchester.

She was roused by a quiet knock at her door. In short order a large tin bath was filled with scented water, her skin and hair were lathered clean with the finest hard soaps, and her best gown was laid out across her bed. Two maids patiently worked her long damp tresses free of any tangles, then brushed her hair before a hearty fire until her waving locks shone with copper glints and golden highlights. After her long night and miserable drenching, it was the most wonderful luxury she could have wished for. If she'd then been able to crawl into her bed, bury her head beneath the covers, and sink into sleep, she would have been truly content. But this was the day of her wedding. Much as she would like to have ignored that fact, she could not.

She was sitting upon a small upholstered bench clad only in a pure white kirtle. The linen was woven of the finest thread and was soft and light upon her skin. Yet she seemed to feel every single place it touched her. Her nerves were on edge and her heart was racing at a fast, fluttering pace. When one maid picked up the heavily figured silk gown, Lilliane waved her away.

"You may both go now. I can manage the rest on my own."

But the women did not make a move to obey, and Lilliane looked up crossly. "I said you may go. Now," she added for emphasis.

"Lord Barton . . ." The one woman looked at her mistress apologetically. "Lord Barton, he said we must stay with ye until he sends word for ye to come to the chapel." She smiled timidly at Lilliane, then gestured to the gown in her hands.

Lilliane did not balk at the rest of their offers of assistance. With her lips tightly compressed, she allowed them to slip the sapphire-embroidered gown on her then lace it snugly about her waist. A gold-and-silver tooled girdle was fastened at her hips, its end symbolically free of any keys. It had been her mother's, and Lilliane felt a stab of intense longing for her.

A pair of rare silken hose were gartered at her knees, and she donned a pair of open-backed slippers that matched her gown. But she was wooden and without emotion as she let the serving women dress her.

It was only when the older woman began to arrange her hair that Lilliane showed a spark of interest in her appearance.

"I'll do that," she insisted as she took the combs away from the woman. A bitter smile played at her lips as she brought her hair up to her crown, twisted it into a heavy coil, than tucked it into a silver caul. The thin metal was cunningly designed and was pierced in an intricate pattern that showed only hints of the rich color of her hair.

She pinned an embroidered linen wimple to drape under her chin, then finally added a small square head veil. When she was content that her hair was completely covered and that she looked the picture of feminine respectability, she nodded to the two baffled servants.

"Now I am ready."

Lord Barton collapsed into his chair with a heavy groan. Thomas was at his side in an instant, and Lord Barton chuckled despite his obvious pain.

"How is it that you who are so scrawny and stooped—and older than I—can still be so quick and spry? While I—" His face contorted in agony and he placed on hand on his stomach. "I appear hale and hearty yet daily feel the loss of my health."

Thomas filled a tankard from a pitcher of goat's milk then brought it to his master's lips.

"Be glad your son-in-law Aldis does not see your illness," he commented dryly as he watched his lord slowly drain the tankard.

"Aye," Lord Barton agreed as he began to feel some relief to the fire in his side. "He would not stand by only fuming if he did not yet fear me. But after today he will have another to fear."

Thomas shook his old gray head and his face reflected his concern. "I fear many changes may be ahead. A Colchester ruling at Orrick," he muttered in disgust.

"Ah, but not just any Colchester. Young Corbett is not to be compared to Hughe. He has his father's shrewdness and strength. And his mother's family's sense of justice. Hughe has always been a careless lad, not given to caution. Although he is cunning, he is a coward at heart. He may not be trusted."

"And Sir Corbett can?"

"Aye. If I did not believe it I'd not have planned so long ago for this marriage between our houses. Even this foolish feud does not change that."

With an impatient gesture he hoisted himself from his chair, grimacing only slightly. "Didn't he come to me today with the truth of his night with Lilliane? It takes much bravery to tell a man to his face that you have been intimate with his daughter. He knows that Lilliane's reputation has already suffered for it. Yet his concern is that she shall not be poorly judged."

Thomas looked askance at his master. "She does not like him one bit. Doesn't her attempt to flee prove that? 'Tis not likely her opinion of him has improved at all considering how he has shamed her now."

Lord Barton waved his old friend's concerns blithely away. "I did not expect Lily to go easily into this marriage. But she has met her match in Corbett. She will learn to appreciate his husbandly qualities." Then his face became more serious. "I will speak to her soon, Thomas. I'll tell her of my illness. When she understands how much Orrick will be depending on her, she'll make her peace with him. She's not one to take her duties lightly, my Lily. She'll come around."

It was hardly her duties that were uppermost in Lady Lilliane's mind as she waited impatiently in her room. She'd sent word to her father twice and still he had not responded. The hour was almost upon her when the ceremony was to begin, and she feared now that he meant not to speak to her at all.

She was not completely certain of what she would say to him. She only knew she must try this one last time to convince him to stop this marriage. A part of her knew it was hopeless. What value would she be in another marriage contract, ruined as she now was? Every time she thought about the way the huge dark knight had seduced her, she flushed with embarrassment. But it only increased her feelings of righteous anger.

Still, Sir Corbett's warning that she might be with child nagged at her. It was the final argument that would keep her father set on this mad course of his, she feared. For Lilliane knew without a doubt that he would not risk his unborn grandchild on what he considered her foolish whim.

She did not have the chance to worry long about

the presence of a babe within her. Thomas's slow, shuffling walk preceded his muffled knock at her door. When she bade him enter, his smile was tender but regretful.

"The company awaits, milady. All are assembled."

"And my father? Will he not see me first?" she cut in anxiously.

"He will walk both of his daughters to their new husbands." He met her fearful eyes with his own apologetic ones.

"I see."

Lilliane's gaze fell away from his. So it was to be, she realized. A shiver of despair swept through her. Sir Corbett had obviously revealed his crude behavior and her father could not change his plans now, even if he wanted to. She felt a flutter deep within her as she realized that in a matter of hours she would again be closeted with that man. This time he would have even more right to use her as he wished.

For a moment she almost regretted that anger that had prompted her to put her hair up in such an elaborate arrangement when he had so expressly asked her to wear it down. But it was the fashion, she reasoned. Still, she was tempted to pull out the delicate looking glass buried so deeply within her trunk. Did she truly look better with her hair free, or was that only another way in which he sought to manipulate her?

She could not answer that. As she was ushered from the room, she fought to quell the terrible fear that suddenly threatened to overwhelm her. She did not want to belong to him. She did not want this union between Orrick and Colchester.

But most of all she was terrified that he would now have the right to exercise the terrible control he had on her—and that she would again bend willingly to the command in his tender touch.

9

Sir Corbett stood near the base of the stone stairwell. He was clad in a tunic of rich burgundy velvet trimmed with an unusual embroidered pattern of silver and gold vines intertwining. The deep slashes on each side of the tunic revealed dark braies and hose, which were tucked into tall black boots of unusual styling. He wore neither mantle nor tabard, but his sword was slung from a wide ornamental girdle at his waist. He stood motionless, his attention seemingly unfocused. Yet when Lilliane descended on her father's arm, she knew his eyes were on her.

And that he was displeased.

Lord Barton was slow and regal in his descent, and Lilliane thought her nerves would not survive the journey. She glanced fearfully at Tullia who walked on her father's opposite side, but her youngest sister's beautifully serene face only caused Lilliane further dismay. Tullia anticipated her marriage with great joy. She loved Santon. For them it was as it should be, Lilliane thought as she kept her eyes averted from the vast, staring crowd. They were marrying for the purest of reasons, and their life together would truly be blessed.

She, by contrast, was being forced into a union for

political purposes and against all her wishes. Could there possibly be any hope for happiness in such a marriage?

Unbidden, she thought of the hours she had spent with Sir Corbett in the shepherd's cottage—and the exquisite pleasure she had found in his arms. If such was to be expected of the marriage bed she did not have cause for complaint, a small voice taunted her.

But there was no love—or even affection—she rationalized as she sought to bury any memory of that night. There was not even respect, for he most certainly cared only for the demesne that went with her hand, and she could never respect a Colchester. That house had brought only death and misery and sorrow to the people of Orrick. To deliver herself to him in marriage was truly madness!

And yet step by step as her father led his two daughters into the great hall, she progressed steadily toward that madness.

At the bottom tread she stumbled. Had it not been for her father's hold upon her, she would most certainly have fallen. Yet his hand was quickly replaced by another, even stronger one, and when Lilliane's startled gaze lifted it was met by the hard slate gray of Sir Corbett's mocking eyes.

He did not speak to her as he led her across the crowded hall and into the smaller chapel. But his silence only deepened her despair. What need had he of words now? All would be his soon enough—Orrick Castle, the entire northern end of Windermere Fold, and the eldest daughter of his bitterest enemy. At that moment Lilliane truly regretted her rash decision to cover her hair so completely. It had been a gesture of defiance, but a useless one, she knew. Still, it was the only symbol of her opposition to this marriage left to her.

With a deep breath she lifted her chin and stared determinedly down the short nave of the chapel. Beneath her hand she felt Sir Corbett's penetrating warmth. Her arm brushed his as they led the marriage procession, and she struggled hard to remain calm. What would be would be, she told herself. Nothing she could do would change it now. She would not think beyond this very moment. She would most definitely not imagine the night to come, nor the other nights—and days—that stretched before her in an endless, unknown stream.

She was firm in her resolve, and yet, when she knelt before the altar and bowed her head, it was not perseverance she prayed for but reprieve.

The mass that she so often found endless today seemed incredibly brief. Father Denys was clearly in his glory, for Lilliane was sure the chapel had never been so filled with devoutly bowed heads. When he bade the two couples approach the altar, she woodenly stepped forward to do so, but Sir Corbett's firm grip brought her up short.

"You may marry Sir Santon and Lady Tullia first," he said to the surprised priest. A quiet hum of whispers filled the small stone chamber but just as quickly died out when the priest nodded then addressed the other couple.

Lilliane hardly heard the ceremony that joined her youngest sister to Sir Santon. Her mind was too preoccupied with Sir Corbett's high-handedness. Had he no respect for any authority but his own? Must even the church amend its ways so as to accommodate his whim? She was incensed, filled with a righteous anger, until she saw Santon slip his ring onto Tullia's hand. When he sealed his vow to her with a sweet kiss, a general murmur of approval went up and Lilliane fogot her own distress. Her littlest sister was now a wedded woman! Only the best sort of future awaited her. A tear escaped Lilliane's eye as she smiled back at Tullia's ecstatic face. How happy this would have made their mother, Lilliane thought.

But then the priest turned to her and Sir Corbett, and all thoughts of happiness fled. The priest was preparing to begin the holy matrimonial prayers once more when Sir Corbett spoke up.

"I would have the wedding performed where all might participate."

The corpulent priest in his gleaming vestments looked up at the towering knight with a puzzled expression. "And so they may. We shall serve communion immediately—"

"You do not understand. I would have this ceremony performed on the front steps of the great hall."

At that Lilliane looked at him aghast. What did he think to gain by this ill-mannered display? she wondered in true amazement.

As if he read her thoughts he continued. "As you will recall, good Father, it was long the custom of the great houses to have everyone from grandest visitor to least servant witness their marriages. So it shall be today. I would have every man, woman, and child of Orrick bear witness to this marriage of Lady Lilliane, eldest daughter of Orrick, to Sir Corbett formerly of Colchester, now also of Orrick. Thus shall they accept me in their midst just as Lord Barton and Lady Lilliane accept me."

To such a request, worded so reasonably and in

such a tone as to refuse any opposition, the priest could only agree. Still shaking his head in amazement, the man made his way up the nave, preceded by his six attendants and followed by the entire company.

Only Lilliane and Corbett did not immediately make their way out of the chapel. When he turned to face her directly, she had to force herself not to back away from the glitter in his eyes.

"Now, my reluctant bride. I will have you appear as I instructed." With that his hand whipped her veil from her head. Before she could stop him he had removed her filet and tugged the veil beneath her chin off as well.

"Stop this!" she cried even as she recognized that he would not stop until he had his way completely. "Why do you do this? Why must you shame me in this way?"

"There is no shame in wearing your hair free," he contradicted. His one hand held her firmly by the arm while his other fumbled with the caul pinned at the back of her head.

"The whole company will see what you have done! That is shame enough!"

"And do you feel no shame to disobey your husband?" he taunted as the caul finally came loose. In a heavy tumble her gleaming chestnut tresses fell free to spill over her shoulders and arms. At the sight Corbett's fierce expression relaxed, and he filled his hands with her silken locks.

He stood only inches from her as his fingers slid through her luxuriant hair. Lilliane trembled anew at his touch. Had he no respect for this holy place, to caress her in such a bold manner? Was there no one that this man bowed to?

"You are not my husband," she replied angrily, but her voice carried little conviction.

Corbett chuckled as he stared deeply into her eyes, and his fingers stilled in her hair. "We are most assuredly wed, my Lily. 'Tis only left for the priest to mumble his words."

"Oh! You truly blaspheme to say so!" she cried as she snatched her hair away from him. Then she lifted her skirts and hurried down the chapel's aisle.

Corbett did not delay in joining her. He took her arm firmly in his as he opened the door for them both. Behind them only a few scraps of linen and a delicately worked caul, abandoned on the floor, gave evidence that anything had gone before.

The priest's words were mercifully brief. He seemed alarmed that the tall, muscular bridegroom would make still another demand on him, and he hurried through the ceremony with no regard for propriety.

When he nervously asked the bridegroom for the ring, he seemed truly to fear for the response. But without word or expression Corbett produced a heavy ring, which he slipped onto Lilliane's left hand. She had no ring for him but she felt no shame for it. She did not wish to bind him to her with a ring, she reasoned. And she did not want him or his ring.

Still, when he spoke his vows of marriage then looked expectantly at her to repeat her own, she knew it was useless to fight. Her voice was quiet and devoid of all inflection as she pledged herself to him. She would not meet his gaze—she did not want to see the smug look of triumph she was certain he wore. But she could not stop the tremor in her hand where he held her still within his possessive grasp.

"I now pronounce you man and wife," the relieved priest quickly intoned. His round face relaxed in a smile. "You may now kiss your bride."

As if in a dream Lilliane turned her face obediently up to her new husband's. Her eyes were hidden by her lowered lids and thick lashes, but when he slipped his hands to cradle her head her eyes opened with a surprised jolt.

"You will kiss me now, my lady wife," he whispered for her ears only. "You will kiss me with enthusiasm and passion." His face was earnest as he lowered his lips toward hers.

"No!" She gasped. Her hands grabbed his wrists but she could not escape his determined hold.

"Oh, but I believe you shall. For if you do not accept me wholeheartedly now, to the contentment of all who witness our marriage, then I shall have no recourse but to lift you in my arms and carry you straightaway up the stairs to our chamber." As her eyes widened in disbelief he continued in a low tone. "You will be my wife, fair Lily. And every man, woman, and child here shall know it."

Lilliane was beyond doubting he meant every word he said. He would not hesitate to do just as he threatened. And who was there to say he could not? For a moment longer she stared up at his lean, determined face. Then despite her every logical instinct, she reluctantly turned her face up to his in mute acceptance of his will.

Corbett, however, was clearly not satisfied with

such passivity. "I said you shall kiss me." His lips lifted in a faint smile. "Kiss me, wife."

Beyond them a low murmur of speculation rippled through the curious onlookers. But Lilliane was oblivious to all but Corbett's presence. His hands were warm and firm on her neck and one of his thumbs gently massaged the sensitive spot just beneath her ear. Her hands were both still gripping his wrists but no longer was her grasp tense with resistance.

She was warm all over as she stared up into his inscrutable gray eyes, warm and quivering with disturbing sensations. She searched his face as she teetered between acquiescence and defiance. He was a handsome man in his own strange, brutal way. His features were harshly masculine, all angles and planes, and tanned from many years spent on horseback. His eyes were beautiful, she realized with a start, their gray fringed with thick black lashes. The scar on his brow she did not think twice about; it was simply a part of him. But his lips she found fascinating.

In that instant Lilliane's decision was made. She swiftly raised up on her toes and lifted her mouth to his, but he was so tall that she could not reach him. Trembling now, she met his watchful gaze with huge, imploring eyes. For that brief, sizzling moment she felt he somehow saw right into her soul. Then he lowered his head and their lips finally met.

She had not meant the kiss to be any more than Tullia's and Santon's, but Corbett seemed to have other ideas. When she would have pulled away, he only held her steady against him, not ready to let her go.

For Lilliane it was an exquisite form of agony. His lips were warm and firm as they moved over hers, and she could not feign indifference to him. Her heart was beating a fierce staccato as her lips clung to his. When his tongue traced the tender corner of her mouth, she gasped and pulled a little away from him. She knew her face was flushed and her confusion plainly evident to him, but to her vast relief he did not choose to gloat over this newest of his victories over her. Instead, he only gave her an odd searching look before turning to face the now-cheering throng.

Lilliane could not precisely remember the ensuing minutes before they returned to the great hall. They had stood there on the top step, his brawny arm wrapped around her waist, waving to the people of Orrick. Her father had kissed her, and she and Tullia had embraced. Odelia, of course, had only given her a grim sort of smile, and that just because their father was watching. But the other faces and their words of congratulations were merely blurred images and jumbled phrases in Lilliane's mind.

It was not until Corbett pulled her slightly aside on the raised landing while the guests streamed into the great hall that she finally regained her senses. Still, she did not want to meet his alert gaze; she feared he would see her confusion and her vulnerability. But Corbett was not one easily rebuffed. He tilted her face up to his with a finger beneath her chin.

His face was solemn as he kept his eyes upon her. Once again she was struck by the rare masculine appeal of the man. She would have looked away had he not spoken first.

"You've a choice to make, my fair Lily." He

reached out for a long rippling strand of her chestnut hair and wound it thoughtfully around one of his fingers. Her skin tingled from the light touch, but she fought to keep her face carefully blank. Then he smiled ruefully, and it was almost as if he knew of the struggle that went on within her. "You may choose to continue your resistance to our marriage— and to me. Or you may decide now to concede a gracious defeat and accept your proper place at my side. As my wife." He uncoiled her hair from his finger then caressed her cheek with his broad palm.

"I am ready to live in peace, Lily. Orrick Castle will be my home. We shall live here many years as man and wife. Think hard on what sort of life you would have, for the choice is now yours." He paused and his eyes became harder. "I can make your life a heaven or a hell. It is up to you."

Before she could think to answer him, they were suddenly beset by jovial guests. In the crush of people whacking the new groom on the back and claiming the good-luck kiss from the bride, Lilliane and Corbett were carried apart from one another.

It seemed at last that the knights of Colchester were being accepted at Orrick. Most certainly Lilliane was soundly kissed by nearly every one of them. It crossed her mind that it was strange no one else from Colchester had attended the wedding, not even Corbett's brother, Hughe. But she did not have time to ponder it for long.

Ale and wine were being poured aplenty as the wedding guests prepared to begin their celebrating in earnest. For the first time Lilliane felt a small glimmer of hope. As the great hall of Orrick echoed with laughter and good-natured ribaldry, she felt an odd tingle of anticipation.

Orrick had for too long been a castle somber and stern, lacking the warmth her mother had always given it. Now it was her turn. But could she truly make a good life with this man—her enemy? Lilliane's eyes searched the crowd for her husband. Due to his great height and the arrogant carriage of his dark head, he was easy to find.

He was speaking to her father, bending down slightly to listen to the older man's words. Lilliane watched her father, for the first time in days able to see beyond her anger and pain to the man he was. He saw this marriage as the best hope for his beloved Orrick. It was for that reason—and that reason alone —he had forced this wedding upon her.

Now as she stared at him standing so near her new husband, she was suddenly aware of his considerable age. Beside the vital Corbett her father was only a shadow of his former self. Oh, he was hale enough, with his florid face and his substantial girth. And most certainly he appeared every inch the powerful baron with his fine velvet tunic and silver-gray hair.

But he was an old man.

Corbett, by contrast, was at the height of his power; youth and experience combined to give him the best of both. He had the strength, the stamina, and the time to make of Orrick what he would. But Lilliane could not be sure he had the wisdom. Still, she could do nothing about that, she reminded herself. He would rule Orrick once her father was gone, and she was certain he would begin even now to take over, bit by bit. He would not long take to another's rule.

As she watched him, she saw his second in command, Sir Dunn, draw him aside and whisper something to him. Almost at once Corbett's face darkened in a frown, his scarred brow giving him a harsh, forbidding look. He exchanged several words with Dunn and his anger was clearly evident. Then he looked up, searching the room until his eyes met hers.

Even from across the crowded hall Lilliane felt the force of his gaze, and a quiver of emotion coursed through her. He frightened her. She knew his strength and the terrible power he wielded over her. Even now the thought of the intimacies they had shared made her tremble in remembrance.

Yet he fascinated her as well.

For long seconds their eyes remained locked. Would she ever come to know and understand this man whose ring now marked her as his? Not conscious she did so, Lilliane rubbed the hefty ring on her finger, all the while staring at her new husband. His face, handsome despite the wicked scar that marred it, softened somewhat, and she wondered what thoughts he had as he studied her. But her musings were interrupted when someone blocked her view of him.

"Lady Lilliane." Sir William bowed low over her hand but did not kiss it. "May I present to you my wife, Lady Verone."

Lilliane smiled automatically at the lovely woman on William's arm, then became more sincere in her greeting when she saw how hesitant the young woman looked. Certainly she appeared too young to be already heavy with child. "I'm so pleased you are feeling well enough to participate in today's festivities. Tullia mentioned you'd been ill." She took Verone's timidly proffered hand. "I have long wished to meet the wife of my childhood friend."

"Oh, and—and may I wish you much happiness in your marriage," the girl stammered shyly.

"As I wish you in yours," Lilliane replied, squeezing her hand.

William was stiff and barely communicative as the two women warmed to one another.

"May I see your ring?" Verone asked as she relaxed in Lilliane's presence. "Oh, 'tis truly lovely," she exclaimed, looking closely.

Lilliane had not yet examined the ring herself. She'd not wanted it at all, and in spite of its unfamiliar weight on her hand, she'd tried hard to ignore it. But now, as she stared at it, she had to agree. A wide filigreed band of twining silver and gold vines circled her finger from almost knuckle to knuckle. Rising from the band, a long multifaceted stone reflected the lights of the many torches in the hall. So brilliant was it that only by twisting her hand was she able to recognize the lavender stone as the same meridian jewel that decorated the comb and looking glass she'd received as a betrothal gift.

She looked up then, searching the crowded hall for Corbett, but he was not to be found. When Verone saw how her eyes sought him, she smiled softly. "He is a fine man. I wish you many children of him."

At that Sir William abruptly took his wife's arm. "I'm sure Lilliane has many others to greet this day. Shall I escort you to your seat?" Without waiting for a reply, he rudely hauled his wife away.

But Lilliane had no time to wonder at his unseemly behavior, for she was quickly beset by many more guests. As she greeted them and murmured the necessary replies and thanks for their kind attendance, her eyes searched again for her husband. But he was nowhere to be found. Finally when she could put it off no longer, she made her way to the place of honor so that the meal might begin.

Where was he? she wondered in angry frustration. Then she recalled that Sir Dunn had whispered something to him that had turned his expression grim. Was that it? Had Dunn told him something—perhaps about her—that had angered him? After all, there was no love lost between her and Dunn. He had made his distrust of her clear, and although she'd received a kiss from most of her husband's men, Sir Dunn had not been among them.

A frown creased her brow as Lilliane made her way to her chair. Was Corbett so unmannered as to ignore his own bride at the wedding feast? Or so cruel? She was simmering with anger and humiliation when her chair was suddenly scraped back before her. Then a hand wrapped around her arm and before she knew what was happening, Corbett had seated her with all the chivalry of the most courtly of knights. As he lowered his long frame into the adjacent high-backed chair, he noted her glower and his scarred brow arched in mild surprise.

"Can I assume by your unhappy expression that you tire of this raucous company?" He stood up abruptly and began to pull her up as well. "Come along then. Let us retire to our chamber—"

"No!" Lilliane's voice was a high-pitched squeak. She snatched her hand from his grasp and sat down hard. "I-I-I am famished," she stammered, all the while avoiding his mocking gaze.

"Very well, then." He sat down as a page filled their goblets with a ruby-red wine. Then he handed her one silver chalice and lifted his in salute to her. "Enjoy this feast that you have seen prepared for our pleasure. Drink well of this wine fermented of the berries that fill Orrick's fields. Greet your guests that celebrate our wedding this evening. This day is yours with all the trappings and show considered so dear by women." He took a deep draft of his wine, then leveled his gaze upon her. "But know this, Lily. The night will be mine, and we will celebrate it as I deem fit."

Her heart lurched within her chest at his blunt words, and a slow heat suffused her entire being. But Lilliane had no reply. Indeed, she was silent throughout the meal they shared despite the boisterous celebration that resounded in the old hall.

She was frightened, she told herself. And angry too. But there was another disturbing emotion dominating those two. She dared not call it anticipation, for logic deemed that she should dread the approaching union with her new husband. But the memories of how he'd raised her to such astounding heights of pleasure could not be ignored. Had it only been last night? she wondered in amazement. Was it truly only a matter of hours since they had lain so intimately entwined up on the pallet of soft sheepskins?

She should be overcome with the very shame of it, she berated herself. But instead of shame she felt again a warm flush upon her skin, and a disturbing knot seemed to coil and twist deep within her belly. Unable to resist, she stole a look at Corbett.

He was speaking to her father again, relaxed back in his chair with his long legs stretched before him.

As her stare lengthened he turned his head to meet her gaze and his conversation ceased. Between them the air seemed to crackle and come alive until Lilliane made herself break the hold of his mesmerizing gray eyes.

Beyond him her father was smiling and nodding softly. His face was beaming with contentment, for he had succeeded at last in binding the two houses together through this marriage. Lilliane knew he expected peace and prosperity from this union, but she was not convinced of it. Still, she had not seen her father look so well since she'd returned from the abbey. It was hard for her to resent him when he so clearly believed in what he had done.

She let her gaze sweep over the crowd, noting the high spirits of the celebrating guests. One person was not smiling, however. William was staring at Corbett with an expression of black fury. Then, as if he sensed her watching him, he looked over at her. Lilliane, however, immediately looked away. She didn't know what to do about William, but she knew she must do nothing to encourage this lingering affection he felt for her. It was wrong and most certainly unfair to his lovely wife.

Her thoughts were interrupted when Corbett rose to his feet. He lifted a goblet of wine in his hand for silence. Only when everyone in the hall had quieted and looked expectantly to him did he speak.

"Good people of Orrick. Honored guests. Respected host." He nodded at Lord Barton. "I bid you join me in honoring my bride, the fair Lady Lilliane." He saluted her with his goblet, then proceeded to drain its contents. When he banged the empty chalice down on the heavy table, everyone began to cheer. But when he then pulled Lilliane up from her chair, the crowd erupted in good-natured hoots and catcalls.

She was sure he meant to kiss her. His eyes were smoky and warm, alive with promise and passion. Lilliane was shaken by the expectant thrill that ran through her. A part of her was appalled at the thought of kissing him here. But another part of her would have risen to the challenge.

"None of that, you young stallion!" a happily slurred voice called.

"Hold your passion in check!" another joined in.

"There's time enough! Time enough!"

Before she could take hold of the situation, Lilliane found herself surrounded by a giggling bevy of women even as Corbett was hauled away by a rowdy group of knights. Up the stone stairs she was swept, Tullia having joined her in the circle of chattering women. Then one group pulled Tullia away to her room while the others continued up the torchlit stairway with Lilliane.

Inside the tower room Lilliane backed away from her laughing tormentors.

"Look at her cheeks, would you!" one matron teased. " 'Twould lead a body to believe she knew already what her lord husband has in store for her."

"Mayhap she does," another less pleasant voice challenged.

At once the chamber fell quiet. To Lilliane's dismay it seemed she now faced a room full of accusers. Her heart thumped painfully in her chest as her wide eyes swept the circle of women. Then, like a guardian angel, Lady Verone stepped forward and took both of Lilliane's cold hands into hers.

"I think perhaps she fears, as we all did, that her husband's vigor will rival that of the stallions and bulls every girl has witnessed." She moved to Lilliane's side and began to unlace the beautiful sapphire gown while she kept her eyes steadfastly fixed on the other women. "Is there a woman among us that can say she did not dread that first joining?" she asked in a soft voice that still dared anyone to contradict her.

It was just what was needed to break the awkward silence. In a rush of teasing banter, maternal advice, and jovial warnings, the women swiftly stripped Lilliane of all but her delicate kirtle and new wedding ring.

Lilliane was pink with embarrassment as she stood among them. They all knew what was to come tonight, she thought. What was to happen in the large bed. Near to panicking, she turned desperate eyes to Lady Verone. But that sweet lady only smiled warmly and gave her a hug.

"Do not fear to meet your husband this night. I have seen how he looks at you and how he desires you. Be glad that your father has chosen such a man as Sir Corbett for you, and not some fat and aging fellow. This battleground you contemplate"—she gestured to the massive bed—"will prove to bring you much delight if you will but let it."

There was no time for Lilliane to reply. With a crash the door was shoved open and, amid many shouts and lewd comments, a crowd of men hustled Corbett into the chamber.

Despite the women who shrieked and squealed and gathered protectively around Lilliane, Corbett's eyes found her at once. The men, warmed by both the wine and the expectations of this traditional wedding vanguard, were bold of glance and tongue as they squeezed into the now-overcrowded chamber.

"Stand away from the bride!" one inebriated knight demanded of the women who still clustered around the scantily clad Lilliane.

"Aye, we would see her delivered to the bride's bed—"

"As we will deliver her groom!" another boasted.

As of one mind, the men began to pull at Corbett's clothes, removing his girdle and tunic before he shoved them roughly away. He still was grinning as he held the raucous group at bay.

"I can manage the rest on my own."

"So he says!"

"Aye—he's taken far too long to take a bride. Mayhap he doubts his prowess—"

"Away!" Corbett roared in mock temper. "I'll see to my bride without benefit of your help or advice." Then he began to push the men back and out of the room. In a high mood, the men continued with their bold comments and lewd advice, but slowly they dispersed.

Corbett stood with one hand upon the door, clad only in his loose shirt, hose, and boots. When he turned his intense eyes on the whispering group of women, they hushed at once. He had no need of words with them. Under his steady stare they silently melted away.

Lilliane would have kept Verone with her, so unnerved was she now that the moment was at hand. But the young woman gently disentangled her hand from Lilliane's desperate grasp and, with a last reassuring look, exited the chamber.

Then it was only Lilliane and Corbett. Slowly he closed the door. His face was serious as he stared at her, and she was captured by the intensity of his smoldering eyes. It was not until he moved lithely toward her that she shrank from him, trying in vain to cover herself more adequately from his view.

"Don't," he said quietly. "I would see what I have won."

"I thought it was Orrick that was the prize," Lilliane whispered in a wavering voice.

"Aye. And a handsome prize it is. But I knew that when I put my mind to marrying you." His lips curved in a faint smile. "But you, my lady wife. You are not what I expected."

As his eyes swept her Lilliane trembled at the appreciation she saw on his face. Like a flame heating her through and through, anticipation caught her in its grip and she could not deny it. Still, she fought the pull she felt from him. Like a frightened doe she backed away. Her eyes were wide with alarm, thick lashes framing their dark golden centers.

But there was no escaping his avid gaze nor his masculine threat. He did not pursue her. With one careless motion he pulled his shirt over his head and tossed it aside. His boots were removed next. All the while he kept his fiery eyes upon her.

Lilliane's pale skin flushed a rosy pink under his ravenous gaze. She watched in dismay as he removed his hose, but when he stood up, clad only in his small cloth, she quickly looked away. Unfortunately, it was the wide bed that her eyes fastened on, and she swallowed convulsively. It was dressed with fresh linens, strewn with pale-pink rose petals, and readied for the wedding night.

Then her eye was caught by his movement. She gasped, fully expecting him to lay his hands upon her. But it was not to her side that Corbett made his way. It was to the bed, where he made himself comfortable. He sat back, his long muscular legs stretched beneath the pure white sheet, then patted the empty space beside him.

"Come to my bed, Lily. It is time."

Lilliane stood against the wall and stared at him in disbelief. Did he truly think she would come willingly to him? That by his simple command he could force her to submit to him?

"Perhaps it is time for you. But not for me. Never for me."

Instead of the anger she expected, he only smiled softly. "You succumbed easily enough last night. You enjoyed it. Why not admit it and let us enjoy ourselves once more?" He paused and his voice grew low and husky. "It will be even better this time, Lily. I promise you."

Lilliane was torn by terribly conflicting emotions. It was true. Everything he said was true, for she *had* enjoyed it, much to her dismay. She looked away from him, confused by her awful predicament. Then she looked cautiously back at him. Her gaze swept from his smoky gray eyes to his well-formed lips, then down across his bare chest to where the sheet hid the rest of him from view. He was her husband now. That much she could not deny. Before the church and God and all the people of Orrick she had spoken her vows, and that bound her to him for life.

It took every ounce of her courage to step toward him. She saw the flicker of surprise in his eyes and she wondered at it. Did he think that she was any less

forced by her vows today than she had been forced
by his superior strength and expertise last night? A
part of her railed at the unfairness of her position:
she would lose to him whether she resisted or not.

But still she shivered with the new knowledge of
what the next few hours held in store for her. His
eyes seemed to grow hotter as she approached the
bed until she felt positively scorched. She knew the
finely woven kirtle offered her scant protection; her
nipples already protruded against the soft fabric,
standing rosy and impudent before him.

At the bed's edge she lowered her gaze, focusing on
one perfect rose petal upon the sheet. When he
reached over and gently pushed her hair behind one
of her shoulders, she could neither move any closer
to him nor pull away. Then he reached his hand out
and ran one finger along her shoulder and down her
slim arm until he reached her hand.

"Come to me," he repeated softly with the lightest
of tugs on her wrist.

There was no reason for her to fight him any
longer, she rationalized as she allowed herself to be
drawn toward him. She had fought him with all her
strength, but it had been of no use. He would be lord
of Orrick one day. And she was now his wife.

With a ragged sigh Lilliane knelt upon the bed. She
would not meet his eyes, and her bent head cast her
hair protectively before her. But her hair was truly
no proof against him, for he seemed to find as much
pleasure from it as from her scantily clad body.

She heard his sharp inhalation of breath as he
filled his hands with the warm silk of her hair. Lilliane's skin tingled at the whisper-light touch and the
sensual slide of his fingers.

"There's no need for hesitance any longer. Last night was only the beginning of the pleasures we may find in each other."

"I did not wish for that to happen," she muttered obstinately.

"And yet you cannot deny the pleasure you received."

"I was not willing. You forced me," she reminded him sharply.

"You may not have been willing at first. But later . . ." His fingers moved silkily through her hair. "And now we are married. Tell me, Lily, do you come to me a willing wife?" His eyes captured hers and she could not break their compelling hold.

"I—I did not want to marry you," she admitted with a hint of challenge in her troubled eyes.

"You made that more than clear." There was a faint ring of amusement in his voice. "But now we are wed. Do you come to me willingly?"

She was conscious that his hands had stilled within her hair. She caught her breath as she contemplated her answer to him. This was, in truth, the moment of her vow, she realized. The afternoon's ceremony had proven to everyone else that they were wed. But her answer now would tell him whether she accepted it as well.

It went against everything she felt for the house of Colchester. She could recount every wrong they'd dealt the people of Orrick, every insult and unfair blow. Was there any hope for a marriage begun so? Her father clearly believed there was. But she did not. Or . . . she had not. But now?

Lilliane searched his face for an answer. He was an enigma to her. Hard as steel, fearsome and scarred, he had terrified her and bullied and threatened her. He had hunted her down like a frightened hare and then forced her into his bed.

But he had not raped her.

Her blood heated at the thought of what he had done with her, but she could not call it rape.

At last she lowered her eyes from his. Her nod of acquiescence was barely perceptible, but she knew he recognized it. Once more she felt the movement of his hands within her hair, but this time he slid his palm to the nape of her neck. With only the slightest pressure he bade her lean nearer him as he tilted her face to his.

Lilliane was transfixed beneath his sure touch. With every fleeting stroke, every nimble caress, her body came alive despite her conscious wish not to let it be so.

Her eyes were tightly closed, as if she might block out the fact of her surrender to this man—her enemy, her husband. But Corbett would not allow her to avoid him so easily.

"Open your eyes." His lips caressed one lid gently then the other. "Open your eyes and look at me, Lily."

In the candlelit room his eyes were the deepest shade of gray, almost black. Yet Lilliane was still able to see tiny flecks of silver and gold in their piercing depths. And a look of absolute possession that took her breath away.

He drew her head down and captured her lips in a kiss that sent her senses spinning. She was dizzy and falling, not sure whether he pulled her down upon him or the other way around. Then he deftly rolled her over so that he lay above her, his hand still cradling her head, their lips still clinging.

Her arms were trapped between them, and her hands pressed against the warm skin of his naked chest. She should push him away, she thought as her lips parted beneath his. She should not want this sultry drowning sensation so desperately. But as his tongue slid enticingly along the sensitive edge of her lips then slipped brazenly into the silken depths of her mouth, all thoughts of resistance fled Lilliane's mind.

Her fingers pressed his chest still, but now they sought only to gather his warmth to her, not to push him away. She was aware of the crisp, curling hairs on his chest, of the hard, muscular stomach that pinned her to the mattress and the iron-hewn thigh that lay now between her own bare legs. She was also conscious of a twisting knot simmering somewhere inside her, and she writhed at the exquisite torture of it.

Her artless movement seemed only to inflame Corbett more for he deepened the kiss and pressed his body more intimately against hers. There was her simple kirtle between them, and his smallcloth as well, but neither of those could hide the thickening between his legs. Like the touch of a flame, it seemed to jolt Lilliane to her senses even as it increased the heat within her. And all the while his kiss was sapping her of any will apart from his own.

When at last he ended the kiss, she was completely breathless. His own breath was ragged and he smiled as he pushed a wayward tendril from her cheek.

"I should punish you for all the ways you have opposed me," he murmured as he cleverly loosened the ties of her kirtle.

Lilliane lowered her thick lashes, unable to maintain such close and intimate eye contact with him. "And . . . and now will you?"

When he did not answer at once, Lilliane hesitantly lifted her gaze back to him. What she saw there caused her heart to flutter in alarm. Corbett already held her beneath him; his superior strength was indisputable fact. Yet at this moment it was not that physical strength she feared so much as the strength of will she recognized in his piercing gray eyes. He would not beat her; she knew that. But he had the ability—and the single-mindedness—to find other, more effective methods to bend her to his desires.

He lowered his head a fraction and stared intently into her clear, amber eyes. "And now . . ." His lips lifted in a faint grin. "Now I think it is hardly punishment I have in mind for you."

She felt his warm, firm lips begin a trail along her jawline and the sensitive curve of her neck to the pulse point at the base of her throat. Oh, how she wanted to remain unaffected by his kisses! But as before, she was completely disarmed by the gentle power he wielded over her. He sapped her will, diffused her anger, and drove all thoughts of resisting him completely away with those clever, knowing kisses.

Then he slid ever so slowly down her softly curving length until he lay completely within her legs, his head upon her stomach. Lilliane's heart was in her throat as she felt the warm tickle of his breath along her ribs and the heat of his hands upon her breasts.

In a matching tempo he circled her breasts, spiraling ever nearer her tensed nipples. Teasing her over and over again, he would stop just short of those aching rose-tipped buds until she was arching off the bed in silent plea. Lilliane was consumed with need for him. Like a tidal wave passion washed over her.

"Oh." She panted desperately. "Please—" Then when he took each nipple between a forefinger and thumb, she moaned in response. Relentlessly he drove her on, planting kisses on her belly as he raised her to a fever pitch. When he moved his kisses up to her outthrust breasts, she shamelessly pressed her belly up to his.

"Oh, no, my fine young minx. You shall not find your relief so easily," he taunted her as he swirled his tongue sensuously around first one nipple then the other. "You still have much to atone for."

Lilliane wanted to ignore his words, but like the demon himself he seemed content to torture her with the promise of more and more pleasure.

"Oh, please," she begged as she ran her fingers through his hair and tugged unsuccessfully to bring his face up to hers.

"Ah, now you say please." He moved his hands to the side of her head and filled them with her chestnut locks. "But tell me, why did you not wear your hair loose as I requested?"

His words brought her eyes wide open and she stared at him in surprise. With agonizing slowness he slid his hard torso up along hers, making certain every sensitive portion of her flesh felt the strength and heat of him.

"I would have your answer, Lily."

"I . . . it was only . . ." Lilliane floundered, not

able to think or even remember now why it had been so important to her to thwart him by wearing her hair concealed.

"It was only that you must oppose me, in whatever way possible. Am I right?"

"Yes," she breathed, torn between the terrible desire he inspired in her now and the deep resentment she still nursed for him. But instead of angering him, her answer seemed to increase his ardor even more. With his knee he brought her legs apart, and one of his hands slid down to her thigh.

"You were not my wife then," he murmured hoarsely as he stared down into her heavy-lidded eyes. "So I will not punish you. But know that I expect absolute obedience from my wife."

Lilliane wanted to block out his words. She did not want to obey him or even be his wife. But he seemed to have taken all control from her and made her body pliant to his will only. Was he a demon to practice such dark arts upon her?

The she felt the sensuous caress of his finger between her thighs, and she arched in passionate response. Back and forth he stroked until she was helpless and limp beneath his expert touch. She wanted him with an intensity that shook her to her very core.

"You will be . . . my most . . . obedient wife . . ." he said, panting as he too was overwhelmed by his own needs. She felt the probing length of him and a small cry of ecstasy escaped her.

"Say it, Lily," he muttered hoarsely in her ear. "Say it."

"I—I will," she agreed, blind with the need for

what only he could do for her. "I will be an obedient wife—"

With a groan he drove into her then, and Lilliane thought she would swoon from the sheer glory of it. Hot and smooth, like steel wrapped in velvet, he moved in long, determined thrusts. She was sure he touched her very soul.

His mouth came down on hers with such passionate fervor she thought she must die of pleasure. His tongue filled her mouth in a demanding rhythm that mirrored their other joining. Then she was no longer a passive receptacle for his passion. With a fire that matched his own, her tongue met his and was drawn enticingly to explore his lips and mouth. She wrapped her arms around his wide shoulders, reveling in the hot, slick feel of his skin. And with every possessive stroke of his body into her she rose in willing acceptance.

She was flying into the unknown, frightened and exhilarated as her body reached for some new indefinable goal. Then like some incredible explosion within her, she felt one exquisite wave after another wash over her. He had pushed her beyond all control. Then she was practically lifted from the bed as his body stiffened and he groaned against her neck.

"Ah, Lily . . . my God, woman . . ."

Lilliane felt the shudders that ripped through him, and she gloried in the knowledge that she had the power to affect him even as he affected her. But as he slowed his frantic pace, she felt a sudden sting of tears against her lids. He would pull away from her now, she realized. Although it was madness, she did not want him to go.

When he rolled to his side, taking her with him,

she kept her face averted from him. She was bewildered by all he made her feel. She was supposed to hate him, but she desired him beyond all understanding. She had fought to be free of him, yet now she clung to him, devastated to think he might leave her so quickly.

But Corbett did not loosen his hold on her at all. Instead he nestled her within his arms, tucked her head neatly under his chin, and pulled the coverlet over them both. Beneath her ear Lilliane could hear the strong beat of his heart as it gradually slowed its pace. He sighed hugely and slid his hand down her arm, then kissed the top of her head.

"You will do very well, wife," he whispered sleepily. "Very well."

His breath stirred her hair and Lilliane felt a delicious quiver deep within her. Despite her wish for it not to be so, she was gratified by his approval of her. She did not like this strange reversal of her feelings, but she could not ignore it. Nor could she deny that her desire for him was stronger than ever.

For a long while Lilliane lay still within the embrace of her new husband. It was a strange feeling, to lie with a man so. She feared that despite her extreme weariness, she would never relax enough to sleep.

But oddly enough, she did feel safe in his arms. Safe and protected. With a small sigh she settled against him and, lulled by his soft, steady breathing, she slipped peacefully into sleep.

10

Lilliane was being pressed down beneath the most delicious of weights. She was heavy with the clinging after-effects of sleep, she truly did not wish to awaken.

Yet the warmth seeping over her was not to be ignored. Even as it forced her awake, it drugged her into compliant lethargy.

She was not all at once aware of Corbett's presence in her bed. Her memory was still too clouded from her exhausted slumber. But the masculine feel of his hard, naked body was impossible to ignore. When his hand slid slowly down her side to rest upon her hip, she squirmed unconsciously against him, still resisting full awareness.

But when his lips began to nibble at her neck and his warm breath tickled her sensitive ear, she could not fight it. Her eyes slowly opened to the dimness of the early morning and the realization of whom she lay with.

"Sleep well?" Corbett's husky words seemed to stroke some chord within her and she took a quick breath. He was half lying upon her; their bellies were pressed intimately together, their legs were entwined. Memories of the hours just past tumbled through her mind, and to her complete chagrin a wave of desire rushed through her.

Hesitantly she peered up into his shadowed face. There was little revealed in the dim light of predawn, only the massive size of him and the way he completely dominated her. But there was no force in his light touch; nor was there any tentativeness. He did not command, neither did he request that she respond. He only smoothed her tangled hair back from her brow then cupped her face between his hands.

Still, that was enough. Like a smoldering fire fanned suddenly by high winds, she felt the full force of her longing for him return. It was as if their previous joinings had only whetted her appetite, she realized as she succumbed to the exquisite torture of it. Against her belly she felt the insistent pressure of his arousal, and without thinking she pressed up hard against him.

"Ah, my little wife," he murmured hotly against her lips. "How you drive me to distraction. I would sooner stay abed with you . . ." His mouth captured hers eagerly, drawing her tongue into a wildly passionate dance. She was ready for him at once, as if their previous lovemaking had not ended at all, but only melted into this new, freshening passion.

"Stay abed," she whispered. She arched her neck as his lips moved seductively upon her tender flesh. " 'Tis yet night. You need not leave."

Corbett raised above her then. She could not clearly make out his expression, although she knew he stared at her intently. She thought he would speak. Certainly he paused as if something preyed upon his mind. But then it appeared he'd reconsidered for he moved down upon her. His knee nudged her legs apart and she willingly complied. Then he entered her with a sureness that took her breath away, so consummately did he fill every part of her.

"Oh, dear God . . ." She panted as he began to move rhythmically within her. Like a fire out of control her blood seemed to rush through her. She was his wife, she thought as she spun in dizzy circles. This was right and good in the eyes of God and the church. But, oh, she was so much more than merely his wife. In some inexplicable manner he had taken her entire will into his own. She who had hated him so violently did now willingly succumb to him. She wanted him. She felt certain she would die without his touch.

His thrusts had become most furious when she felt him begin to tense. He had reached the zenith of his passion, and she knew now that it would soon end.

"Oh, wait." The words were a soft, frustrated whisper; she hardly realized she had said them. But as Corbett shuddered in passionate release, she knew he had heard.

Lilliane was mortified. Why had she said such a thing? Despite her new knowledge of what might occur between them—what might occur within her—she could not fathom saying such a thing. Her hands slid slowly from their grasp around his powerful neck and down his damp shoulders and arms. It was a wonder to her that she could lie so with a man. Especially *this* man. Yet honesty would not let her deny the pleasure she received from him. Still, to beg him to wait! It seemed the words of a wanton, not a wife.

When Corbett propped himself on his elbows and looked down into her face, Lilliane kept her eyes carefully averted. But he would not have it and firmly tilted her face up to his.

"I should not have rushed you so," he began, his face earnest and intent. "I am most pleased with you, Lily. Despite all that has gone before, I think ours may be a marriage of mutual contentment. If I did not let you . . . If I was too . . . ah . . . too hasty with you, then my only excuse is that I find much more pleasure in my wife than ever I had hoped."

He grinned then and she caught the flash of strong white teeth against his shadowed face. "A virgin and yet a woman of passion. You're a rare find."

She was uncomfortable with his direct words. But there was a vague disappointment too. His words of "mutual contentment" rang hollowly in her ears, and yet she knew she had no sound reason for it. Mutual contentment was as much as she could ever have expected in a marriage, and yet, now that she had it, it seemed a poor expectation.

But she was hardly going to reveal that to him. "Have you forgotten the main reason you married me?" she retorted defensively. "Have you forgotten that I'm an heiress?"

He laughed then and planted a lusty kiss upon her startled lips. "My passionate, virgin heiress. Yes, you will do quite well, Lily." He paused and she felt his weight settle even more intimately against her feminine length. Then he slid slowly down along her and her heart began to pound.

Last night he had done this. He had moved down her body like that and then teased her and touched her and kissed her to the point of madness. Her head was thrown back, her eyes were closed in tremulous anticipation as she felt his hot wet kiss move past her breast to her belly. Then a horn sounded from some-where without and he lifted his lips from her sensi-tive flesh.

"Corbett," she whispered, willing the distraction away. But then they were interrupted by a heavy pounding on the door and the moment was ruined.

She heard his short muffled oath and his sharp re-ply to the knock, but she could hardly believe it when he rolled to his side then rose from the bed and crossed to where his clothes still lay.

It was the last thing she expected, and for several shocked seconds Lilliane could do no more than lie there, staring at him. Then cool air washed over her heated skin and she was even more painfully aware of the absence of his strong, warm body.

With an angry jerk she pulled the coverlet over her. She wanted to bury her head beneath its protec-tive warmth, but pride would not allow it. When she finally risked a glance at him in the soft light of the breaking dawn, he had already donned his braies and was securing his hose over his well-muscled calves.

Despite her anger—and her hurt—Lilliane could not deny the masculine beauty of this man. Oh, she recognized well enough that his beauty was not the same as Sir William's. He was too scarred, too marked by the hard life he'd lived. Yet that only seemed to strengthen the attraction she felt for him. He was hard as granite, as unyielding as the oak, as tested as the steel of his war tools.

"I must leave you now." His abrupt words inter-rupted her thoughts.

" 'Tis clear enough already that you leave," she an-swered in a more petulant voice than she intended.

He looked up then and she could see the frown that creased his brow. "No, Lily. I mean I must leave Orrick. I've business that cannot be delayed."

As pained as she had been at his removal from the bed, it was as nothing compared to the shock of this new blow. Her disbelief was so great she did not at first react, but only lay there staring dumbfounded at him.

For his part, Corbett seemed quite busy with his garments, and there was a prolonged silence between them. Lilliane's heart seemed to plummet as she finally absorbed his words, and she could barely restrain her tears. As it was, she turned her face away from him and squeezed her eyes tightly against the telltale stinging she felt.

Damn him! she silently railed. Damn him for treating her so! Barely married and already abandoned, she would appear quite pathetic to the guests who rightfully expected at least another full day of celebration. Yet it was not the thought of their pity that left the awful hollowness within her chest. From the heights of passion to the dreadful depths of abandonment he had plunged her. He'd given her hope that their marriage might succeed, then turned right around and proven his lack of concern.

She'd been so filled with wonder and delight, and now she felt only empty and drained. But she would not cry, she vowed as she fought back the tears. He would never make her cry again.

"Where are you going?" Her voice was low, held under tight control. It took all her effort to sit up in the bed.

He did not answer at once, but only concentrated on the lacings of his boot. "I've business to attend to.

A matter of duty to the king. Something you would not be interested in," he added offhandedly.

He finally looked over at her as he settled his short leather tunic over his wide shoulders. His expression was unreadable, and it nearly broke her composure. Duty to the king? What could possibly be so important? And what of his duty to his wife? Why, oh why couldn't he care just a little for her? He'd seemed well pleased with her, yet if that were so he would not leave her this way. What business could be so pressing that he must leave his very marriage bed?

All her insecurities came to the surface as Lilliane sat on the edge of the bed, the linen sheet held tightly up to her chin. He had wanted a virgin heiress, and she had come to him so. The passion had been a surprise to him—and to her—and it had helped to heal the wounds their marriage had started with.

But now it was even worse. At least before she'd harbored no foolish hopes for them. She had been wary, her guard had been up. Then he had broken through her defenses with his tender touch and whispered words. He had drugged her with his kisses then swept her away with his ardor. She had been lulled into sweet complacency by his false-hearted deceit.

But morning with its hard light brought reality back into focus. Now he showed his true self, and all she could do was try to defend her heart from him.

Corbett buckled on his sword of Damascene steel then shouldered his leather satchel. "I regret leaving you so, Lily." His voice was husky and it sent an unwilling shiver up her spine. Not trusting her voice, Lilliane only shrugged. But when he crossed to the bed in three long strides, she flinched away from him.

He frowned but she forestalled any questions. "Hurry on your way. Your business awaits." She stared up at him, trying hard to mask her feelings with a show of indifference.

Corbett rocked back on his heels, and for a moment she thought she saw indecision in his expression. But so quickly was it gone that she wondered if it had really existed at all. He studied her for a second longer with his impenetrable gray stare before he reached to finger one wayward lock of her chestnut hair.

"I cannot say with certainty when I return. I apologize for any inconvenience this causes you." He paused and Lilliane held her breath. Already her anger had weakened under his casually possessive touch. She wanted to beg him to stay, but pride held her back. Still, she hoped for some word from him— anything at all—that would fill this hollowness she felt.

It was not meant to be. With a vague frown Corbett released the silken strand and took a step back from her.

"Keep well, Lily." Then he was gone.

The sun was but a red glow beyond the distant forests when Lilliane hurried into the bailey. She had dressed hastily, throwing on the same sapphire-blue gown she had been married in but this time without benefit of kirtle, then had slipped on her embroidered silk slippers and draped a woven wool shawl over her shoulders.

She was not sure why she had followed Corbett.

Part of it had been the silence in the empty bedchamber. His absence had made it feel even colder than it was. Part of it had been her decision that she would look less pathetic to their guests if she were there to see him off. At the least she could give the illusion of a united front with him. No one else need know how she'd been abandoned so abruptly.

She did not want to admit to herself that she still sought some sign of his approval, so she firmly pushed that idea aside. Yet, when Corbett turned to watch her approach, she could not deny the heavy thumping of her heart or the fear and uncertainty that gripped her.

He had paused in the midst of conversing with a select group of his knights. After only a brief hesitation he finished his instructions to them. Then he immediately strode across the busy yard to where she stood alone in the fresh morning air.

Lilliane's heart quickened as he stopped before her. He was dressed as he had been when he'd first ridden into Orrick, in the garb of the warrior. She'd been awed by him then. Now she could hardly believe that this fierce knight was the same man who had held her so tenderly.

"I did not expect you to see me off."

Lilliane looked up into his serious face. She pursed her lips uncertainly then hugged the shawl tighter about her. "I do not want to appear abandoned," she answered grudgingly.

"I'm not abandoning you!" He reached for her but she stepped back.

"Then why must you leave?" she blurted out.

"Do you want me to stay?"

Lilliane had no ready answer for that. But as the

silence stretched out between them his lips curved in a faint knowing grin.

"Do you want me to stay?" he asked again, more softly.

Unable to face his curious stare, Lilliane turned her face away, pushing her wind tossed hair back from her cheek. "It doesn't . . . it isn't seemly for a bridegroom to ride off so abruptly from his . . . from the . . ."

"From the marriage bed?" Corbett asked. This time he did take her into his grasp with one warm hand on each of her shoulders. "Believe me, Lily. If it were not so important I would not go."

"What could be so important?" she cried, unable to stop herself. "Surely it could wait at least one more day!"

For a moment he only stared at her. Then a slow grin lighted his face. "Does this mean you shall miss me? Perhaps if I promise that my first duty upon my return will be to take up where we left off in our bed, I might coax a little smile out of you."

But Lilliane could not jest when she felt herself unaccountably being torn apart. She tried to pull away but his hands tightened on her.

"It cannot wait," he said more seriously. "You must trust me in this matter."

"Trust a Colchester?" she scoffed. "I'd be a fool to do that."

He frowned at her words and his scarred brow lowered. "As I would be a fool to trust the very wench I found digging through my belongings," he reminded her harshly. "Make up your mind, Lilliane. Either be my wife truly . . . or else declare your opposition to me now. You may not have it both ways."

Lilliane was torn. She should not trust him. She should not! Yet there was a directness about him that she could not help but respect. A shiver shook her.

"Well, Lily, which is it to be?" His eyes were wary, their gray darkened almost to black. They seemed to pierce almost to her very soul.

"I am your wife," she finally admitted. Despite the reluctance in her tone and the challenge yet lingering in her eyes, she knew she could not ignore reality. They were married and they would remain so for many years to come. It would be foolish to antagonize him constantly.

He pulled her closer then, and without realizing it her expression softened. "When will you return?"

"As quickly as is possible," he murmured as his eyes swept her face. "Knowing what awaits me here will give me wings." Then he bent down to her and took her lips in a deep, stirring kiss. Like one drugged, Lilliane was incapable of resistance. Indeed, as the kiss deepened, she found herself clinging to him in the most wanton and willing of fashions. When they finally broke apart she was breathless and flushed and, to her complete bewilderment, consumed by desire for him all over again. Was she mad to want him so?

Then, still dazed, she let him lead her to the gatehouse where several people, including her father, William, and Aldis had gathered to watch the knights' departure. She saw the disapproval on William's and Aldis's face and the delight on her father's. If only her own feelings about her husband could be so simple, she thought as she watched Corbett return to his waiting band of men.

Corbett was traveling with only half his knights

and a handful of his retainers. As he mounted his great destrier to depart, he raised a hand in salute to Lilliane. Then his attention was drawn by Sir Dunn's hand on his steed's bridle.

"I like nothing about this expedition," Dunn said with a growl.

"Do you think I do?" Corbett answered curtly.

"Then let me go in your stead. I've no wish to lay about in this place . . . as you clearly do."

Corbett looked down at his disgruntled second in command. "I must handle this, as you well know. Besides, I need you here to keep a watch on things." Corbett's eyes lifted to where Lilliane stood, flanked by her father and Sir William. "William bears watching."

"And your new wife does not?"

Corbett's gaze dropped furiously to Dunn. "Be careful what you say! She is mistress here now— yours as well as everyone else's—and deserving of your loyalty."

"But not my trust. Have you already forgotten her spying? How she hid her identity? And what of her love for William?" he continued despite Corbett's fierce glower. "She could well be as much a part of this as William."

"Hold your tongue, Dunn! I warn you once only." Enraged, he wheeled his heavy horse away. "Time will flush out the villains," he said with a growl. "You know your duties. See them done."

As the contingent of men rode across the heavy drawbridge, Lilliane climbed the steep stone stairs to the battlements. She was bewildered and confused, still torn by the many conflicting emotions that beset her. The last thing she needed was her father's robust praise of her new husband or William's undisguised dislike of him.

William had been fuming ever since Corbett had kissed her, and she knew he wished to get her alone. But Lilliane was too baffled by her response to her husband to try to justify her feelings. Besides, she decided as she hurried up the last flight of steps, she owed William no explanation. He had married another. So had she.

She found a spot between two crenels and leaned out beyond the face of the stone. The double line of men proceeded down the turnpike in an orderly fashion, all the men clearly trained as warriors. But there was no mistaking Sir Corbett. Tall and straight, he sat a dappled-gray destrier. But it was more than his physical presence that set him apart. More perplexed than ever by this strange man she had wed, Lilliane ran her tongue lightly over her still-sensitive lips. He was harsh and demanding; he was tender and gentle. He had forced her into this marriage and into his bed.

But she could not be honest and yet deny the pleasure she received from him. He revealed very little about himself; even the purpose of this journey was a complete mystery to her. But although she knew he was an enigma and very likely a most dangerous man, still, she could not truthfully say that she did not await his return with considerable anticipation.

11

"Lie still. Lie still," Lilliane crooned to Lady Verone. Quickly she mopped the beads of sweat from the younger woman's brow, wincing from the tight grasp she kept on her other hand.

"Here's the brew Mother Grendella sent," Ferga said as she hurried to the bedside. While Lilliane held Verone's head up, the stout serving woman fed her the thick decoction of yarrow.

It had been more than a week since the wedding and all of the guests, including Odelia and Tullia, had departed. Lady Verone had not felt up to traveling, and she and William had lingered awhile longer at Orrick. But Lady Verone had not improved. Then this morning the pains had begun.

They all knew it was too soon. Grendella had come at once, much to Lilliane's relief. If anyone could prevent a too-early birthing, surely it was Grendella. Using her hands more than her eyes, the wisewoman had examined Verone.

"We must prevent the birth, else the babe will not survive," she had mumbled, more to herself than to Lilliane. "Yarrow is the thing. Mayhap it can stay the pains."

To everyone's relief, it had indeed seemed to do the

trick. In the early afternoon when Verone finally fell into an exhausted slumber, Lilliane wearily descended the broad stairs.

In the main hall only a few people were about. Two maids cleaned the tables so that the men could stack them aside. A boy clambered into one of the massive hearths, cleaning away the ashes and soot. At a table under one of the few windows at Orrick that boasted glass, her father and Sir Dunn sat with a chess board spread between them.

"Ha! If your strategy against the infidels was as poor as your strategy today, 'tis a wonder you made it back alive," Lord Barton crowed as he took another of Sir Dunn's pawns and stymied his opponent's plan to move one of his bishops. "Look to your defense, man, else I'll soon threaten your king!"

"I defended my king in the East. I'll defend this stone piece equally well," Dunn muttered as he searched the inlaid board for his best move.

It was a wonder to Lilliane that the taciturn Sir Dunn, of all people, should be the one her father most enjoyed. Both men professed to mistrust each other, yet every afternoon once Lord Barton's business had been attended to and Sir Dunn's daily exercises with his men were complete, the two would settle down for a game of chess. Amid much grumbling and constant accusations they would challenge one another, and yet Lilliane clearly recognized her father's delight with the contest.

With a tired sigh Lilliane turned toward the far hearth. After her long vigil at Verone's side, she needed a bit of broth to restore her energy. But she was halted by William's sudden appearance.

"Have all of you then succumbed to Colchester?" he asked sarcastically.

Annoyed by his constant ill temper, Lilliane brushed past him. "There's no harm in a game of chess," she snapped in irritation.

"And what of the game of love?" He barred her path, forcing her to face him.

Lilliane sighed again. She was exhausted and hungry, and she was tired of dealing with William's constant sniping at her. "Love is no game," she began. "If you—"

"Ah, but that's how he views it, Lilliane. He will woo you to his side and use you to his advantage." He took her hands in his. "But a woman like you deserves to be loved. To be idolized. I would have idolized you. I would do it still if you'd let me—"

"Stop it! Stop it, William!" Lilliane tugged her hands free of his grasp and looked at him, appalled. "What are you saying!"

Lilliane could hardly believe her ears. How could he presume to say such things to her? she wondered. Had he no loyalty or honor left?

"Are you mad, William? You should be thinking of Verone who even now struggles with bearing your babe!" Then thoroughly disgusted with him, she broke away and fled the hall.

At her sudden departure Lord Barton and Sir Dunn looked up. Barton was vaguely annoyed by William's presence at the far end of the hall, but Sir Dunn was clearly angered.

"Yon pup seems hardly concerned with his wife's confinement."

"William is concerned only with himself; neither his wife nor child, nor even his own holdings have value to him beyond the wealth and comforts they provide him." Lord Barton hunched his massive shoulders and reached to move his bishop. "It was for that very reason I denied him when he would have married Lilliane."

"He hangs after her yet. Can you be sure she does not encourage him?"

Lord Barton brought his fist down so hard on the ancient oak table that the chessmen jumped. "Watch what you say!" he said with a fierce growl. "She is my daughter—your mistress—and the chosen wife of your liege!"

Dunn's scowl deepened and he pursed his lips. "She has my loyalty because she is wed to Corbett and he is bound to see this valley at peace. But William . . . he is one I will watch closely."

Lord Barton was somewhat mollified by Dunn's words. But when the game at last ended, his face was pale and he held his side. After Sir Dunn left he lingered a long while just sitting in the hall.

It was not much later as Lilliane was stepping from her bath that a maid burst into her room. "You must come, milady! Quickly. 'Tis Lord Barton—"

Lilliane's heart turned to lead at the panicked tone in the girl's voice. As she frantically threw on a gown, she was able to determine no more than that her father had been found in his chair, seemingly asleep. But he would not rouse.

Lilliane was unmindful of the chill in the castle as she fled barefoot down the stairs. Her wet hair was wild, streaming down her back and leaving her un- laced gown damp. But all she was conscious of was the crowd clustered at the far end of the great hall.

"Oh, milady . . . milady." Ferga moaned at Lilliane.

Lilliane pushed her way through to her father. "Dear God, what has happened?"

He was sprawled back in his favorite chair. His normally florid complexion was pale with a grayish tinge, and his breathing was hardly discernible. His skin was dreadfully cold when she felt his brow. Lilliane's throat tightened in fear.

"Get him to his chamber. Build a strong fire," she ordered with far more confidence than she felt. "And find Mother Grendella at once!" Lilliane anxiously followed the four men who lifted Lord Barton between them. "And someone try to find Thomas."

But even as they worked frantically to make Lord Barton comfortable, Lilliane could feel him slipping away. Still, she could not give up hope even when the wisewoman shook her head soberly. Refusing to believe it, Lilliane blocked the priest as he moved to her father's side.

"You can't let him die, Grendella! There must be something we can do!"

"There is a time for each of us. When God calls." The old woman fixed her half-blind stare on Lilliane. "He needs the priest now more than he needs me."

Like a blow the wisewoman's words fell on Lilliane, harsh and punishing. She rebelled against them and would not have accepted them. But it was her father who made her face the truth.

"'Tis done," he mumbled hoarsely. Immediately Lilliane bent over him and pressed her shaking hand to his brow. At her tender touch Lord Barton managed to open his eyes and smile weakly at her. Then a frown creased his brow and she felt a shudder rack his body. " 'Tis done . . ."

A long slow sigh followed and he seemed almost to shrink beneath her hand. When he did not take another breath she knew he was gone.

"Father! Father!" In desperation she tried to gather him into her arms, to somehow share her strength and youth and health with him. But it was no use. With firm yet understanding hands Mother Grendella pulled her from the still form of Lord Barton.

"He cannot be dead," Lilliane insisted numbly as the wisewoman handed her over to William. In shock she let him lead her from the chamber. "He cannot be dead, William. Why, he was hale as ever, sitting at chess with Sir Dunn . . ."

"Sir Dunn," William scoffed. He turned her abruptly to face him. "Didn't you hear what your father said? He accused his killer even as his soul departed his body. He said ''tis Dunn.' It was Dunn, Lilliane. Your husband's man killed your father. Corbett got his revenge as he'd always intended."

Lilliane was staggered by his accusation. For a moment she could not respond; she could hardly think, her emotional turmoil was so great. Then her father's words seemed to echo in her ears. " 'Tis done," he'd said. Or had it been " 'Tis Dunn"? She stared at William's angry face as she fought to control her careening emotions. "You can't be sure of that," she whispered in dread.

"I'm sure," he hissed back at her. "Have you become so blinded by him that you can overlook your own father's murder? God knows it is widely known that the sons of Colchester have long wanted revenge against him."

Lilliane did not have the strength to answer his accusation, for hadn't she once wondered if that had been Corbett's motivation from the beginning? Her father himself had acknowledged that Lord Frayne's sons still sought revenge. Everyone knew that was so. And yet . . . and yet somehow it was hard for her to believe it of him

She put one hand to her head. She was so confused; she needed to think. Yet she was terrified of what the truth might be. Still, she could not rest until she knew. Stricken, she tore from William's grasp and sought out Grendella. Her eyes were huge as she faced the withered old woman, and her voice trembled with emotion.

"Did . . . did my father ever consult you for any ailment?"

Grendella peered sharply at Lilliane's pale face. "He had little use for my talents, although I know he suffered the rich man's ache—the gout. Thomas had asked for a poultice from me." She thought a moment. "And I removed a tooth for him this spring past. But nothing else known to me."

"You see, Lilliane? It is as I said. He was healthy as ever, until that . . . assassin of your husband's stole the life from him."

William's words caused Lilliane to shiver in terrible dread. "It was Dunn," she slowly admitted to herself in horror. But could it truly be? Dunn had befriended her father. And yet that might have only been in order to gain the opportunity to poison him. Then his master, her husband, could rule Orrick free of any opposition and with the satisfaction of having brought down the man he believed had murdered his father.

Lilliane shook her head at such a thought. Still, Corbett was conveniently gone so no blame could rightly fall on him.

She was so confused. If only Aldis was here, she thought. Or even Santon. They would be able to help her defend Orrick from this evil within.

But at least William was still here, she thought in relief. Although she felt awkward around him these days, still she knew he would help her. Nonetheless, Orrick's defenses now lay primarily with her, she realized, and her heart grew hard within her at the thought.

In the hours that followed, her father's body had to be prepared for burial; the mourning room had to be prepared and messengers had to be dispatched. Over the entire castle a somber pall had descended. Lord Barton had been well loved, and there was much wailing to be heard. But no matter how beset Lilliane was with sorrow, she could not avoid the words that circled and circled in her mind. " 'Tis Dunn," he had said. " 'Tis Dunn." The accusation was plain. Her father was dead and by Sir Dunn's hand. And if that were so, then there could be no doubt that it was at the instruction of her husband.

She wanted to succumb to tears, for the hollowness she felt within was close to consuming her. Still, Lilliane knew she could not afford to be so weak. Especially now. She was in charge of the castle, and everyone was looking to her for guidance in this dire time. Even mourning brought her little ease for she had no family there nor even good Thomas to comfort her. He had gone just that morning to visit his son in Sedgewick.

By the time Lilliane finally retreated to her chamber, she was trembling from exhaustion. The room was cold, for Ferga had been too occupied with attending Lady Verone to manage her normal duties. For Lilliane, however, the chilly room was welcome respite. Her head was throbbing and her fingers shook as she undressed for bed. She was too weary to even braid her still-unbound hair. Yet once she had slipped beneath the heavy cover, she could not find the rest she so desperately sought.

As had occurred every night since her wedding, her mind was filled with memories of Corbett and the intimacies they had shared in this bed. But where before the memories were becoming welcome, despite her confusing feelings for her husband, now those thoughts brought nothing but pain. He had made love to her in the most expert and winning fashion, bringing her to an almost complete acceptance of him, while all the time he must have been plotting murder. He'd cozened her father to his side then seduced her as well.

Unable to bear the thought of his deviousness— and her own stupidity—Lilliane pressed her hands to her face. But even that brought haunting memories of Corbett for his heavy ring still circled her finger.

With a bitter cry of frustration she ripped the intricately worked piece from her hand and threw it sharply from her. She heard it clatter across the stone floor to rest somewhere in the dark. But then silence reigned once more, almost mocking her with its empty waiting.

It was only then that her tears finally came. Hot

and stinging, they blinded her eyes and choked her breathing. Her slender body was racked by hard, crushing sobs as she mourned her father. He was gone, just when they had finally reconciled. She had wasted two years at the abbey avoiding him. Now, when she at last realized how much he loved her—and how much she really loved him—he was gone.

Lilliane gasped for breath as she wiped the tears from her face. She had never truly shown him her love, she thought sorrowfully. He had wanted what was best for her and for Orrick. It was that fact that had brought him to this dreadful end. Now it was left to her to look out for Orrick's well-being and to avenge his death.

She sat up in the big bed, still sniffing and gulping for breath. She *would* avenge his death, she vowed. Sir Dunn could not be allowed to escape punishment for such a heinous crime.

It had been easy to avoid Sir Dunn in the bedlam of the past hours, but the morrow would see him instructing the knights and foot soldiers in their duties and she would not be able to bear it.

Lilliane shivered as she pulled the coverlet over her shoulders. Despite the overwhelming presence of the Colchester men, they were still outnumbered by the Orrick guards, she thought. And those guards would follow her lead over an outsider's.

She paused as she contemplated the enormity of what she plotted. She would imprison Sir Dunn and the rest of his cohorts, but then what? Corbett would return eventually, and what would she do then? Even in the dark she could picture his hard face made even more cruel by a scowl. Fear made her tremble anew. How frightened she'd been at their first meeting. And then again when he'd foiled her escape attempt.

Still, he'd always been gentle with her, she thought as she recalled his tenderness and the warmth of his caress.

But that was all lies, she reminded herself harshly. She slid from the high bed and paced the room on bare feet. It didn't matter what Corbett of Colchester did now, she could not idly accept her father's murder. He might consider it an eye for an eye, but what he'd done was plain murder.

She would have Sir Dunn and all the other Colchester followers thrown in the dungeon. Then she would prepare the castle against her husband's return. Orrick was well provisioned; they could withstand a lengthy siege if need be.

If only Aldis was here, or even Santon, she fretted. But at least William was there for support. He disliked Corbett intensely. Surely he would aid her in this plot. Relieved at that thought, she turned back to the bed only to step squarely on her cast-off wedding ring.

She gasped in pain. Then she kicked at the offensive jewel. Once more it clattered across the hard floor, coming to rest somewhere beneath the raised bed.

Only partially mollified, Lilliane clambered back onto the high mattress. It was cold and dark in her room as she lay there, longing for the peace of sleep. Her father was dead; her husband was a murderer. She was now the one who must keep the people and lands of Orrick safe.

It was a terrifying thought, and yet she knew she had no alternative. She did not know what the future held: not how she would overpower Sir Dunn, nor how she would repel Sir Corbett.

In desperation she clasped her hands tightly together. "Dear God," she whispered to the dark, silent room. "Please help me!"

12

On the fifth day after Lord Barton's burial, Corbett and his men were sighted. In an instant the castle was in an uproar of preparation. From the fields and the village everyone in Orrick responded to the tolling of the alarm bell.

Lilliane ran as quickly as she could to the gatehouse. South of the village she could see the knights were at least a league from the castle, yet she had a dreadful foreboding. Despite all the planning she and William had done, she felt unprepared for this confrontation. Corbett would not take this easily—she knew that. He would use every weapon at his disposal to take back Orrick.

But what could he do! she reasoned as she watched the villagers streaming up the hill to the castle. He had only a small group of knights with him. All the rest of his fighting men were securely locked in the donjon beneath the north tower of Orrick.

How furious Sir Dunn had been, she recalled with an unpleasant shiver. No matter William's accusations and her pointed questions, he had maintained his innocence adamantly. But he'd certainly appeared capable of murder as he'd glowered wrathfully at her.

Remembering his vow that they would never keep Corbett out of the castle, her brow creased in concern. She was not reassured even when William joined her at the battlement.

"Sir Corbett has been bested this time," William boasted, a grin lighting his smoothly handsome face.

"I would not celebrate too quickly," Lilliane muttered. Then she sighted two riders leaving the village at a hard gallop.

"Dear God, who is that so far ahead of the rest of them?" She gasped, but she knew—even as she asked the question she knew.

"Raise the bridge! Close the gates!" William shouted, then spat a foul stream of curses for he too recognized the massive lead rider.

Lilliane could not move as she watched Corbett's rapid approach. He had ridden ahead of the rest of his men. But why? Had he known what she was doing? Had he ridden ahead just to surprise her and foil her plan? If so, he'd come very near to doing just that, she realized as the bridge over the moat finally began to inch upward.

But if he'd known the castle would be closed to him, would he and his men have come riding in so boldly at midday? Wouldn't they have been more covert and cautious?

A frown creased Lilliane's brow as she watched her husband. He had clearly been surprised to see the ancient bridge once more being raised against him. As his horse thundered down the last stretch of the hard, gravelly road, the villagers who were now locked out of the castle fled into the fields. When he brought his powerful destrier to a stiff-legged halt at the moat's bank, Lilliane could feel the fury that emanated from him. It took all her strength not to cringe behind one of the battlements.

But she was a daughter of Orrick, she told herself. And she was right in turning him away. Still, a quiver of fear coursed down her spine as she gazed at the glowering form of her husband.

"Ha! We have him now!" William crowed as he leaned over the battlement.

"You'd best let me deal with him," Lilliane interrupted. "We can't know what revenge he might take against those who aid me."

At that William quickly stepped back from the embrasure. " 'Tis unlikely he'll be in a position to take any revenge." But he sounded more sullen than boastful.

"He is still well favored by Edward," Lilliane murmured uneasily. She watched the second rider reach Corbett's side. "We can only hope that King Edward will not condone such a foul crime as murder."

After conferring briefly with Corbett, the other rider departed as quickly as he'd come. To rally the trailing knights, Lilliane suspected. Her heart was fast sinking as she stared at her husband, so composed as he still sat his steed at the abrupt end of the road. As his silence continued her nerves seemed to stretch almost to breaking. Then his eyes swept the crenellated battlements until they found her.

Lilliane swallowed convulsively as his eyes locked with hers. She thought she'd remembered the force of that stare and the strength of will behind it. But her memories paled next to the reality of it. Then he addressed her and it was as if no one was there but the two of them.

"Lower the bridge, Lily," he ordered.

A hush settled over the entire castle as he awaited her response.

"Orrick is closed to you. Go away." Although her voice rang out clearly, she trembled from head to foot.

"Orrick is mine by dint of marriage to you. Do you forget so quickly that we are man and wife?"

At that arrogant reminder her composure fled. "I forget nothing! Most especially I do not forget the murder of my father!"

When he seemed taken aback by her accusation, she was even more incensed. "Are you so surprised then that we found you out? Have you nothing to say for yourself?" she snapped sarcastically. "At the least I expected a very clever profession of innocence."

Corbett's dark-gray stare had not wavered from her at all. When he spoke his very calmness disturbed her even more. "This is a subject better discussed in private, Lily. Your father particularly understood such matters."

"My father is dead at the hand of your hireling!" she cried, sobbing. "You're the only one to gain from that!"

"His death gained me nothing that I did not already have. Most certainly I would not leave my man to do such a task. Had I wanted him dead, it would have been done by my own hand!"

"Liar! Liar!" she screamed.

"Come away, Lilliane." William placed an arm protectively around her. "You need not deal with him any longer."

Corbett did not outwardly appear to react to William's unexpected presence, nor to his solicitous handling of Lilliane. But she sensed his fury at once.

Like an impending storm, it filled the air between them with a crackling intensity. She shook William's arm off with a nervous gesture then turned to cast some final accusing remark at her tensed husband.

It was then that she saw the rest of his men approaching. Spread out like a fan across the meadow, they herded the hapless villagers before them. Slowly but relentlessly they forced the villagers into a large cluster just beyond Corbett. Although he did not turn to view the deed, Lilliane knew he was sure of what was happening. She was certain it had been his idea, and he trusted his men to see his every whim carried out.

"What—what is it you plan to do?" Lilliane asked fearfully, her voice thin in the silence that gripped the castle.

His eyes were steady upon her and she imagined she saw a bitter smile twist his lips. "I plan to enter Orrick, have a bath, and eat an excellent meal." He paused. "Lower the bridge, Lily."

There was a terrible silence.

"And if I do not?" Her voice trembled despite her every effort to sound calm.

His face grew harder. Then he turned to face the tightly bunched villagers. "Whosoever of you is oldest, step forward now."

There were murmurs and much shuffling among the poor group. Then two slight forms separated from the rest and Lilliane cried out in horror. Thomas had finally returned from his journey to visit his son, but at what a terrible time. And he was joined by Mother Grendella!

"What are you doing?" Lilliane called down, truly frightened now.

"I'm not doing anything. Yet." Corbett smiled grimly up at her. "The next move is yours, my lady wife."

It was Lilliane's first inclination to seek her father out. But with the fresh realization that she could never do that again, a new and terrible fear swept over her. Corbett of Colchester sat before her, mocking her poor attempt at opposing him, and she knew she could do nothing about it. He held the lives of Thomas and Grendella and so many others as a threat before her. Her wide frightened eyes met his again and she sought desperately to find some chink in his hard demeanor, some sign of compassion in his fierce expression. This was the same man who had been so tender to her. But he was also the man everyone called the king's Bird of Prey. He was a harsh, brutal knight, and he was determined to best her.

A sob caught in her throat as she broke away from his intense stare. But William blocked her path.

"Don't give in to him, Lilliane." He gripped her shoulders.

"And then what? Watch as he slaughters my people?"

"He'll do it anyway. If you let him in, what's to stop him from doing anything he wants?"

Lilliane backed out of William's grasp. Her amber eyes were damp with tears. "I can't believe he would go that far. They're just innocent villagers. He has no quarrel with them—"

"Was your father guilty of anything? No! But he died anyway! Do you truly believe Colchester places any value on a handful of pitiful old villagers?"

"He may not. You are right in that. But *I* value

them. And I'll not see them slaughtered. Not now. Not ever." With that she lifted her skirts and hurried out of the gatehouse toward the captain of the guard.

By the time the bridge was down, Lilliane was in the bailey. She stood alone, waiting for Corbett's entrance. What would follow she did not know. But she had instructed the guards to stand well back and offer no symbol of opposition. It was her last hope that her husband would take no reprisals against anyone but herself. And she was prepared to endure those reprisals, no matter what they were. She would endure and some day, in some manner, she would have revenge on him for his mounting list of crimes against Orrick.

There was an unearthly quiet in the bailey. Only a capricious wind that tugged at her heavy caddis skirt and neatly coiffed hair interrupted the stillness. When Corbett entered the castle, his men close upon his heels, Lilliane was reminded of his first arrival at Orrick. Like then, the entire populace was intimidated by the powerful knight and his arrogant manner.

But Lilliane's apprehension of that other day was as nothing compared to this deep-seated dread. If he'd seemed fierce and brawny then, he appeared absolutely invincible now.

He rode his destrier straight toward her. It seemed every last person in the bailey caught his breath in anticipation and dread. Given a choice of feeling fear or anger, Lilliane much preferred the latter. But she could not prevent a shiver of fear snaking down her spine as she raised furious eyes to him. As was so often his wont, he did not speak at once. In the uncomfortable silence his eyes swept over her. Unwillingly her own gaze roamed him, noting his dusty, travel-worn appearance and the ill-disguised weariness in his face. But his eyes, gray as granite, were sharp and as discerning as ever. For a moment they darkened, and she thought she saw a smoldering light deep within their hooded recesses. Then his lips lifted in a chilling smile.

"I want a bath and a meal. Also, see to my men's needs." He shifted his weight and the leather saddle creaked beneath him. "And heed this warning, my sweet wife. You have been nothing but trouble so far. You'd best consider proving your value as a wife."

"Or what?" Lilliane challenged, but in little more than a whisper. "Shall you be as easily rid of me as you were of my father?"

He straightened up at that, but his scar darkened as he frowned. "See to your duties," he ordered curtly as he turned his steed from her. "Then return to our chamber and await me there."

It was worse than if he had punished her outright. She did not dare cross him, for she feared his vengeance if not against her, then most surely against her people. Yet to meekly submit to his selfish orders was galling indeed.

As she hurried about her tasks, ordering the water heated for the tubs and food prepared for the table, her emotions veered between overwhelming anger and a sinking desperation. Her efforts had been for nothing. Her father was still dead and Corbett had control of Orrick, just as he'd planned from the beginning.

There was no conversation in the kitchen as she made a cursory check of the trays of cold sliced meats and the baskets of breads. Two men pulled the creaking ale cart behind them as the silent column of servants made their way to the great hall.

But Lilliane refused to follow them into the hall. That she just could not do. Using a narrow back stair, she made her way up the musty passage to the tower room, there to await the wrath of her husband.

She did not doubt his fury, for all his well-contained appearance. Still, at least Thomas and the others were safe, she thought. William was the only other person she feared might taste Corbett's vengeance. If only he had not lingered here, she fretted. But although Verone fared a little better, there could be no moving her until well after the birth of the babe. Lilliane paced the room nervously. If Corbett punished William, it might have dire effects on Verone's frail health. And there was the babe to consider as well.

The minutes stretched interminably. The room grew dim but Lilliane could not muster enough interest to light a torch or even a candle. Too many worrisome thoughts circled in her head.

What would her punishment be? Would Corbett seek to hurt William or any others? But overriding that still was the question of her father's death. Was Corbett capable of such a foul deed? At times she was certain of it. But at other times . . .

She shook her head hard. Who else could it be? If he was guilty, then it was her duty to avenge the crime. But how could she know for sure when he so adamantly denied it?

She was so caught up in her troubled thoughts that she did not hear the approaching footsteps. When the door to her chamber opened, however, she whirled quickly from her place before the fire.

In the doorway Corbett stood, a great, towering shadow. Her heart lurched in her chest as she stared at her husband. He had bathed and changed into fresh clothes; his hair was still damp and slicked back from his face. The meager glow from the fire in the hearth cast dancing golden lights over his harsh profile.

Lilliane's breath quickened as he stood there unmoving, only watching her with his dark, inscrutable stare. Uncomfortable with his unwavering silence, she clasped her fingers tightly together and lifted her chin bravely. His lips curled sardonically at her show of bravado. With a slow, sure move he stepped further into the room and closed the door securely behind him.

"Come attend me, wife," he ordered as he tossed his leather satchel onto the trunk. "Show me your wifely concern. I confess I've found it sorely lacking thus far."

She bristled at the sarcasm that edged his voice. "I've no wifely concerns for you at all."

Lilliane knew she risked much with her defiance, but she was unable to do anything else. She hated him. She would always hate him. She would never cease trying to be rid of him.

Although his jaw tightened at her words and his scarred brow lowered in a scowl, Corbett did not respond at once. Instead he crossed to a chair and sat down. "I will tell you this one time, Lilliane. Only once. You may believe it or not. 'Tis your own choice." He paused and pulled off his boots. Then he looked at her sharply. "I did not have your father killed."

He stared at her hard as if to gauge her reaction.

Then he drew his tunic over his head. "I have questioned Dunn and all the rest of my men. I am convinced there was no foul play in Lord Barton's death. Furthermore, your father's own man—the old one—tells me his master suffered greatly with a rot in his gut. He knew his days on this earth were numbered." One corner of his mouth turned up ironically. "He says it was for that reason that he consented so quickly to our marriage."

Lilliane stared at him in stunned silence as he tugged his shirt off over his head.

"I don't believe you," she whispered. She was taken aback by his last words, and her thoughts could not rally to contradict his preposterous statement. Her father had been perfectly well. In fact, he'd been better than ever since the wedding ceremony.

"Thomas wouldn't lie—" She faltered when he stood up. "You must have forced him to say such a thing." She backed away from his steady approach, still trying to make some sense of it all.

"You may question him yourself on the morrow, Lily. Right now he is drowning his own sorrow in ale."

Lilliane shook her head in stubborn refusal. "It is not as you say! You had every reason to kill my father."

"I had no reason at all."

"You hated him," she accused in a voice shrill and unnatural. She felt the sting of tears but could not fight them off. "You wanted revenge for your father's death and now you have it. You planned this from the very beginning!"

Corbett's jaw tensed at this, and even through her

tear-blurred eyes she saw his scarred brow lower in a frown.

"Damn it, woman! Even had I plotted his death, poisoning is not my way, I am a knight of no little pride. I meet a man squarely in battle."

She clenched her eyes shut and turned away from him. She did not want to hear his words. She did not want to credit him with any honor whatsoever, yet she could not deny that what he said bore some remnants of truth. He would not resort to poison. He would no doubt easily thrust his wicked blade cleanly through a man's chest, but he would stare his victim in the face as he did so.

That admission let loose a flood of emotions—all her repressed sorrow for her father and a terribly confusing relief that perhaps Corbett was not a murderer after all. But then why had her father died? Was it merely as Thomas had said, an ailment he'd kept concealed from them all? A sob caught in her throat and she buried her face in her hands.

At once she felt Corbett's grasp on her shoulders and his strong arms encircling her. "Hush now," he murmured as he held her awkwardly. "Don't cry, Lily. Don't cry."

But that only made her cry harder. Terrible wracking sobs tore through her as he held her close. It had been so hard, these days since she'd buried her father. She'd been strong and made the decisions that needed to be made. But she could be strong no longer.

Lilliane could not say precisely how Corbett maneuvered them to a chair and then sat down with her in his lap. She might have been a pet or a child in his arms as he soothed and comforted her. His hands were gentle and his bare skin cool against her over-heated cheeks. But as her storm of tears began slowly to subside, she knew his tender touch was nonetheless that of a man upon a woman.

" 'Tis a hard thing indeed to lose a parent." He spoke quietly.

"I've lost them both now. They're both gone."

"As are my parents." He paused and his fingers slid up her back to the soft nape of her neck. "You must learn to rely on me. I'm your husband. I'll see to your needs."

The low rumble of his voice was soothing to Lilliane's overwrought nerves, and for a weak moment she let her aching head rest against his shoulder. She was confused and upset, torn in two conflicting directions. Logic deemed that he was the cause of all her woes. And yet . . .

She struggled against the lulling comfort of his gentle embrace and with the back of her hand wiped her tears away. "I must speak to Thomas. He and—"

"Tomorrow."

Lilliane peered warily at Corbett, suddenly discomfited by their intimate position. "I must see him tonight," she insisted. "If it is true—"

"It is true. Tomorrow will be soon enough to seek him out. He was well into his cups when I left him anyway."

Lilliane sighed sorrowfully. "Poor Thomas. He loved Father well." She turned her pale face toward the fire and stared sadly into the low, flickering flames. For days she had been caught up in the frenzy of preparing the castle against Corbett. It had been more difficult than anything she'd ever done before. But now she could see it had just been a way to avoid the aching emptiness her father's absence created. She had wasted two years away from him, and that made his loss even harder to bear.

"Thomas will be lost without him." She smiled wanly. "My father was a good man."

"I've no doubt he was a good father."

Lilliane sensed at once the meaning of Corbett's words. She turned her wide, dark-lashed eyes on him. "He was a good man," she insisted. "He had nothing to do with your father's death."

Corbett's jaw tensed at that and his fingers stilled their gentle circling upon her neck. She continued before he could speak. "He would not strike a man unaware, giving him no chance for defense. He lived by a code of honor, much as you say you do," she added.

For long seconds he did not reply as he considered her words. He only stared at her with eyes dark and smoky. Yet that steady, searching stare unsettled her more than any words might. She did not know if he believed her or not. She wasn't even sure whether she completely believed him. Still, her heart began to race in her chest as his eyes held hers captive.

Despite all the doubts, all the hatred between their families and the struggles between them, she could not quell the warmth his nearness stirred within her. Swift and urgent, it quivered up her spine with sudden awareness of each place their bodies touched.

He was harsh and ruthless, she told herself sternly. The king's Bird of Prey.

But it was useless. Like a live thing some spark crackled between them, and she knew he was as aware of it as she.

Then his hand moved to her head and he pulled

the wooden hairpins from her carefully arranged hair. "Your welcome today left much to be desired."

"I was . . . I was not eager to have you return," she admitted in a small voice.

"Nonetheless, I am here." He removed her fillet and wimple, and she felt her hair tumble free. "We have unfinished business to settle between us," he murmured against her hair, and she felt the damp heat of his breath against her temple.

Disturbed, Lilliane squirmed unconsciously upon his lap. But the press of his quick arousal against her bottom only flustered her further. As his hands found the laces at her waist, she mustered her wits as best she could.

"You—you have not said what repercussions there will be for what I have done today."

He paused in his sensual assault and looked at her with a faint, cynical curve to his lips. "I have taken the necessary steps to make sure the responsible parties are punished."

Lilliane's heart began to pound nervously. "But it was I. I'm the responsible one. William had nothing to do—"

"Don't speak to me of William." Corbett's eyes had turned hard. "He is confined, as is your captain of the guards. As for the others, all you need to know is that there will be no chance for insurrection again."

"No. Please don't harm them. They were only following my orders," she argued.

"They know now not to make that mistake again."

"But that's not fair to them, for they've not done anything wrong. Nor is it fair to make me appear no more than a servant in my own home."

"You're hardly a servant, Lily." To emphasize his

point he slid his hand slowly along her thigh, but she slapped it away.

"What have you done to my guards?" she demanded angrily.

Corbett's eyes narrowed. "First of all, they're not your guards any longer. Any man not loyal to me—*me*—may shed his guard duties and go back to husbanding sheep or tilling the soil."

Lilliane was infuriated by his high-handedness. "You have no right!"

"I have every right!"

She was silenced by his angry words. For a long moment their gazes remained locked in silent conflict. Then Corbett took a slow breath and seemed to calm.

"Things will be different at Orrick now," he began in a reasonable tone. "Accept it and you will find life to be far easier."

He didn't have to say "Fight me and you will lose." She already knew how he felt on that score. Still, Lilliane could hardly resign herself to seeing everything at Orrick turned upside-down on his whim.

In frustration she sought to rise, but he easily stopped her.

"We have unfinished business between us," he reminded her.

"To what business do you refer?" she asked, wondering angrily if he had some further punishment in store for his willful wife.

"You bade me wait, when last we lay together. Tonight I will do just that, wait until you reach your complete pleasure."

Lilliane's amber eyes widened at that; she was caught completely off guard by his astonishing words. On too many painful occasions she had recalled precisely those frustrated words of hers. She had not known why she'd revealed her feelings in such a wanton manner. Indeed, she'd hoped he had forgotten her shameless cry. But it was terribly clear he had not. As she stared at him, mortified by the memory, his stern expression eased and she caught the trace of a smile upon his lips.

"Come now. Why such a shocked mien? Surely you have not forgotten how much you enjoyed the pleasures of our marriage bed?"

"All I remember is how I was forced into this marriage against my will!" she replied angrily, unwilling to admit the truth of his words.

"I don't deny that is how it was." She felt his warm breath against her hair. "But why must you deny that you now find as much satisfaction in our joining as do I?"

It seemed at once that he kindled a flame within her. In place of her anger a new, even more volatile emotion now seethed. Like fire she burned everywhere he touched her: his fingers within the loosened laces at her side; his palm resting above her knee; and most markedly his masculinity beneath her bottom.

Something within Lilliane tightened and twisted with her new knowledge of what was to come. But there was a part of her that still fought such all-consuming submission to him. Instinctively she tried to get free of his hold, but Corbett would have none of it. His hand tightened at her waist to keep her still upon his lap.

"Do not flee, Lily. And do not deny the sweet pleasure we took of one another."

He turned her downcast face up to him then slid his finger slowly along her full lower lip. "What we shared before was only the beginning of the pleasure we shall find in one another."

Lilliane blushed heatedly. Both his words and the sensuous slide of his fingers over her lips set her to trembling. Memories of their earlier joinings besieged her and, indeed, she felt an intense rush of desire for him.

As their gazes held she could clearly see the smoky desire in his eyes. She quickly averted her stare, afraid her own wanton desires might be just as plain to him. She was mortified by her uncontrollable emotions. Hadn't he just flaunted his victory over her? Hadn't he mocked her by robbing her of every authority she held at Orrick? How could she then feel this terrible, overwhelming desire for him?

She was perched on his lap, trembling with longing yet unable to face him and the plain truth of her confusing feelings. But Corbett was not so shy nor so hesitant.

"Show me what you want," he murmured in her ear. Then his lips moved down to her neck and she felt the hot whisper of his words against her oversensitive skin. "Show me."

She gasped in pleasure and her breath quickened as his hand slid along her thigh. With just such a light touch he ignited her, and all vestiges of reason fled her mind.

"Show me what you want," he demanded once again, his voice low and husky.

"I—I don't know," Lilliane cried softly. "I don't know."

In a sudden motion he stood up, lifting her high in

his powerful arms. His dark eyes were alive with light as he stared into her heavy-lidded ones. "I know, Lily. I know just what you want."

He crossed to the high, draped bed and she closed her eyes in silent acceptance of his words. He did know, she realized. A tremor shook her.

At the bed he sat down, still holding her close against his chest. She was pliant in his arms as he cradled her; resistance was beyond her now. Then he tilted her face up and captured her lips in a warm, persuasive kiss. His mouth was firm and mobile on hers, sweet and knowing. When his tongue swept sensuously along the curve of her lower lip, fire seemed to dart from her belly, heating her entire being in sudden response.

She remembered these torrid, drugging kisses. Only too well. They made her weak and wet, and made her long for so much more.

Without conscious thought her arms crept up to circle his neck. Beneath her fingers she felt the warm firm skin, slightly damp now with sweat. As she arched closer to him, pressing herself intimately against him, she heard his low groan of desire.

"Ah, woman, how you have tormented me these long, long weeks."

Something in Lilliane exulted in those words, something feminine that she'd never felt before. "Is that why you rode ahead?" The whispered question was out quite before she could stop it.

Corbett laughed at that, then leaned back to better see her. "It was," he conceded with a wicked grin. Then without warning he lifted her from his lap and put her on her feet before him. His eyes gleamed with anticipation as he took in her pretty, flushed features.

"I made intolerable haste to return to my bride." He paused and his hungry gaze drank in every inch of her soft, womanly form. His voice grew huskier. "Show me your welcome, Lily."

She wanted him. An ache had begun in her and she knew that only he could ease it. Yet as he sat there, like some finely carved statue, resplendent in his own masculine beauty, she was swept with acute shyness.

How to welcome him? she thought distractedly. She'd fought him and hated him. Now it seemed he might not be a murderer as she had suspected, yet he was still a hard and ruthless man. The king's Bird of Prey. She shook her head in confusion and took a step backward but Corbett caught her wrist.

"Leave off this coyness," he warned. "You may not avoid your wifely duties any longer, Lily."

"I—I'm not being coy. And . . ." Her face heated and she lowered her eyes. "And I'm not trying to avoid . . . anything."

The sternness left his face then. He pulled her to stand between his legs and placed his broad palms at her waist.

"You need not be shy before me, my sweet little wife." He smiled and pushed a curling strand of her hair behind her shoulder. "But if you prefer that I help you disrobe, so be it."

Lilliane was caught between painful humiliation and a dizzy exhilaration as he set to his task. Her wrist laces were first; then her girdle was taken away. When he helped her lift the gown over her head, she blushed violently. She quickly removed her slippers and stockings, well aware of his fervid gaze upon her pale curving legs. Then she stood up covered only by her thin bissyn kirtle, and looked at him.

In the firelight Corbett appeared a dark, golden shadow, some vision conjured up by her own wanton thoughts. How many times while he'd been gone had she closed her eyes only to see him precisely so? How many prayers had she sent desperately aloft in the hopes of quelling the terrible desires that had overwhelmed her? She had kept her solitude in this very same bed, and yet his memory had been alive in it.

Now, though, it was no memory. Her entire being tensed in awareness and expectation for he was here, flesh and blood, bone and muscle. His skin would be the same, warm and firm, marked with the scars she knew already by heart. His lips would be as sensuous as before, whispering endearments, kissing her, licking and biting . . .

Lilliane's breath quickened and her eyes grew wide. Sensing her clear arousal, Corbett pulled her nearer. "Now this kirtle." He put his hand just above her knee and began to draw the soft linen fabric up.

Her heart thundered in her chest as he slowly bared her legs. She swayed toward him, dizzy with the rush of emotions that had her in their grip. When his hand found the tender flesh of her leg, she leaned against him, her hands braced on his wide shoulders.

She closed her eyes helplessly as his hand slid up her thigh. She could take no more of this, she thought weakly. No more.

Then she felt the warm pressure of his other hand at her nape, pulling her face down to his. When their lips met she could have expired from the sheer pleasure of it. Fire seemed to leap between them, and she needed very little coaxing to open to his insistent kiss. She was drowning in pure delight, falling further into some magical chasm where only she and Corbett existed. Her thin gown disappeared. Then he pulled her tightly against him. Her belly and breasts pressed hard against his chest as he drew her relentlessly down onto the bed.

He rolled them both over, imprisoning her beneath him. "At last I have you, my wild Lily. You play the ice maiden so well, but I shall melt that winter heart of yours."

Lilliane felt anything but icy. Corbett's hard masculine body pressing down upon hers had started the most torrid of fires in her blood. Yet still his words brought her eyes wide open.

"It was never my heart that you sought," she whispered. Then before he could respond she pulled his head down to hers and kissed him. It was passionate and desperate, a shamelessly bold move on her part. But Lilliane could not bear to hear his reply. If she could have taken back her words she would have, for she knew they revealed far too much to him.

Her passionate response seemed to fire Corbett even further. From her lips, down her neck he planted hot fervent kisses, as if branding her his and his alone. Lilliane felt she was surely being devoured by him. She threw back her head and closed her eyes, a willing martyr to this wonderful torment. Everything in her responded to his skillful touch, to his clever fingers and knowing lips.

Slowly he slid his hard body down hers so that he could nuzzle her breasts. She gripped his shoulders tightly as he took one aching nipple between his lips and then the other. Back and forth he went, teasing, biting, and sucking until she was dizzy with excitement and mindless with ecstasy. She pressed her belly up against him, pleading mutely for some relief to this swelling pleasure deep within her. But Corbett was not quite ready to ease her driving need. His face was flushed with his own passion as he stared at her from smoky, heavy-lidded eyes.

"Tell me what you want, Lily." He tortured her with a light wandering trail of kisses up her throat and neck. "Tell me," he breathed in her ear.

Lilliane moaned in boundless pleasure. "I want you." She gasped. "Oh, come to me now . . ."

With a low groan of his own Corbett at last capitulated. They were both slick with sweat as he raised up over her. The heavy weight of his masculinity burned against her belly and she squirmed in delicious anticipation.

"Ah, my fiery girl. Now you hurry me. But there is no need for such haste." He paused as he probed the silken entrance to her feminine being. Lilliane arched up, eager to feel the relief of his fullness within her. But he would not be rushed. "Tonight I want everything from you, Lily. Everything."

Then with a sureness that stole her breath away, he pressed his full length into her. Lilliane gasped at the intense pleasure; at that moment she was willing to give him all he wanted of her. That, and even more. He slowly began to move over her, a studied torturous rhythm that fired her to unimaginable heights. Her hands grasped his sweat-slick shoulders as he urged her higher and higher.

She was trembling in ecstasy, filled with a wonderful, terrible anticipation. In a moment of sudden fear her closed eyes came open and fastened on Corbett's face just inches above her.

"Don't hold back, my lovely Lily." He thrust deep within her, then pulled out with agonizing slowness. Then again and again. And all the time he watched her every expression.

She could not hide from his possessive gaze. Nor was she able to resist the powerful sensations that were building within her. Then it began and she cried out in mindless bliss. Like a tidal wave it washed over her. She was sucked down into a dizzy swirling vortex, then when she could hardly breathe for the very intensity of it, she was cast back up into the light.

As if in a dream she felt Corbett's powerful body tense over her, then he shuddered and she heard his low groan of pleasure. Lilliane's eyes were closed, her body was drenched with sweat, and she had never felt so completely limp and drained. Yet her lips were curled up in a soft smile when he finally slowed his torrid pace.

"A smile?" Corbett kissed her lips lightly, then rolled to his side and pulled her snug against him. He had not yet caught his breath and his heart was pounding beneath her ear. Lilliane slid her hand along his steel-muscled side, marveling at how right such a light and intimate caress felt. Then she laughed softly at her fanciful thoughts. Surely this was nothing as compared to the other intimacies she had just shared with this man.

"She smiles. Then she laughs." Corbett's breath tickled her ear. "Ah, the rare delight of a man whose wife truly relishes the pleasures of their bed."

It was his turn to laugh at Lilliane's heated embarrassment. His palm was warm as he gently slid his hand along her arm. "I hope that tonight eases the frustration of our last time together."

She raised her eyes shyly to her husband's shadowed face. He was propped up on one elbow watching her, a half smile playing on his finely carved lips. Yet the sincerity in his eyes was apparent.

Slowly she nodded, her eyes held captive by his steady stare. When he bent over to kiss her, she closed her eyes in contentment. It was heaven to have his lips moving so seductively upon hers. It was a pleasure she'd never dreamed of to feel his iron-hard thigh move to rest between her own bare legs. She lifted her arm to circle his neck, but he caught her hand and brought it to his lips instead. He kissed her wrist warmly, then moved his lips past her curled fingertips to her sensitive palm.

But in the midst of this tender, passionate display, he suddenly halted. She started to speak when he opened her hand wider and ran one finger along her ringless finger.

"Where is it?" He looked at her sharply with eyes that had turned dark and cloudy.

"I . . . It is . . ." Lilliane faltered, trying desperately to recall where in her anger she had thrown her wedding ring. But Corbett's suspicous stare only flustered her more. "I was . . . I wasn't sure of you. My father was dead—"

"Of natural causes," he interjected curtly.

"Yes," she agreed nervously. "But I didn't know that, and when William . . ."

Lilliane's heart sank at the stony look William's name brought to Corbett's face. For a long tense moment he loomed over her. All vestiges of the pleasant warmth between them had fled. Then he rolled from her and sat up on the side of the bed.

The flickering remnants of the fire gleamed on his damp shoulders and edged him with gold. Yet she was certain there would be no warmth from him now. She shivered as the cool night air touched her bare skin and pulled the heavy coverlet up to her chin. She feared he would leave her, and she struggled to find words that would smooth over her rash actions. When he spoke she was troubled by his somber tone.

"William is under guard in his chamber this night." He turned his head and locked his dark eyes with hers. "Give me one reason not to throw him in the donjon. Give me one reason not to seek revenge on him for his deviousness."

"It wasn't for deviousness that he helped me," Lilliane argued softly.

"No?" His scarred brow arched in mocking doubt. "Then tell me why he did it."

"He . . . he did it merely to help me."

"He did it to help himself." His jaw clenched. "And to help himself to you."

"That's not true!" She started to sit up but he stilled her with a fierce look.

"You are my wife, Lily. Mine! I've been more than lenient with you for I know what it is to lose a parent. But mark my words, woman. Today you went too far. There are some things I will not countenance."

She had no reply. When he finally lay back and pulled the cover over him, she remained still and quiet. In the dark they lay thus until he spoke once more.

"He goes tomorrow. I can offer him no more leniency than that." It was said without inflection, and yet she knew his emotions seethed beneath his contained façade. Still, she could not leave him unaware of all the circumstances.

"Lady Verone cannot travel," she said quietly.

He moved in the bed but she kept her eyes fixed on the high shadowy ceiling. "Her child threatens to be born any day, but it is too soon," she continued. "She must not travel."

There was a low, muffled oath. When he finally spoke, however, his tone was restrained.

"Don't make me appear the villain, Lily." He reached out for her and pulled her close to his chest. "I am lord of Orrick now. You are my wife and mistress here. But I am your lord."

"Yes, you are now lord. But am I truly mistress? You strip me of any authority. You turn my own guard against me!" she muttered heatedly.

His hand moved possessively to her belly and he pulled her snug against his loins. "I warned you before not to fight me. But you refused to listen. Maybe now you'll not make that mistake again."

Lilliane knew it would be useless to argue with him, although her anger festered sorely within her. She tried to convince herself that perhaps time would ease the conflict between them. They would adjust to one another and life at Orrick would become more settled. But even so, she knew it would not come easily.

As she reluctantly relaxed against him and accustomed herself to sleeping in such an intimate embrace, she sighed deeply. She would just have to face each of their encounters one at a time. He wanted William gone. In truth, so did she. But Lady Verone was another matter entirely. She was fighting for her child. Lilliane knew she could do no less for her new friend.

She shifted and Corbett's leg slid between hers. Much had passed between them this day, she realized. From mistrust and hate to hesitant belief, and then this unexpected, explosive passion. She yawned again as his head settled comfortably at the corner of her neck. Today had been a revelation. Tomorrow anything was possible.

But her first task would be to find her ring.

13

Lady Verone grasped Lilliane's hand weakly. In her pale face her eyes were huge and sunken, terrible evidence of the battle she fought. Her pains had begun in the early hours before dawn and were now coming with frightful regularity.

"Just hold on, Verone. It's almost past. Just hold on," Lilliane encouraged her suffering patient.

"Oh . . . oh . . ." The woman panted as the pain began finally to subside. Then she shifted her gaze to Lilliane's stricken face. "Do not fret so, Lilliane. What God wills we must accept."

"Don't speak in such a manner. Your child may yet be strong and healthy."

"Yes." Verone closed her eyes in utter exhaustion. Her words were hardly more than a whisper. "Yes, I pray it will be so. But you must promise me . . ." At this she raised her eyelids once more.

"You know I'll do whatever I can to help you."

"Then help my child," Verone murmured. "If it's a girl . . . William wants a son. He will be so displeased . . . Please, if it's a girl, please take her to your heart. Raise her for me."

Lilliane caught her breath at the finality in Verone's words. "Why, you shall raise her yourself. Or him. William will want his child and his wife."

Verone managed a wan smile then patted Lilliane's hand. "He would want his son. But not a daughter. And I know I shall not be here."

Despite her wish for it not to be so, Lilliane could not long deny the dire prophecy of Verone's words. Neither Mother Grendella's ministrations nor Father Denys's prayers could alter the terrible progression of events.

By midafternoon Lilliane could no longer restrain her tears. Verone was slipping in and out of consciousness, her face a deathly white from her dreadful loss of blood. It was only when the babe's head slipped free and then its tiny body followed that Verone managed to rouse from her delirium.

"Bring her . . . to me . . ." she murmured as Grendella hastily separated the child from the cord, then swaddled it in the waiting linen cloths. "Let me see."

Lilliane took the wee bundle into her arms and bent close to Verone. "Look at her, Verone. You see? You have a beautiful little girl. She's tiny but she's perfect."

"She breathes well?"

"Oh, yes," Lilliane answered through the tears that choked her. "She let out a lusty cry when she made her entrance into this world. She is strong and—" Lilliane's voice broke and she could not continue. Grendella moved quickly to her side and laid the baby in the curve of Verone's arm. Disturbed, the tiny girl let out a small cry of protest. But she calmed almost at once.

Verone's lips were almost blue and she trembled

from a sudden chill. But she smiled at the tiny cry of her child. "Remember, Lilliane. Remember that I've given her to you now. Elyse is yours."

Then, as if content at last, Verone let go of her last hold on life.

That women died often in childbrith was hardly unknown to Lilliane. Her own mother had gone in just such a fashion. Yet Lilliane had felt a bond with Verone that she was not willing to sever, and she could not accept her death.

"Grendella!" she cried in panic. "Quick! We must rouse her. If we keep her alert she can fight it and—"

"It is too late to help her in this world, Lilliane. She needs only your prayers now." Then Grendella lifted the sleeping baby from her mother's still embrace and placed her in Lilliane's arms. "Take the baby from here. She needs a nursing mother to nourish her, but for now take her to your own chamber."

Lilliane was too numb to protest. When Ferga took her arm and led her from the room, she followed along meekly. As they crossed the great hall, William approached her. He had been freed from his chamber for Lady Verone's sake, although Lilliane knew Corbett would prefer to banish him from Orrick completely. Now William looked more annoyed than anything else.

"She bore me a daughter, then," he remarked, sparing only a glance for the swaddled child.

"Yes," Lilliane whispered, staring at him through tear-blurred eyes. "You have a daughter but—" She faltered, then placed one hand on William's arm. "Verone is gone, William. I am so sorry to tell you that she died in the birthing."

William was silent and his eyes stared unseeingly

across the quiet hall. Then he focused back on Lilliane. "Did she ask you?"

"To raise the baby?" Lilliane took a shaky breath, then nodded as she stared at the tiny features of the child.

"And will you?" he prodded.

"Of course I will." Lilliane looked up earnestly at William. "Unless you wish her raised elsewhere."

"Oh, no. No. If that's what Verone wanted."

Lilliane had not expected such a rush of relief at his agreement. She hugged the child more closely to her. "I'll raise her as my own. She'll grow to be a fine lady. You'll see."

"If your husband allows it," William cut in sarcastically.

It was just that comment that was worrying Lilliane not an hour later. She had left the child in her chamber under Ferga's motherly eye. After giving instructions for the care of Verone's body, she had then hurriedly washed and groomed herself. Corbett would return soon, and she knew it would not be easy to gain his approval to keep little Elyse.

Lilliane paused as she thought of the poor child. William had not asked a word after his daughter's well-being, not even asking about her name. Lilliane twisted the trailing ends of her girdle in agitation as she pondered the matter. It was true he had just lost his wife. She'd heard that some men blamed the babe for the mother's loss. But she could not condone such a callous attitude. As she thought of that tiny puckered face, so innocent of any blame, she could not accept William's coldness toward his own child.

Her musings were quickly turned away from William's lack of feelings for his new daughter, however. From her place near the the hearth in the great hall she clearly heard the ringing sound of heavy hooves upon the stone paving outside. Corbett and his knights had returned. Her heart began to race as she contemplated how she might approach her husband on this delicate subject.

It didn't make her plight easier to think of their passionate lovemaking of the night before. She'd not truly faced him since then as she'd risen early to attend Verone. Now as he strode confidently across the smooth stone floor, she felt a blush rise on her cheeks.

"Ah, just as any man could wish, I am met in the evening by my good lady wife." Corbett grinned dryly at her, then casually lifted one of her hands to his lips. " 'Tis certainly an improvement over the greetings I received yesterday."

"My . . . my lord," Lilliane began in a faltering voice.

"I have a name. Will you not use it?" His face was half serious, half mocking as he stroked her cheek with one finger. But his expression became concerned when he saw the sadness in her eyes. "What troubles you, Lily? Does your patient yet suffer?"

"My patient . . . Lady Verone is beyond all suffering now. It is her motherless child who . . ." Lilliane could not finish. She turned to hide her weeping from Corbett, but he caught her by the shoulders and pulled her against his chest. At his tender gesture the last of her composure fled. Unmindful of the servants and retainers in the hall, Lilliane buried her face in her husband's broad chest and wept.

"Hush. Hush, love. Please don't cry so, Lily."

But Corbett's compassion only seemed to increase

her sorrowful outburst. Curled within his powerful arms, she clung to his wide chest. He was strong and reliable, something stable to hold on to while she was falling apart. She'd had to be strong for everyone else, but he would be strong for her.

Corbett sat her on his lap with her head against his shoulder. There was something wonderfully comforting about the way he held her, Lilliane realized as she struggled to contain her sobs. It was as if she might actually mean something to him.

Hesitantly she lifted her face from his now-damp tunic. In the hall the servants peeped curiously at their lord and lady, but she did not care. It was her husband's concerned expression that drew her, no other's.

"Are you calmer, then?" Corbett's slate-gray eyes searched her face. Then he smoothed a loose strand of her thick chestnut hair away from her cheek.

Not quite trusting her voice, Lilliane nodded, then wiped at her damp eyes.

"Can you tell me now what has caused this flood of tears? I thought you hardly knew Lady Verone, save for the past weeks."

Lilliane took a shaky breath. She was grateful for Corbett's tender concern, but she wondered how well he would react to her request. Still, there was nothing to do but to ask.

"Lady Verone managed to bring forth her child before she—" She stopped, then continued on determinedly. "The baby is tiny but perfect. Healthier than ever we could have hoped."

"At least William may take some comfort in that."

Lilliane stared at Corbett, wondering how to best ask him her question. She had left his side before dawn, but he had addressed her before she'd slipped away to Verone's chamber. His voice had been husky and warm. Clearly he'd wanted her to stay, but he'd let her go when he knew her task. It was only when she'd paused and asked him to let William attend his suffering wife that his mood had cooled. Still, he'd reluctantly done as she asked, and now she took heart at that knowledge.

"Verone asked me to raise the child."

Beneath her hand she felt Corbett tense, but when he spoke he remained reasonable. "No doubt William will want to take his son with him when he departs."

" 'Tis a daughter he has," Lilliane revealed. "And he has already agreed."

Her words were followed by a terrible silence. As it lengthened she grew more and more uncomfortable.

"It is not such a great thing, nor so very rare," she argued more determinedly. "Many children are raised in the homes of others."

Still he did not speak.

When she could finally bear his silence no more, Lilliane moved to stand. But Corbett stayed her on his lap with one brawny arm about her waist.

He fixed her with his sharp stare. "Why would he agree?"

"I—I don't know," she stammered.

"Don't you?" Corbett commented enigmatically. Without warning he placed her on her feet, then rose from the chair. "William and his child will leave as soon as it is safe for the little one to travel."

"Oh, no!" Lilliane grabbed her husband's arm before he could turn and leave. "There is no cause for you to be so cruel!"

"Cruel?" His scarred brow lifted sardonically. "Is it cruel to let a child live with her natural parent? William will no doubt marry again. Let his new wife raise the child."

His eyes were hard as he dared her to respond.

But Lilliane would not waver and she met his suspicious stare with an honest reply. "It would be cruel to me."

"Pray explain that," he said with a growl. But he did not step away.

"I cannot precisely explain it," Lilliane admitted. "It's just that . . . when I held her . . ." She stared at him beseechingly.

Corbett searched her face then pulled her nearer with a hand on each of her shoulders. "You're just tenderhearted, Lily. It is natural that you should want a child in your arms. But God willing, we shall have one of our own soon enough. Content yourself with that."

"But she has no mother!" Lilliane cried. "I have asked you for nothing before this. Nothing."

"That's not true. You asked me for your freedom that night at the cottage. Or rather, you demanded it."

Lilliane's brow creased and she bowed her head. "Please give me this child, Corbett. I cannot explain how she has touched my heart. I fear for her. Her father does not want her, but I do. If you give me nothing else, please give me this."

"I gave you a ring but you—"

"I have it," she broke in, raising her hand to show him the heavy silver and meridian band. "You see?"

Corbett stared at the ring, then finally turned his somber gaze back on her. She knew her request troubled him deeply, but she sensed that he might be wavering.

"Please, Corbett," she pleaded unashamedly. "I know I have much to atone for—"

"But will you atone for it?"

Lilliane nodded slowly. "I'll be a good mistress to Orrick, if you let me and . . . and a good wife to you."

Corbett's lips compressed tightly and he looked away from her. His gaze swept the now-deserted hall before he looked down at Lilliane's sincere face. "I hope you mean all you say, Lily."

"I do," she whispered, fearing to believe the acquiescence in his voice.

"Then keep the child."

"Oh, Corbett!" Without pausing to think, she threw her arms around his neck and pressed a grateful kiss against his mouth. If he was startled by her reaction, however, Corbett was not tardy in enjoying her gratitude. His arms held her close against his hard body as he responded to her innocent kiss.

Lilliane was even more surprised than Corbett by her behavior. When she felt his lips move over hers she struggled to regain her composure, but by then it was too late. Corbett's kiss was hungry as he teased her lips apart, and his hand was bold as it slipped down to cup her bottom.

"Oh, Corbett, you must stop this," she whispered urgently, casting her eyes wildly about for witnesses to their byplay.

"Must I?" he murmured huskily in her ear. "When you throw your arms around me, when you kiss me so passionately and whisper my name so sweetly, can you truly mean for me to stop?"

Lilliane could not prevent her blush as she realized how forward she must appear. She knew well the pleasure to be had in his arms. Despite his stern appearance, he had proven on more than one occasion that he could be most tender when need be.

Nonetheless, she hardly thought it wise to hand him yet another means of control over her. She was supremely relieved when the noisy entrance of a group of knights brought them abruptly apart.

Sir Dunn made no secret of his displeasure as he strode toward them. Even his tawny beard could not disguise the rigid set to his jaw. When he stopped before Corbett, he did not even spare Lilliane a glance.

"The last group of guards await your review. In addition, I have the reports from the other two bands of scouts."

"Good. When I return to the hall I'll hear them." Corbett turned to Lilliane. "Right now I must attend another matter."

"But there is much you should know of," Dunn insisted, shooting a suspicious glance at Lilliane.

Lilliane was embarrassed by the situation and torn by her emotions. She knew Sir Dunn disliked her. Since she'd accused him of murder and imprisoned him, his distrust of her had clearly deepened even further. As mistress of Orrick, it put her in an awkward predicament. Logic deemed that she should do whatever she could to ease the tension between them. But she could not help but anger at the way he strove to dismiss her importance in her own home.

"What review of the guards?" she asked, ignoring Dunn and staring directly at Corbett.

He gave her a long, considering look before answering. "They decide today just where their loyalty lies. And whether they shall continue as guards or become farmers."

He'd told of this before; she knew her anger was pointless. Yet when Dunn's dour expression lifted in a faint, smug smile, she could not contain her wrath.

"Should you limit yourself to the guards only?" she snapped. "Why, the stableman might harm your beloved horses, or the cook might somehow serve you spoiled food. Heaven knows, I might devise any number of other cunning methods to overset you. Shouldn't you demand my vow of loyalty?"

Although Corbett's expression had hardened, his words were nevertheless mocking. "I seem to recall receiving that promise not minutes ago. Do you renege on your word so quickly?"

She was silenced at once by his terse jibe. He did not need to remind her again that the baby Elyse stayed at his consent only. Frustrated anew, she lifted her chin and stared at him with ill-concealed hostility.

"Pray then, see to your duties. There is much that I must arrange for the baby." She stepped back, fully intending to escape their unbearable presence. But Corbett caught her hand.

"There is no need for the child to sleep within our chamber." Although he said no more, his potent gaze left her with no doubt of his meaning.

It took all Lilliane's control to silence an angry retort. "No," she muttered once she'd regained her composure. "She will sleep with her nurse."

Both men watched as she hurried away. She had no doubt that Dunn would feel free to express his mistrust of her. Well then, let him. She felt no great trust for him either despite his innocence in her father's death.

As for Corbett, Lilliane did not know what to think. At one moment thoughtful and kind; at the next cold and unyielding. He was thoroughly exasperating.

Still, she did have Elyse now. Corbett might question the guards and doubt her at every turn, but he had not denied her request. She slowed her rapid pace and took a calming breath. She must try harder to curb her sharp temper, at least in his presence. It was clear she could not win any overt battle of wills with him. Whether in matters of the castle, or even in their private chambers, he was inevitably the victor.

Yet she was not without her own strengths, she reminded herself. She was not about to surrender all authority at Orrick to him. One way or another, she would have at least the household matters run as she deemed fit. Even Dunn would not be able to influence Corbett should she decide to entice her virile husband into seeing things her way.

That knowledge gave her heart, and she smiled despite the trauma of the past days. Her life seemed to be changing almost daily, but perhaps that was not entirely bad.

Sir Dunn clearly did not share Lilliane's mood.

"How quickly she diverts you from your task," he accused as Corbett watched until Lilliane disappeared up the stone stairs.

But Corbett was too content to rise to his friend's

baiting. "It would not be seemly for a man to ignore his wife. Especially one as sweetly formed as mine."

"Aye. She's sweetly formed. And words may flow like honey from her smiling lips, though I've yet to hear her be anything but a shrew. I know better than most how deceptive she can be."

Corbett laughed at that then slapped Dunn on the back. "Come now, man. Can you not forgive her that honest mistake?"

Dunn only frowned. Then he looked up questioningly. "She spoke of a child. William's brat is born?"

"His wife delivered him a girl. But only the child survived." Corbett sat down in a heavy oak chair and stared thoughtfully toward the fire. "Lilliane will raise it."

"What?" Dunn scraped another chair around then sat facing Corbett. "You will let her raise William's brat knowing everything you do about him?"

Corbett's jaw tensed and he looked challengingly at Dunn. "It's my brother's suspicious ties to William and his 'friends' that you refer to, no doubt. Certainly you imply nothing about Lilliane."

It was a statement, not a question, and Dunn heeded his lord's warning.

"Aye. That's all I mean. But it is sufficient. William will have every reason to linger at Orrick. If he is spying for Hughe, he will have knowledge of our every movement."

"As I will have of his. 'Tis better to have a known enemy close at hand than to have an unknown one God knows where." Corbett ran one knuckle along his scarred brow. "The dissidents must make their move before Edward returns. *If* Hughe is involved, William will be our connection to him."

"Do you still doubt Hughe's participation in this treason?" Dunn scoffed.

Corbett's gaze darkened and his brow lowered in a frown. "The truth will out. If he's guilty then I'll spare him no pity. But I must have proof before I accuse my own brother. I must have proof."

14

❧❦❧❦❧

Winter set in with a vengeance. The wind blew in harsh, unremitting blasts through the valley, moaning along the battlements, carrying sleet and freezing rain into every corner of Orrick.

Lilliane would have preferred snow. She could accept the icy weather and bitter cold if the countryside at least lay quiet and pristine beneath a beautiful blanket of feathery white snow. But the brutal cold that gripped Windermere Fold now offered no such mitigation.

In the village there was little activity; both men and beasts huddled for warmth in their shelters. In the castle the routine of life went on much the same, except that the fires in the hearths burned higher and the servants clustered more closely around them. The daily tasks of cooking and cleaning and tending to the demesne's business required the same attention as always.

But for Lilliane life had taken an abrupt turn. Castle matters she had well in hand. There was not a servant who dared take liberties, for her temper was well known to all of them. The hard visage of her warrior husband did not encourage any laxness on their part either. Even the care of tiny Elyse did not drastically alter Lilliane's life, for the babe had a wet nurse as well as both Magda and Ferga to see to her needs. Indeed, the baby was nothing but a pleasure to Lilliane, and she spent as much time as possible in the nursery.

It was the men of the castle who frustrated her endlessly.

Sir Dunn was dismal enough, what with his constant frown and watchful stare. She'd never felt so thoroughly disliked as she did when faced with his daily presence.

William was a more complex problem, however. At her request he had been allowed to remain at Orrick, although Corbett had made it clear he did so reluctantly and only because of the baby Elyse. As a result, William was constantly in attendance in the great hall, affording Lilliane no escape from him at all.

He was at his most charming during those cold, frozen days. He entertained everyone with amusing stories, tantalizing gossip, and astounding acecdotes about the London court. During the long evenings in the torchlit hall, Lilliane was once again reminded of the young man she'd once been so enamored of.

But she was also well aware of Corbett's festering anger.

By day her husband was a tireless lord. He had the carpenters clear a practice area within the barns so that he and his men might daily maintain their fitness for battle, no matter the weather. He studied every corner and twist of the meandering old castle, then translated that knowledge into drawings for improving both the defenses and comforts of the centuries-old structure. He examined Lord Barton's tally sheets and even, to her irritation, her own household books until he was thoroughly familiar with every facet and detail of Orrick's complex management.

In almost every area of the castle's stewardship he made some change or another, much to her aggravation. They clashed frequently. But he was adamant that they never argue in public.

Yet that was another problem as well. After venting her fury at him, she could not fathom how he could calmly ignore her wishes and then expect her to come willing to him at night. The very thought of his unerring ability to silence her with his kisses infuriated her. Each time she would be determined to resist him and somehow impress upon him the importance of her opinion. Yet invariably she succumbed.

He used his hands and his lips as effectively as any weapon, robbing her of her will and bending her to his own. He remained always the victor, supremely confident as he planted his stamp more and more firmly upon Orrick. And upon her.

There was only one subject that unsettled him. Lilliane saw it every night as the entire castle sat down to sup.

He would be unfailingly polite and solicitous with her. With his men he was ever ready for a joke or a shared toast. But her least display of friendliness or even civility toward William soured him at once. As the days went by Lilliane could not ignore his increasingly bad temper. She began to dread the outburst she sensed was in the offing as their confinement to the castle lengthened.

When a fair afternoon finally presented itself, she decided on impulse to take a ride. Fresh air and a hard gallop were just what she needed to break the tension she felt from all sides.

Once in the stable, she ignored the flustered stableman's mumbled words that she should not take a horse out. She simply led Aere to a low bench so that she could mount the mare unaided.

But she could not ignore Corbett's angry appearance at the foot of the gate tower, nor his sharp words as he grabbed the reins from her hands.

"Where in God's name do you think you're going?"

Although taken aback by his high-handed approach, Lilliane was quick to respond. "I plan to give Aere and myself a hard run. We've both a need to be rid of this place, if only for an hour."

"You can't go."

She had known that would be his response. Perhaps that was why she'd not even considered informing him of her plans. Yet even still, she could not prevent her surprise when he turned the horse and began to lead her back toward the stable.

"What do you think you're doing? Why, you horrible brute! Let me go. Let me go, I say!" At that she tried to yank the reins free. When that failed, she abruptly freed her leg from the pommel and swung neatly to the ground. Then she began to walk stiffly toward the gatehouse.

She got no farther than five paces before she was rudely hauled around to face him.

"Stop acting like a little fool," he snapped.

"It's not me who is acting the fool," she hissed readily. "You treat me like some hound you keep on a chain. But I will not be confined so. I will not!"

Lilliane was in a rage. All the pent-up frustrations of the past weeks served only to fuel her anger as she faced her husband's fierce glower. He had a harsh grip on each of her shoulders and she knew she would never be physically able to escape him. But he would not silence her this time, she vowed. She would vent her fury here, in the bailey where any eye or ear might freely see or hear what passed between lord and lady.

"I do not confine you, Lily. You exaggerate on that score," he said in a quieter tone.

"Ha!" she scoffed. "I may not leave Orrick even for a pleasant ride. You check on every task I perform, always seeking to change my methods. You frown and glower the live-long day. I might as well be confined in the donjon for all the—"

"This is not the time nor place for such an outburst," he interrupted as he tried to steer her back to the keep.

But Lilliane shook off his hand and faced him squarely. "What would be the time and place?" she mocked. "Perhaps at the evening table?"

"Don't play the lackwit with me." Then he seemed to reconsider his words. "Listen to me, Lily. I do not mean for you to be unhappy. We can talk about this tonight in the privacy of our chamber. Then you—"

"That is always your solution! Always! But that's not enough."

Corbett's expression became grim. "You should be glad to be treated so well. Any other husband would have beat you within an inch of your life for locking him out of the castle. Any other husband would have sent that baby on its way—the winter cold be damned. And yet for you that is not enough!"

Lilliane was silenced by his angry outburst. For a moment she considered his words, for she knew she could not argue with him. So what was it she wanted from him?

"I want . . ." she began in a soft, trembling voice. Then she stopped. She wanted Orrick to be a happy place. But she didn't have any idea how to make it so. She wanted them to be at peace with one another, and she wanted him to see her in a different light.

Her confused thoughts could go no further. She swallowed hard as she stared into his angry gray eyes. Then she turned abruptly and hurried back to the keep.

Lilliane did not go down for the evening meal. She drank the broth Magda brought her and dutifully ate the square of white cheese, but she refused to join the company. Instead, she dismissed the nurse and tended the baby. The small chamber boasted a hearty blaze, for Lilliane refused to take any chances with the tiny girl. Holding the baby warm and comforting in her arms, she settled into a wooden chair before the hearth.

"Far away, far away, child; When will you give me a smile . . ." she crooned softly to the baby. But the blurry infant gaze that met hers seemed as unlikely to smile warmly at her as was Corbett's piercing one.

She sighed as she thought of her difficult husband. She did not know what he wanted of her any longer. Once she'd thought she knew. He'd wanted Orrick, of course. Then she'd thought his clear pleasure with her in their marriage bed would be enough to keep them both content. But that was no longer sufficient for her. And obviously it was not enough for him either. But what did he want of her?

She bent her face down to nuzzle the baby's soft

cheek. Elyse smelled of milk and mint oil and baby,
and it was strangely reassuring. When the door
creaked slightly she did not even look up but only
murmured, "You need not return so soon. I'll stay
with her awhile."

"And neglect your duties in the meantime?"

Lilliane's head jerked up at Corbett's quiet remark.
He stood within the door opening, almost as if he
hesitated to enter. A part of Lilliane, something deep
within her, leapt to see him standing there. He had
come to find her, and she could not ignore the feelings of satisfaction that gave her. But she cautioned
herself not to make too much of it.

"The castle will not be neglected by my absence on
this single occasion. Magda will see that naught goes
amiss."

"Magda cannot sit beside me."

Lilliane peered warily at him, trying to decipher
the meaning behind such odd words. Then she gave
him an arch look. "If you fear the gossip springing
from our—our disagreement in the bailey, well, I
have much familiarity with the gossips. Believe me
when I say you will survive."

To her surprise, he did not rise to the sarcasm edging her words. Instead he took a step further into the
room and closed the door to the drafty corridor.
When he still did not speak she peered at him curiously, unable to fathom his strange mood.

Finally he came nearer then stood before her, his
legs planted apart, his hands behind his back. "Is this
some new method you have adopted to annoy me?"

Lilliane knew he referred to her absence from the
table, but she took perverse satisfaction in feigning
innocence.

"How selfish you are to begrudge this little mother-less baby a few minutes of my time," she replied in her most injured tone.

"Damn it, woman! That is not what I meant." He stared accusingly at her. "And you're well aware of it also."

It was all she could do to stifle the laugh that bub-bled to her lips; she had to look down quickly at Elyse's puckered face so that he would not see her expression. She knew she would have to say extra prayers this evening to atone for the wicked delight she took in frustrating him this way. But then, he deserved it, she reminded herself, recalling how abruptly he'd spoiled her ride earlier.

"Well, if it is not the time I spend with Elyse that bothers you, then what?" she persisted.

Corbett's scowl deepened. "How long shall you stay away from the evening gatherings?"

"It is not my intent to irritate you by my absence," Lilliane finally answered more soberly. "It was just that today . . ." She trailed off as she thought once more how unreasonable he had been.

"It is just *today* that you wished to irritate me," he finished curtly.

His self-centered complaint was the last straw. She stood up quickly and laid the baby back in her wooden cradle. After tucking the soft wool blanket securely around her, she slowly turned to face Cor-bett. She was furious all over again at his selfish atti-tude.

"Today," she began vehemently, "today I simply could not abide one more minute of the farce we call a marriage." She smiled bitterly when his brows raised in surprise.

"This castle has a long history of strife. But I've never felt it so keenly as now. Not even when our families were embroiled in fierce combat! And it's all your fault!"

"My fault!" he exploded. "My fault? From the first moment I laid eyes on you you've been nothing but trouble!"

"Then leave here!"

In the silence that followed her shrill cry they stared at one another. He looked furious, his face darkened in a frown. But her vision was quickly blurred by the tears that sprang unwanted to her eyes. Mortified, she turned abruptly away. How she wished she could take back those rash words. But once said they could not be banished. Indeed, she was not at all certain what she would say in their place.

"You'll not be rid of me so easily, Lilliane. No matter how much you may wish me gone."

A lump lodged in her throat at that and she wrung her hands together. "I don't . . . I didn't mean that," she admitted in a small, quiet voice.

When there was no reply from him, she peered cautiously up at him. He had not moved. Not an inch. He was just staring at her as if he struggled to understand just what sort of woman it was that he had wed.

"I confess, you leave me continually baffled, Lilliane." For once he truly seemed not in control of the situation. "What is it that you mean? Shall I leave or shall I stay?"

She would not believe he would actually leave Orrick if she so demanded. She was certain he would never do that. Yet perhaps it was their marriage he referred to. Still, whichever it was, she took some comfort in knowing he wished to know how she truly felt.

As she struggled to find words, he ran his hands through his hair and released a weary sigh. "Will you at least give me an honest answer? You need not fear my reprisal."

"I feel so . . . so alone," she confessed softly.

"Alone? God's teeth, but we are surrounded day and night! By servants and retainers. And unwanted guests."

"That's not what I meant," she interjected softly. With her nerves in a tangle, she began to restlessly roam the small chamber. "I too feel the strain of the last weeks here. But I am nonetheless alone. I don't know . . ." She shook her head sadly. "I don't know what you expect of me."

He was silent a moment. "But do you want me to leave or stay?" he asked once more in a quiet tone.

The low rumble of his voice seemed to strike some chord in her and a quiver shook her. She knew her answer. It was foolish of her to pretend otherwise.

"I want you to stay," she admitted, watching him guardedly. At the quick lifting of his expression she hurried on. "But we cannot continue on as we are. Some things must change."

Corbett nodded slowly, keeping his smoky gray gaze locked thoughtfully upon her. "Perhaps . . ." he began. Then he smiled and it was almost as if the sun suddenly shone upon her. "I must depart for London very soon. Would you leave Orrick to travel with me?"

"Leave Orrick?" Lilliane was completely taken by surprise.

"Dunn will see to the defenses. Ferga will tend the babe. Magda will keep everyone else well in line. Orrick will survive your absence, Lily."

"I do not doubt that," she revealed, a hesitant smile beginning to curve her mouth.

"Do you doubt the sincerity of my invitation?"

Lilliane did not answer. Perhaps a change of scenery would be good for them, for away from the routine of Orrick—and the oppressive presence of William and Dunn—they might indeed be able to work out some of their problems.

"But why so far away? Why London?"

He shrugged. "I have business to attend there. Besides, does it really matter to you where we go so long as we are together?"

Lilliane could hardly believe his words. He wanted her with him! It was impossible to credit, but it was true nonetheless. Her amber eyes were fixed upon him and she did not pause to debate her answer. "Yes. I would like to go with you."

At her acceptance, Corbett let out a hearty laugh. Then he crossed to her and pulled her gently to him. "So my lady shall go to London. No doubt you think it a treat, but I warrant you'll tire of court very quickly."

"I am sure I shall love it," she contradicted, regaining her composure somewhat. "So many important lords and ladies. So many fine things to see."

"We shall not be staying overlong," he cautioned.

"Good." She finally smiled up at him. "As much as I shall enjoy it, I shall still enjoy returning home all the more."

For a moment he did not reply but only stared at her unseeingly. Then he focused on her and forced a smile to his lips as well. "As shall I," he murmured. "As shall I."

15

❧❧❧

London was at once fascinating and terrifying. Lilliane was amazed at the magnitude and the size of the many buildings crowded together near the banks of the Thames and stretching out into the green countryside. She was dumbfounded by the throngs of people, by their constant motion and their utter nonchalance at their surroundings. Her nose wrinkled at the heavy scent of smoke—and slop—but even that could not dim her enthusiasm.

The entire journey had been a wonder to her for, once they'd passed Burgram Abbey, she'd been in territory completely foreign. For the first two days they'd followed the old road through the Pennine range. The mountains were beautiful in their early mantle of snow. But once they descended into the midlands, the snow gave way to mud and drizzle and the going was more difficult. Still, each day brought new places, different people, and a dawning awareness of how truly large the world must be.

They found shelter each night at castles eager to offer the new lord of Orrick and his lady their hospitality. The castles and the many lords and ladies she'd met were beginning to blur now in her mind—Sir Frederick of Bexhill, Lord Rufus and Lady Anne of Tutbury, the drunken Herbert of Wolston. She'd been most relieved when they stayed at the abbey at Woburn, for the spare mode of living there was a blessing after the opulent feasting of the previous five nights.

At Berkhansted the accommodations had not been so comfortable, but by then Lilliane had not cared for she'd known London was only another half day's journey.

Now as the entourage of heavily armed men-at-arms made their way into London, Lilliane could hardly contain her excitement. On impulse she urged her mare forward, ignoring the alarmed cries of the two knights assigned to her. Before they could prevent it she had pulled abreast of Corbett and she turned to him eagerly.

"Oh! Look, see the fair! Why, who has heard of a fair so late in the season?"

At once Corbett grabbed her reins, clearly annoyed that she was ignoring his instructions to keep herself always surrounded by the knights when they rode through towns. But his sharp reprimand died unsaid. Her eyes were so bright and her smile was so gay within her wind-pinkened face that his scowl would not hold.

" 'Tis not a fair as you are familiar with," he answered, signaling a man to ride up along her other side. "In London there are markets continually open. In the warmer months, though, there are fairs that bring rare and precious goods—fine jewels and oils, silks and cottons."

Corbett chuckled at Lilliane's wide-eyed wonder. "And now, have you a yen to spend my coins at the market? Well, I may be inclined to escort you there.

But mind you, Lily." His face grew more serious. "Do not venture anywhere without my express consent and an ample guard about you."

Lilliane scarcely heard his warning, so excited was she by their surroundings. Corbett had been most considerate during their journey, and the long ride had gone far toward easing the tension between them. He had not changed; she knew that. He was as careful and watchful as ever, as his warning had just proven. But he had begun to relax around her. It was the first chance they'd had to spend any time together outside of their bedchamber, and he'd proven to be a most entertaining companion. He'd told her tales of the various towns and churches and castles they'd passed. He'd further kept her amazed with stories of the crusades and Prince Edward's campaign, chuckling sometimes at her wide-eyed wonder and naive questions. Even when she'd asked him hesitantly about the scars that marked him he'd answered her: the sword that had glanced off his brow at Byzantium; the bear that had clawed him so viciously when he'd fought it away from Edward near St. Blasiens; and the spear that had come close to separating his arm from his shoulder.

With every tale came another revelation. Slowly she began to see him in a different light. He was stern and demanding, yet he took his duties seriously, never shirking a task. He was proud to the point of arrogance, yet he'd proven himself in battle and tested himself against steel. He was harsh and yet . . . Lilliane smiled to herself as she thought of their recent nights together. He was always a tender lover, even from that first terrifying night in the shepherd's cottage. But now there seemed a completeness about their joining, a wholeness, meeting in equal eagerness. In equal desire.

Oh yes, he was a harsh man. But never cruel. And he was learning how to bend.

In what was becoming a most natural gesture, she reached her hand to grasp his. The quick squeeze he gave her leather-gloved fingers warmed her through and through, and confirmed what she was beginning more and more to realize. Her heart had no defense against this fierce warrior husband of hers. Despite the bitter wind and the damp, seeping chill, she was warm and happy as she passed through the Bishop's Gate at Corbett's side.

Lilliane had not given a thought to their accommodations in London; she knew Corbett would attend to those details as he'd attended to the other facets of their journey. She was not prepared, however, for them to stay within the imposing complex surrounding the White Tower.

When they were waved entrance into the Tower Green and then were met by a full complement of eager attendants, she was speechless with surprise. She knew little of the world and hardly more of England and English politics. Yet even she knew that Tower Hill was the seat of the Kingdom. And here was her husband being greeted with such obeisance and attentive respect. The retainers seemed almost to compete for the honor of serving him.

Corbett took it all in good stride, as if he were quite accustomed to such attention. However, when an ornately uniformed man made to help Lilliane dismount, he stayed the man with a quick gesture. Then he lifted his own hands up to her, waiting patiently with a smile curving his firm lips.

In Lilliane's eyes he was the most handsome of men. The wicked scar that had horrified her on first viewing now only made him more masculine and appealing. She knew he was physically powerful; his arms and shoulders bulged with iron-hard muscles and his back and legs were equally endowed. But now, seeing what respect he commanded, she knew his power extended far beyond his battle prowess. It may have been at war that he'd received the title king's Bird of Prey, but it was clear it was a role in which he was equally cast here in the center of English government.

Slowly she placed her hands in his, but her face had lost its wondering look and grew more serious. As if her weight were no more than a kitten's, he lowered her to the ground, but he did not remove his hands from her waist. His eyes were half amused, half curious as he looked down on her from his excessive height. It crossed Lilliane's mind that she knew not one thing about why they'd come to London for he'd deftly parried all her queries. In so many ways he remained a complete mystery to her.

Then her serious thoughts were ended by his quick kiss to her lips. "I can understand your gaping at London in all its beauty and filth. But why do you now gape so openly at me? Have I suddenly sprouted horns?"

Without thinking Lilliane's hand went up to his wind-ruffled hair and smoothed back the raven-black locks. "No." She smiled wryly. "No horns at all. It's just . . ." Her cheeks grew warm with color. "It's just that you seem so . . . so different here."

His eyes, which had been so lively and teasing, turned dark and opaque at her words, and his jaw tightened. He looked up at the solid three-story tower beyond them for a moment, then his gaze returned to her. "I *am* a different man here, Lily. Remember that well. I caution you again to do nothing—indeed, say nothing above the most minor of exchanges without my permission."

From charming and teasing he'd become somber and secretive, much to Lilliane's dismay. She was bewildered and more than a little annoyed. "But I don't understand—"

"You don't need to understand. It's better this way."

"Then why did you bring me here?" Lilliane burst out in frustration. "I may not go anywhere nor speak to anyone! Am I free to think my own thoughts?" she added caustically.

To her surprise he paused and his tone became more gentle.

"It is not as bad as you make out." He slid his hands placatingly up her arms. "As to why I brought you here, can you not believe that it is simply because I want you near me?"

It was difficult to argue with such a flattering sentiment. Still, Lilliane was troubled as Corbett guided her to the chamber set aside for their use. As much as she truly wished to believe him, she feared that, above all, it was his distrust of William that caused her to be in London now. No doubt he hoped that William would have left Orrick when they returned. Indeed, for the sake of everyone she wished the same thing. But no matter where William chose to spend the winter months, Lilliane resolved not to let anything ruin the tentative bonds that were forming between her and her enigmatic husband. It was bad enough that Corbett sometimes still kept her at arm's length. She did not need William exacerbating the situation.

Their chamber within the king's palace was impressive indeed. As the serving men brought in their trunks, she wandered the thick-walled room marveling at the furnishings and comforts alike. Above a wide hearth, etched forever in stone, old King Alfred and his hound cornered a stag of immense proportion. In the warmer hues of a colorful silk tapestry William the Conqueror received fealty from Harold, King John accepted the barons' oaths, and Richard routed the infidels at Acre.

Lilliane might be merely the daughter of a minor baron from the northernmost regions of the English kingdom, but she'd paid close attention to the exhilarating stories told in the evenings at Orrick. Amazing deeds of honor and courage, bloody victories on the field of battle, and even, on occasion, a tale of enduring love and loyalty. But nothing she'd seen at Orrick or even Burgram Abbey could compare to these wonderful carvings and needlework, which brought to life the stories that had always captivated her. Even the high wood bed showed a fanciful scene of a marvelous feast being served. From honored guests at a head table down to young serving pages and the hungry hounds beneath the tables, it faithfully detailed every aspect of a vast dinner.

" 'Twas King Henry's coronation."

Lilliane let her fingers run across the smooth wood, stopping just short of the monarch's likeness. Then she looked at Corbett curiously. "I confess that I never suspected you would warrant such princely consideration."

At Corbett's snort of amusement she continued on even more boldly. "The servants all know you. This chamber is no mean accommodation. Shall I then be considered a great lady because you are my husband?"

Her last words abruptly banished Corbett's negligent attitude. "You will be well courted and fawned over. But do not make too much of it, Lily."

"I know. I know." She grimaced. "Speak to no one. Go nowhere." She sighed and sat petulantly upon the high bed.

For a moment she thought he might relent, for the expression that passed over his face was compounded of both amusement and fondness. But as if only with great effort, he marshalled his features and grew more stern.

"Keep those instructions well in mind," he told her. "Now, however, you may relax. I've ordered a bath for you, and I'll have a maid sent in to attend you."

"You are leaving?" Lilliane started to get off the high comfortable bed but his slight frown kept her in her place.

"I would like nothing better than to stay here with you. To join you on that bed. To bury myself in your sweet softness," he added in a voice grown husky. Then he took a harsh breath. "But I had a purpose in coming to London. I must attend it."

Without further explanation he removed a slender packet of papers from his leather pouch, shoved it safely within his tunic, and left.

Although physically freshened from her bath, Lilliane's humor was not in the least improved by the luxurious soaking. She was determined to make her inflexible husband understand how frustrated she was by this confinement he pressed upon her. But with few resources of her own, she was left with showing her displeasure by dawdling at her bath, lingering at her toilet, and stretching out all the other necessary preparations for her first appearance at court. But even in that she was thwarted, for despite the exceedingly long time she spent brushing her hair dry and the time-consuming process of trying on every one of her gowns, then rejecting each of them until even the poor, subservient maid was close to voicing her complaint, he still had not come. In the end, she sat waiting upon a narrow upholstered bench. She was well dressed in an intricately figured gown of celadon silk; the cream-colored linen of her kirtle showed prettily at the neckline and at the three gold and green embroidered slashes in the upper sleeves. She'd woven her hair into a thick knot at the back of her head with a gold netted caul containing the gleaming wealth of her tresses. Now she sat with the barbette, a wimple, and a filet upon her lap, toying with them as her irritation increased.

She should wear them all, she fumed. Let him object if he would, but she would not appear at court with her hair streaming down her back like some half-grown child. But before she could decide whether to afix those chaste garments to her hair, she was interrupted by Corbett's tardy entrance.

With a look he dismissed the maid. Then he crossed silently to the deep-set window alcove and stared out into the early night sky.

For all her anger with him, Lilliane was at once disturbed by her husband's brooding silence. Her thoughts of complaint fled as she contemplated his tense posture and scowling profile. But it was the lines of weariness marking his face that broke her resolve. She moved to his side, then placed one of her palms against his cheek. "Corbett, is something wrong?"

"Something is always wrong in London," he muttered. Then he dragged his gaze away from the window. "This is town peopled with vultures. You think my words of warning unnecessary, but believe me when I say they are quite able to slaughter you and pick your very bones clean before you are even aware of it."

"I don't understand. Who is it that troubles you so?"

Her concerned tone seemed to bring him up short, and his eyes focused on her upturned face. As if by pure will he banished all trace of weariness, anger, or worry from his expression. " 'Tis nothing you need worry about. London always affects me so."

When it was clear he would say no more, Lilliane sighed. "You're tired. Shall I at least send for a bath to refresh you?"

"No, there is not the time now. They must accept me as I am." He chuckled grimly. "At least it is honest sweat and dirt. Besides, you are quite enough to draw all eyes. No one will be aware of my presence at all."

Lilliane blushed at his pretty compliment. But her concern for him was too strong for her to be that easily diverted. "We may delay our entrance until tomorrow if that is your will. You appear so tired."

He seemed almost to consider her suggestion but then he grined ruefully. "What? You would have me miss tonight's performance? All the players are assembled. Save the king, of course. It remains only to see who it is that plays the leading role."

"I don't . . ." Lilliane shook her head in confusion. "I don't understand. Wouldn't the king always be the most important person?"

At this his hard-edged amusement banished. "The king—and his welfare—must always be of paramount importance to his loyal subjects. Don't fret about my words, Lily. This does not affect you."

"But it affects you. And I'm your wife."

"Yes." He studied her face seriously. "You are my wife. And as such, I bid you stay near me and do nothing without my express consent."

Obviously back in his previous inflexible mood, he deftly escorted her to the door. Lilliane accompanied him willingly enough, but she was disturbed by his strange behavior. As they made their way across the green to the tower itself and then up to the state banqueting hall, she contemplated the abrupt change in him. From weary and resigned he had become almost predatory. Like a wolf stalking, a dangerous light gleamed in his eyes now. He moved like a hunter, cautiously but without fear, all his cunning and power carefully restrained. But she knew he was ready for whatever was to come.

Much to Lilliane's relief, Corbett paused on a narrow landing. She badly needed to compose herself before entering such a grand and noble company. For a moment her concerns for Corbett were forgotten as she contemplated her own meager importance. Surely they would all know at once that she was only an unknown daughter of a relatively unknown baron of the far northern demesnes. But Corbett interrupted her terrifying thoughts.

"Come now, Lilliane. I would see a smile on your lips." He turned to look at her and tilted her face up to his.

"You're not smiling," she retorted nervously. "And you never call me Lilliane unless you're quite serious."

If he was taken aback by her observation, it did not show. But neither did he comment on it. Instead he drew a small velvet bag from inside his tunic.

"I meant to give you this earlier but I let myself become distracted." Then he pulled the cords free and spilled a glittering necklace into his palm. Like golden fire it caught the torchlight, seeming almost to wink and sparkle at her.

Lilliane was speechless with surprise as she stared at the fortune he dangled between his fingers. From a delicately worked gold chain a series of loops fashioned in the same intricate style were suspended. But at the corner of each fanciful loop an opulent sapphire flanked by two smaller rubies was set. Corbett smiled at her reaction, then took advantage of her silence to fasten the unusual piece around her slender neck.

"Oh, Corbett! Thank you, thank you! It's so beautiful!"

"The more fitting that it should be yours. I knew it would suit you." He ran one finger along her collar bone, tracing the necklace's outline. "The meridian ring marked you as mine. This gold-and-sapphire necklace will mark you a great lady of the realm and make you a part of this court."

There was something in his tone, some shadow in

his eyes when he said those last words that caught Lilliane's attention. Troubled anew, she studied his face more closely. "Is that all that is necessary at court, a display of wealth?"

For a moment he seemed not to have heard her. "Wealth is helpful," he finally answered. "A keen, observing mind is better. But to have knowledge—" He smiled grimly. "To have knowledge is to have true power at court."

He would elaborate no further but drew her without warning into a hard embrace, kissing her mouth fiercely until her senses were reeling. Then he abruptly placed her hand upon his arm and led her into the state banqueting hall.

Lilliane hardly remembered their entrance, for his unexpected kiss had left her quite faint. Added to that was his strange behavior and troubling moods. In the course of one afternoon she had gone from exhilarated to annoyed to frustrated and angry, all due to him. Now she was no longer angry but she was more bewildered than ever. Still, she consoled herself with the thought that he did seem to care something for her. After all, he'd brought her here with him, and now he'd given her this fabulous necklace.

She fingered the golden prize around her neck, then lifted her chin a notch and looked around the well-attended chamber. London was going to be difficult, she realized. Unconsciously she clasped Corbett's arm tighter. She would just try to behave as Corbett had instructed, and perhaps by the time they left he would be more trusting of her.

With that thought warming her she forced a smile and began to examine the place more closely.

The White Tower was well known throughout England, for it had been the first mark William I had made on the land he had so newly wrested from Saxon domain. Alternately called the Conqueror's Tower and the Palantine, it was now generally referred to as the White Tower although little remained of its whitewashing. But by any name it was still the heart of English law, and Lilliane respected that fact. Despite Corbett's clear dislike—and ill-disguised disdain—of the place, she knew that even he did not underestimate the cumulative powers vested in the Tower.

In truth, she was surprised at the smallness of the banqueting hall. Orrick's great hall came near to matching it in length and breadth, for they were both of the old Norman manner of construction. Certainly the newer cathedrals she'd seen from afar almost dwarfed this chamber.

But nonetheless, she was properly impressed. The intricately knotted tapestries depicting England's grand history, countless candles scented and flickering, and enormous rugs stretched over the floors lent true majesty to the otherwise simple space. The myriad of finely clothed lords and ladies moving easily from one cluster of people to another made her hesitate once more.

As if he understood her feelings, Corbett murmured quiet reassurance. "They are no more than you, my lady wife: entitled by rank or birth or marriage to enter this place. And no more likely to have lasting impact than you or I," he added more dryly.

Then it was time for her to begin her role as wife to an important lord of the realm. As she'd been prepared by her mother, Lilliane met her task with that proper mix of feminine reserve and noble hauteur. She was grateful to stay on her husband's arm as he made his way through the throng greeting his acquaintances on all sides. She was introduced to one and all, suffering alternately their curious scrutiny or their careful assessment.

The men were most avid in their gazes, but few pursued their interest so far as to draw her into private conversation. Corbett's dark gaze forbade it. With the few ladies he was more lenient, allowing her to chat briefly with Lady Katherine of Hereford and Lady Elizabeth of Littleton. But even still, she sensed his restlessness. His eyes scanned the assembled group constantly. Lilliane almost thought he searched for someone. Then they were approached by a broad, beaming fellow.

"Ho, young Corbett! What is this I hear? You've brought a wife to court? Why, she needs be truly saintly to agree to such a union!"

Lilliane's wary surprise changed swiftly to relief when she saw the genuine smile of pleasure that lighted Corbett's face.

"Gavin!" He grinned at Lilliane. "Do not be alarmed at his noise nor taken in by his charm." Then he belied his words by embracing the older man heartily. "This is my godfather, Lily. Lord Gavin of Durmond. Gavin, I give you my wife, Lady Lilliane of Orrick."

"Yes, the lady Lilliane. Barton's child."

"You knew my father?" Lilliane exclaimed, already liking the man. Despite his muscular build he looked like an aging cherub, all plump cheeks and twinkling blue eyes.

"Indeed, Barton was fostered in my father's household. I was but a lad, too young yet to participate in the manly arts he learned at Durmond. But we remained fast friends through the years. It brings me much happiness to hear that his fortune has been joined with my own godchild's." Then his smile faded. "I only wish he could have lived long enough to see a grandchild of the union."

"Thank you, Lord Gavin," Lilliane responded warmly. "It does me good to know he is as much missed by his friends as by his family."

"He will be sorely missed at the council. Although I hear"—and here he cocked one eyebrow at Corbett —"I hear your husband is likely to be as noisy and belligerent a member as ever your father was."

Corbett shrugged, his good humor not strained by his godfather's jibe. "I'll not hesitate to speak when it is a matter of importance," he conceded. "But my pretty wife is not interested in matters of state."

There was a note in his voice, almost as if he were warning Gavin not to speak too freely. The two men's eyes met and Lilliane's smile faded at her husband's subtle lack of faith in her. But that emotion was short-lived as Corbett suddenly went very still. Had she not had her hand on his arm, she would never have recognized his rigid stance. She looked up in alarm to see him staring at a tall, gaunt man just entering the hall. There was a strange look on Corbett's face. His expression was fierce yet his eyes were dark and troubled, even vulnerable. Without thinking Lilliane blurted out, "Who is that?"

It was Gavin who answered. "Your brother-in-law is here. Have you not met him before?"

"We married without much fanfare," Corbett answered curtly. "Hughe was not forewarned. It appears now that I must make amends. You will excuse us, of course?"

Lilliane was sorry to leave Gavin's pleasant company as much for Corbett's sake as her own. All Corbett's enjoyment of the company had fled, and she almost dreaded meeting the man who clearly troubled him so.

There was little to note in their approach to Hughe, nor anything meriting remark in the polite greetings that passed between the two men as Lilliane was introduced to Corbett's older brother. It even appeared to Lilliane that Hughe of Colchester did not note his younger brother's wariness. But then she realized it was because Hughe was examining her with an interest she found disturbing.

"So, Orrick's daughter is fallen into Colchester hands." His narrow eyes flicked rapidly over her with a scrutiny that made her skin crawl. "I'm sure Father will forgive you mingling our blood with that of his murderer, given the wisdom of linking our holdings to Orrick." He turned his gaze to Corbett, dismissing her presence entirely. "Have you seen Charles of Harwick yet? He and his brother Roger wanted a word with you."

Lilliane had to choke down her rage. Hughe of Colchester was all she'd been led to expect: a hard-hearted, mean-spirited man, cruel to all he did not need to fear. But her anger was directed more at Corbett than at Hughe, for she could not believe he would take this slighting of his wife so easily. Hurt and angry, she tried to catch Corbett's eye, but his interest was clearly focused on his brother.

In frustration she would have pulled her hand from his arm, but he placed his other palm firmly upon it and would not let her go. Had she been at her own home she would not have let that stop her, but here, in these strange and impressive surroundings, she was hesitant to be so bold. Angry and humiliated, she resigned herself to remaining at her husband's side. But her growing faith in him was sorely shaken.

As she watched the men converse, Lilliane could not understand Corbett's almost solicitous attitude toward this man—this brother—whom she was so certain he disliked. Then it struck her that perhaps he distrusted Hughe. Perhaps Hughe was one of the "vultures" Corbett had referred to with such disgust but with whom he still must associate for business purposes.

"Have you just arrived then?" Hughe's eyes slid over the crowd as he maintained polite but disinterested conversation with his brother.

"This afternoon," Corbett said tensely. "I have goods arrived at the docks that I am eager to check."

"Goods? Riches from Turkey, no doubt?"

Hughe's interest was obviously piqued, but no less than Lilliane's. This was the first she'd heard of such goods. Could he possess even more than the caravan of riches he'd already brought to Orrick? Her fingers sought the fabulous necklace he'd given her. Or perhaps, she thought, he said that only to distract Hughe from his actual purpose in London, whatever that might be.

Corbett shrugged nonchalantly. "I traveled many places. I sent back many things."

"Do you hear aught of King Edward?" Hughe asked casually. "Does he ever plan to return to England?"

Lilliane felt the sudden stiffening of Corbett's arm

beneath her hand. But when she looked at him he seemed only marginally interested in the question. "Eventually he must," he replied offhandedly.

Yet she knew there was nothing offhanded in Corbett's loyalty to his king. He was not dubbed the king's Bird of Prey for nothing. If he feigned indifference there must be a reason. And clearly, his brother was not someone he was inclined to trust.

Though it was little real knowledge and left much still open to speculation, Lilliane took some comfort in it and vowed to be more understanding of her husband's secretiveness about his comings and goings. But someday he would learn that she *was* worthy of his trust.

Just then they were joined by two other men to whom she was introduced. Charles and Roger of Harwick were twin brothers, little older than she was. Slender of build, they both had elfin faces that alternately looked ridiculously young or amazingly mature.

"We're glad you're back." Roger clasped Corbett's hand eagerly.

"But irate not to have received an invitation to your wedding," Charles joined in.

"It was hastily done," Corbett replied, but the quick glance he gave Lilliane was cautionary.

"Nevertheless, you must make reparation," one of the pair cut in.

"Yes," the other quipped. "You owe all of your friends a celebration. At your expense, of course."

"Perhaps Corbett will sponsor the Christ's Mass and celebrations at Orrick this year," Hughe suggested smoothly.

It was said quite casually, as if an idea of the moment. Yet Lilliane sensed there was some motive behind the seemingly harmless suggestion. She felt also Corbett's slight tensing and knew he sensed the same thing.

Charles and Roger immediately warmed to the idea and clamored for Corbett's consent. When he finally agreed, however, Lilliane was struck with the certain knowledge that for some reason, Corbett was more pleased with the idea than any of the others. She hardly understood his strange reaction, but she was certain it was tied somehow to his distrust of his brother. Corbett planned something, but what she could not fathom. Nonetheless, she much preferred that he—and therefore Orrick—be in command of the situation, and not the other way around.

From there the evening progressed well enough. Corbett's mood was oddly light as he renewed friendships with more people than she could later remember. He was unfailingly courteous to her, never letting the conversation become too obscure or political. She would have suspected that it was done more from mistrust of her than consideration had his mood not been so high. As it was, she could not fault his behavior at all.

Lilliane was drooping with exhaustion by the time they departed the banqueting hall. She had no concept of the hour for, although the many candles and torches had burned low, an army of servants had been on hand, constantly refreshing the lights so that the gathering might linger until dawn if any were so inclined.

"So, what tales shall you tell of London when we return to Orrick?" Corbett asked as they made their weary way up the stairs of the king's palace.

Lilliane covered a yawn with one hand, then rested even more heavily on his sturdy arm. "I've seen very little, but what I've seen is most strange."

Corbett chuckled. "And what was it you found so strange?"

"Do you not think it strange that at such a festive gathering there was no call to sup? Why, whoever heard of a meal where one eats from trays carried about by servants, meanwhile never pausing in the endless talk? And when one tires of one group, one progresses on to another."

At that Corbett laughed out loud. "This was no meal we attended, my little country wife."

Lilliane's brow creased as she looked into his smiling face. "Then . . . then why did I dress in my finest—why did all the women dress so well—if not to dine in the banqueting hall of the White Tower?"

"That was actually an informal session, my sweet innocent. And the talk, while often of no consequence, was at other times of paramount importance."

Lilliane was silenced completely by such an astounding revelation. Certainly her perception of a meeting of the council was far different from the casual conversation and erratic circulation that had gone on this evening. It was not until they entered their chamber that she spoke again.

"If that is so, then great matters of state might have been decided just beyond my shoulder."

"Or even under your pretty little nose."

Lilliane turned her wide amber stare on him. "Was your acceptance of Hughe's suggestion for the Christ's Mass feast one of those matters?"

Corbett's abrupt silence confirmed her suspicions

despite his tardy response. "It was a good suggestion and will go far in settling the discord in Windermere Fold."

She smiled softly. "I cannot disagree with you."

"I would have made the suggestion myself eventually," he insisted.

"That would have been most wise of you, my lord."

Corbett sent her a dark look. "Do you mock me, wife? Are you angry that I did not consult you on this decision and so try to infuriate me now?"

"I am not angry. Nor do I mean to infuriate you by going along with your plans so agreeably." Lilliane turned away from him. She was pleased to have read him so well, even if she did not yet know why he wanted this gathering at Orrick. "Now, where is my maid?"

Without warning she was swept up into Corbett's arms, then spun around until she felt dizzy and clung to his neck.

"You've no need of a maid. I'm quite able to undress my wife without someone else's help."

Lilliane had to lean against him for support as he lowered her to her feet. "Oh! But that is not seemly," she protested, her head still spinning. "You don't realize how servants talk. Why, what shall be the gossip in the morning—"

Corbett's lips were warm against her neck and his breath hot in her ear when he answered. "Come morning the maids shall twitter and talk of how enamored Lord Corbett is of his new bride. By noon the ladies shall be sending you sorrowful looks for the burden you bear of your own husband's lustful attention."

He moved his mouth to hers and slid his tongue

seductively along the tender edge of her lips. "But come the council meeting in the afternoon, I shall have the congratulations—and the envy—of every man here. For I have my beautiful wife to myself with no complaints from her."

Lilliane opened her mouth to Corbett's seductive lips, reveling in the sensuous pleasure of his heady kiss. It was true, she thought before she succumbed completely to his rising passion and her own. They would hear no complaints from her.

16

❦

One afternoon, Lilliane sat in a third-floor solar, surrounded by a bevy of court ladies. The chamber was warm, made so by the close company as much as by the fire that blazed so brightly in the stone hearth. Conversation buzzed, laughter burst forth often, and gossip passed back and forth discreetly between heads bent near. Yet Lilliane felt no satisfaction in the amiable setting.

In the eight days they'd been in London, she'd been accepted well enough into court society. She knew now who was who, who was aligned with whom, and who detested whom despite every appearance of friendship. Corbett had thought to keep her innocent of such knowledge, but even he had been surprised at the information to be had through the other women.

Now as Lilliane thought of Corbett and his stern admonition to her not to stir from the king's palace for any reason while he was gone, she was frustrated anew. Restless, she put down the fine linen headrail she was applying a pattern of silken knots to and rose from the bench she shared with Lady Elizabeth. Her lips were pursed in displeasure as she picked her way across the jewel-toned Bijar rug, littered now with women reclining on great embroidered cushions. She leaned into a deeply recessed window and cleared a spot on the damp window glass.

Outside the sun shone despite the chill of the early December weather, and she longed more than ever to be away from the stuffy solar. Whether it was the close atmosphere or the company or the enforced lethargy she detested most she could not decide. But she knew that if she did not get out to walk, or ride, or whatever, she would surely scream.

The thought of Corbett's anger should he learn of her disobedience caused her to hesitate. But then she became even more determined to get outside. After all, he went to and fro quite freely. Why shouldn't she, a woman accustomed to the outdoors and the freedom to roam the countryside at will? Why shouldn't she be allowed at least some brief reprieve from the closeness of castle life?

Convinced, she quietly slipped from the room and hurried down the much chillier hallway. Besides, she rationalized as she made good her escape, Corbett would never know. He had gone to see about some ship and would be away until the evening. She would be back long before then, and who would notice her absence, let alone mention it to him?

When she stepped into the sunshine, Lilliane felt an enormous relief. It was bitterly cold despite the deceptive sunshine, but she was dressed in a neat caddis work gown, a warm sarzil mantle, and a knitted woolen hood. She paused once she'd crossed the bridge and approached the gardens along the river, and took a deep breath of air.

The smells were so different here, she thought. No pungent forest odors or fresh scent of mountains. In

London the smell of smoke from a thousand hearths drowned out all the other smells. Although it was not truly unpleasant, she still could not help but miss Orrick. Magda would have the household tasks well in hand by now. Bread would be baking; a large pig or hind would be turning upon the spit. Or perhaps she had a stew bubbling in the big iron pot. Ferga would be with little Elyse, seeing to the tiny baby's every need. Thomas . . . Thomas, she realized, would be dreadfully lost now that her father was gone. Oh, how she wished she could be with him right now.

Lilliane walked slowly along the gravel path until she came to a wooden garden bench. In spring it faced a green lawn flanked with rose vines, but now it looked over a faded and desolate yard. With a heavy sigh she sat down and stared unseeingly at the barren garden.

A part of her must have heard the crunch of approaching footsteps, but it wasn't until a familiar voice hailed her that her sad thoughts were brought up short.

"Why, Lilliane, you must be half to frozen!" Before she could respond, William had seated himself next to her and took her chilled hands between his own gloved palms.

"Whatever are you doing out here alone without even a maid or a page to see to your needs?" he admonished.

It occurred to her that Corbett would be terribly displeased to find William in London, but for the moment, at least, she was happy to see a familiar face. "I've no needs to be seen to." She laughed, her mood lifting somewhat. "But tell me, what brings you to London?"

"I've business matters that need my attention," he answered noncommittally. Then he squeezed her hands more tightly. "But I would hear more about you. Have you enjoyed court? It appears your new husband neglects you already."

"Corbett does not neglect me," Lilliane stated quite firmly. "He also has business matters to attend. Besides, he knows I am safe here within the reach of the royal guards."

For a moment William did not reply. His blue eyes seemed to take in every aspect of her appearance, although she could not have defined his expression. At once wistful and cunning, she knew his eyes hid a myriad of confusing emotions.

But her own emotions were not confused any longer. She knew her loyalty must be with her husband; certainly her heart was beginning to be well attached to him. William must banish thoughts of any feeling save friendship between the two of them now.

Lilliane was set on making him understand just that when he released her hands and looked at her most seriously. "Yes. You are safe enough here, Lilliane. But even within the royal residence there are those who may not be trusted. I have no doubt your husband is concerned with your safety. I hope, however, that my equal concern will not be misinterpreted by him. Nor by you."

She was much relieved by his conciliatory little speech. "Oh, William. I am grateful for your concern. Never think I am not. It has been so difficult for me when the two men I care most deeply for are at such odds with one another."

"He is a suspicious man. In that he is much like his brother."

"Yes. He's very jealous," she admitted. "But although I know very little of Hughe, I see few similiarities between the two of them. Are you well acquainted with the family of Colchester?"

William leaned back. "Their father was an impossible taskmaster. But although he and Hughe disagreed on many things, Hughe held his tongue. Once Colchester was his, however, he changed everything. Corbett, as do most second sons, always sought his father's approval. He would be the best warrior, the best at his letters, the first to volunteer for a task." William grinned mockingly. "My own brother Albert was much the same. As if he might at least gain a larger portion from my father by winning his affection, for the inheritance was already mine. So it was with Hughe and Corbett. But now that Corbett is settled at Orrick, I think Hughe is none too pleased." William's gaze narrowed thoughtfully. "Does Corbett speak of his brother or of Colchester?"

Lilliane hesitated. She had been much concerned by Corbett's close attention to all of his brother's affairs. Although he was subtle in his observations, and he never brought Hughe's name up in conversation, she knew somehow that it was Hughe's presence in London that had prompted their journey. Still, it would be wrong of her to reveal such thoughts.

"He talks fondly of Colchester," she finally replied. "But he and his brother have only infrequent contact. Do you see Hughe often?" she added, trying to steer the conversation away from Corbett.

"We supped just last night—" William stopped abruptly, then he slowly continued in a more off-hand manner. "No doubt we may see him again this very evening in the council chambers."

"No doubt," she agreed. Then she stood up and pulled her mantle closer about her shoulders. "My, but it is colder than ever."

With that hint William stood up as well. He did not notice the neatly folded parchment that fell from his girdle, but Lilliane did. When she stooped to retrieve it for him, she saw that the paper bore the symbols of Normandy. She could not help but remark on it.

"You have lost this letter, William. Do you correspond with Normandy now? Have you business concerns so very far away?"

At the surprised respect on her face, William beamed. "Not business in the most common sense. But I do hear regularly from my cousin in the king's entourage."

"Oh, and how does the king? When shall he return?" she asked eagerly. She'd never met old King Henry, but she had high hopes now of meeting King Edward some day. She noticed the small pleased smile that lifted William's lips at her questions, but she did not place any great importance on it.

"Actually, I believe he does rather poorly. His health is tenuous at best." When her eyes widened in concern, however, he added, "But my cousin is his physician, and he will no doubt see Edward well tended. Now tell me how you've spent your time in London."

Lilliane would rather have heard news of Orrick, which she missed sorely. But she realized that if she spent too much time with William, Corbett would surely hear of it. Besides, she thought, perhaps William's new attitude would appease her husband. If she could just get the two men to discuss Orrick or any other neutral topic in a noncombative mood.

Nonetheless, as William escorted her back within the walled compound, she decided it would be wisest for her not to mention their brief, accidental meeting. Corbett was too suspicious and jealous. No need for her to fan such flames further.

To Lilliane's relief, Corbett was in a most jubilant mood when he returned from the docks. She had just finished her bath and was dressed only in her light kirtle when he entered the chamber. On seeing her he dropped his leather satchel and leaned against the stout door frame.

"Ah, my lovely Lily. What a feast you are for the eyes." A wolfish light gleamed in those very eyes then and an appreciative grin spead across his face.

Lilliane blushed a pretty pink at his words, for she was still not accustomed to such casual intimacy between them, even in their private chambers. "I-I'm sorry I am so late in dressing . . ." She signaled to the silent maid who quickly helped her step into a rich, peach-hued gown of Tartaryn linen. Corbett did not voice objection as she made herself presentable, and Lilliane was dismayed by the small prick of disappointment this roused in her. Did she expect him to seduce her every time they were alone? Why, she was becoming quite wanton in the desire she felt for her virile husband! There was certainly a better time for what she wanted of him than such an early hour as this!

Still, no amount of self-berating could stifle the sweet longing she felt for him so long as he was watching her with that dark, unsettling gaze of his. It was only when she removed her precious necklace from its velvet purse that he waved the maid from the room. Then he approached Lilliane.

"You smell as delicious as you look," he murmured as he gently pushed her long, thick hair aside. When he fastened the jewels at her neck, every touch of his fingers sent heated tingles shooting through her.

"I hate having to share you with anyone tonight," he added. Then he pressed a sensuous kiss to the nape of her neck.

"Must we go to the council chambers tonight?" Lilliane breathed as she let herself sway against his solid form. For a moment she thought he might agree with her, for he gathered her in his powerful arms as if he would never let her go. Then she felt his slow sigh.

"Tonight I must be there." Then, at her own sigh of disappointment, he added, "But if all goes well tonight, tomorrow we shall depart for Orrick."

Lilliane's complete delight with that news carried her happily through the evening. If anyone had doubted the contented state of affairs between Lord Corbett and his exquisite wife, this night convinced them otherwise. He was never far from her side, though he spoke with any number of lords during the long evening hours. Her merry laugh was always in his ear, her lilting voice ever within his conscious awareness though he may have addressed another. His eyes constantly wandered toward her.

For Lilliane's part, she did not stray far from Corbett, though she shared conversation with lords and ladies alike. She felt as if she were floating with happiness, and nothing would stifle that lovely feeling.

When she had a few moments to herself, she tried to understand her strange jubilance. Certainly she was happy they would be departing for Orrick on the morrow. She'd longed for that almost since they'd arrived in London. It was odd, though, that on the eve of her departure she was finally enjoying one of these normally difficult evenings.

Perhaps she was enjoying herself simply because she was happy, she thought. But it was more than their imminent departure that had settled this effervescent mood upon her. Once more her eyes sought Corbett, only to find his turbulent gaze already on her. He was standing a little distance from her, speaking to the archbishop of York. Yet despite the other man's animated discourse, Lilliane knew Corbett's thoughts were on her. That knowledge sent a sweet, secret thrill through her. Who would have thought she could ever be this happy with him? For a moment her eyes misted as she recalled how adamantly her dear father had stood by his decision for the two of them to wed. She had fought him every step of the way, yet if she had been successful in her flight to Burgram Abbey that terrible night, where would she be now?

Being courted by William.

It was an abrupt realization, and a distasteful one as well. Her other choice would have been to spend the balance of her days at the abbey or as the spinster sister under the watchful eye of her brother-in-law Aldis, which was equally unpalatable. With a tiny shudder she sent a grateful prayer aloft. Then her eyes refocused on Corbett and her lips curved in a contented smile. At once he ended his conversation with the mighty archbishop and crossed to her side.

"You must cease such enticement," he murmured for her ears only.

Lilliane laughed at that. "Am I enticing you, then? I thought I was merely gazing at my husband. Would you prefer that I did not?"

"What I would prefer . . ." His thumb ran tenderly down the slope of her cheek then lightly caressed her lower lip. It was only with great effort that he forced his hand away from her. "What I would prefer," he whispered huskily, "is to know what thoughts . . . what emotions you hide behind those innocent amber eyes."

For a moment she considered his words, pondering also just what those emotions were. Then in a sudden moment of clarity she knew.

She loved him.

It was not just respect. Nor desire. It was far more intense than either of those emotions, and the very knowledge left her awestruck. At some point in their difficult, turbulent marriage she had fallen deeply and completely in love with her husband.

It was something she'd never expected, and the truth of it was almost too incredible to believe. *She loved him.*

But how was she to reveal such emotions to a man whose own feelings were an enigma to her? For a moment longer she stared into his smoky gray eyes before she lowered her gaze in confusion. She was far too transparent with her feelings while he hid everything too well.

"I am happy," she admitted a little breathlessly. Then she bravely looked back up at him. "Aren't you?"

"Yes."

One short sweet word and yet it meant more to Lilliane than even she could have expected. He was happy with her. She had thought as much, but his easy admission was welcome confirmation. She could not speak for the giddy emotions that filled her. But her tremulous smile and glistening eyes revealed her inner feelings.

Clearly pleased, Corbett bent near and whispered softly, "How tempting you look, my Lily. It takes all my willpower to avoid whisking you up those stairs right this moment to a more private place."

"You have my permission," she murmured without thinking. They were bold words, she knew. And yet when she saw the hot glow that leapt in Corbett's eyes, she would not take them back.

Corbett groaned low in his throat, then took a deep breath. "I've one more matter to attend, then nothing shall keep me from taking you in my arms and doing just that."

"Corbett!" She gasped, convinced by his lusty expression that he truly would not hesitate to be so bold, even in front of this company. "You must not think to really do such a thing!"

"Ah, but you have tempted me beyond any man's endurance."

"Oh!" Lilliane was caught between delicious anticipation and a very real fear that he might truly do as he said. "You would not humiliate me so," she said, taking a cautionary step backward.

"Humiliate you? I would hardly call it that. Why, every man here envies me my beautiful wife. And there's not a woman at court who wouldn't turn

green with envy to be so desired by her own husband."

At this Lilliane had to laugh. Her eyes were dancing as she faced her husband's wicked tormenting.
Two could play at this game, however.

"I shall leave here this very minute, then. While
you continue your boring discourse with the archbishop or the earl of Gloucester, or whoever else you
must see, I shall be across the green, upstairs in our
chamber."

Corbett took a step toward her, but she stepped
backward as he came, and all the while she taunted
him. "While you speak of sheep and wool, I shall be
letting my hair down, brushing it loose over my
shoulders." Her voice grew more husky. "And while
you discuss ships and soldiers, I shall be unlacing my
gown and stepping out of it."

Her eyes sparkled with delight for Corbett's face
was a study in frustration as he stalked her step by
step across the crowded hall. "And while you worry
over the king's poor health, I shall slip into our bed.
If you stay away too long, though, I shall fall asleep."

"The king's poor health?" Corbett drew up in surprise. "What do you know of such things?"

She did not hear his words, however, for she had
inadvertently backed into a stout older gentleman.
Nor did she see the suspicious expression her final
words had brought to Corbett's face, because she was
making her apologies to the other man. When she
finally did smile back at her husband before escaping up the stairs she only saw him watching her, his
face frowning, his eyes dark. She was not aware that
his gaze remained fixed and staring long after she'd
disappeared from his view.

* * *

It was almost midday before they departed the tower. Lilliane had awakened quite late to find Corbett already gone to prepare for their departure. She had no time for disappointment, however, for the maid was immediately at her side, urging her to rise and prepare herself for the day. She did not even see Corbett until she had descended to the Tower Green where the horses had been brought around. Then the very sight of his tall, muscular form brought vivid memories of the previous night rushing back.

He had not come to her until late, much to her frustration. But for all that he'd made her wait, he had been most conscientious in his attentions to her.

There had been no playfulness in his lovemaking despite the teasing that had preceded it. He had, in contrast, been strangely serious, seemingly bent on bringing her every pleasure almost to the neglect of his own enjoyment. It had been intense and silent, and they had both been drained when their mutual culmination had come. It was as if Corbett had been trying somehow to absorb her, mind, body, and soul. Afterward he had held her close against him all through the night.

Now, surrounded by his men and the various servants who loaded the animals, he displayed no signs of affection—or intimacy—toward her. But Lilliane was beginning to read him a little better, and she knew his gaze, though brief, was not wanting in attention toward her. She waited patiently beside her dappled palfrey as he saw to the last details of their departure. It was only then he approached her with a tonsured friar in tow.

"Brother Claverie will give us a blessing for our

journey," Corbett announced. He gave her no greeting, but his eyes seemed to drink her in so avidly that she had to fight down a blush. She was relieved to bow her head dutifully as the stout friar gave his longwinded words of safe journey. They prayed for fair weather, good roads, safety from attack, and as always, the king's good health.

As the friar waddled away from them, however, Corbett murmured quietly. "Yes, we should all pray devoutly for the king's good health."

"Is he truly so very ill, then?"

"Why do you think he's ill?" Corbett replied as he led her to her horse. "Who put such an idea in your head?"

For a moment Lilliane faltered. She'd heard it from William, of course. But he'd not been present in the council chambers last night, and it seemed pointless, now that they were leaving London, to bring his name up. "I'm . . . I'm not really sure who mentioned it to me. Perhaps I overheard some conversation . . ." She waved her hand airily. "With everyone I've met here it's a wonder I can recall their names, let alone who revealed what particular bit of gossip."

"Yes, it is quite easy to forget who says what . . . and whose word may be trusted in this place," Corbett agreed.

There was an odd note in his voice, and for a moment Lilliane feared he might not believe her. To her anxious eyes, however, he seemed to accept her explanation well enough. She was extremely relieved when he saw her properly seated, then mounted his own steed. She was only too happy to be leaving London, and she hoped her presence there would not be required for quite some time.

The day proved fair enough albeit chilly with a brisk breeze blowing. The land lay still and fallow, the crops long reaped, the new planting months away. Shepherds husbanding their sheep roamed the wide meadows as their woolly charges searched for diminishing forage. Woodcutters with their oxcarts worked deep in the woods, taking full advantage of the lenient weather before the next winter storm struck. Their children, gathering twigs and branches for kindling, ran excitedly toward the road when they saw the caravan of knights pass by. Their shyness made them hang back behind the trunks and bushes until they saw Lilliane's smile and friendly wave. Then they scampered forward like kittens, tumbling and running and elbowing one another aside for a better view of the fine lady and fierce knights.

Corbett was quiet during the ride, seemingly sunk in his thoughts. Lilliane was still feeling guilty about her small lie to him, and she was almost relieved not to have to face him any further.

They stopped in a meadow just beyond St. Albans for a light repast then continued on, planning to make Woburn by nightfall. As the afternoon wore on, clouds began to gather in the west. Although rain did not threaten, the wind grew more biting and dusk seemed to descend more quickly than usual.

They were traveling a narrow section of road that wandered through the forests. Lilliane recalled that there was an ancient stone bridge over a stream just beyond the curve in the road. Then not too much farther to the abbey at Woburn. Her mind was dwelling on the warm meal and soft bed waiting for her when she was startled by shouting and a loud commotion behind her.

It happened so quickly she hardly realized it. She heard Corbett's bellow "To arms! To arms!" Then the reins were suddenly snatched from her hands and she was surrounded by knights. A brawny hand forced her to bend low over the frightened palfrey's neck, and in the crush of horses and knees and raised shields she could see nothing at all.

"Stay low, milady! Keep down!" someone ordered. But Lilliane was too terrified to obey. She was safe enough, she sensed, surrounded by guards as she was. But Corbett was not among them. His voice, clear and loud, could be heard shouting curt instructions. Then even that was drowned out in the ringing clang of metal on metal—blade upon blade, mace upon shield. In vain she struggled to see him, to make sure he was safe. But all she could see was a melee of men on horseback. Dust obscured them beyond recognition so that any one of them might have been either friend of foe.

Then she saw him, tall and awe-inspiring as he fought in the thick of the battle. In one hand he swung his long steel blade with wicked accuracy, while the other wielded his shield almost as effectively as a weapon. One armored horseman came upon him broadside, but before the man could strike, Corbett's huge war-horse put a mighty shoulder into the other steed's chest. With one deadly swipe Corbett severed the unbalanced man's arm at the shoulder and the screaming fellow fell beneath the destrier's hooves.

At once there was another foul attack on Corbett's

back. But like a devil who sees behind as well as forward, Corbett hunched suddenly to the left, then cut back with his sword. There was a sudden cry of agony, but it was quickly lost in the curses and grunts and other cries of pain.

Lilliane was too stunned to be truly frightened. It was happening almost too quickly to be real, and she stared at the awful scene before her more with amazement than any other emotion. Her eyes could not break away from her husband as he made short shrift of his would-be assassins. Like a machine trained only for war, he cut down his opponents while his men rallied around him.

It was only when three of the enemy knights galloped off, followed by four riderless horses, that Lilliane was able to take a breath. Her heart was pounding in her ears and her nails had cut her palms, so tightly had she clenched her hands.

But that did not matter, for Corbett had survived!

"Corbett!" she cried, her voice only a dry, cracked whisper.

Yet he turned to look at her as if somehow he'd heard. His expression was frightening in its fierceness. The light of battle had not yet died in his eyes, and she shivered at the dark emotions she saw there. If she'd ever wondered why he was called the king's Bird of Prey, she now knew the answer. He was a fierce and deadly warrior, a man never to be taken lightly.

And yet his loyalty was something to treasure.

She would have gone to him then, but at a quick gesture from him she felt her mount being turned. Then, as one man, the guard that hemmed her in so tightly made off toward Woburn Abbey.

17

Corbett drew off his heavy traveling birrus and flung it on the floor.

Sir Dunn watched his lord's restless pacing, but he wisely held his words. Instead, he poured two large tankards of ale and silently handed one to Corbett.

Corbett wiped his forehead with the back of his hand, took the tankard, and drained it in one long pull. It was only then that he turned his troubled gaze on his friend. "Things are beginning to move quickly now."

"Then you have the proof the king requires?"

"I will soon. I've invited all the actors in this farce to celebrate Christ's Mass at Orrick. We will flush them out once and for all—"

" 'Twould be easier by far if they were simply to meet with an 'accident,' " Dunn said with a grunt. "Then there would be no traitors left to worry about."

"That might have been King Henry's way," Corbett retorted. "But Edward would rather they answer to the law of the kingdom. His revenge, when it comes, will nonetheless be hard, but it will also be within the limits of the law."

"Then it seems we will be forced to stomach this 'festive' gathering and ferret out the rat."

"They're getting worried." Corbett began to pace the low-ceilinged hall where his knights were housed. "We were attacked just hours out of London."

"What! By all that is holy! Who was it?"

Corbett shrugged. "A band of knights errant. They had been hired by an intermediary, so far as we can tell from the dying words of one of them. We could not prove who actually planned the attack."

"But you have your suspicions," Dunn prompted.

At this Corbett grew quiet, and once again he rubbed the ridged scar on his brow. "Aye, I have my suspicions. The web is tightening. The same ones who would see Edward dead have no use for me either. There is much gossip and speculation in London about the king's lengthy delay in Normandy. But we kept the fact that he was poisoned out of common knowledge. Only his most trusted advisors knew of it at all."

"He yet lives?" Dunn asked anxiously.

"Eleanor is with him and he grows stronger daily. But there is a leak somewhere." Corbett paused then and turned a cynical gaze on Dunn. "I heard from my own wife about the king's illness."

"From your wife!" Dunn's thick blond brows lowered in confusion. "How did such vital information slip into the women's gossip?"

"I hardly think she heard such secret news from the women." Corbett paused once more and stared unseeingly at the pitted stone wall. "The king's physician, Richard of Gorham, is cousin to Sir William of Dearne. Richard is suspect in the attempt on Edward's life, although he is unaware of it. And I've determined already that he corresponds frequently with his cousin."

"William is no longer at Orrick," Dunn put in, his brow creased now with worry. "He left not three days after you did."

"And he turned up in London. Only he kept well out of my way. I learned, however, that he sought out Lilliane."

"Then it was from him that she learned of the poisoning!"

Corbett moved restlessly across the room. He fingered a heavy wool window hanging before finally turning back to his friend. "She made no mention of poison."

"That would very nearly be a confession of guilt." Dunn snorted. "She must be exceedingly stupid even to let on she knew anything of Edward's doings. But then few women have the sense to curb their prattling tongues. William is a fool to reveal such a thing to her."

He stopped abruptly as another thought occurred to him. "Or maybe it is more than that. Perhaps she is a part of the plot. After all, Orrick stands squarely in the midst of these dissenting northern shires."

"I have no reason to suspect her of treason."

"If not treason, then perhaps—" Dunn stopped at the angry glare Corbett sent him. "You cannot afford any foolish loyalties. You already know that William is involved. And perhaps even your brother."

"Aye, William is involved. And he is a fool, which is our good fortune. It only remains for us to prove his guilt and that of his accomplices."

"And if those accomplices include your brother? Or your wife?" Dunn persisted.

Corbett did not answer at once. When he finally spoke his voice was grim. "Then they may expect no pity from me."

Lilliane lowered herself onto a narrow hide-covered bench and rubbed the aching small of her back. She was exhausted. She hurt all over from sitting in that wretched sidesaddle, and she wasn't sure which she wanted more: a bath or her bed.

"You smell of horses and you're caked with mud." Magda fussed as she removed Lilliane's travel-stained cloak then began unlacing her coarse woolen tunic.

"And you smell of fresh bread and . . . and baby." Lilliane smiled despite her utter weariness. "How is little Elyse? I should like to see her at once—"

"She is in her bed asleep, as you will be very soon also. Once you are bathed and fed you will go straight to bed."

Lilliane sighed, as much in contentment as anything else. How good it was to be home. Magda and Ferga had kept the household in good order, and even Thomas had been on hand to give her his familiar smile. Orrick would always be home to her, she decided. Let other, grander ladies than her have London. She would be content to stay a simple country mouse.

The trip from London had been far more arduous than their initial journey. Corbett had driven them at a furious pace. He spared neither men nor beasts in his determination to see them safely on the lands of Orrick. Lilliane's face lowered in a thoughtful frown.

Corbett had been quite distant throughout the journey, hardly spending any time with her at all. She
understood, of course, that he had been most concerned with their safety. Even now she shivered to
think how viciously he had fought off those fool-
hardy knights who had attacked them. But now they
were home and everything would be all right.

Of course there was still the dreaded Christ's Mass
festivities to get through. Why Corbett wished to entertain people he did not even like, and so soon after
her father's death, was still a mystery to her. But he'd
been in a difficult mood during their journey and
she'd not dared to question him.

At Magda's prodding she lifted her arms so that
her tunic would slip over her head.

"We've a considerable task ahead of us." Her muffled words came from beneath the smothering gown.

"Whatever it is, 'tis naught that can't wait on another day," Magda retorted as she pushed Lilliane
toward the steaming tub set before a hearty blaze.

"So you say now," Lilliane answered as she let the
woman remove the remainder of her clothes. "But it
will take every pair of hands at Orrick to see my lord
husband's will done."

"You can cajole him with just a smile."

Lilliane grinned and sank gratefully into the warm
water. "I hope that is true," she admitted. "But it is
the festivities of Christ's Mass I speak of. He has invited near a hundred guests! Think what that means,
Magda. We must entertain them on the feast of St.
Thomas, prepare gifts and a huge banquet for
Christ's Mass, then toast them anew on the feast of
St. John. If the weather precludes travel they'll linger
for the feast of the Holy Innocents—or perhaps we

may encourage them to fast that day. And of course there are those who will stay through Twelfth Night." She pursed her lips, already feeling daunted by the enormity of the task that confronted her. "We shall be fortunate if they leave before Candlemas!"

But for all Lilliane's fear of entertaining on such a grand scale, there was nonetheless a secret satisfaction in her heart. Corbett trusted her to see the castle ready and every detail of the weeks-long celebrations attended to. When at last she settled into her high bed, she had already composed a list of meals and accommodations, and decided on the forms of entertainment she must arrange.

She was determined to stay awake until Corbett joined her, but she had no sooner lain down than an overwhelming sleepiness took her. Though she fought to stay alert, her waking thoughts seemed to jumble with very odd dreams. Wait up for Corbett, she told herself. Yet the last image she recalled was of a huge black bird circling a snow-covered field where a single white flower dared lift its delicate head.

Sir Dunn watched her more closely than ever, although he tried mightily to be nonchalant about it. But Lilliane ever felt his eyes upon her. She would have complained to Corbett, but his mood was strangely tense. Sometimes she felt he also was trying to see quite through her as if what he saw on the surface was still not enough.

In every other matter things seemed well enough. The servants had been conscientious about their tasks during their lord and lady's absence, and even frail little Elyse seemed to be thriving.

And yet Lilliane knew something was amiss.

On the afternoon of their third day home, she resolved to approach Corbett about it. He was out with his fighting men, as he'd been every daylight hour since they'd returned.

Lilliane locked the kitchen storeroom, then made her way up the four short steps. At the top she felt a momentary light-headedness, but after a brief pause it passed and she continued on her way. Corbett had been most short-tempered with the poor castle guards. the crossbow men, and his own mounted knights. She should be glad, however. Better that he drilled them until he and they were exhausted than bring his poor humor to her. Still, each night when he had come to bed late he had fallen quickly into a restless sleep, and she could not completely bury her frustration.

But not tonight, she vowed. Not tonight.

For all her resolve, however, Lilliane found herself drooping with unaccustomed weariness before the evening's supper had even commenced. Despite his distracted mood, Corbett noted her obvious exhaustion.

"How do you labor that such an early hour finds you yawning?" he asked in a lighter tone than she'd heard in a week.

" 'Tis labor very unlike your own, but tiring nonetheless."

He seated her at the high table and took his place beside her. "I confess to knowing very little of how noblewomen occupy their days."

"I know even less of how you spend yours," Lilliane replied in a voice more plaintive than she'd intended.

Corbett gave her a steady, almost searching look. "I learned much of defense in the East. And of treachery." He paused. "I want Orrick to be unassailable. To do that the guards must be well trained and the castle defenses well maintained."

It occurred to her that Orrick had never had a serious enemy save Colchester. Logic deemed that threat gone now. But then, how to explain the attack on them?

"Have you . . . have we so many enemies, then?" she asked haltingly.

Again Corbett's keen gray eyes seemed to watch her most sharply though his answer was wry. "I doubt our attackers were motivated by robbery."

"You have always avoided my questions about that day," Lilliane accused, her confusion combining with her weariness to make her completely frustrated. "Have you learned who it was?"

For a moment she was certain he was going to confide in her, to tell her just who it was he suspected of so foul a deed. But then a commotion at the end of the hall drew his attention.

When Lilliane looked up she saw Sir Dunn bearing down on them, a most furious expression on his face.

"Sir William of Dearne has just arrived. He expects to be admitted and treated as a guest."

Lilliane looked at Corbett for his reaction, but he was staring at Dunn. Some understanding passed between the two men, something that excluded her completely.

"And why shouldn't he be treated as a guest?" she demanded, goaded more by their lack of trust in her than by any lingering friendship for William. "His daughter is under my care. He deserves every consideration as a guest. I suggest you keep in mind your position here, Sir Dunn. It is I who attends the guests."

She signaled two servants to see to William, but she did not stay to see her orders carried out. His arrival seemed the last straw in a long and grueling day. What little appetite she'd had was now gone. Dunn was scowling at her. Corbett was treating her most strangely, and she knew she was not up to keeping matters between her husband and William civil.

As she rose to leave Corbett caught her hand and peered at her closely. "Do you flee your duties as hostess and mistress of this table?"

From nowhere tears started in her eyes, and she had to blink them away. "The servants are well trained enough to serve the meat," she managed to say. Then she shot Dunn a disdainful look, lifted her chin a notch, and glanced back at Corbett. "Besides, I doubt my company will be much missed."

Lilliane wanted Corbett to follow her, but to her vast disappointment he did not. Once in her chamber, she dismissed the young serving girl who had hurried after her, then doused the two torches and the five candles in the heavy branched holder. In the dim light of the hearth she slipped out of her simple rust-colored kersey tunic and pulled an old woolen blanket around her shoulders.

A large sheepskin lay on the floor before the glowing fire, and with a disconsolate little sigh she settled herself upon it. Something was terribly wrong, but for the life of her she didn't know what. Before she would have thought William's presence and Corbett's jealousy to be the cause. But Corbett had been remote ever since they'd departed London. Certainly that could not be blamed on William. Then there was that strange look that had passed between Corbett and Sir Dunn.

To make matters worse, she must be ill for she was sorely lacking in both energy and good temper. It was one thing for her to snap at Sir Dunn, for he could try her patience acutely. But she had snapped at Cook twice, and even Magda had been the recipient of her bad mood.

The only one who brought her any peace, it seemed, was little Elyse. She had held and rocked the child at midday and had felt truly content to see the tiny girl's trembling yawn and then her restful sleep. For a while at least, all had seemed right with the world.

But now William was back and Corbett would surely turn even more remote.

Corbett was no less occupied with dark thoughts. He had finished the evening supper in silence, but to the cook's eyes seemed not to enjoy any aspect of the well-prepared meal. When he rose to depart the table, he signaled the others at their meal to continue. But Dunn quickly followed his retreating form.

"Where is he?" Corbett muttered when they had quit the hall.

"The puppy has gone to change from his traveling clothes." Dunn snorted in disgust.

"Puppy he may well be. But he is not to be taken lightly." Corbett hesitated as if he dreaded what he was about to say. "He spent several evenings in London in long conversations with Hughe."

Dunn peered keenly at Corbett although he did not

appear truly shocked. Then Corbett continued. "There is much evidence to support the idea that William is Hughe's dupe, not the other way around as I had hoped." When Dunn made no protest of that idea either, Corbett rubbed his scarred brow as if he were suddenly weary.

"See that William is given a squire to attend him. Someone completely trustworthy. Then keep me informed of any strange doings on our guest's part."

"Where do you go?"

Corbett glanced only briefly at his man, then turned to stare at the narrow back stairs. "I think I owe my wife a visit."

Holding Elyse was like a balm to her soul, Lilliane thought. She had abandoned her bedchamber, seeking some reprieve from her disturbing thoughts. Now, holding the warm baby, she felt some small relief. At least here was someone she could shower her love upon without fear it might be used against her. Here was someone who would love her back and be contented by her very presence.

As she eased herself into a wide settee upholstered in an exquisite silk cloth of eastern pattern, she waved Ferga away. "I'll call you when I leave. Right now I shall enjoy this solitude."

But she was not destined to have solitude. Only minutes after Ferga had left, Lilliane was disturbed by a knock on the door. When William entered, cautiously at first, then more boldly as he spied her, it was all she could do to force a smile of greeting to her lips. Still, she could not help but be warmed by this evidence of his concern for his little daughter.

"You have come to see your sweet motherless child. Well, she is strong and growing every day. Here, come nearer and look at her." She gently nudged the swaddling cloth away from the tiny chin so Elyse's face could be seen better. "I vow, she favors her beautiful mother already."

William sat beside her and peered dutifully at the sleeping child, then lifted his eyes to look at Lilliane. "Clearly she is thriving under your care."

"Actually, it is Ferga who deserves all the credit—"

"You are too modest, Lilliane. As ever." His eyes swept over her. "Do you know what a model of feminine beauty and responsibility you are? And now, seeing you holding my own child in such a sweet and loving manner." He paused—almost dramatically, it seemed. But Lilliane had lowered her face in dismay at his warm effusiveness and did not see the look that now heated his eyes.

She suspected that William longed for her still—or for what they once might have had. But she longed only for her husband. She was certain that William's eye would soon be caught by someone else. But she could not be so certain for herself. She was inextricably connected to Sir Corbett of Colchester—of Orrick —and nothing could prevent the pain she felt when he kept himself remote.

Unexpected tears stung her eyes and little Elyse's face blurred before her. Oh, Corbett, she thought. Why can you not sit beside me and tell me how you love me . . . how you long to see me cradling our own child . . . ?

"What is this? Tears?" William turned her face up to his and cupped his hands about her checks. "Oh,

Lilliane. I cannot bear it either! How I would like to steal you away from him. We could be happy together. You and me . . . and the child as well," he added.

Lilliane was too stunned by William's words, and too choked by her perverse tears, to respond at once. As if her shocked silence were tacit agreement with him, he rushed on.

"I could take you away from here. You could seek protection at the abbey . . . or somewhere else. I promise you, Lilliane, it wouldn't be long before we could be open about our love."

Angry words bubbled to her lips but before she could correct his ridiculous misconception he threw his arms around her. "Oh, I know you've been unhappy with him. But now I'll make you happy."

With a wail the baby began to squirm, protesting the uncomfortable pressure of William leaning so heavily against Lilliane.

"Oh, William, do be gentle," Lilliane protested breathlessly.

"Be gentle?"

The hard mocking words came from the low-beamed door of the nursery. Lilliane's heart seemed to drop to her feet as she recognized Corbett's voice. William jumped as if stung. But to her complete dismay, he stayed at her side and even placed his hand quite possessively around her shoulder.

"My, my. How sweetly domestic this looks. How unfortunate that this is my house. And my wife."

"The child, however, is mine," William threw back cuttingly. "And Lilliane is now mother to it."

Corbett had been leaning against the door frame,

seemingly at his ease. But at William's words he came away from it and advanced menacingly into the room. His eyes were on William but his words were meant for Lilliane.

"Leave the child and go to our chamber."

"Corbett! Please listen to me. Things are not as you imagine!"

For a moment only his dark-gray stare turned to her. Yet Lilliane knew at once that she was on very dangerous ground.

"And what is it that I imagine?" he asked her silkily. Then his face grew colder and he did not let her answer. "Put the babe in its cradle and leave us."

Lilliane clutched at Elyse as she stared into Corbett's hostile face. He was not in a mood to listen to her, and she feared he would do something drastic.

"I-I will go," she stammered. "But please, I beg you. Do not send this child away. Please, Corbett. Say you will not be so cruel—"

"But he is cruel," William cut in caustically. "He wanted Orrick and so he took it—and you—"

"And I shall not stand by and let you take it all from me!" Corbett thundered.

With that he crossed the room and flung William away from Lilliane. William landed against a low bench, toppling with it to the floor.

Meanwhile, as if William were of no further concern, Corbett rudely pulled Lilliane to her feet. "Put the child down!" he ordered, snarling furiously.

Terrified now, she complied at once. Then he dragged her to the door and bellowed for a guard.

She had no chance for protest or pleading. Elyse was swiftly handed to a passing maid who took the child away while Lilliane herself was whisked off to her chamber by a pair of her own burly guards. The last thing she heard before they rounded the corner was the ominous thud of a slamming door followed by the high-pitched wail of the crying baby.

18

"Don't ruin everything because of her."

"Since when are you William's protector? Or my wife's?" Corbett lashed out at Dunn. "Perhaps killing him now would be the best solution. No one to plot against the king. No one to tempt my pretty little wife!"

"There are others besides William involved in this treasonous plan."

A cynical smile lifted Corbett's lips. "I notice you do not go on to add that there may be others involved with my wife. But then, she has not shown herself to be free with any other man. It is only William I've ever had to worry about. It's always been William."

"That doesn't make her a traitor."

Corbett's eyes narrowed. "What is this? You, singing a new tune about Lilliane? I'd have thought you would be the first to say her treason is confirmed. There's been no love lost between you and her."

Dunn grimaced at that, but his brow was creased thoughtfully. "I'll not dispute that fact. But she's an odd one." He rubbed his bushy blond beard. "She was furious at being confined. And frightened too.

But though she raged at you and cried for the child, she said not one word regarding William."

Corbett shrugged. "Perhaps you read too much into it. Perhaps she is as guilty as he but sees no need to go down with him."

"I suppose that could be it," Dunn admitted slowly. "But nonetheless, I'm beginning to think all is not necessarily as it seems."

"There is one way to determine that," Corbett declared with a meaningful glare at the heavy door, beyond which William had been cast. "It would take very little to force the truth from him."

"But is now the time?"

Corbett's answer was a long time coming; he seemed to wrestle with his emotions. Revenge was clearly uppermost in his mind. Yet when he spoke, his words were reasonable despite the hard, caustic ring to his voice. "I'll proceed with caution. There will be no discussion of Edward or of treason. At least for now."

Corbett entered the damp chamber alone. William was languishing on a crude stone bench carved into the wall, but he jumped to his feet at the sight of his captor.

"The lord of the castle at last," William said with a sneer. "Are you so uncertain that your bidding will be done that you must see to my imprisonment yourself? Or do you delight in torturing those within your grasp?" He laughed bitterly. "How foolish I was not to steal Lilliane away from you in London."

"Indeed. Surely it was not honor that prevented you," Corbett scoffed, but his jaw was clenched in anger.

"My child was still at Orrick. Who knows what revenge the king's Bird of Prey might take if his wife were to publicly scorn him for another!"

"Lilliane would never shame me—or herself—in such a manner. And you are beneath contempt to imply it." Despite his even delivery, however, Corbett's hands had tightened into fists.

"She is a lady," William conceded. "But she is a woman first. And she does not love you."

Corbett smiled coldly. "You miss the point entirely. Love is not in question here. She is my wife. She will remain my wife. And you cannot change that. No, I think it is time for you to depart Orrick once and for all." He turned stiffly as if to leave, but William started forward furiously.

"I'll have my daughter if I should leave! I'll not have her raised in your household."

"You'll have no one. Not Lilliane, nor Elyse. 'Tis winter. That babe could not survive a trip to Dearne in such frigid air. No. She stays here—with Lilliane."

William's face was livid with rage. "She may stay with Lilliane. But you delude yourself if you believe Lilliane will long stay with you!"

Corbett glanced at the disheveled men as if he considered William's words completely inconsequential. But his eyes were alert as he goaded William further. "Lilliane knows where her duty lies. And that is with me."

"But it's her heart she'll follow. And I have that!"

"You cling to that as if it's of importance," Corbett snapped impatiently. "It's well known I did not marry her for love."

"No, you married her for Orrick and for the children she could give you. Well, consider this." William sneered, an evil smile beginning to curve his lips. "When she does bear you a child . . . it might not be yours."

For a moment the chamber was absolutely still. No one moved. No breaths were taken.

If Corbett had wanted to goad William into some careless admission, he'd clearly received more than he expected.

If William had wanted to strike Corbett a painful blow, he'd succeeded. But by his wary demeanor he obviously wondered at the cost to his own well-being.

For an eternity they stared at each other, a stunned expression on one face, a fearful expression on the other. Then without a word Corbett turned on his heel and quit the donjon, slamming the door hard behind him.

The entire castle lay in wait. Everyone knew that Lady Lilliane had been confined to her chambers and Sir William had been locked in the seldom-used donjon. No one could say precisely what had happened, but everyone knew the master was enraged. And so the gossip buzzed interminably.

Ferga was in tears as she sat in the kitchen surrounded by the inside servants. "He asked me if the child could travel." She sniffed, dabbing at her eyes with a worn linen cloth. "Could she survive the cold winter days."

"And what did you say?"

"Why, no, of course. Young as she is, and bein' so tiny. Why, it would be the death of the wee thing."

"How did he answer you back?" Magda asked quietly.

"He . . . he didn't say anything, really." Ferga

blew her nose and sat up straighter. "He just went over and stared at the poor child while she lay sleeping. He stared at her the longest time. Then he left."

"That was all?" the cook pressed. "He didn't say anything else?"

"No. Nothing. I called out to him to ask what I should do, but he didn't answer. I don't even know if he heard me."

"And what about milady?" a young serving girl asked in a tremulous voice. "She's so good to everyone. And now she's locked where only he can get to her."

"She has been short-tempered lately," Ferga put in. "Perhaps she knew something was in the wind."

"She's nothing but kind!" The girl defended her mistress stoutly. "If she's tired, or cross, it wouldn't surprise me if it were because she is with child."

And so a new wave of speculation was born. In the kitchens, in the stables, in the storerooms, and the weaving chamber. Wherever two or three folk gathered the quiet whispering began.

But it was a different story entirely in the great hall. Only two figures sat there, and all was silent save for the hissing of the fire that burned low in the hearth.

Dunn was cautious in his perusal of his lord. Corbett, however, was completely unaware of his friend's concern and was steadily and deliberately drinking himself into oblivion.

"Get me more ale," he said with a growl as he poured the last drop from a wide-mouthed jug into his tankard.

"You've had enough," Dunn replied. He shook his

head, stopping Thomas as the aging servant started to shuffle in with a fresh jug.

Corbett turned his head slowly so that he could focus on Dunn. He smiled cynically at the unmistakable disapproval on his friend's face.

"Get me more ale," he demanded once again. "Are you forgetting who's lord here?" Then when Dunn still did not move, he pounded his fist furiously on the wide-planked table. "I'll tear you apart if you don't do as I say!"

Dunn rubbed his chin as he eyed Corbett. There was a measuring look on his face. "Sober, aye, you could do it—though none too easily. But tonight?" He leaned back in his chair. "I don't think so. You're too drunk to face a mere woman. How can you expect to fare against a knight of the realm?"

For a moment it appeared Corbett would attack his friend, so enraged was he by the insulting appraisal. Then Thomas made his presence known.

"You must not mistrust the lady Lilliane," he ventured in a thin and quivering voice.

At that Corbett turned his furious gaze on the slight servant. "On your word?" he scoffed. "If the mistress is false, why shouldn't her servant be?"

"You can't see what's right before your face," the old man muttered, his face creased in a frown.

"Begone from here, old man!" Corbett said, snarling. Then he grabbed his tankard and drank one last, almost desperate pull. When he stood up he placed both hands on the table and leaned toward Dunn challengingly.

"What's between me and Lily is none of your affair. Nor anyone else's." On legs surprisingly steady, considering the vast amount of ale he'd consumed, he then turned and headed for the stairs that led to the tower room.

"And what of William?" Dunn called out.

Slowly Corbett turned. His angry belligerence had disappeared, leaving in its stead a dark and disturbing calm. A bitter smile curved his lips.

"William will be released tomorrow—quite early." He chuckled coldly at the bewilderment on Dunn's face and added, "I shall let my pretty little wife talk me into it."

"But I told you, she didn't say a word in his behalf before. What makes you think she will plead his case now?"

Corbett didn't answer at once. His thoughts seemed to turn inward before he continued more slowly. "Perhaps she is true." Then he shook off his odd mood. "But whether she is faithful or not, William will think she holds me within her control. He'll think me so besotted by her that I would do anything to please her." He released a dark, mirthless chuckle. "He'll very likely treble his efforts to ingratiate himself with her during the Christ's Mass celebrations." Then, as if content now that all was truly going as he planned, he strode up the stairs.

Left alone in the empty hall, Dunn thoughtfully finished off his ale. But there was a wry expression on his face when he too rose to leave.

"Aye, William will think she holds you in the palm of her hand. Everyone will." He laughed to himself. "It is only you, my good lord of Orrick, who does not recognize the very truth of the situation."

Lilliane was curled upon the trunk, peering out into the dark countryside. She'd railed and wept,

then railed again at Corbett all during the long hours
since he'd had her confined. Imprisoned in her own
chamber! In her own home! She planned, in her impotent fury, to accuse him and threaten him and
. . . and throw the candle holder at him when he
finally faced her. She would never forgive him if he
sent Elyse away, she vowed. Never.

It was one thing for him to go into a jealous rage
over William. Certainly William encouraged just
such a misunderstanding, and it was difficult to
know which of the two men to be more angry with.
But if Corbett banished Elyse with William . . .

Lilliane lowered her face to her knees at that
thought, unable to stop the tears that sprang once
again to her eyes. She was utterly exhausted by her
emotional trauma and, coupled with the general
malaise that had been plaguing her, she felt drained
of every bit of energy from her body.

She did not mean to fall asleep there, wrapped in a
blanket, leaning back against the stone mullions. She
had meant to greet Corbett as a furious virago, showing him her temper and the strength of her will.

Instead, when he strode belligerently into the
room, he found her relaxed in slumber, her dark
lashes casting shadows over her pink-flushed features, her thick chestnut tresses a rich tangle across
her shoulders.

Corbett's forbidding expression was not able to
hold as he gazed at his vulnerable wife. For long seconds he stood in the doorway, watching the play of
the firelight upon her as if it entranced him. When he
finally moved nearer he appeared almost reluctant,
and yet it was clear that he could not fight the inexo-

rable pull that drew him ever closer until he stood silently above her.

Lilliane was barely conscious of the gentle touch upon her cheek. Her beleaguered senses were too clouded by her deep need for sleep. Still, she stirred at the tender sweep of a broad palm along her hair, and the faintest smile curved her lips. She had been dreaming of birds: of kestrels and falcons and curlews. And of their prey, helpless against the swift birds' determined pursuit. Then she had somehow become the prey, running terror-stricken from the fearful strike of cruel talons. But now, this familiar, provocative caress.

In her dream she was lifted in strong arms, and she turned smiling, knowing now that the hunter was Corbett and that she was glad to be caught by him. Yet in that moment her captor seemed to change and her gray-eyed husband's image altered. From scarred brow to smooth. From raven hair to blond. And as William's face seemed to loom before her, she began to to shudder in terrible confusion.

"William?" The word trembled from her lips and tears of disappointment sprang to her eyes.

Lilliane felt the hands fall away from her. With a violent start she awoke, her mind confused and her body heavy and lethargic. She thought she heard a step. But when she shook the cobwebs from her mind and awkwardly pulled herself upright, she realized that although she was now in her bed, she was nonetheless alone. For a moment longer she remained confused. But then memory returned and every terrible detail of the past hours came flooding back to her.

She felt old and tired as she curled into a tight ball

on the feather mattress. Despair settled like a dark gloom upon her. Corbett was not coming to her. She knew that with awful certainty. He had judged her guilty and she would not be able to sway him.

With an effort she pulled a heavy coverlet over her trembling shoulders. He was not coming to her and he never would, she thought disjointedly. She could not think beyond that point—not to what the morrow would bring, or the days that stretched beyond that. She only knew that he was not coming and there was nothing she could do about it.

Nothing but weep.

19

⊰⊱⊱⊰⊰⊱⊰

Lilliane paused at the stone work balustrade and looked down into the great hall. She had slept far beyond her normal waking hour, yet still she did not feel refreshed. Instead she was tired and sluggish and completely confused.

Something was terribly wrong, and she had an awful feeling that it went deeper than merely Corbett's jealous possessiveness. Yet she could not fathom precisely what it could be. In the weeks since the wedding, she'd come to love and respect her husband. He was fair-minded and even-handed; he was a good lord for Orrick. And as a husband . . .

Lilliane trembled when she thought of his horrible expression at finding William's arms about her. She'd hoped so much that he might grow to love her. But now he seemed to hate her and had made her a prisoner in her own home.

Yet even on that score he had bewildered her. She had been certain a guard would still be posted at her door, but to her surprise no one had been there. She had descended cautiously and now, though a few servants moved about the hall, she sensed an odd and somber mood. But then, that was to be expected when the mistress of the castle was imprisoned, she thought in returning vexation.

Still, what had happened since Corbett's furious outburst the evening before? Had he sent Elyse away with William? Or had he, in his rage, deprived that poor babe of her one remaining parent?

Frustrated, nervous, and more than a little angry, she finished her descent to the hall. Though the servants saw her and even bobbed their heads courteously, they did not pause in their tasks. For a moment Lilliane wished she could inspire them to labor so swiftly and with so little chatter. But she also knew that it was fear that drove them today. They feared their lord's ire.

Lilliane's brow creased with annoyance. Well, she was not afraid of his ire. Or at least she was not so afraid that she would cower before him, she amended.

But though she sought him in the great hall, then the castle offices, and finally the bailey, Corbett was nowhere to be seen. She was fuming when she finally crossed to the kitchens, and the entire group of cooks and assistants jumped in alarm when she abruptly pushed the door open.

"Oh, milady . . ." The cook trailed off awkwardly. Then he rallied. "Did you wish to know the day's menus? I confess to taking the liberty of planning—"

"Blast the day's menus! Just tell me where he is!"

There was a dreadful pause and for a moment Lilliane was certain that something awful had happened. Then the pantler cleared his throat. "He's left, milady. He was put out this morning even before dawn."

"Put out? Put out of the castle?" Lilliane stared at

the timid faces before her and wondered if she had finally gone mad. "How could . . . who would dare put the lord of Orrick from his own castle?"

"Oh, not Lord Corbett," the portly fellow corrected. "It was Sir William that was put out of the castle. The master is likely still off with the guards." At once there was a babble of voices joining in, competing suddenly for the honor of informing her all that had passed since the previous evening.

Lilliane hardly heard a word. She was too surprised by the clear relief they all felt that she had been inquiring about her husband and not William. Did they all believe, like Corbett, that it was William she longed for and worried about?

At once she felt even more depressed than before. She was suspect in everyone's eyes, it seemed. No matter that she cared nothing for William beyond a fast-fading friendship, they seemed only to recall her childish longing for him from years before.

With an angry clap of her hands Lilliane silenced the chattering group. "So William is gone. Did his child travel with him?"

"Oh, no, milady. Ferga tends her as ever."

Lilliane did not wait to hear any more. As she hurried from the kitchens, she took a deep breath, only now aware how long she had caught her breath in anxious anticipation of that knowledge. William was gone and yet the baby, Elyse, still remained. It was what she had wanted all along, and she felt a wonderful relief.

But what of Corbett?

Lilliane stopped beneath the bare limbs of the ancient chestnut tree. The wind whistled along the high granite walls of the bailey, and she shivered and pulled her short mantle more snugly about her shoulders. She was confused and perplexed.

Corbett suspected her of a terrible thing, and yet he had not come forth and accused her. But although he had not stated it outright, she did not feel the lack of his accusation. Every least servant at Orrick seemed even more aware of what was going on than she. She looked around her once more, glad there was no one near to disturb her thoughts, muddled as they were. And yet still she felt an odd mood over the castle, even to the very walls.

If only she could clear her mind and think things through, she brooded. Then she looked beyond the open gatehouse. She could walk down to the forest. No one was there to prevent her if she decided to follow the path through the woods to a curving stretch of the river Keene, she realized.

It was precisely what she needed, and she felt better immediately. She wished she'd brought her long mantle, but she would be warm enough once she began to walk, she reasoned.

To her relief, she was not stopped when she passed under the gate tower and crossed the narrow drawbridge. She was certain the sun seemed brighter and the air fresher once she saw the stubbled fields stretching before her, and she strode along the road with more energy than she'd felt in days. In truth, she half expected to be followed and ordered back. But she was determined to ignore any such command. After all, who could command her now? Only her husband, and he was nowhere near.

If that fact bothered her, Lilliane pushed it sternly from her mind. Instead she breathed deeply of the cold December air, marveled at the cheeky thrushes feasting on the winterberry bushes, and wondered as she did every winter at how the drifts of gold and red and brown leaves had so quickly returned to the earth. It was a miraculous cycle, she reflected as she made the turn in the road. When she came abreast three towering cedar trees, Lilliane moved with easy familiarity onto a narrow dirt path that wound into the thick forest. In the summer she would have been swallowed up at once by the dense growth of towering oak and beech trees. But the forests were barer now, with only the glossy green leaves and bright berries of the small hollies showing amid the stark white branches of the beeches. As she moved along, the rust color of her short mantle was easily visible through the trees.

She was lost in thought, trying to untangle her conflicting emotions about her difficult husband. Things had been going so well between them in London. Until that last night there. William had arrived by then. Could he and Corbett have had a run-in of some sort? Corbett certainly seemed to despise the man more than ever.

She was prevented from following that line of thought by the sharp crack of a dry twig. With a start she whirled around only to find Corbett sitting his favorite black destrier and staring at her.

Lilliane felt a rush of relief, followed by quick self-reproach. How could she be so happy to see him sitting there, his gray eyes cold and hooded, his mouth set in that familiar, grim line? And yet she was happy to see him and to know he had come looking for her.

Afraid that her feelings were surely apparent to him, Lilliane deliberately looked away toward the slow-moving river. As the silence between them stretched out, she was conscious of the rapid pounding of her heart and a peculiar tightness building within her. It took all her resolve not to glance back at him when he urged his mount nearer.

"Do you plan to flee me once again?" His words were curt, said with little inflection. The dearth of emotions in them goaded Lilliane's anger.

"I wasn't married to you then," she said, shooting him a sharp glare. "Despite what you think, I know my duties as a wife."

"Do you?" He lounged back on his horse and stared insolently at her. "So you are not fleeing because we are married now."

This time she could not miss the tension in his voice. For a moment she felt a wild flicker of hope. Could he want her to stay for more than only a sense of duty?

But his expression was inscrutable. He sat so tall and imposing upon his huge steed, so powerful and unmoving, that it seemed impossible that he could ever feel a mawkish emotion. Swallowing the lump that had suddenly formed in her throat, Lilliane turned away from him. She would not let him taunt her, she vowed. She would not.

Trying her best to ignore him, she walked down to the riverbank and stopped, bracing her hand on a young beech. There was no ice upon the river yet, although she knew the water must be frigid. But it could not possibly feel any colder than the dreadful sadness welling up within her. More than anything Lilliane wished Corbett would go away so she could succumb to the tears rising so embarrassingly in her eyes.

"How can I be certain I haven't interrupted a tête-à-tête between you and your . . . you and William?"

At last it was out in the open. She felt a strange relief that he'd finally accused her. And yet she was terribly sad. Still, now she was justified in turning all her pent-up anger loose upon him.

"I've no reason to meet with William," she began. "He's gone. And you've no reason to be so suspicious!" she ended sharply.

"No?" Corbett swung down from his destrier in one fluid movement. Then he turned a smooth, mocking expression upon her. Only his eyes revealed the fury that now possessed him. "For myself it seems perfectly clear why I suspect you of—" He stopped abruptly and took a harsh breath. Then he approached her almost warily. "You loved him once. Do you deny it?"

"Once," she answered honestly in a shaky tone. "But that was long ago—"

"You did not wish to marry me," Corbett interrupted. "In fact, you denied your own father, so desperate were you to avoid me!"

"Yes, but—but you *know* that was because of the trouble between our families. Besides, *you* didn't want to marry me either! All you wanted—"

"All I wanted was a peaceful home and a dutiful wife. Instead I've a woman who cannot be trusted and someone overly eager to strike me down."

Lilliane was temporarily silenced as she recalled the surprising attack on them outside London. Did Corbett think she was somehow involved in that? Or William? At once her anger disappeared.

"Corbett." She stepped nearer him and placed a hand upon his arm.

But he shook off her tender gesture and looked even more suspiciously at her. "Soft tones and a smile will not win me over."

Crestfallen, Lilliane let her hand fall to her side. "I'm not trying to 'win' you over."

His lips lifted in a slight, sardonic smile. "More's the pity," he murmured. Then he became more terse. "William is gone. I sent him packing like the craven fool he is after he told me all I wanted."

"He told you all . . . ? You tortured him?" Lilliane's face grew pale with horror.

Corbett's expression remained cynical, but his eyes seemed to become as cold as granite in winter. "He is easily manipulated. I know the truth now."

"If you know the truth, then you know I have done nothing wrong."

Corbett's quick laugh was harsh and without any trace of mirth. "Then your truth and his are sadly at odds. If it were not for the unwanted complications it would entail, I would have killed him last night."

William had lied about her to Corbett! That sudden revelation coupled with the crushing reality of Corbett's animosity made Lilliane light-headed. She stumbled back and would have fallen down the muddy riverbank had Corbett not steadied her with a quick hand upon her arm.

For a moment she stared into his eyes, so close to her now, and she was sure she saw a flash of concern. Of compassion. But then just as quickly it was gone, and she knew with awful certainty that it had only been wishful thinking on her part.

"Do you grieve so for his loss?" He bit the words out. "Then take comfort in the fact that I kept his brat for you."

Tears glistened in Lilliane's eyes as she looked up into his harshly handsome face. "Th-thank you for that. But if you hate me so much, why didn't you send her away too?"

She felt his hands tighten on her arms, and he seemed to struggle for words. When he spoke it was a low, taunting whisper. "I wish to see whether you will make a better mother than you are a wife."

With an angry cry Lilliane struck out at him. But he caught her hand before she even came close. Then he jerked her roughly against him. "As ill-tempered as ever. But I shall tame you, my little demon of a wife."

"You are too crude and . . . and too stupid to ever tame me!" Lilliane panted as she fought to be free of his paralyzing grasp. But it was to no avail. As if he took pleasure in her useless struggles, he only pressed her more intimately to him.

"You've liked my crudeness well enough in the past," Corbett muttered as he deftly stilled her flailing arms. Then she felt the possessive slide of his broad palm down to her backside, and she gasped at the confusing mixture of emotions that rose in her belly. He didn't care about her at all; he didn't trust her and, indeed, believed only the worst of her. And yet his first touch threatened to dissolve all her anger and leave her instead longing helplessly for him.

"Don't do this," she warned, trying to fight off the fire beginning to flare deep within her.

"You are my wife." His voice was low and husky, buried somewhere within her hair as he nuzzled her neck. Then he tilted her face up and took her mouth in a kiss of brutal intensity.

Lilliane felt his anger. It was there in the way his

lips took ruthless possession of hers and in the way his tongue boldly searched out every intimate place in her mouth. But there were other emotions too. She couldn't clearly identify them or determine what they meant for she was too overwhelmed by her own unwilling response to him. Still, when she could no longer resist and her tongue came forward to meet his, she sensed the change in him from demanding to beguiling, from aggressive to enticing.

It was this more than anything that proved Lilliane's undoing. She could fight his anger. But she had no defense against the tender side of his passion. Without conscious thought her arms crept up to encircle his neck.

At the new pliancy of her body against his, Corbett let out a low groan. "My God, when you show me this sweetness . . ." The rest was lost to her, and yet there was still a part of her that feared the exquisite pleasure they found in one another might mean nothing at all once the passion had passed.

The thought that he would have her his wife in their bed yet keep her his enemy otherwise stabbed sorely at Lilliane's heart. In desperation she clung to him, willing him to love her and need her as much as she now loved and needed him. For a moment Corbett seemed taken aback by her sudden display of ardor. But he was quickly caught up in the fire that ignited between them.

She did not know how it happened, how they came to be on the hard, wintry ground, her sitting on his legs, half lying in his arms. "Oh, my love," Lilliane whispered as he pushed her mantle aside and slid his warm hand along her side. He had started to kiss her again. But he hesitated when she spoke. Lilliane sensed a new tension in him and she opened her eyes. But the gaze that met hers had lost that smoky, glazed look of just moments before. Instead, Corbett's eyes had cleared to a dark, unreadable gray.

"Am I your love?" he asked quietly. But there was a hard, biting edge to his voice that brought a blush to Lilliane's face. When she did not answer he grew more caustic. "Then if I am not, who is?"

At that Lilliane struggled to rise. "Why must I love anyone?" she snapped, frustrated by this sudden turn of events. "You most certainly do not!"

"Ah, but I'm not the one whispering such endearments," he replied blandly, watching her now as she stumbled to her feet.

"No, *you* would not do such a thing." Despite her anger, it was the pain Lilliane felt that came through in her trembling voice. Humiliated by that inadvertent admission of her feelings for him, she tried to turn away. But Corbett was too quick. With a single grasp of his hand he caught her skirt, forcing her to an ignominious halt.

"So it is as I thought. You *are* trying to flee your wifely duties." His sarcastic words fell as harshly as blows upon her, and Lilliane had to struggle to prevent her tears from spilling over. How could he be so tender one moment and so cruel the next? How could he touch her so lovingly then accuse her so wrongly of infidelity?

Caught as she was in the tangled sweep of her skirts, she had no choice but to respond to his taunt. "It is not one of my wifely duties to grovel in the dirt with you!"

"It is your wifely duty to please your husband."

"And I clearly do not." Then she jerked hard at her

skirts, ignoring the ripping sound of the wool in her relief to be free of his hold.

Lilliane wanted to run as far and as fast as she could to some hidden, private place where she could succumb to the hot tears stinging her eyes. But that would only prove to him how much control he wielded over her emotions. She had to content herself with stalking stiffly away from him.

She did not get very far. Before she could even reach the road, she heard Corbett on his huge black war-horse behind her. But she was determined to thwart him, and she darted behind a linden tree on the pretext of gathering holly limbs.

She could feel his eyes upon her but she could not risk returning his steady gaze, for she knew his eyes would have that cool and mocking distance. It would be another blow to her battered heart, and she was sure she would not be able to bear it.

Lilliane bent down for the lowest holly branches, letting her loosened hair fall protectively about her face. She tugged at one branch ineffectually, then tried another, only to prick her fingers as she accidentally stripped off several of the glossy green leaves.

"You have servants aplenty for that sort of work. Your duty is to see them perform their tasks, and you've been away from the castle long enough. Come here and ride before me."

Lilliane lifted her head proudly although she stared carefully at the road and not at Corbett. "The servants at Orrick are well enough trained that they do not turn slackards should I be absent from the castle. You need not tell me of my duty on that score. I'll return to Orrick in my own good time."

She knew that last would infuriate him, perhaps even goad him into some violent reaction. But she was too overcome with the pain of rejection to be cautious. It was only when the great war-horse came crashing through the underbrush that she looked up in alarm.

As easily as if she were but a slight child, Corbett plucked her from the midst of the holly and winterberry bushes. With complete disregard for her shrieks of protest, he sat her quite unceremoniously before him, then deftly turned the animal toward the road.

"Let me down, you great oaf!" she cried as she tried to twist from her husband's grasp.

With a sharp tug Corbett drew her close against his chest. "Ride before me properly," he muttered, "or enter Orrick a captive, facedown, tied hand and feet before me!"

Despite her fury, she was still aware that Corbett's threat was no idle one. Stiff with anger, she stayed woodenly where he'd put her, but inside she was seething.

The ride home was pure torture for Lilliane. She was sitting sideways before Corbett, balanced somewhat precariously as the big horse picked his way along the path. With every slight change of direction she was thrown off balance and she might have fallen had it not been for Corbett's sturdy arms around her. But every touch of him was a new form of pain for her, and her anger swiftly gave way to heartbreak once more. Pride would not let her clutch at him when the horse scrambled up a short embankment or stepped over a fallen log. Yet the feel of his broad chest, so warm despite the wintry air, and the

rock-hardness of his arm steadying her only intensified the hollow feelings inside her.

He had proven to have every quality she desired in
a husband, save one. He did not care for her at all.
And the saddest part was that she had come to care
for him beyond all reason.

An involuntary shiver shook Lilliane. At once she
felt Corbett's arms tighten around her. But that only
made things worse for it was not the cold that made
her shiver so. It was Corbett's devastating nearness
that was affecting her so profoundly.

His warm breath moved in her hair; the scent of
his clean skin haunted her. Her bottom was pressed
most intimately against his lap, and a drugging
warmth seemed to be rising in her. He was the man
who had taken her innocence and then lifted her to
heights of passion far beyond her wildest imaginings. The thought of the exquisite pleasures they'd
shared caused another quiver to shoot up her spine.

"Are you cold?" Corbett's voice was gruff, almost as
if he did not wish to inquire about her comfort. Lilliane did not answer but she sat up straighter, trying
to get as far from him as she could.

At that futile response Corbett chuckled. Then he
tightened his arm around her waist and pulled her
closer than ever. "Shall we ride about our lands, my
sweet lady wife? A good lord and lady should concern themselves with the well-being of their people."

"You do not care about any of us!" Lilliane
snapped as she tried to loosen his grip on her.

But Corbett only pressed his palm more firmly
against her waist. "I care about every citizen of Orrick."

"For what they may gain you!"

"My duty is to protect Orrick and make it prosper."

"Yes," Lilliane replied heatedly as she tried to lean as little as possible against him. "You will protect the shepherd so that you may have more wool. And the farmer so that you may have more crops. If you protect me it is only so that you may have your heir!"

There was only the briefest pause. "And will I have my heir soon?"

Lilliane had not expected such a question, and for a few moments she was at a loss for words. She wanted a child for them with an intensity beyond explanation. And yet . . . and yet she wanted him to desire her for more reason than simply to beget an heir. Her face set in a slight frown and she focused determinedly on a group of village men repairing a stone wall between two fields.

"I cannot be certain," she finally replied in a low monotone.

"Then perhaps we must try harder."

Had Lilliane not been so mortified by his blunt words, she would have noticed the tension edging his voice. But all she heard was the casual way he discussed their future children, much as he might discuss the breeding of his war-horses.

In self-defense she tried to mimic his careless attitude. "I'll meet my marriage duties so long as you meet yours. I shall give you the heirs you desire and you shall keep Orrick safe for them."

"Yes, I'll keep Orrick safe for my children. But just mine."

At that strange comment Lilliane chanced a look at him. "Of course . . . Oh. You mean Elyse. Why, she will be well provided for."

Corbett did not reply and, after a hard searching

stare that left her feeling completely exposed, he looked away. It was only then that she understood. William had made Corbett doubt her fidelity, and now he could not help but wonder about any child she might bear him. For a moment Lilliane felt sympathy for Corbett's plight. He was a proud man and would want his own child. But she had been a faithful wife, she reminded herself. She did not deserve such suspicion.

As they rode on in an uncomfortable silence, Lilliane searched for the words to make him believe her. Finally as they approached the solid towers of Orrick she ventured to speak.

"You must not doubt my . . . you must not doubt me," she faltered.

"Why not?"

She felt the chill of his suspicion far more keenly than that of the biting wind as she shrugged for the right words. "Because I was raised to be a lady. And a lady would never behave so wickedly as you believe I have."

For a few hopeful seconds she thought he might believe her. But then he let out a dark laugh.

"Were you raised to disobey your father as you did when you fled our wedding?" He grabbed her chin and made her face him. "Yes or no?" Then he laughed again.

"Any girl so disobedient as that should be suspect. But then, knowing your father's devious way, it would not be surprising if you learned such deceit at his knee."

Corbett did not flinch at the sharp slap she landed on his cheek. Perhaps he knew he deserved it, but Lilliane would attribute no such decency to him.

Taking advantage of his momentary pause, she slid recklessly from the horse's withers. She stumbled to her knees but in an instant she was up and running toward Orrick.

Corbett did not follow until she had passed over the drawbridge and was well into the bailey. She did not linger there, however. Without a word to anyone she stormed through the great hall, up the drafty stone stairs, and into her chamber. There she slammed the door, dragged the chest to block it, then finally crumpled onto the floor in a torrent of tears and heartbreaking sobs.

20

~~~~~~

He came to her every night.

In the darkness and silence he came when the entire castle lay quiet and asleep. But Lilliane was never asleep.

It might have been a pact they shared, although they never spoke of it. By day she worked herself nearly to exhaustion preparing for the lengthy entertainments to come. Accommodations must be prepared. Torches and candles must be allotted. Menus and the food stores must be calculated. These preparations on top of the routine daily tasks she saw to kept her occupied from before dawn until well after nightfall.

She saw little of Corbett during these long, wearing hours. He was always gone before she rose, and except for the midday meal she rarely saw him at all.

But he came to her every night.

He would be freshly washed. His hair would still lay in damp curls along his neck and he would smell of soft soap, clean skin, and ale.

Lilliane knew he drank every night before he came. At first she thought it was because he could not stomach lying with her and that he came only to assure himself an heir. But his tenderness and his passion belied that reasoning.

Then she thought he drank to forget her supposed crime, so that he could come to her with no memory of his terrible suspicions. Yet his words whispered so hotly in her ears too often negated that idea. "You are mine, Lily. Only mine," he told her every night, just before he took final possession of her.

Oh, how she wanted those words to be true. More than anything she wanted to be his, in every way possible, and to have him be hers forever. But she feared it was only his pride speaking: what was his was his, and he would share it with no man. But that didn't make her really his. As much as she wanted them to belong to one another, he was the one preventing it with his suspicions and his accusations. Yet despite the terrible emotional distance between them, Lilliane took him gladly in her arms each night.

The first night he had come she'd been half asleep, hardly aware when he entered the room. It was only when he tossed his tunic over the trunk and removed his boots that she realized she was not alone. By the time he had slipped beneath the cover, Lilliane had been fully awake and her heart had begun to race.

He had paused slightly and Lilliane had been in a whirlwind of conflicting emotions. Everything logical had said to send him away—to deny him or at least respond with complete indifference.

But her heart had said otherwise.

When he'd finally drawn the heavy woven coverlet down from her shoulder then let his hand slide slowly back up her arm, a sharp quiver had shaken her.

"Turn to me, Lily," he'd whispered hoarsely.

She'd been unable to resist.

That first night their lovemaking had been fierce and explosive, in a wild, almost desperate fashion. Since then it had become no less passionate, but somehow more serious, as if each time might be the last chance they'd have.

Each morning Lilliane had awakened alone to a myriad of conflicting emotions: she loved him and wanted him; she hated him for using her this way; she was sure she would die of mortification when she saw him at dinner.

And each morning she made a feeble vow to herself that they could not go on this way. But as the afternoon sun cast long shadows over Orrick, the slow-building tension would begin. Anticipation for her night with him would tighten like a feverish knot deep in her belly, and time would drag interminably. Any thought of sending him away would vanish in the heat of her all-encompassing desire for him. But she never abandoned the wish for settling matters between them.

She knew the minutes after their lovemaking were when he was most relaxed and perhaps the most open to her overtures. She was loath to ruin that sweet aftermath by bringing up the difficult subject that divided them. But she was wise enough to know that she too was less likely to anger when they were lying naked and entwined together.

Promising herself that tonight they would sort things out between them, Lilliane gave little Elyse a gentle hug. "Sweet baby, I hope to give you a little companion sometime during this next year. It would be a shame for a nursery not to be filled with contented babies and laughing children." Renewed by such happy thoughts, Lilliane stood up and donned her mantle. Then she wrapped a warm knitted blanket about the child.

"I'm taking her out for a bit of fresh air," she called to Ferga who was busy stitching a dress for the fast-growing little girl.

"In this cold?"

"In the sunshine, protected from the wind, it's actually quite nice," Lilliane countered. "Besides, it will do her good and pinken her cheeks."

The air was cold, but crisp and clear; sunlight bathed the bailey with gold, and Lilliane appreciated it all the more given the dreariness of the previous few days. She cradled Elyse protectively, whispering sweet songs as she strolled leisurely toward the now-leafless chestnut tree.

"Perhaps I'll have a seat hung from the tree for you," she crooned as she smoothed a wispy lock from the baby's brow. Then she laughed as the baby's serious gaze crinkled into a funny, toothless grin.

From the parapet near the gatehouse Corbett had a clear view of Lilliane. He was unaware that he had stopped in midsentence to stare at her, but Dunn did not miss his friend's preoccupation.

"She is the picture of motherhood," Dunn commented wryly, watching the play of emotions on Corbett's face. "Or is it something other than her motherly qualities that occupies your thoughts?"

Corbett reluctantly dragged his gaze from Lilliane's willowy form and gave Dunn a dark scowl. "You forget yourself. She is my wife, not some wench that you may jest about."

At his bristly response Dunn crowed with laughter.

"You are clearly in a worse way than I ever imagined. I speak of serious matters like treason, and you growl like a jealous dog! Does this mean you've now given up your foolish suspicions about her?"

Corbett's jaw tensed and he frowned in aggravation. "You make no sense at all. You've reason enough to mistrust her. You know as much as I do about her connections to William and her dangerous knowledge of the king's affairs."

"I know more than you do." Dunn snorted. "But only because I have my wits about me while you've clearly lost yours." Then his tone changed. "She's innocent, Corbett. I've not a doubt in my mind."

There was a long pause as both men stared at the woman and child in the bailey below. "She's a passionate woman," Corbett began. Then he halted and slowly shook his head. "She fought me hard because she believed I was her enemy. She imprisoned you when she thought you'd killed her father. She fortified the entire castle against me because she was sure I'd planned Lord Barton's demise."

His face started to relax at that memory but then he stiffened. "If she is with William, then I have to believe she will do everything in her power to help him. And that puts her squarely against my king. And against me."

"What if she *is* innocent?"

"Then that will be good," Corbett replied slowly.

"Yes, perhaps. But I see you around her. She will not easily forget the strain of these past weeks."

"I make her forget every night!" Corbett snapped, clearly annoyed at this turn in the conversation.

But Dunn was like a stubborn hound worrying a bone, and he would not let it drop. "She was raised a lady and for her that will never be enough. Treat her like some favorite whore and you'll lose this chance to win her love."

Corbett turned his head sharply to view Dunn. "What has love to do with this? I married her for her inheritance. She knows that. Love has never been a consideration!"

Dunn did not reply to Corbett's vehement words. Instead, he turned his attention back to the task of checking the cranking mechanism for the drawbridge. But there was wry amusement on his face as he watched Corbett still staring down at his pretty wife.

That night Corbett did not come.

Lilliane lay awake in their shadowy chamber debating what she should say to him and how she should begin her overtures of peace. Perhaps she should broach the subject before they became too carried away by passion. Perhaps he would be too exhausted afterward to take careful note of her words.

But then if she approached the subject too early, he might be too distracted by desire to really hear her.

It was a dilemma she debated long and hard with no firm conclusion. But when the fire settled to glowing embers, and the solitary candle sputtered and died, she knew he would not appear this night.

Had he grown tired of her? she fretted. Had the passionate hours that had meant so much to her been only a momentary easing of his lust for him?

That thought caused Lilliane's heart to tighten painfully. If he did not come . . . She closed her eyes against that dreadful thought. But still she could not avoid it. If he did not come tonight . . . If he never came again.

She sat up and thrust the heavy coverlet from her. The chill of the room seemed sadly appropriate, and for a moment she was tempted to crawl back into the warm cocoon of her bed. There she could bury her head and hide from the terrible reality of her life.

But Lilliane fought that cowardly idea and swung her feet down from the high bed to the cold stone floor. She would seek him out, she decided. He had not come to her so she would go to him. She would find him and convince him to come back to their chamber and then . . . and then . . .

How did you convince a suspicious man to trust you? Or an indifferent one to love you?

She did not know but she was too frightened of a future without Corbett's love to dwell on it. She would just find him and then she would decide what to do.

The castle was still and the silence oppressive. Save for the several servants who slept curled in the rushes before the hearth in the great hall there was no sign of life. It might have been the castle of the legendary sleeping princess that a long-ago minstrel had entertained them with. But in this version it was not a princess who slept, but the prince. And it was up to her to find and awaken his heart with the strength of her true love.

Lilliane was not certain where to begin. Corbett might have decided to sleep anywhere: in the stables on a pile of sweet-smelling hay, on a bunk amid the guards. Perhaps even in a vacant chamber in the keep. She bit her soft inner lip in frustration and wondered if perhaps she was pursuing a hopeless quest. What if she didn't find him? What if he became angry and sent her away from him? How would she ever face him—or anyone—again if he came right out with his rejection of her?

She shivered and a cold lump lodged high in her throat. She could not think like that, she told herself. She must simply find him and then deal with the consequences afterward. For she knew she could not go on in this suspended state any longer.

Outside the night sky was clear, brilliantly lighted by a silver crescent moon. Stars littered the night sky like sparkling gems strewn upon velvet of the darkest blue. The bailey was all silver light and ebony shadows with not a soul about. For a moment she feared that she would be seen, for then she would have to explain her nocturnal mission. But then she remembered that the guards' gazes faced outward. They sought no enemy from within.

Despite her silent search, Lilliane was unable to find her missing husband. Not anywhere in the stables, or in the kitchens or outside storage rooms. The visitors' chambers were as they should be, clean and readied for the coming guests, but vacant.

She was trembling with disappointment. Fighting back tears, she stood in the shadows before the soldiers' quarters. Did she dare to enter there? She took a step forward, then turned away in indecision. It went against everything her mother had taught her. But then she seemed unable to do anything right on that score. She had flagrantly disobeyed her father. She had barred her own husband from his castle. And now she crept through the night like some wanton, searching for a man who did not feel anything for her but occasional lust.

Lilliane wiped away two hot tears then turned her gaze up to the sky. Dear God, she prayed as the brilliant stars swam before her eyes, please help me. Then her vision cleared and she stared at the crenellated silhouette of the look-over. Something had moved there. She squinted, trying to make it out. Had it only been a trick of the shadows, or perhaps her imagination? But then she saw clearly: a man lifted something to his lips.

Lilliane's heart lurched within her chest at the sight. Corbett had been so near, just another flight of steps above her while she lay worrying in her bed. It occurred to her that he must prefer his solitude to her company. But she refused to listen to such depressing thoughts.

The climb up the curving steps to the look-over seemed endless. Yet when she stood before the iron-hinged door, she hesitated. For a moment she considered retreating to the safety of her bedchamber. But other emotions far more powerful than fear drove her on, and after only a brief hesitation she forced the heavy door open.

Corbett was sitting between two high, pointed crenels. One leg dangled from his precarious stone perch. The other was cocked as a rest for his arm. He held a round pewter jug in one hand, but he was not drinking now. He only sat there in silence, staring out over the moonlit countryside.

In that moment Lilliane recognized too clearly her husband's unhappiness. Had he been thus when he'd first come to Orrick? She could not say, for she'd not been able to see beyond his powerful image as a knight—and as an enemy. He had been the king's Bird of Prey, and she'd been the prize he'd set out to snare. Well, he had her now, but he'd obviously not found contentment in his victory.

That knowledge almost sent her running away in defeat. Would she ever be able to make him care for her? As she stared at his hard, unmoving profile, it seemed somehow impossible.

She turned away. At the door her fingers were clumsy as she fumbled with the lock. When Corbett spoke to her she shook her head hard, willing him to forget she was there and let her leave quietly with her shattered heart.

But Corbett was as uncooperative as ever, and with a simple command he made her go still.

"Come here."

Lilliane's very heartbeat seemed to stop at his words. More than ever she wished to flee and avoid this further humiliation. But she could not break the hold he had on her that easily. Instead she bowed her head against the weather-beaten door as if it might lend her support.

"I said come here," he demanded more harshly. This time she heard the slight slur brought on by the wine.

Still she did not obey but only stayed where she was, a pale, slender shape trembling against the dark stonework. When it was apparent she would not respond, Corbett left his place between the crenels and crossed the small enclosure to her. Then he turned her sharply and backed her against the rough door.

"Why are you here?" he barked. "But that's a foolish question, isn't it?" His hands tightened on her arms before he released her. Then he braced one hand against the door and leaned nearer. She could smell the wine on his breath, and she knew he'd had much more than on the previous nights.

"You know, you disprove all my theories about women," he began in an unexpectedly amiable tone. Lilliane watched him with wide, wary eyes. She was confused by his odd mood, which seemed to jump from pensive to angry to almost teasing.

"Wives are not supposed to be passionate, you know. They only endure their husband's attention out of a sense of duty. 'Tis mistresses who are sweet and responsive." He ran his finger along her cheek then began to toy with her hair. "Too bad you could not have been simply my mistress. How much happier we might have been."

"And you're not happy at all now," Lilliane whispered.

"No more than you. We married because duty bade we must. But lovers . . . lovers obey no such duty."

"It was not your duty to marry me. No one forced you into it," Lilliane reminded him reproachfully.

Corbett smiled grimly. "There are many types of duty, Lily—"

"Yes, and having an heir—and something to leave that heir—was your duty," Lilliane snapped, hiding her pain behind anger. "How I wish you had picked someone else."

Corbett's face was just inches from hers. His eyes appeared black as coal and as impenetrable as stone. She tried to turn away from his disturbing stare but his hand, still tangled in her loose hair, prevented her.

"Indeed, it would have been much easier if I could have. All I wanted was a proper little wife. What I got . . ." He stopped then he pressed close to her. "What I got was a fiery little temptress. Tell me, Lily, would you have consented to be my mistress only?"

"Oh, you are blackhearted!" Lilliane cried as she tried to twist away from the heated length of his body against hers. "You have only one wicked thought in your head!"

"As do you!" He deftly stilled her frantic struggles. "What reason brought you to seek me except lustful ones? You can accuse me of no worse than you are guilty of."

Each word hurt her terribly, doubly so because they were partially true. But she could not admit that to him. Not now when he was finally being honest about his feelings for her.

"I'm guilty of nothing but trying to be a proper wife."

Corbett let out a dark laugh. "A proper wife tends her duties, accepts her husband as her lord, and quietly endures her husband's amorous demands. But not my Lily. You hold me off at arm's length as long as you can and then cry with passion until we are both trembling and spent. So which are you, wife or mistress?"

She lowered her thick lashes to hide the tears rising in her eyes. How could she answer such a thing? "I no longer want to fight you," she whispered.

"No," Corbett finally murmured. "You may no longer want to fight me. But then, things have changed."

"No, *you* have changed," Lilliane accused him shakily. "You are distant. You avoid me. And you wallow in ale and wine every evening."

He seemed a little taken aback by her words. "I

have my reasons." He paused and added with a rueful twist of his lips, "Ale provides strength. Wine provides courage."

Lilliane could not take such words seriously. "What have you to fear?" she scoffed furiously. "It is the rest of us who must walk gingerly in fear of your anger or your least whim!"

Corbett's dark gray eyes searched her face for what seemed an endless time. Something grave disturbed him and Lilliane could not fathom the source. Some demon he held inside. But as she stared back, partly frightened, partly fascinated, she saw his expression change.

"Tell me, Lily. Are you frightened of my anger now?"

Lilliane was instantly wary. Something had changed. Some note in his voice, or perhaps the slant of his scarred brow gave her a vague warning.

"Perhaps you're worried about my least whim?" he persisted when she did not answer right away.

"You—you won't hurt me. I know that," she stammered.

"Would that I could be so sure of you," he murmured. But before she could question such an unfair comment, he suddenly dragged her away from the rough wood door. "I have a whim tonight. And I wish you to humor me."

Then he pushed her mantle back from one of her shoulders and fingered the soft wool of her gown. She caught her breath and waited tensely for him to continue.

Finally he spoke in a low, almost tortured tone. "Show me which you are, wife or mistress. Let me see which it is you are to me."

"I-I am your wife, Corbett," she whispered. "Why do you dwell on such foolish thoughts?"

"Why, indeed. Show me," he demanded again.

"I don't know what you want of me!" Lilliane cried in confusion. He was treating her as callously as he might some tavern wench. He was doing it quite purposefully and he was breaking her heart.

"Surely you must know. Your mother could not have neglected such an important part of your training. A wife will always do her husband's bidding, and he has the right to to beat her if he does not. A mistress, however, is free to leave her man at any time—there is always another man available. But if she stays, it is for love." His eyes grew narrow as he taunted her further. "You did not love me when we wed. You loved another. Sir William, I believe," he added caustically.

"No, that's not true—"

"And though you were innocent at the time, William now taunts me with his conquest of you."

"He lies! I don't know why—"

Corbett caught her by the wrists and pulled her cruelly to him. "I don't know why he would lie either. He would have to be mad, for I could easily have killed him. Therefore I must believe his words are true."

Lilliane's tears were falling freely. It was hopeless and she knew she had lost him. Truly, she'd never completely had him. But for a while she'd had so much hope. Now, though, there was nothing to hope for.

"My wife. His mistress." His grip tightened and his jaw tensed. "By right I should beat you. I should mark that pale, smooth flesh so that no man would have you again."

"I was never . . . never his mistress." Lilliane choked on a sob, closing her eyes against his terrible anger.

At that he released her abruptly and she stumbled back a pace. In the dark, moonlit look-over they faced one another. With one hand she wiped her tears away, then she took a shaky breath.

"I don't know what you want of me—what you want me to be. If I am passionate . . . if I think lustful thoughts, then you deem me guilty. Does this mean you prefer me to be cold and unresponsive?" She shook her head and stared at him with huge, reproachful eyes. "Can't I simply be your wife? Can't you just be content with the passion that flares between us without judging me so unfairly?"

Lilliane was trembling from head to toe as she faced him. When he took a step nearer she did not flinch at the anger still smoldering in his eyes. He reached out and gathered her thick, loosened tresses into his hands. Then he pulled her hair back so that her face was turned up to his.

His eyes traveled from her tear-filled eyes down to her lips, then further along the vulnerable length of her throat to where the neckline of her gown covered her.

"Then show me," he whispered hoarsely. "Show me you can be both wife and mistress."

With those wrenching words Corbett lowered his head and took her lips in a hard, domineering kiss. He held her rigidly so that her arms were pinned between them, and at first she was too startled to respond. But if his anger was a terrible wild fire burning everything in its path, it quickly escalated into an inferno of pent-up passion that she had no defense against. Like one unable to resist the very thing that must consume her, she yielded to the harsh demands he made of her. As if none of what had gone before mattered, she became a soft foil for his unrelenting hardness.

Corbett groaned deep in his chest as she caught the wool of his tunic in her fists and clutched him to her. He seemed to be a man in agony as he raised his lips from hers, then took her face between his hands and forced her head back. His eyes were as black as the night yet within them Lilliane saw the terrible doubts that racked him.

"Show me, Lily," he muttered hoarsely. "Show me how a woman comes eagerly to her man. Entice me." He groaned and took her lips once more. "Make me believe it."

He doubted her. He would always doubt her, Lilliane realized, and a sob rose in her throat. Yet even that all-consuming sorrow could not stifle the flames he stirred in her. A part of her knew it was hopeless. And yet she wanted to believe—even if she was only fooling herself—that he loved her. At least this one last time. He needed her in some desperate private way, and although it was not love, for this moment she would pretend it was.

As she rose to him her sob was lost in a kiss that wrenched her very soul. "I love you, Corbett. Oh, I do," she whispered as he backed her against the crenellations. They were not words she meant for him to hear, and once said they could not be taken back. But she could not tell if he'd heard her, and, indeed, as she began to drown in the dizzying rapture of his kisses, she ceased to care.

Lilliane lost all connection with time and place as Corbett drew her deeper and deeper into a splendid delirium fired by pent-up hunger and intense desire. She wanted him with a fierceness that shook her to her very core.

Corbett wedged his knee between her thighs most intimately, heating her with his aggressive possession of her. One of his hands cupped her breast most sensually while the other arm supported her as he bent over her between the heavy crenels. Lilliane's arm encircled his neck, one holding his head down to hers, the other clutching at his wide shoulders.

She could have succumbed to him then and there, in the dark night against the cold stone walls of Orrick. But even as she became more and more pliant and began to press herself most wantonly against him, she felt him pulling away.

Frantically she clutched him, willing him to stay. But though his lips clung to hers, and his tongue met hers in a hot, erotic dance, she could not make him stay.

Lilliane was in complete disarray. Her skirt was hiked up, baring her legs, her dress was loose at one shoulder, and her hair was a wild tumble in the chill wind. She was partially leaning back in the space between the crenels where he'd been sitting before and she knew she looked the complete wanton. But if that was what he wanted of her . . .

Corbett was breathing hard. His expression was wary as he stepped farther away from her. Then his eyes moved slowly over her, and she blushed at the thoroughness of his perusal. Shaking as much from passion as from the departure of his warmth from her, she struggled to rise. When she was upright she shook out her skirt and tried to refasten her mantle. But she could not raise her gaze to Corbett's face for fear of the condemnation she would see there.

When he finally spoke his voice was an unfamiliar rasp as if he grappled with his words. "This is not what I want," he said, and Lilliane felt as if a cold fist had tightened around her heart. Then he rubbed one hand along the scar on his forehead. "It's not enough for you to respond to me, Lily. I want *you* to show me your passion."

At her look of utter confusion Corbett took a slow, shaky breath and looked away from her. "Shall I be crude and tell you precisely what I want of you?"

Comprehension dawned on her in a sudden flash. Her belly tightened at the knowledge that he wished her to become the aggressor, the one to initiate their lovemaking. It was such a happy realization that she could not help but smile. "Oh, Corbett, I tried to do this very thing that last night in London, but you—"

"Don't speak to me of London," he cut in abruptly as his eyes pinned her to her spot. "Don't ever speak to me of London. Just do as I ask."

Lilliane had to bite her lip to prevent herself from crying anew. In some ways he wanted her so badly, just as she wanted him. But in other ways . . .

She pushed one wind-driven lock from her brow as she tried to compose herself. In other ways he seemed determined forever to keep her at arm's length.

She crossed to the door. Corbett opened it for her and then followed close behind her as they went down the steep stone steps. The stairwell was cold but Corbett's nearness seemed to create an aura of warmth. Still, for all the physical heat they generated together, Lilliane could not mistake the emotional chill between them.

When they reached the door to the tower room Lilliane turned to face him.

"I have one caveat upon which I must insist," she started as bravely as she could.

Corbett stood very near her. His great size blocked the light from the single torch so that only his silhouette was clear to her. "No."

The word, though spoken quietly, seemed to roar like thunder in the empty stone tower. Lilliane wanted to clap her hands over her ears to shut out that obstinate, angry sound. But instead, with no forethought, she put her hands up to his cheeks and pulled his head down to meet her kiss.

It was a bold move, one she'd had no chance to weigh the merits of. But perhaps for that very reason it seemed to placate him as nothing else would have. She'd only wanted to ask him to leave his anger behind when they went through the door, to allow them to meet without the emotional encumbrances that tortured them both. But as their lips clung in a kiss at once both passionate and sweet, Lilliane felt as if he'd already given in to her unspoken request.

She was aware when he backed her into the door. Then the door opened and she started to fall. But Corbett caught her up in his arms. The touch of his tongue was like a stroke of fire along her lips and within her mouth. The solid feel of his body cradling hers so easily was like floating off into heaven, for she knew just what a heaven awaited her.

But Lilliane fought off the mind-stealing lethargy

brought on by his passion. That was not what this night was about. When Corbett lowered her feet to the ground, she put one palm flat against his chest to hold him at bay.

"Wait," she said, panting, although waiting was hardly what she wanted to do. "You must let me do as . . . as you said."

Corbett did not smile, but his eyes were smoky with desire and he was breathing hard. "Then go ahead." He gestured to the bed.

Lilliane shook her hair back as she looked over her powerful husband. He was tall and strong, and in spite of the scars that marked him, she thought him the most handsome and desirable man alive. Her hand slid slowly across the breadth of his chest, feeling the definition of his muscles there and the reassuring beat of his heart. It was a steady beat, strong and reliable as he was. If only he could see that she was strong and reliable too.

But she pushed that painful thought away and took a step nearer him. With hands that trembled only a little, she loosened the brooch that held his short mantle on. Deliberately she stood as close to him as she could, and although she did not see his face, she knew the effect she caused on him. Her hair was a loose cloud, tumbling wildly about her face and shoulders. She knew how he loved her hair, and as she bent even closer she felt his fingers stroke down through the long chestnut length.

Before he could gather it into his hands, however, she moved to take hold of the gold-braided hem of his tunic. As she tugged the blue serge up and over his wide shoulders, he raised his arms obligingly and she was reminded of their first meeting.

It had been in this very room and she'd had to undress him then as well. But where she'd been frightened and filled with dread then, now she felt only love.

His shirt was next. She cast it carelessly aside, for she was feeling eager as he stood before her bare-chested.

"Now it's your turn," he murmured huskily, and he reached for her.

"No." Lilliane stared at him seriously, putting up one hand to keep him at a distance.

But Corbett caught her hand and twined his fingers with his so that their palms were pressed warmly together. Somehow it seemed the most intimate of gestures, and Lilliane felt a rush of love for this man go over her. For a moment she could do no more than stare into his deep gray eyes.

"If I may not remove your clothes until mine are gone, then you must hurry, Lily. I'm only human and you tempt me beyond endurance." Lilliane did not delay although her cheeks burned when she removed his braies and then his small cloth. Yet when she looked at her husband standing so erect and proud in his naked glory, she could feel no shame for her brazenness.

She kept her wide, golden gaze locked upon his as she slowly began to remove her own clothes. Corbett's face took on an expression approaching torment as she struggled with the tight lacings at her wrists and at either side of her waist. But as she finally put the full-skirted garment aside, Lilliane was more than pleased to see the rigid evidence of Corbett's arousal. She let her hair fall before her as she bent to remove her hose and then her delicately woven kirtle. It was a gesture done more for the scanty protection it gave her from his gaze than to be provocative. Yet it proved to be the final straw for Corbett.

"Come here, Lily," he murmured in a low, tortured tone.

She started to go to him, as meekly and obediently as a wife should. But then she stopped; she wanted to show him so much more than just obedience.

It took all her mettle to raise her head bravely and shake her hair back. Only when she stood before him proudly in her nakedness did she at last come to him.

Corbett's eyes seemed to devour her. She was trembling with excitement, her own arousal now clearly displayed to him. When she reached him he stood as one entranced until she slid her hands up his chest to encircle his neck and then fitted herself intimately against him. It was an unmaidenly thing to do, indecent by any lady's standards. But Lilliane knew instinctively that it was the right way to show her love to Corbett.

In an instant he gathered her into his steely embrace with a fierceness that took her breath away. She'd had plans to seduce him, to try to imitate all the ways he'd kissed her and touched her in the past until this time he would be the one begging her to come to him. But she'd underestimated both the power of her seductive preparations and the strength of his raging desire.

Corbett's lips were like fire on her skin. Everywhere they passed—over her eyelids and her cheeks, down to the corners of her mouth, and the lobes of her ears—she was inflamed. Then he moved in sweet delicious kisses along the sensitive curve of her neck and lower, to the high outthrust swell of her breasts.

Corbett sank to one knee then and one of his hands moved to cup her derriere. His mouth became more deliberate as he began to kiss the pearly skin of first one of her breasts and then the other. Nearer and nearer he circled until her nipples were aching with need and Lilliane was arching toward him desperately.

She caught his head between her hands, marveling that his hair could be so soft when the rest of him was so hard. She bent to kiss the top of his head and then, using all her waning strength, guided him most demandingly to take her nipple in his mouth.

The exquisiteness of his lips upon that tight rosy nub as he sucked it into his mouth then teased it with his teeth and tongue sapped the last of Lilliane's strength. Had he not held her so snugly to him, she was certain she would have fallen. As it was she sagged against him, crying at the acute pleasure and yet still wanting some ease for the voracious need building in her belly.

But Corbett was relentless. First one, then the other of her breasts received his total devotion. Then, when she thought surely he must bring her to the bed or she would die of longing for him, he moved his kisses lower still.

Lilliane stood leaning over him, her hands braced upon his massive shoulders as he bent to kiss her belly. When his thumbs tenderly opened her most feminine center to those extraordinary kisses, she cried out in ecstasy. "Corbett, Corbett! My one sweet love!"

Then she began to shudder with the explosive

power of her release. Her hands gripped him blindly as she arched back in that perfect, perfect agony.

It lasted forever. It ended too soon. She only knew that Corbett was on his knees grasping her so tightly to him that it hurt. His head was bowed just beneath her chin and she rested her tear-streaked cheek on his damp, raven locks.

She was crying and unable to stop when he finally raised his head to look at her. Their eyes seemed to meet forever, and in a brief moment of clarity Lilliane thought that his gaze had never seemed so clear. Then he lifted her high in his arms and laid her down upon their bed.

His entry was swift and sure. Lilliane wrapped herself completely about him, wanting more than anything in the world to give him whatever he wanted. If he wanted an obedient wife, then she would become that wife. If he wanted a mistress to provide him with the most carnal of pleasures, she would be that mistress. If he wanted an heir, oh, please God, let her bear him their child.

And if he wanted to be rid of her . . .

She could not think of that at all. Instead she rose to meet his powerful thrust, taking all he had to give over and over again.

When he pulled her upright to straddle his thighs so that they were face to face, she was certain he touched the very center of her being. Her fingers dug into his shoulders as she felt the passion rising within her again. As he strained in an increasing tempo and then began to stiffen, her own passion peaked once more and, as if in a violent storm, they reached their zenith together.

There were no words afterward. They lay quietly

together after catching their breath, but neither of them sought to break the intimate tangle of their limbs.

Lilliane lay with her head on Corbett's chest, his heart beating strongly beneath her ear. One of her arms lay across his chest and under her hand she felt the three scarred ridges on the back of his shoulder.

That heartbeat. Those scars. At that moment they seemed somehow to symbolize everything about him. He was a warrior, scarred outside and perhaps inside as well. Yet his heart pounded so adamantly, so constantly within his chest. Could that heart ever love her? she wondered wistfully.

The words came to her lips unbidden. Her soft "I love you" was less than a whisper in the quiet night air. But she meant it as nothing she'd ever meant before. Whether or not he was awake to hear, whether or not he would even believe her, it was nonetheless true.

She loved him and she always would.

21

It was a fragile peace.

Lilliane was truly grateful that Corbett has ceased his nightly drinking and had regained a modicum of his earlier, easy mood. But she knew at the same time that she had but won a skirmish. The enemy was not yet defeated. The war was not over.

She saw it in the way his eyes followed her, although he always had a smile ready for her. She sensed it in the way he concerned himself with every least detail of the castle preparations. The only odd note in his otherwise careful behavior was his annoyance with his friend, Sir Dunn.

Dunn, it seemed, had suddenly grown to like her. Gone were the suspicious stares and the watchfulness. Now he greeted her most cordially, always inquiring after her health, or little Elyse's. And if Corbett was about, Dunn always sent him a smug, almost triumphant look. This would bring a scowl to Corbett's face. But no words would pass between the two men. Just those strange, telling looks.

Despite the relative calm at Orrick, however, Corbett's tension seemed to increase up to the day the guests began to arrive.

Tullia and her husband, Sir Santon, came first, and the two sisters met in a warm embrace.

"How content you look, sister!" Tullia cried as her soft brown eyes took in every aspect of Lilliane's appearance.

"And you look quite the happy wife."

"Soon to be a mother," Tullia confided with a most rapturous expression. "I hope you are soon so fortunate as I."

"So do I," Lilliane whispered as she hugged her sister anew. Her gaze sought out Corbett who was greeting Sir Santon most hospitably. All the signs were there to indicate that she might, indeed, be with child. Her second monthly flux was even now overdue. And yet she still held back from telling Corbett. She told herself she just wanted to be sure. But a little part of her lived in dread of the doubting look she might see on his face. He'd never again brought up William's accusations—lies was a more accurate term. But she feared he still believed them. Would he doubt the true parentage of this child she bore?

Lilliane shook off those troubling thoughts and smiled at her youngest sister. "You must be quite exhausted from your journey. I had your own chamber prepared so that you may be most comfortable."

She barely had them settled before more guests appeared on their heels. Sir Roger and Sir Charles come from London along with Lady Elizabeth and her father. Lord Gavin from Durmond and the earl of Gloucester. Even Odelia and Sir Aldis from their home in Gaston, their greeting meek and hesitant. Although there was still a reserve between her and her sister, Lilliane was relieved that Odelia and her husband seemed more accepting of her marriage to Corbett.

The castle was filled to overflowing and was in a constant hubbub, for aside from the invited guests, there were also their guards, their personal servants, and their horses to be housed and fed. The kitchen was filled with activity at every hour of the day or night as breads were baked, huge haunches roasted, and every manner of fish and fowl cleaned and prepared for the guests.

Despite the endless supervision and the myriad of details the servants plagued her with, Lilliane took a profound pleasure in hosting the Christ's Mass festivities. When she had prepared the castle for Tullia's wedding feast—and unexpectedly her own—she'd felt a certain detachment as well as a sense of loss, for she had thought Orrick would never again be her home. And then the wedding feast itself had been a complete sham.

But the preparations for these lengthy festivities were another matter entirely. She was determined to enjoy every aspect of Christ's Mass: the feasting, the games, the entertainments, and the gift giving. She did not feel at all the same trepidation she'd felt among the crowds in London, for now she was on home ground. Now she was at Orrick.

It wasn't until after the feast of St. Thomas that Lilliane felt the first qualm about the festivities. Corbett had taken the male guests on a hunt in the winter woods quite early. Most of the ladies were taking advantage of this winter reprieve from their own wifely tasks to stay long abed. So it was that Lilliane was alone with her kitchen books when the chamberlain announced the arrival of still another guest.

Lilliane hurried to the bailey as the small retinue of riders crossed the bridge, but when she recognized Sir Hughe of Colchester, her smile began to fade. Still, there was nothing to do but greet him as cordially as possible despite the instinctive dislike she felt for the man. And even though she worried about Corbett's strange interest in his brother's every move, she nonetheless hoped her husband would soon return and relieve her of any lengthy discourse with the ominous Sir Hughe.

"I bid you welcome, Sir Hughe." She curtsied as he dismounted and tossed his reins carelessly to a waiting groom.

"What is this!" he exclaimed with a joviality not reflected in his narrow gaze. "I bid you greet me as a loving sister-in-law, Lilliane." With that he gave her a forceful hug and a hard kiss directly on her mouth.

Lilliane was more than shocked by his unwonted familiarity. She stepped back quite startled and stared at him warily. But Hughe seemed determined to befriend her.

"Don't be so shocked, my dear. Despite all that has passed between our houses, I am certain that Orrick and Colchester shall now be at peace. Why, it will almost be as if we were one united demesne." He grinned.

"Y-yes, so it shall," Lilliane stammered, quite certain now that something was afoot. Corbett and Hughe were far from affectionate brothers. Neither Corbett's attempt at only a casual interest in Colchester, nor Hughe's unexpected friendliness toward Orrick could quite disguise that. But Lilliane was intrigued.

When Hughe inquired about a number of the

guests and then finally asked after William of Dearne, her curiosity only intensified.

"William is not here," she murmured as she offered him a tankard of ale in the great hall.

"Indeed?" Sir Hughe swished the dark-brown ale thoughtfully in the tankard. Then his watchful gaze rose to her face. "I am surprised he was even invited. Some say he may forgo the pleasure of Orrick entirely."

He sought information. Lilliane was certain of it. Well, so did she, she admitted to herself. It could be quite enlightening to linger at conversation with Sir Hughe.

"Oh, I'm sure he must come." She fingered her heavy meridian ring, then affected a faint, knowledgeable smile. "After all, his daughter, Elyse, remains at Orrick."

"But not with his consent. I heard Corbett was quite ruthless toward William." This time he smiled. "And toward you as well."

Lilliane could not prevent the frown that creased her brow, nor the color that stained her cheeks. Did the entire kingdom know of William's lies and Corbett's suspicions? Did the ladies even now whisper of it in their rooms and the men jest crudely at the expense of her reputation?

She fought down angry words and faced her bland-faced tormentor. Plainly he delighted in the troubles between her and Corbett, as if somehow he benefited from his brother's problems. Well, how much more would he delight if she magnified them even further?

Lilliane did not pause to consider the consequences as she declared war on Sir Hughe. She knew only that he was still her enemy—in spite of her marriage to his brother. She suspected that for some reason, he was Corbett's enemy as well.

"I'm afraid Corbett has a suspicious nature," she revealed slowly. Then she gave him a long, steady look. "I would not ask . . ." She faltered, then had to restrain a laugh at the avid expression on Hughe's face. "Has . . . has Corbett always been inclined to drink?"

Any humor Lilliane felt fled at the quick flash of satisfaction that lighted Hughe's gaunt face. If she'd had any doubt of Hughe's true feelings toward his brother, they were now banished. For all his pretense of civility and even brotherly concern, it was apparent to her that he would take perverse pleasure in Corbett's downfall.

Hughe smiled expansively and let his eyes slip assessingly over her. "He has always had a wild and ruthless streak. He was a jealous and cruel boy. No doubt he's become a jealous and cruel man." The last was said as a statement yet the arch of his brow lent it a questioning air.

Lilliane would not confirm it and thereby lie outright, but she did not hesitate to blush prettily and lower her gaze in apparent agreement. When Hughe took her hand and patted it reassuringly, she had to grit her teeth to prevent her revulsion from showing.

"Take heart, my dear. Despite the unfortunate past between Orrick and Colchester, rest assured that you may always turn to me should Corbett's vile temper get out of hand. Just send word to me and I shall see to your safety." His smile became more knowing. "And despite his absence, I know you may count on William's unwavering loyalty as well."

With that clear innuendo Hughe excused himself and retired to his chamber with many reassurances and smiles. Once he was gone Lilliane remained in the great hall fighting down a wave of nausea that might have been caused as much by the vile Sir Hughe as by her suspected pregnancy.

What was Hughe up to? she wondered in agitation. He and William were somehow tied together in this, and they both saw Corbett as their adversary. But why?

Her musings were halted by someone approaching. When she looked up she saw Sir Dunn's curious face.

For a moment there was silence. They'd never actually sought one another's company despite Dunn's recent overtures of friendliness. Still, the suspicious expression on his face was more a reflection of the old Sir Dunn, and Lilliane almost felt relief as she snapped, "What is it?"

He did not respond at once and Lilliane was sure he debated in his mind how to begin. He finally drew a long breath. "I hope I'm not wrong about you."

"Wrong? What is that supposed to mean?"

"You spoke a good while with Hughe. He seemed well pleased when he left you."

Lilliane stood up in exasperation. "He is my brother-in-law. Should I not speak to him or put him at his ease? Besides, what right have you to spy upon me?"

His face grew grim and he watched her closely. "Your loyalty lies with your husband."

At his solemn expression Lilliane drew back and her annoyance fled. "My loyalty is with him," she vowed most earnestly. "Believe nothing else but believe that."

The blond knight's face was inscrutable as he weighed her words. When he spoke it was slowly and with much feeling. "I believe you. He is not so sure of it, but I leave it to you to convince him. Still, I caution you to be careful of Hughe."

"Can't you tell me what the trouble between them is?"

But Dunn only shook his head and, with a last intense look at her, quit the hall.

Lilliane did not have time to ponder Dunn's vague warning. Much too soon she was called to inspect the four pigs roasting in the huge kitchen hearths. By then the ladies had begun to rise, and no sooner were they being entertained than the men returned from the hunt.

She dispatched a servant to see the game cleaned and dressed, then sought out her husband in the great hall. Corbett was laughing at some antic of Gavin's when she entered, but though he retained his interest in the company she knew his eyes followed her.

"Good lady Lilliane," Sir Roger boomed as he took her hand most gallantly. "Perhaps you can answer this puzzle. Your husband swears the woods of Orrick contain the wildest of creatures. He had us all watching our backs lest some strange animal attack us!"

"I never said the creature attacks," Corbett countered. "Indeed, I told you repeatedly that it was quite shy and would flee at any pursuit."

"But there was nothing there more than any greensward might hold: deer, the occasional hind or boar.

I say he is just spinning some fantastic tale for his own amusement!"

"But I myself have seen the flighty creature." He grinned then lowered his gaze to Lilliane's puzzled face.

"But no doubt never caught it!" Sir Charles accused wryly.

Corbett hesitated and his eyes seemed to warm as he looked at her. "I don't believe it can be caught, at least not as other creatures might be."

Lilliane could not prevent a blush as she realized to which wild creature he referred. To her relief none of the others seemed aware of Corbett's meaning as they continued in their boisterous conversation.

Once the servants appeared with ale for the guests, she beckoned Corbett away from the others. She wanted to tell him about Hughe's arrival, but it appeared the raucous company had brought Corbett's brother downstairs. When Corbett's arm became rigid beneath her palm, she did not have to turn around to know who he had seen.

How she wished this animosity between the two brothers could be dissolved. But as Lilliane looked up at her husband, it was not so much dislike she saw as it was regret. That and an expression akin to pain.

But then that rare glimpse of his feelings was covered by a mask of polite greeting.

"Welcome, Hughe." Corbett strode toward his brother. If he was surprised by Hughe's broad smile and hearty slap on the back, he hid it well.

"Glad I am to share these festivities at Orrick with you and your lovely wife. It's far too long that this valley has been torn apart by mistrust. Now the two of us can see Windermere Fold united."

It should have been perfect, a pretty domestic reunion, Lilliane thought as she was drawn into the crowd that encircled the two brothers. Yet she could not escape her suspicious thoughts about Hughe; she was certain he planned something.

Corbett was behaving in a manner equally confusing, for he was maintaining a farce of his own. Unbidden, Dunn's words exhorting her to keep her loyalties solely with her husband came to mind. Did that imply more than she had at first realized?

She truly did not know her husband well enough to decide. He held his feelings in check. Once she'd thought him capable of murdering her father. Lilliane stared at him thoughtfully and felt a twinge of doubt. If he'd had any part in her father's death, then he was most certainly capable of plotting against his brother. She knew that to hold both Colchester and Orrick castles would give him immense power in northern England. And Corbett was most definitely a man who relished his own power.

But he had not contributed to her father's death, she told herself sternly. That had been a natural occurrence, well attested to by old Thomas. What lay between the two brothers she could not say. She would just have to keep faith in Corbett.

Lilliane wearily rubbed the small of her back. It had already been a long day and the evening feasting was still to come. Then two more days until Christ's Mass. At that moment Lilliane lost all enthusiasm for entertaining. She was exhausted by the preparations and tired of the endless machinations among the nobility. More than anything she wanted everyone simply to leave her and Corbett alone at Orrick. They might have a chance if Hughe and all the others were gone. Then she could tell Corbett about the child she carried and they might finally be happy together.

A short time later the head table was well filled, for Hughe, Odelia and Aldis, Tullia and Santon, and Sir Gavin joined them along with the earl of Gloucester, one of King Edward's triumvirate. The seating arrangement had perplexed Lilliane sorely, but to her relief Sir Gavin was charming Odelia and the earl of Gloucester was keeping both Corbett and Hughe well entertained. Once the meal was underway she relaxed.

"How I wish Father were here," Tullia said wistfully. "Everything has turned out as he hoped."

Lilliane squeezed her sister's hand. "You knew all along that he planned this?"

"I knew that you and the man you wed would rule at Orrick. That's why he was so inflexible in the choice of your husband."

"But he couldn't have held out hope for my betrothal agreement with Corbett all those years."

"No, perhaps not. But he didn't truly hate the house of Colchester. Even after all the misery they brought to Orrick, he always respected their motives in avenging their father's death."

"But they were wrong in accusing him," Lilliane insisted.

"Yes. I know. But that is all past now. All that remains is for you to bear an heir for Orrick."

"Then our father shall soon be most content," Lilliane confessed in a whisper.

"Oh! I knew it. I just knew it!" Tullia exclaimed, bringing a curious look from both Corbett and

Santon. Tullia quickly composed her features, but her bright brown gaze was brimming with happiness for her sister. "Have you told him yet?"

Lilliane bit her lip and glanced at her handsome husband. He was speaking to Hughe and it appeared a most peaceful scene. But she knew much still brewed beneath the surface, for this festive occasion had not been planned by accident. She shook her head slowly. "I've told no one but you." Then she looked at Tullia intently. "Say you'll keep my secret for now."

"Of course I will. But you might do well to tell Odelia also."

"Odelia? She feels no good will toward me. Why, she and Aldis would be quite annoyed to see their right to Orrick further eroded."

Tullia shrugged. "Perhaps that was the way of it once. But Aldis has heard much of Corbett's connection to King Edward. He is wise enough to accept things as they are. Besides, his father now seems more willing to hand some of the responsibilities for Gaston over to him. Plus," Tullia added with a secretive grin, "Odelia is also with child. But do not let on I told you!"

Three little cousins to be borne of three sisters. Lilliane smiled at the thought of the three families sharing many years of festivities such as these. When Sir Hughe retired early from the table, it seemed the best of omens. Those who then remained in the great hall were all of good nature and fine company. In her happiness, Lilliane finally pushed all thoughts of strife or plotting from her mind. They gathered to celebrate the Christ's Mass, the birth of the son of

God, the baby that had brought peace to all the world.

Lilliane let her hand slide down to rest comfortingly on her belly. Her eyes sought out her husband. God willing, this baby of hers would help bring peace to Windermere Fold.

Sir Hughe's mind dwelt on Windermere Fold, but his version was far removed from Lilliane's. Under cover of a moonless night he made his way toward the gate tower, startling the pair of guards who maintained the lower watch.

"Do you go without, milord?"

Hughe shook his head then groaned and put one hand to his brow. "Sweet Jesu, but the wine flows freely tonight," he muttered.

At that the guard who had spoken began to chuckle. "Aye, it sounds to be a considerable feast."

"And you stout fellows left out in the cold." Hughe gave them each a sympathetic look. He took two more erratic steps then leaned heavily against the stonework of the gatehouse. "I'll tell you what, my good fellows. I've a flask here. I'd intended to curl up with it and find my sleep—" He groaned again and this time held his stomach. " 'Tis time to quit the wine." He gave them a lopsided grin and struggled to stand upright. "Here. You take the rest. 'Tis sure to keep you warm despite the bitter cold."

"We can't drink during the watch," the same guard replied reluctantly.

Sir Hughe stared at them both then shrugged. "Oh, well. 'Tis only a little left anyway." Then he seemed to brighten. "Perhaps the creatures in the moat would like to drink as their betters do." He pulled the stopper from the flask and began to make his way toward the bridge.

"No, wait!" The second guard grabbed Sir Hughe's arm, then looked back at his partner. "'Tis but a taste left for each of us. Surely there's no harm in just a swallow or two."

Sir Hughe stood very still as the other guard weighed the matter in his mind. It was all he could do to restrain a grin of triumph as the two guards reached for the bottle. Within a matter of minutes they both had collapsed to the ground, victims of the strong dose of redroot he'd added to the wine.

Before any note could be taken of what he'd done, Hughe dragged the two men into the shadows behind a flanking wall and then assumed their position at the gate. When a single figure approached the bridge some time later, the upper guards hailed him. But when one of the lower guards questioned him then bade him enter, there was no further comment from the ramparts. Only then did Sir Hughe relax.

"You see, William, 'tis as I said. My brother is but a mortal man. And as easily as you have gained access to Orrick, so now shall you gain access to your child. Also to the fair Lady Lilliane. She will not hesitate to flee Orrick if she knows both you and the babe await."

William pushed back the hood that covered his head. His face was grim but his eyes had come alive at the mention of Lilliane.

"Aye. She was so close to coming before. But that demon cast me from the castle." His voice shook with emotion. "This time he'll never know until it is too late!" Then he paused. "But he'll follow. He'll not lose easily."

"I told you to leave that to me. Once he is dead you will be free to take Lilliane. Then you'll have Orrick and we'll be a force that Edward must reckon with."

There was a stirring in the shadows and Hughe looked around furtively. "The guards will not sleep forever. Hurry to your task. Everyone is yet at the feast. You know where the babe lies. Be quick about it!"

The ladies retired when the men began to gamble at dice. There was much boasting and ribaldry as well as numerous oaths to be heard when a large group of men drank and gambled. Lilliane deemed it best to escort the ladies from the great hall before things became unruly; she relied on Corbett to keep the men reasonably in line.

Corbett bade her a fond good night when she rose to leave, kissing both her hands then holding them more tightly when she would have left.

"Shall I wake you when I come to bed?"

Lilliane's eyes fell away from his intense gaze and she felt her cheeks color. "Yes."

"It may be quite late. You'll not be too tired?"

At that Lilliane looked up into his serious face. "I'm never too tired to attend you, my lord."

Again there was a pause. "You've been most weary lately."

So he had noticed. Lilliane resolved then and there to tell him about their child. Tonight, after they had made love, she would confide in him. Then she would know where she stood with him.

"I'll be waiting for you," she vowed.

Once in her own chamber, Lilliane paced restlessly. She was as eager as a new bride, she admitted.

Surely it must be a sin to desire your husband so. Yet she knew no church admonition that clearly forbade her this deep-rooted longing for Corbett.

He would be a long time coming. She knew that some of the men would happily remain at the gaming until almost dawn's light. At the thought of that possibility she frowned and wrapped her arms about her waist. Her sweet secret lay cradled deep within her. Corbett did not know of it.

But he could not be as unaware of her love for him. Even if he'd not heard her whispered words of love, he must at least suspect how she felt. She was an utter failure at hiding her emotions, quite unlike him.

He'd never really sought her love. Still, there had been times when he would look at her in a certain way, or perhaps say something unexpected. She bit her lip in uncertainty. Perhaps it was time to tell him exactly how she felt.

A quiver of nervousness shivered up her spine at the thought of such a revelation. She could win all she hoped for, or her dreams could be dashed forever.

Lilliane began to pace again. Then she stopped. Perhaps she could while away the time with Elyse. Ferga still gave the child a nightly feeding, but tonight she would do it herself. Satisfied with that idea, she slipped her tunic back over her kirtle. When she realized her hair was streaming loose across her shoulders in the most wanton manner, she donned a short, hooded mantle and quickly tucked her thick hair inside the woolen garment. Then she quietly made her way down the stairs and across the loggia to the wing where the nursery was.

The scene that greeted Lilliane was hardly one of juvenile repose.

"Ferga! Ferga!" Lilliane rushed to the bound figure lying upon the carpeted floor.

"She's gone, milady! He's taken her!" the weeping woman exclaimed, sobbing, once Lilliane removed the cloth that gagged her mouth.

"Elyse? Someone's taken her? But who? Who?"

"Sir William! He said she was his and no devil of King Edward's was going to raise her."

"Oh, dear God in heaven," Lilliane whispered as she helped the frightened woman to rise. "He must be mad to take such a tiny infant into the winter night like this. Hurry, Ferga. We must go to Corbett with this. He can—"

"But, milady, wait. Read this first." Ferga grabbed her arm and showed her a bit of paper. "Sir William was most adamant that I give it to you when no one else was present."

Lilliane's hand trembled as she took the single piece of parchment and then read the words William had written.

She is my daughter. She was given to you to raise. We may yet do that together. Join me at the crossroad to Burgram Abbey, sweet Lilliane. We have been denied our happiness too long. But now we must act. Come to me at once. Tell no one of your destination. Do not fear to leave all behind for I've made plans to rid you and Orrick of your cruel husband once and for all.

William

Lilliane stared at the parchment long after she'd read over the words. He'd made plans to rid her of

Corbett? Dear God, dear God! He must truly be mad! Did he really think she valued her wedding vows so lightly? Even had she been married to a man she detested she could not so easily betray him. But she loved Corbett with her whole heart and soul. With every fiber of her being. She would never leave him. Nor would she allow William to hurt him in any way.

Lilliane looked up at Ferga. "How did he seem? Was he crazed or distraught?"

"No. No, he was calm and polite. He even apologized for binding me. But then, you know he was never a violent man."

Lilliane did not respond. William might not appear to be a violent man, but his threat said otherwise. She balled up the parchment and flung it into the fire, not knowing whether to be more furious with him or with herself. She'd never explained to William how deeply her feelings for Corbett ran. She'd foolishly allowed his affection for her to continue long after it should have died. He had every right to his child, she knew. But he was terribly wrong to take her like this and thereby endanger her life. And to threaten Corbett's life!

In agitation she weighed her alternatives. But given William's hatred of Corbett, Elyse's delicate condition, and William's dire threat, Lilliane could come to only one conclusion. No matter how she debated it, the answer was the same. She must meet William as he'd instructed and then try to make him see the futility of what he was doing. If she could just appease him, he might abandon his foolish threat. And perhaps even let Elyse stay until the spring. She would promise to deliver the child to Castle Dearne then. She would not deny him his child, no matter how much she had grown to love the little girl.

Resolved on this, Lilliane faced Ferga. "Lie down and seek your rest, Ferga. I'll see to William and Elyse."

"Shall I fetch milord?"

"No!" Lilliane's startled cry drew Ferga aback. With an effort she made herself sound more calm. "No, it would be best if he did not hear of this at all. Sir William is only misguided in his devotion to his daughter. But if I go to meet him as he asked, I can soothe his fears and persuade him to bring Elyse back. Besides, you know my husband's temper would not hold were he to face William now."

It was that last that convinced Ferga to keep silent. That and Lilliane's promise to take two guards with her. But although Lilliane made the promise, it was one she had no intention of keeping. Not pausing to weigh the consequences, she hurried to the stable, saddled her favorite, Aere, and without a word to the two hunched-over guards, thundered from the castle.

22

The night was pitch black and bitterly cold. Had Lilliane not known the road so well, she would surely have lost her way. No moonbeam glinted off the bent stalks of dried grasses, no starlight caught in the bare, reaching limbs of the oaks and beeches. It was a night fit only for wolves and owls, those deadly hunters and their hapless prey.

Lilliane tried not to think of all that might go amiss with her pitiful plan. Aere could stumble and fall upon the road, although Lilliane kept her at a nerve-rackingly slow pace; thieves could beset her from the forest, although it seemed unlikely that even highway robbers would be out this night.

She would not dwell on the possibility of not finding William nor on Corbett's anger when he found about her escapade. She would simply locate William and straighten things out with him. Then she would smooth everything over with Corbett.

It was her determination alone that kept her going through the cold, murky night. She knew from the curves in the turnpike that she was nearing the river and then the Middling Stone. The crossroads would not be much beyond there.

She and Aere were going along at a fast walk while

she peered ahead into the darkness when she heard a cry. At once she pulled Aere up. Had it been just a hunting bird, or perhaps a rabbit caught beneath the deadly talons? She strained to hear, holding her breath. Then it came again and she was certain. It was a child, a baby crying out in fear or cold or hunger. At once her flagging spirits were renewed and she urged Aere on.

"William! William, please wait! It's me, Lilliane!"

When his call came in reply, Lilliane's heart surged with relief. Following the direction of his voice, she cautiously guided the mare off the road. She did not see anyone at all; she could barely make out the upright shape of an ancient yew tree when William spoke again.

"Stop there, Lilliane. Dismount." There was a pause. "I trust you came alone as I instructed?"

"Oh, yes. Of course, I'm alone. But how is Elyse? I heard her cry."

As if on cue the baby began to whimper, and Lilliane immediately hurried toward the sound. But William blocked her path and put his hands on her shoulders. "I knew you would come," he murmured. Then he enveloped her in a smothering embrace.

"Please, William. Let me breathe," Lilliane muttered as she struggled to be free of his unwelcome grasp. She was tired and angry, and frightened half to death. With a final yank of her arm she was free, and she moved back a step and tried to make him out.

"Forgive my eagerness, my love," he began, stepping forward even as she backed away. "It's just that I've dreamed of this day for so long."

Lilliane's first inclination was to lash out at him

for his foolish notions toward her and his selfish lack of concern for Elyse. But something warned her—perhaps the tone of his voice, perhaps only her sense of self-preservation—to proceed cautiously with him. It was her goal to bring Elyse to safety, she reminded herself. To do that she must reason with William, not berate him.

"I-I know you've waited," Lilliane whispered most reluctantly. "But we must see to your daughter first. She might be cold or hungry. Have you any changing rags?"

"Changing rags?" William turned his head toward the sound of Elyse's cry. "Harold? Have we changing rags?"

Lilliane was startled by this first indication that there were others with William. It might make her task even more difficult.

A burly fellow stepped forward carrying a large basket from which the child's angry cries were coming. At once Lilliane knelt on the ground and carefully lifted little Elyse from the jumble of blankets. She did not speak as she swiftly removed the soaked linen from the baby and fastened fresh cloths around her. Then she tucked her neatly within the protective wicker and warm wool.

Lilliane's mind had been working rapidly as she'd attended the child, trying to form some plan. Now when she looked up at William she saw he was flanked by two men, their forms more discernible as the clouds thinned and the moon showed feebly in the haze.

"I think she's already ill," Lilliane lied. "She's much too young to be out in such cruel weather. If she's not put before a warm fire soon she will not survive. Babies are frail creatures. You can't drag her around—"

"She'll survive. And if she doesn't do not despair. I know *you* will give me a son."

The very callousness of his words struck Lilliane speechless, even more than his outrageous assumptions about the two of them. He didn't care at all about Elyse. She was simply the bait he'd used to get her to come to him.

With an effort she managed to subdue her fury. She stood up with the basket in her arms. "William, we must find her shelter."

"We ride to Burgram Abbey. She'll manage well enough."

"But, William, I hardly imagine Mother Mary Catherine will take us in if she believes I've deserted my husband."

"You need not worry on that account for long, Lilliane. Besides, you forget that he's a murderer. He murdered your father and no one has taken him to task for it. But he'll pay for everything he's done. I've seen to it."

The icy rage in his voice sent a shudder of pure terror through Lilliane. She hugged the now-quiet baby closer to her as her mind raced desperately for some way to escape him.

It was clear he intended more than simply to flee with her and Elyse. He wanted to wreak his revenge on Corbett. He'd used Elyse as the bait to draw her in. Could she now be the bait to draw Corbett into his trap? Suddenly, she saw how foolish she'd been to come to him so easily. An icy dread filled her as she realized she might be used to cause Corbett's downfall.

Lilliane was wooden as William took her arm and led her to her horse. There would be no talking him into changing his mind, she understood now. Her only hope was that she might somehow escape with Elyse.

But as William took the baby and helped Lilliane mount, he must have sensed her hesitation. Instead of giving her the reins, he led her horse to his, then wrapped the reins about the raised pommel of his cloth-covered saddle. It was only then that he handed her Elyse's basket.

"Keep the child quiet as we ride," he ordered.

"Please, William. You cannot do this," Lilliane pleaded. "It's wrong and it will never work."

"Ah, but that's where you're mistaken. We have always been right. It was that hideous second son of Colchester who was wrong for you. But your father just would not see it."

He swung up onto his own horse. "And as for not getting away with it, I told you, you will soon be a widow. I need a wife. You'll need a husband. You're already mother to my child. No, it will all turn out as it should have years ago."

Lilliane had turned pale at William's confident threat against Corbett. "What do you plot against him?" she cried.

William frowned at the frightened note in Lilliane's voice. When he spoke this time, his anger was directed at her. "So he has turned you against me! Well, you will get over him, Lilliane, I assure you. Your Sir Corbett will be brought down by his own brother. Then you and I shall rule at Orrick."

It was a madman's reasoning, and Lilliane could make no sense of it at all. If Hughe were desperate enough to kill Corbett, then why would he allow William to rule at Orrick? And then, why should Hughe want his brother dead? Lilliane did not doubt that Hughe had such treachery in him, but she could discern no motive for such a vile act.

William led the way with Lilliane and Elyse directly following. His two henchmen were silent as they rode along behind them. As they regained the turnpike and continued south, the situation seemed unreal to Lilliane.

Corbett was no less unbelieving as he towered over the quaking Ferga.

"Both she and the babe?" he thundered as the woman cowered before his fury.

"She . . . she went after the child," Ferga mumbled with her head bowed low and her shoulders hunched against the expectations of a blow. But no blow came. When she chanced a terrified glance at Corbett, the pain she saw on his face gave her the courage to speak further. "William came first. He took Elyse and gave me a note for milady."

"What did the note say?" It was Dunn who broke in.

"I-I don't know," the maid admitted sorrowfully. "But she was certain she could convince him to return."

"So your wife is run away with William."

Corbett stiffened at the sound of his brother's voice.

"How inopportune that she should do so amid such merry-making and with so many guests present." Hughe paused and, despite his attempt at solicitousness a spark of malice crept into his tone. "Of course, she and William no doubt planned it in just such a fashion to take advantage of the confusion within the castle. You cannot forget that she is the daughter of a murderer, no matter how enamored you may have become of her pretty face."

With a fierce growl Corbett lunged toward him. Had not Dunn prevented it, he would have struck his brother down. As it was Hughe fell back several paces before regaining his composure.

"Your anger at me is sorely misguided!" he exclaimed, sputtering. "Better that you accept my aid in finding her than strike out at me so unfairly!"

Corbett's anger was a terrible thing to behold, and yet with a supreme effort he fought it down. Then he turned to Dunn. "Order the horses. Bring four of the guard." He turned abruptly to go, then stopped and stared intently at Hughe. "Will you ride with us, brother?"

It was said unemotionally, as if there were no misunderstandings between them or years of bitterness. But the very calm of his voice seemed to chill the room.

"I'll ride with you. After all, we must maintain a united front. Colchester and Orrick together create a mighty force. If your wife is successful in her flight, it would only cause a new wave of discord in Windermere Fold."

Corbett did not deign to reply. He watched as Hughe and Dunn both left to prepare for their imminent departure to search for the missing Lilliane. But as he donned his own short leather tunic and reached for his knife and sword, he spied Ferga huddled still in the corner.

"You may go," he ordered curtly as he stooped to lace on his tall leather boots.

"You must not be angry with milady," Ferga murmured in a small, frightened voice.

"Indeed?" Corbett bit the word out. "It seems her very purpose in life is to anger me. To mock me, to thwart me, to make a fool of me." He finished with the ominous slither of his sword into the leather scabbord at his side.

"She loves you."

The maid's words were but a whisper. Yet they froze Corbett in his place. His emotions could not be contained as he stared at her, and Ferga took heart at both the longing and the doubt she saw etched on his hard features.

"You cannot know that. Did she say such a thing to you?"

"Some things are not always said with words. But if you were paying attention, then you would know it nonetheless."

At Corbett's doubting look she smiled faintly and nodded her head. "Aye, she loves you."

Corbett started to speak again then stopped and stared intently at her, as if he might somehow be able to see the truth or falseness of her words if he only looked hard enough. Finally he took a heavy breath and reached for his mantle.

He did not speak to her as he quit the room, but Ferga heard his quiet plea as he strode away. "Pray let it be so, for 'tis certain that I love her."

In the bailey there was much confusion and curiosity among those guests who had not yet sought their beds. But Corbett's thunderous expression forbade any questions. As the men mounted their nervous steeds, Dunn pulled Corbett aside. "I do not like this at all. It behooves you to watch your back."

"That's why I keep you with me," Corbett answered dryly. "To watch my back for me."

Dunn scowled. "Do not treat this lightly—"

"Believe me when I say I do not!"

Corbett started to mount but Dunn caught his arm. "You should know that your wife and your brother had a long 'private' conversation this afternoon."

Corbett stared at Dunn. "Does this mean you reverse yourself once more where Lily is concerned? Or do you now believe Hughe is innocent of any scheming as well?"

Dunn opened his mouth then closed it. Finally he took a weary breath. "I don't know what to believe. I only know that nothing about this night is an accident. Anything could await us out there. We should not go out with such a small force."

"We must travel swiftly," Corbett snapped. "A full contingent of men would only slow us down. If you're frightened then stay behind. But I must find Lily before any harm befalls her."

With that he shook off his friend's arm. The other men were right behind, with Hughe and Dunn bringing up the rear.

Lilliane rode as slowly as she could. Despite the lead rein that William kept on her mare, she managed to guide Aere into bushes, snag her skirt in shrubs, or alternately urge Aere to crowd William's horse and startle it. Yet despite the meager satisfaction she received from her actions, she knew they were useless. With every pace they drew farther and farther away from Orrick. Even the clearing sky seemed designed to thwart her, for in a storm she might have managed to escape. Now, however, the moon aided their flight to Burgram Abbey. She could only hope that Corbett had somehow found out and was coming for her. Even if he was angry and jealous and completely mistaken about her motives, she prayed that he was coming.

They were at the river beginning to ford it when she chanced another glance backward.

"You need not fear his pursuit. Hughe will prevent him from ever bothering us again."

Lilliane fought to still the panic his boastful words roused in her. "What does Hughe plan? Why is he . . . helping you this way?"

William slowed his horse as they cautiously made their way through the nearly chest-deep water. "Hughe knows Corbett will not rest until he purges this area of all but the king's staunchest supporters."

"Doesn't Hughe support King Edward?"

William shrugged. "We in the north have more often than not been forgotten by old King Henry. His son is too interested in affairs abroad to concern himself with us any better than did his sire. But there are nearly enough of us now . . ."

He trailed off at a shout from one of his two men. "Someone moves along the road behind us!"

"Where?" William squinted into the darkness, searching for some sign that they were indeed being followed.

"It could just be Hughe," Lilliane said in an effort to relax William's guard.

"Perhaps." He grunted. "But we can't be sure. Hurry. If we can't outrun them then we shall hide at the base of the stone."

Lilliane felt equal measures of fear and hope as she hugged the sleeping Elyse close. Please let it be Corbett, she prayed fervently. And dear God, please keep him safe . . .

Corbett urged his stalwart mount to an even faster pace when the moon, glancing off the river, illuminated several figures.

"So you have caught up with your wayward wife and her lover." Hughe grunted as he kicked his horse to keep up with Corbett. "You can easily slice William apart, but that will hardly endear you to your wife."

Corbett did not even spare a glance at Hughe, so intent was he on reaching Lilliane. It was as if nothing mattered in the entire world—not England, nor Edward, not even Orrick and Colchester—so long as Lilliane was returned safely to him.

He did not pause in his headlong flight when he reached the river. By the time Qismah had made the other side, he could see the small band of riders approaching the Middling Stone at a mad gallop.

Hughe was somewhere behind him. Dunn and his men were farther back still when he heard Dunn cry "To arms! To arms!"

Corbett drew up at once, turned and saw a group of mounted men attacking his small band. William had planned well, he thought with a vicious oath. For a moment he hesitated. Dunn and the others were his trusted comrades. They'd fought together and saved one another countless times.

And yet there was Lilliane, and he could not turn back.

His decision was made in an instant. He did not hear Hughe's foul oath when he turned Qismah toward the ominous shadow of the Middling Stone. He did not second-guess the orders Dunn shouted as, blade against blade, his knights fought back the men who'd laid in wait for them. He only leaned low over his stallion's neck and prayed for Lilliane's safekeeping.

The first of William's henchmen was no opposition at all. With one whistling stroke of his long blade Corbett severed the man's arm at the shoulder. He did not wait to watch him fall.

His quarry had reached the base of the jagged outcropping before Corbett caught them. This time the man who faced him was ready for the attack. Yet he fared no better than his comrade. One stroke, a second, and then a third time the broadswords clashed in a grim dance of death. But as the men closed quarters Corbett drew his knife. With one swift upward stroke he deftly disemboweled the man. There was a terrible gurgling sound as he wrenched the knife free. Then he kicked Qismah away from the other horse and started up in earnest after William.

He was not mindful of Hughe's steady pursuit, nor of the now-muffled sounds of the battle beyond the river. His every sense was focused on the sound of hooves on the rocks above and of the thin wail of a child.

Lilliane was terrified as William whipped her horse to climb before him. The darkness, the awful sounds of battle carried in the chill night wind, and his desperate persistence filled her with dread. That it was Corbett who trailed them so doggedly she did not doubt. But even as he closed in on them, her fears for him magnified.

When the horses could go no farther, William

jumped down and dragged her down as well. "Climb!" he ordered wildly. "Climb!"

Too frightened to disobey, Lilliane scrambled upward, holding the basket with the now-wailing baby inside tightly before her. In the dark she stumbled and almost fell yet still she went forward, oblivious to the pain. At a wide space on the meager trail she paused for breath, then dodged William's hand as he grabbed for her.

"I'll go no farther!" she cried as she backed into a narrow crevice, sheltering Elyse in her arms. "You must stop this madness now, William!"

"Madness! You call it madness when all I want is to love you? To marry you?"

"I am already married to another. And I love *him*!"

Her words were lost on the wind as a huge figure leapt forward to confront William. There was no mistaking Corbett, and Lilliane could have wept with relief. But the scene was far from played out, and she held her breath as the two men faced off against one another.

"Back off. Back off, I say!" William screamed.

In contrast to William's desperate tone, Corbett's voice was low and controlled. "Back off? Or what? Shall you threaten your daughter? Or *my* wife? Is that the kind of man you are?" He sneered in contempt.

"She should never have married you!"

"But she did. And what is mine is mine."

"Yes. You would keep her. But only as a possession! Only as something to own! But I love her. I always have. And she loves me!" He moved to cut off Corbett's approach to Lilliane.

"You delude yourself, William, in this as in so

many other things. Lilliane does not love you. She loves me." He paused and even in the dark on the windswept ledge his eyes found hers. "And I love her."

Lilliane could hardly breathe for the tightness in her throat. Her dear, sweet love! He was here for her, fighting for her, declaring his love for her in spite of all that had gone wrong between them.

"Corbett," she whispered. Then it became a scream of warning. "Corbett!"

How he avoided the deathblow Hughe intended she did not know. From a quick feint to his left he rose to a wary crouch, watching two figures now.

"You said he'd never catch us!" William screamed at Hughe. "Where in the bloody name of God were you!"

"Shut up!" Hughe snarled. He kept his eyes on Corbett. "It doesn't matter. We have him now and he will die."

Although Corbett did not appear surprised by his brother's foul action, it was clear he was baffled by his motives. "What has led to this? What has led you to embrace treason . . . and fratricide?"

"Is it treason to defend your home? To seek to strengthen it?"

"If it is only for your own personal gain, then yes, it is treason. You have no need to fear Edward as king. He is a man of the law. He'll unite England."

"His father was a bumbling fool! He created nothing but dissension, and Edward was his fist in keeping power away from the barons."

"So you use that as reason to foment trouble in the northern shires? Did you truly believe Edward would let the lot of you break off on your own?"

"He would not be able to stop us. We're too strong already."

"And since I stand for Edward and for England, then I must go first?"

It was William who answered. "You stole Orrick and Lilliane from me!"

"You already have a home. And you had a wife!"

William advanced a step with his sword waving dangerously before him. "Lilliane has always been mine. I know it. She knows it. But you had to ruin everything."

"Tell him, Lily." Corbett's voice rang out clear and strong, and it strengthened Lilliane's faltering courage. "Tell him how it is between us."

She feared her voice would fail. She feared her tears would drown the words and that Corbett would never hear. But his eyes were steady and his fearlessness reinforced her. "I love you, Corbett. I've loved you since—"

The rest was cut off by William's frenzied cry of rage. Like a madman he flew at Corbett, his blade held high.

Lilliane screamed in terror as Corbett tumbled back under the onslaught. Like a man berserk William followed him down, and the two men lurched to the side as each one struggled to gain the advantage.

Hughe did not delay in joining the battle. With a razor-sharp dagger he struck out at Corbett. Lilliane nearly swooned at the blood-curdling cry of pain. But it was not Corbett whose blood gushed forth upon the moss-covered stone. In the last moment before Hughe's deathblow had come, Corbett had twisted away. The blade had buried itself in William's side, leaving the two brothers alone in the fight.

At once Hughe lifted his sword, but Corbett was too swift. In one lithe movement he was on his feet, his own wicked blade at the ready.

"You devil!" Hughe screamed. "The heathens should have finished you off long ago!"

"Why do you want me dead? It's more than just Edward. It's me. But why? Why!"

"Because you were Father's favorite. I knew it, you knew it. Everyone knew he would have left you Colchester if he could have!"

It was clearly the last thing Corbett had expected, and at his stunned expression Hughe began to laugh.

"Ah, yes. You thought I didn't know. Well, neither did he. But in the end he admitted it."

Lilliane was huddled in the crevice, confused by Hughe's rantings. He is mad, she thought. But that only made him more dangerous than ever.

"What do you mean, 'he admitted it'? Our father never played favorites. He expected the same from us both. But then, you've never been one to be content with merely equal treatment."

Hughe's face became smug. "You see. Even your words mimic his. But you're both wrong. I showed him who had the strength and cunning to lead Colchester. Now I shall show you who will lead all of northern England."

At that he feinted to the left and reached deep with his sword. But Corbett was ready and deftly parried the stroke.

"How did you show him?" Corbett asked in a grim, even tone. "How did you show him your strength and your cunning?"

Hughe smiled evilly. "He fell when we were hunting. You remember the day. He fell and called for help. It was almost too easy. With a single stone I crushed the life from him."

His smile faded uneasily as he recalled the crime. "He said you'd learn of it. But you never did. You believed my accusation of Lord Barton just like everyone else did. But it was me. Me!"

For a moment Corbett let down his guard. His brother's confession far exceeded his expectations of Hughe's depravity. His voice was raw with emotion as he faced Hughe. "It was yours anyway. Colchester was yours. Why did you do it?"

"To show him that I had the stomach to do whatever was needed. I showed him. Now I'll show you."

With a cry that sounded more like a beast's than a man's, he lunged forward. Metal crashed against metal. Muscle strained against muscle. Then one of them slipped on a loose stone and they both fell in a twisting tangle of limbs and swords.

Lilliane heard Corbett's grunt of pain. She saw the sudden dark stain upon his thigh. Then he gave a mighty heave and sent Hughe flying over his shoulder. But when the two men scrambled to their feet, Corbett had his back to a cliff that fell sharply to the valley below.

Hughe could hardly catch his breath, yet he chuckled when he realized his advantage. "So the end has come. The end for you, that is. For me it's the beginning."

"What of Lilliane?" Corbett interrupted him. "And the child. Will you kill them both? How will you explain that? Then there are my men. How will you explain the attack on them?"

At Hughe's confused expression Corbett taunted him further. "You have lost everything, Hughe. Your greed has ruined all your plans."

Hughe looked from Corbett to Lilliane then past him to the river far below. Without warning he suddenly lunged toward Corbett, his long steel blade aimed straight at his brother's heart.

Lilliane screamed at the move, but Corbett seemed to have expected it. With a quick twist of his body he dodged the vicious blow.

Hughe tried to swing around and finish him off, but in the dark he had misjudged. His foot pivoted but then it slipped over the edge. With a high-pitched shriek he disappeared from sight.

The silence that followed was deafening.

Lilliane was too shocked to react. She could only stare at Corbett, who was peering over the rim of the cliff. Then he sagged and went down on one knee.

In an instant she laid the baby's basket down and was at his side, hugging him to her and trying frantically to pull him away from the dangerous edge of the stone outcropping.

"Corbett! Corbett!" she cried over and over again, holding him as close to her as was humanly possible. Tears streamed down her face as she kissed his cheeks, his eyes, his lips. He was trembling from exertion and pain as well as from the terrible trauma of the last minutes. But he quickly enveloped her in his arms and held her fast against him.

"I thought I'd lost you. I love you, Lily. My God, I love you! I couldn't bear to lose you. I never want to be without you!"

"You never will. You never will. I'd die if I couldn't be with you forever! I love you, I'll always love you!"

They were the perfect words of love. Lilliane's heart filled with the wonder of it all. How long had she waited to say them? How long had she prayed to hear him say them to her? Forever, it seemed, yet now they were said. He loved her. She could hardly believe it and yet . . . she knew it was true.

In the dark, in the cold, with little Elyse beginning to wail and the sound of Dunn's bellow from the base of the Middling Stone, she managed a smile.

"I want to go home, Corbett. I want us to go home to Orrick together."

EPILOGUE

Hand by hand
  we shule us take,
And joy and blisse
  shule we make . . .

Anonymous medieval verse

Lilliane stood at the edge of the field. The barley was beginning to ripen and in the warm summer breeze the field undulated like a gentle, golden lake. Along the narrow brook that bordered the field, Magda and Ferga had spread a blanket for the babies. Now both maids were fast asleep, as were their little charges. Even old Thomas who had accompanied them was dozing as he leaned back against a sturdy beech tree, his fishing line forgotten in his hands.

In the lulling warmth of the late August sunshine everyone was relaxed and content. Everyone except Lilliane.

She'd walked along the brook for a while, tossing leftover bits of bread to the fish and the ducks. But her restless mood would not abate, and now she had circled all the way to the road.

Lilliane held back a wind-blown tendril of hair from her cheek as she stared down the smooth worn road. Since first waking she'd been sure Corbett would return today. She had known it with a certainty that would not be shaken. Yet now, as the sun began its slow, western decline, her hopes were beginning to fade.

How she longed for him. He had been gone almost four weeks now, off to London to meet with Edward and attend his coronation. She'd not accompanied him due to the recent birth of their little boy. But each night she'd prayed for his safe return, and every morning she had knelt again in the hope that this would be the day.

With a heavy sigh she looked down at the dusty road. It was just as well he did not come today, she thought as she stared at her two bare feet. She'd long ago cast off her slippers; her feet were muddy; the hem of her apple-green linen gown was still wet; and her hair was an impossible tangle. After his weeks at court amid the grandest lords and ladies of the land, he was sure to find her pitifully rustic.

Feeling quite sorry for herself, she began to walk along the road, kicking aimlessly at an occasional stone. It was not until she felt the rumbling of the ground beneath her feet and heard the heavy thunder of hooves that she came out of gloomy thoughts and spun around.

Coming toward her at a headlong pace was a lone rider upon a huge, dark destrier. With a happy cry Lilliane brought her hands to her cheeks. She did not need to see his face to know it was Corbett.

She stood there in the middle of the road, a slender, dusty figure with her skirts lifting in the breeze and the afternoon sun glinting red and gold in her long, wild hair. As he bore down on her she felt as if every happiness in the world had somehow been bestowed upon her.

Then Corbett was there, flinging himself down from Qismah before the winded steed had even stopped and catching her in his arms in a fierce embrace.

"Oh, my love. My love! It seemed you would never return!"

His reply was lost in a long, stirring kiss that left them both breathless. When he finally pulled a little away, Lilliane ran her hand tenderly along his lean cheek then rubbed one finger along the beard stubble on his chin.

"I have missed you . . ." Her voice choked with emotion, and in embarrassment she bowed her head against his broad chest. The intensity of her emotions was almost frightening as she savored the wonderful feel of him and the familiar scent of him, flavored now with leather and dust and horses. She loved him so!

With a low chuckle Corbett tilted her face back up to his. "And here I feared that I might find the castle barred against me once again."

Lilliane tried to give him a reproachful look, but it was lost in her happy tears. "You know I can deny you nothing," she whispered.

Corbett stared deep into her eyes, his own eyes a vivid gray, as clear as crystal. "All I shall ever want is your love; just never deny me that."

"You shall always have it."

Their lips met again and this time she felt as if he were devouring her whole. With his lips and his tongue, with an urgency that bordered on pain, he took her and she was more than willing. If she could have she would have sunk down upon the road and showed him her welcome and her love in every way possible. But it was Corbett who, with a groan of agony, tore himself away from their passionate embrace.

"My God, how I have longed for you!" His callused hand smoothed along her russet curls. "I love you, Lily. I love you with an intensity that tortures me." Then he took a shaky breath and smiled ruefully. "Unfortunately, my men are not too far behind me."

Lilliane laughed in pure happiness. "Yes, we must behave more properly. After all, Dane and Elyse are both sleeping nearby." She waved her hand toward the brook. "And of course Magda and Ferga and Thomas—"

She shrieked as he scooped her up and spun her around and around. "You may not put me off for long, wife."

"Nor do I intend to," she whispered as she began to nibble on his ear.

With another groan he put her down, but he kept his arm around her as they began to walk toward the brook. The barley parted peacefully as they walked, then easily filled back in after they had passed. In the distance the walls of Orrick gleamed brightly as the sun spread its golden haze over the valley.

She had been back a full year, Lilliane realized as they walked along arm in arm. It was a year since Tullia had begged her to return. A year since a huge, scarred knight had descended on Orrick, demanding his betrothal rights to her. A year of strife and sorrow and even terror. Yet rising from it had come the peace and happiness her father had always wanted for his valley.

Still, that would mean nothing without the love she'd found. With a contented sigh she leaned her head against Corbett's strong shoulder and felt his grasp tighten warmly about her. She was home at last.

FREE FROM DELL

with purchase plus postage and handling

Congratulations! You have just purchased one or more titles featured in Dell's Romance 1990 Promotion. Our goal is to provide you with quality reading and entertainment, so we are pleased to extend to you a limited offer to receive a selected Dell romance title(s) *free* (plus $1.00 postage and handling per title) for each romance title purchased. Please read and follow all instructions carefully to avoid delays in your order.

1) Fill in your name and address on the coupon printed below. No facsimiles or copies of the coupon allowed.

2) The Dell Romance books are the only books featured in Dell's Romance 1990 Promotion. Any other Dell titles are not eligible for this offer.

3) Enclose your original cash register receipt with the price of the book(s) circled plus $1.00 **per book** for postage and handling, payable in check or money order to: Dell Romance 1990 Offer. Please do not send cash in the mail.
Canadian customers: Enclose your original cash register receipt with the price of the book(s) circled plus $1.00 **per book** for postage and handling in U.S. funds.

4) This offer is only in effect until March 29, 1991. Free Dell Romance requests postmarked after March 22, 1991 will not be honored, but your check for postage and handling will be returned.

5) Please allow 6-8 weeks for processing. Void where taxed or prohibited.

Mail to: Dell Romance 1990 Offer
P.O. Box 2088
Young America, MN 55399-2088

Dell

NAME_____

ADDRESS_____

CITY_____STATE_____ZIP_____

BOOKS PURCHASED AT_____

AGE_____

(Continued)

Book(s) purchased:_____

_____

_____

I understand I may choose one free book for each Dell Romance book purchased
(plus applicable postage and handling). Please send me the following:

(Write the number of copies of each title selected next to that title.)

☐ **MY ENEMY, MY LOVE**
Elaine Coffman
From an award-winning author comes this
compelling historical novel that pits a
spirited beauty against a hard-nosed
gunslinger hired to forcibly bring her home
to her father. But the gunslinger finds
himself unable to resist his captive.

☐ **AVENGING ANGEL**
Lori Copeland
Jilted by her thieving fianceé, a woman
rides west seeking revenge, only to wind up
in the arms of her enemy's brother.

☐ **A WOMAN'S ESTATE**
Roberta Gellis
An American woman in the early 1800s
finds herself ensnared in a web of family
intrigue and dangerous passions when her
English nobleman husband passes away.

☐ **THE RAVEN AND THE ROSE**
Virginia Henley
A fast-paced, sexy novel of the 15th century
that tells a tale of royal intrigue, spirited
love, and reckless abandon.

☐ **THE WINDFLOWER**
Laura London
She longed for a pirate's kisses. . . even
though she was kidnapped in error and
forced to sail the seas on his pirate ship,
forever a prisoner of her own reckless
desire.

☐ **TO LOVE AN EAGLE**
Joanne Redd
Winner of the 1987 *Romantic Times*
Reviewer's Choice Award for Best Western
Romance by a New Author.

☐ **SAVAGE HEAT**
Nan Ryan
The spoiled young daughter of a U.S. Army
General is kidnapped by a Sioux chieftain
out of revenge and is at first terrified, then
infuriated, and finally hopelessly aroused by
him.

☐ **BLIND CHANCE**
Meryl Sawyer
Every woman wants to be a star, but what
happens when the one nude scene she'd
performed in front of the cameras haunts
her, turning her into an underground sex
symbol?

☐ **DIAMOND FIRE**
Helen Mittermeyer
A gorgeous and stubborn young woman
must choose between protecting the
dangerous secrets of her past or trusting
and loving a mysterious millionaire who has
secrets of his own.

☐ **LOVERS AND LIARS**
Brenda Joyce
She loved him for love's sake, he seduced
her for the sake of sweet revenge. This is a
story set in Hollywood, where there are two
types of people—lovers and liars.

☐ **MY WICKED ENCHANTRESS**
Meagan McKinney
Set in 18th-century Louisiana, this is the
tempestous and sensuous story of an
impoverished Scottish heiress and the
handsome American plantation owner who
saves her life, then uses her in a dangerous
game of revenge.

☐ **EVERY TIME I LOVE YOU**
Heather Graham
A bestselling romance of a rebel Colonist
and a beautiful Tory loyalist who
reincarnate their fiery affair 200 years later
through the lives of two lovers.

Dell

**TOTAL NUMBER OF FREE BOOKS SELECTED ____ X $1.00
= $_____ (Amount Enclosed)**

Dell has other great books in print by these authors. If you enjoy them, check
your local book outlets for other titles.